LOVE UNCOVERED

DIANE HOLIDAY

CITY OWL
PRESS

LOVE UNCOVERED
Love Beyond Danger, Book 2

CITY OWL PRESS
www.cityowlpress.com

Cover Design by MiblArt. All stock photos licensed appropriately.

Edited by Mary Cain.

For information on subsidiary rights, please contact the publisher at info@cityowlpress.com.

Print Edition ISBN: 978-1-944728-94-6

Digital Edition ISBN: 978-1-944728-93-9

Printed in the United States of America

For my husband Steve,
Because his unconditional love and support inspires and humbles me.
Thank you.

PRAISE FOR DIANE HOLIDAY

"*Love Uncovered* blends the tension of a high-stakes corruption case with the charm of a well-realized small-town setting to create a fun, fast-paced story." — Publisher's Weekly

"Diane Holiday's debut, *Love in Hiding*, kept me hooked from the first page to the last." — *USA Today Bestselling Author of Historical Romance, Renee Ann Miller*

"Holiday delivers another fast-paced read with heart and humor in *Rock Bottom Romance*." — *USA Today Bestselling Author of Historical Romance, Renee Ann Miller*

"*Love in Hiding* combines the laid-back atmosphere of country life with the suspense angle of a crazed stalker beautifully. Great characterization, perfect pacing and witty dialogue top off this exceptional read." — *Jessie Gussman, author of Sweet Water Ranch*

"Full of moments that will make you smile. *Rock Bottom Romance* is a feel-good novel that will have you rooting for the hero and heroine right from the moment they meet." — *Young Adult Romance Author, Miguella Twosias*

"This was an amusing read with relatable characters I couldn't stop rooting for." — *Historical Fiction Author, KA Nelson*

"A fast-moving, exciting novel. The main characters are the perfect combination of charming and complex. This contemporary romance delivers electrifying heat between characters with a sprinkle of humor." — *InD'tale, Tina Donovan*

"A strong heroine, sexy hero and downright scream-worthy villains—a page-turner with spunky dialogue and suspense that kept me up way past my bedtime because I just couldn't put it down." — *Contemporary Romance Author and Golden Heart® Award Finalist, Christina Hovland*

"Solid storytelling featuring a classic hero and a daring heroine." — *New Adult Author and Golden Heart® Award Winner, C.R. Grissom*

"A man scarred by guilt, a feisty woman, and a villain who is totally evil make Diane Holiday's *Love Uncovered* a fast-paced read that sizzles with both romance and suspense." — *USA Today Bestselling Author of Historical Romance, Renee Ann Miller*

"Diane Holiday's well-crafted romantic suspense stories keep readers turning the pages, ready for the next twist! I always look forward to her books." — *Contemporary Romance Author and Golden Heart® Award Finalist, Christina Hovland*

"Holiday writes romantic suspense with just the right balance of heart and heart-pounding action." — *USA Today Bestselling Author, Dylann Crush*

"*Love on the Line* is an excellent story in the vein of time-honored romance--suspense, love, and characters who keep you turning the pages." — *Contemporary Romance Author and Golden Heart® Award Finalist, Christina Hovland*

"Two people looking for the opposite things in life find out they might be a perfect match. But danger lurks when they fall under the spotlight of a madman. *Love on the Line* is a suspenseful read." — *USA Today Bestselling Author of Historical Romance, Renee Ann Miller*

"*Love on the Line* delivers a romantic suspense with strong characters you'll remember long after you read the last page." — *New Adult Author and Golden Heart® Award Winner, C.R. Grissom*

"Well-plotted, beautifully written and completely engrossing, *Love on the Line* is absolutely the best romantic suspense I've read this year." — *Jessie Gussman, author of Sweet Water Ranch*

"Both intense and hot, *Love on the Line* keeps readers flipping the pages! Sexy romance and thrilling suspense--there's nothing else one could ask for!" — *Young Adult Romance Author, Miguella Twosias*

"What begins as a cruel bet...soon becomes a terrifying, life-threatening game of cat and mouse. The chemistry between Holiday's protagonists is intense and believable." — *Publisher's Weekly*

LOVE BEYOND DANGER SERIES

BY DIANE HOLIDAY

Love in Hiding

Love Uncovered

Love on the Line

CHAPTER 1

MADDIE COOPER OPENED her laptop and typed so fast she misspelled her password. No surprise, with shaking fingers and only two hours of sleep under her belt.

At last, pictures from yesterday's excavation filled the screen. She leaned closer, her gaze riveted on the images, and zoomed in on the one that took her breath away.

The clay-baked animal she'd uncovered stared back at her. The piece, small enough to fit in the hand of a child, had been sculpted to resemble a wolf. Maybe a father had made it for his son or daughter. Good chance the toy belonged with the Iroquois collection.

She clicked another photo, a close-up of the wolf boxed on the shelf. After double-checking the catalog number to her records, she eased back in the chair. Good. No mistakes, despite the long day and the late hours.

The safekeeping and accurate documentation of each piece in the climate-controlled storage room fell to her as the project manager. Every time she entered the cool, dark building, her pulse quickened. Her team had almost filled the facility with clay pots, arrowheads, tools, and weapons over the last year. So much history to share. Wait until the Seneca Nation tribal leaders saw the figure. They'd be ecstatic.

This rare find would be part of a special exhibit in the proposed museum that could put the small town of Tuckerton, New York, on the map. Sure, she missed traveling on digs, but she'd trade that in a second for the wealth of history her team had uncovered. Each piece gave a glimpse into the past culture of the Native Americans. Now the tribal leaders, working with the museum, would have the opportunity to share that culture and educate people.

She stood and stretched. In one month, the grant money would run out, and they'd have to be done. Too bad she wouldn't be around to help set up the exhibits. She'd check in to make sure the tribal leaders were happy with the displays and return to visit the finished museum next year.

All of this had been a big boost to her career. At twenty-nine, she'd earned the respect of the archaeological community, but making sure the history was preserved mattered more.

Early May meant cool weather in the Finger Lakes region, so she grabbed a jacket. She'd given her team the morning off after the long, late night, but she had responsibilities and deadlines to meet. Her tired body screamed for caffeine.

She drove into town, her body still amped from the thrill of the find, and parked her car in a slushy, gray puddle in front of the Corner Café. Mist accumulated on the windshield and drops merged, sliding down like tears. But it would take more than dreary weather to squelch her spirits.

One step out of the car and her keys plopped into a puddle. With a curse, she bent to retrieve them. Before she could, a man's hand reached down and plucked them out.

"Here you go."

She froze. That voice. Deep, but as smooth as honey.

It had haunted her dreams for two years. It couldn't be him. His fingers brushed hers as he handed over the keys, sending shivers through her body that had nothing to do with the temperature. She raised her head to stare into the unforgettable sea-green eyes of Scott Evans. Her bruised heart slammed against her rib cage. Where had he been for the last two years?

He'd left for an undercover DEA job and promised to call.

Only he never had.

He blinked as if shocked to see her and then rubbed his forehead. His dark hair fell over the tips of his fingers.

Her gaze traveled down his fit body. Well-defined chest muscles outlined the crisp, white button-down shirt and tie. A black leather belt cinched his narrow waist. The gun he always carried hung in a holster on his hip. Muscular thighs stretched the fabric of his dark suit pants. She'd once sat on those strong legs, cradled in his lap, while he'd stroked her hair and watched the sunset over Central Park. They'd made sweet love that night, their first time together.

He straightened. "How are you, Maddie?"

Polite. It took guts to do polite after she'd bared her soul to him, something she'd never done with another man, and he'd left her with a hollow heart. Two years had passed without a word from him. Not a call. Not a text. Not a letter. She shoved her keys into her jacket pocket. "Shouldn't you be in Mexico catching bad guys? What are you doing here?"

He grimaced. "You haven't changed. Right to the point."

"Excuse me. I'm in a hurry." She tried to step around him, but he blocked her way.

"I owe you an explanation."

"Two years ago, you owed me an explanation. A year ago, an apology. Now, you owe me nothing." This time she managed a step around him before he placed a hand on her arm.

"Wait."

"What, Scott? What can you possibly say? I thought the time we spent together meant something. Clearly, you didn't. It's fine. I know when I've been kicked to the curb."

"It wasn't like that."

The lines of his face hardened, and pain flashed deep in his eyes.

He glanced at the ground and then back to her. "It's...complicated."

She fisted her hands to stop herself from reaching out and touching him. Even pissed, she still had the urge to smooth away the sad creases. If she didn't leave now, he'd suck her back in for another round of hurt and disappointment. "I'm sure. Well, I gotta go."

She dropped her gaze to his hand, still on her arm. Warmth radiated from his touch right through her coat. Damn his effect on her.

"I didn't realize you were here." His mouth drew into a thin line. "And now I need to ask a favor."

He had to be kidding. She'd given him everything, and it hadn't been enough. Painful memories threatened to swallow her whole. She shook her head and focused back on him. "I really can't help you. I have to go."

"I wouldn't ask if it weren't important."

His grave expression made her pause. Despite their history, she couldn't turn her back on him. "What?"

"Please don't talk to anyone about my former job with the DEA."

"What do you mean? You don't work for them anymore?"

"No. I've been in the States for a while." He let go of her arm.

And there it was. The stinging slap to the face. Her hope that he hadn't called because he'd been off the grid in Mexico disappeared like a stone dropped into a lake. Her chest ached. "You've been here?"

He waved a hand at the coffee shop. "Not here."

She wouldn't have this conversation. Didn't need the details. He'd been in the country. "Sorry. I'm out of time."

With tears stinging her eyes, she pushed past him and headed to the shop. She swung open the metal-framed door and hurried inside, shutting out the cold morning fog. The comforting aroma of cinnamon buns and hazelnut coffee filled the air, but her erratic pulse refused to calm. She took a deep breath and set her priorities.

Get coffee. Go to the storage building. Forget Scott.

Yeah, right. That hadn't worked when he *wasn't* around.

She glanced about the room. The five small tables were empty, but Tom, dressed in his police uniform, stood by the register. Ugh. They'd been friends long enough that he'd know something was up, and she'd rather chew glass than discuss Scott. If only she could fall for someone nice and reliable like Tom. Tall, athletic, with sandy hair and brown eyes. Women revved their engines and sped past him on purpose so he would stop them. Except for Maddie. He reminded her of a big, strong teddy bear. Not her type. Nope. She'd left her type standing outside on the sidewalk.

Tom, who always had a smile for everyone, wore a grim expression.

Nikki came out from the kitchen, wearing her pink-and-white waitress outfit. She held a finger up to Tom. "Your breakfast sandwich will be ready in a sec. You want your usual, Maddie?"

Maddie did a doubletake before nodding. Nikki sported yet another hair color, this one blond with bright magenta streaks. She changed her looks more often than a chameleon. Then again, so did most nineteen-year-olds.

Nikki filled two cups, put lids on them, and slid one across the counter to Tom. "I'm sorry about the promotion. It really sucks that you didn't get it."

He frowned at her.

"Oops, sorry. I didn't know it was a secret." She scrunched up her face and bit her lip.

Maddie blinked. "What? You didn't make detective?"

"Nope. Looks like I stay on patrol." His shoulders slumped.

"I'm really sorry." Her heart sank for him. Everyone had expected Tom to take the place of the retired detective. "Who filled the spot?"

"Some hotshot New York City cop. Name's Fisher. No one knows him."

Maddie shook her head, paid Nikki, and stuffed money in the tip jar. "Well, whoever he is, he can't be as good as you. I'm so sorry."

"Eh, life goes on. I don't want to talk about it."

Nikki snatched a foil-wrapped sandwich from the kitchen window counter and handed it to Tom. He thanked her and called over his shoulder, "Catch you guys later."

Damn it. Tom had been so excited about that promotion. Maddie fought the urge to follow him, but he'd made it clear he didn't want to discuss the subject.

Nikki wiped the counter. "I don't care how hot the new guy is. Tom should have gotten that job."

"How do you know the new hire is hot?" On second thought, she didn't have time for gossip. "Never mind. I need to get on the road. Thanks, Nikki."

Maddie's phone rang with an unknown caller ID. She stepped to the corner of the café.

"Hello?"

A woman asked for Madeline Cooper and then continued, "I'm Gina, calling from the office of Victor Mole, the developer of the proposed resort property next to Lake Caswego."

"Yes. I'm familiar with the area and project." Maddie frowned. The tribal members were concerned about the construction, with good reason. The land had a high probability of containing Native American artifacts. All the publicity over her team's successful excavation had drawn attention to the area. People were buying private land left and right, no doubt hoping to dig up and sell whatever they could with no regard to the historical importance of the objects. Infuriating.

"Your name was on the list of practicing archaeologists of New York. We need a field survey before we can get our permit to build, and we'd like to meet with you to discuss this."

Maddie nibbled at her lower lip. This could be big. If she found historically significant pieces, she could help preserve Native American history. But she'd planned to travel for work again in a month. "Can I get back to you?"

"I'm sorry, but time is of the essence. If you aren't available—"

"Hold on." She pinched the bridge of her nose. It couldn't hurt to meet with the woman and figure out how long the job might take. She hadn't committed to another dig yet, and the tribal leaders would appreciate having someone they knew and trusted conduct the survey. "Okay. I can fit a meeting in on Wednesday morning. Around eight?"

"I was hoping for something sooner than two days. I'll put you on the schedule, but please call me if anything opens up."

"That's the best I can do right now."

"Okay. Can you meet us at the site?"

Maddie agreed and hung up. After spending a year in one place, she itched to be on the move. She wasn't a put-down-roots kind of person, but until she knew what might be at stake, she couldn't walk away.

Coffee in hand, she hurried from the café to her car. She balanced the cup on the roof and dug out her keys.

"Maddie?"

She whirled around, and her almost-back-to-normal pulse quickened again. Scott hadn't left. "Now what? Are you stalking me?"

"We have to talk."

"Well, you had lots of chances over the last two years. So—"

"I know you don't want to talk about us"—he held up a hand—"but what I asked you a few minutes ago has nothing to do with us."

She hit the unlock button on her waterlogged remote. Nothing happened. Great. As she inserted the key into the lock, she glanced up at him. Big mistake. Those eyes that changed shades depending on his mood made her insides flutter.

He gave a slight shake of his head. "Look, I'm sorry to press, but can you please do me a favor and keep my past quiet?"

Quiet. The irony again. All she'd had from him was silence. So close, and yet so far away. Once, he would have drawn her into his arms and kissed her senseless. Now, an invisible wall stood between them. But her foolish heart kept pounding against it.

To break eye contact and end the agony, she yanked up her sleeve and checked her watch. "No time."

"Maddie—"

"Gotta go." She opened the car, dropped into the seat, and slammed the door shut. Her hand shook as she threw the vehicle in gear. When she pulled away, the coffee she'd left on the roof tumbled down past her window. She hit the brakes and cursed as she glanced in the rearview mirror.

Scott stood by the curb, a hand on one hip. The mist blurred his features, but it didn't matter. She'd memorized them.

Pressing the accelerator, she left him in the fog.

CHAPTER 2

SCOTT STRODE past a lady pushing a stroller on the sidewalk beside the police station. A chipmunk scampered between the lilac bushes lining the path. Tuckerton couldn't be more different from busy, manic NYC or arid Mexico.

Despite the peaceful setting, tension revved inside him after his encounter with Maddie. Damn it. What the hell was she doing in Tuckerton? He'd kept his cool, but she'd rocked him. Even in muddy work boots and a dusty coat, she'd jump-started his heart.

She hadn't held back. Not that he could blame her.

Not a day went by that he didn't think of her. He missed the way she nibbled her lower lip when she couldn't make a decision and the twinkle in her eyes as she challenged him—which was all the time. The woman had a knack for driving him crazy right before she kissed him into oblivion.

When he left her two years ago with a promise they'd work out a future together, he'd meant it, but then his life had gone to hell, and he'd convinced himself he had to live without her. For both their sakes, she'd be better off. She might understand if he explained, but he couldn't.

Too complicated.

Too painful.

Too dangerous, for both of them.

Maybe she was only in town for a short time. She traveled all over the world, or used to, anyway. Right now, he had a drug-dealing son of a bitch to take down, and that's where his focus needed to stay.

Scott swung the station door open and glanced around the room. Fluorescent lights embedded in the dropped ceiling flickered. Four empty desks and a vacant holding cell filled the room. Neatly stacked files rested beside turned-off computer monitors. Nope. He wasn't in the Big Apple anymore.

A noise came from the adjacent room, and Scott turned. The sight of his old mentor had its usual calming effect. A seasoned narcotics detective, Lee had shown Scott the ropes working joint operations with the DEA. The man was unflappable. Scott nodded. "Hey, Chief."

Lee's mouth curved into a look-what-the-cat-dragged-in smile. "Hey, yourself. Come on in."

Scott entered the office only big enough to hold a desk and two chairs.

Lee stood, and they shook hands. In the last four years, he hadn't changed much. More gray hair, but he still had the same strong build and those cool, blue eyes that could stare down the meanest badass. "Want some coffee?"

"I'm good for now." Scott dropped into the hard, wooden seat across from Lee, who picked up an oversize coffee mug and took a drink. No doubt the contents were sky-high octane and thicker than molasses. That's the only way they'd gotten through their stakeout nights. Caffeine and adrenaline, a wicked combination.

Scott waved a hand at the empty station room. "It's like a morgue here."

"Usually is. Four cops, including you. We're talking small. No nine-one-one service. Hell, we go by first names and don't even use ten codes on the radio. Takes some getting used to. Nothing but petty crime in this town."

Scott's gaze went to the framed picture on the desk of Lee's wife. Her hair had grown back after the chemo treatments. He touched the side of the photo. "How's she doing?"

Lee stroked a hand across his chin. "Great. In remission. I think moving out of the city and my leaving narcotics lowered her stress level. Helped to return here, where she has family."

Family. The knot in Scott's stomach tightened.

A muscle ticked under Lee's jaw. "This is a nice town full of good people. I got this job because the former chief was a friend of my wife's family. He was ready to retire but hung in for another month until I could take over." He glanced at the framed picture. "When she underwent chemo, I couldn't fit another casserole into the refrigerator. This piece of shit Mole isn't going to set up shop here and endanger these folks. That's why I asked for you. You're the best DEA agent I ever worked with."

Sometimes the best still wasn't good enough. Scott swallowed and stood. "We were damn close to putting Mole away in the Southwest, but the guy's as slippery as an eel and twice as slimy." He paced to the window. "We'll get enough evidence this time. It's going to be harder for him to smuggle drugs here. Mexico isn't right across the border."

Lee tapped a file on the desk. "This has the aerial photograph and address for the land where Mole plans to build his resort. Your guys tell me he intends to use the place to launder drug money like he did in the Four Corners, and they wager that what he really wants is to dig up artifacts and sell them on the black market."

Without a doubt. That was his MO. Scott returned to the desk and sat. "We're working that angle. Have an agent set up as a buyer. No offense to your force, but this goes beyond small-town police. Mole is brutal. He would chew your guys up and spit them out."

"I'm not interested in a pissing contest with the DEA. You have my cooperation. Gotta tell you, though, Tom Waslinski was gunning for this detective job and took it hard." Lee swigged his coffee. "He's a good guy and well-liked. Thirty-four—same as you— but a patrol cop. You have your work cut out with the locals, since you're filling this spot."

Scott nodded. Sometimes life wasn't fair. "Small-town loyalties run deep. No one wants an outsider taking a job. I feel bad for him, but I didn't come to win a popularity contest. I'm here to put Mole behind bars."

"Well, the sooner we do that, the sooner you'll move on to the next case, and Tom can have this job."

"That's the plan. In the meantime, I'll play the dirty-cop role and see if that bastard takes the bait."

Lee pointed to the computer screen. "I checked your records, and they've been altered to say you've been a beat cop and detective in NYC for the last thirteen years." He leaned across the desk. "No one here knows that we ever worked together or that you're still DEA. We need to keep it that way. Can't chance any slip-ups."

Scott's shoulders tensed. "Well, Houston, we have a problem, because someone here does know about my DEA job."

Lee's eyes widened. "Who?"

"Maddie Cooper." Scott's throat constricted. Just saying her name took him back. "I met her before I left for Mexico the second time. She knows me as Scott Evans, not Scott Fisher."

"Damn. This complicates things. I'm guessing you were more than friends?" Lee raised an eyebrow.

"Yes. I met her at a bar in Maryland. We hit it off and ended up spending a pretty intense summer together. She has reason to be pissed at me. I left her hanging."

"That doesn't sound like you."

Scott closed his eyes and let out a long breath. "Shit happened when I was in Mexico last time." The pain still wrenched his heart to the point of losing his breath. "I couldn't keep my promises to Maddie. I tried to call, but she was off the grid. And then I was in too deep to risk outside contact."

"What happened?"

"I'll tell you about it later." If he could get the words out. Never talked to anyone about it. "Right now, I need to see Maddie. This whole operation could be compromised if she says anything to anyone about me. Are we caught up for now?"

"Yeah. Go do what you need to do." Lee typed something into the computer and printed out a sheet. "She's probably at work. Here are the addresses of the excavation site, her apartment, and her phone number."

"Thanks." Scott stood. "Do you have any idea if she's going to be here long?"

"All I know is she's been doing an excavation for the last year. You'd have to check with Tom or talk to her yourself about future plans."

Tom and Maddie? Scott ground his molars together. Better not to know. What she did with her love life was no longer his business.

Right. If he clenched any harder, he might shatter his teeth.

Lee stood. "Good luck. Maddie's a feisty one. I wouldn't want to be on her shit list."

Feisty was an understatement. The woman had a quick temper, a bad habit of acting before thinking, and no reason to want to help him after what he'd done.

He needed more than luck.

CHAPTER 3

MADDIE STOMPED across the field between the parking lot and her storage building. No coffee, but after running into Scott, she didn't need caffeine to rev her body.

Damn him. He'd swept her off her world-traveling feet and given her a hint of what having a real, lasting relationship might be like. Right before he'd turned into the Invisible Man and dashed any hopes of a happy future together.

He'd mentioned being in the States for a while. Clearly, at some point he could have contacted her. Whatever brought him to town, it'd required a dress shirt and tie. Scott didn't hang out in suits. Correction. The old Scott didn't. With any luck, he'd be passing through.

Never again would she let carefree, don't-get-too-deep Maddie vacate the building. Serious relationships only led to pain. She'd learned the hard way. These days she kept her heart to herself and her dates casual.

She typed in the security code to the storage building, let herself in, and flicked on the lights. Her gaze went to the stack of paperwork on her desk. That could wait for a few minutes. She needed to see the wolf again. Excitement fluttered in her chest. The tribal leaders had asked for more pictures, elated over the discovery.

A knock sounded.

She stilled. Who would be coming by in the morning? Kyle and the other members of her team weren't due until noon. With a frown, she headed back to the front.

"Who is it?" she called through the door.

"Scott."

Her nerves jumped, sending a quick sizzle through her before she could smack them down.

The man was persistent and resourceful, if nothing else. She sure as hell hadn't told him where she worked. If she ignored him, he'd probably come back. Once and for all, she needed to tell him to go away. She opened the door and raked her gaze over him before she could stop herself. The man did justice to a suit. Damn her mouth for watering. She fixed him with a glare.

"I need to talk to you. Can I come in?"

She crossed her arms. "I thought I was clear earlier. We have nothing to discuss."

He took a breath and leveled a look at her with fierce green eyes, ready to battle. Same as always before an argument. Hot as hell. Only this time there wouldn't be make-up sex. Her pulse skipped even as she itched to slam the door in his face.

On second thought, he deserved the earful she'd saved up. She stepped back. "I changed my mind. Come in. We have some unfinished business."

He entered the building. "Yes, we do. You go first."

Oh no. The indulgent let-her-blow-off-steam approach, and then they'd talk for real. That wouldn't work on her. Not anymore.

"When we met two years ago, you only had three months in the States, and I *still* let you in." She brought her face close to his. "I don't let anyone in. I thought we had something. If you changed your mind about wanting a relationship, you should have at least called. I…waited. Like a damned fool."

He winced and then said in a soft tone, "I did call. You didn't have service."

She'd only been off the grid for a month on travel. One month out of two years. "So you tried once and gave up?"

"I'm sorry."

The familiar ache in her chest grew. "That's it? That's all you have to say?"

"About this, yes."

His stoic expression threw ice on her heart. Something had happened to him. His indifference hurt worse than anger. "I see." She took a step back. "Then let's move on. Forget about me. Which, obviously, you had no problem doing. Why are you here?"

"I'm the new detective. My current name is Scott Fisher, and I need you to keep my previous identity as Scott Evans quiet. No one knows me by that here."

She blinked. "Fisher? You're the one who stole Tom's promotion?"

His eyes flashed for the briefest second at the mention of Tom. "I applied for several jobs, and this one came through. It's imperative you don't reveal my former DEA alias."

Whoa. This shit was getting deep fast. And now, the new detective job meant he'd be staying in town. Freaking wonderful. None of it made any sense. She folded her arms and gazed up at him. "Since when are you a cop, and why didn't you go back to work in the city?"

"Things changed for me, and I took advantage of this opportunity."

A breeze blew through the open door. His clean scent of Irish Spring mingled with the fragrant pine of the woods. She forced herself to focus. "What things?"

He squared his broad shoulders. "Nothing I can discuss."

More like nothing he trusted her enough to divulge. She'd bared her soul to him when they were together, and he'd held secrets then and now. The ragged edges of her heart frayed even more. "Your real name was never Scott Evans?"

"No. That's one of many." He stepped inside, pulled the open door closed, and lowered his voice. "Agents are placed in situations where we piss off some bad guys. If they come looking for payback, an alias protects our families."

"So, you lied to me? Pretended to be someone you weren't?" She squinted up at him.

"I didn't have a choice."

"You could have trusted me."

"I'm sorry. Nothing personal. It goes with the job."

Nothing personal. Like hell.

He scrubbed his hand across his jaw. "I need an answer. Can you keep my past private?"

She glanced at his fingers. They had once stroked her skin, traced her lips, and wound in her hair. Never again. Much as she'd love to make his life miserable for hurting her, she wouldn't risk harm to someone. "For the safety of your family, I'll keep your secret."

A look of complete anguish crossed his features before he stiffened and gave a terse nod. "Thank you."

"I assume you got what you came for, so you can go now." She waved a hand at the door.

His mouth drew into a firm line. "I don't blame you for hating me. I appreciate your cooperation."

He turned and opened the door.

"Wait." Dammit. She had to know. In a soft voice, she asked, "Was anything about us real?"

His shoulders stiffened.

She held her breath.

Keeping his back to her, in a casual tone she'd never heard before, he said, "Let it go, Maddie. It was fun while it lasted."

He left, shutting the door firmly behind him without so much as a backwards glance. Her eyes blurred with tears. She blinked fast and cleared them away only by sheer will.

She'd never known him at all. The man she'd fallen for had been a fake. A liar who'd never cared about her.

Nothing personal.

Well, two could play that game.

CHAPTER 4

STUFFING her arms into the sleeves of her jacket, Maddie fumed. Scott's words from yesterday still stung. They'd had "fun while it lasted." What bullshit.

He'd talked to her about doing one more rotation in Mexico and then coming back so they could work out a life together. That screamed anything but casual. Damn him. She'd been willing to wait and had even considered changing her work travel plans for him. She grabbed her backpack, locked up her apartment, and headed to her car.

The man should have gone into acting, because he'd sure convinced her she was special. She couldn't count how many times he'd held her close and told her she meant the world to him. Sure, the sex was phenomenal, but they'd connected on a deeper level, too. Or so she'd thought.

Before him, with all her work travel, she'd kept men at arm's length and only dated for fun. No commitment meant no pain when it came time to move on. But he had changed everything.

He made her laugh and could turn even the most mundane task into a joke. Once while she'd been reading a magazine in the grocery store line, he'd loaded the conveyor belt with cans of whipped cream and boxes of condoms he'd snuck into the cart. He'd disappeared, leaving her to face the elderly, male cashier. Later, they'd laughed, played, and made good use of the purchases. She took a deep breath and pushed away the feelings that once had made her giddy.

Enough of him. Winding through woods loaded with deer at five a.m. required concentration. When she reached the parking lot, she squinted at the lone storage building across the field. The outside lights were off. They'd been on when she'd left last night at ten. Maybe a circuit breaker had tripped or something. The air and heat cycled all the time to control the temperature. That could be trouble if the system malfunctioned. Her hands turned cold.

She grabbed her backpack and got out of the car. Shining a flashlight on the dew-covered field, she picked her way toward the building. A beam of light flashed from the front window.

She froze mid-stride.

Another glimmer flickered from the window.

Her gut clenched. Anyone on her team would have turned on the overhead lights. Something was wrong. But if a prowler had broken in, the security system should be activated.

Think. Think. No nine-one-one service. Who was on duty? Maybe Tom. She fumbled in her backpack, fished out her cell phone, and speed-dialed his number. If he was asleep, he'd forgive her for waking him in an emergency like this.

He answered on the second ring. "Maddie?"

"Tom, I'm at my storage building, and I think there's someone inside. A burglar maybe. Did the security service send any alerts?"

"No. I'm on duty and any alarms would have come to me. Leave and get to a safe place. I'm on my way. I'll call in backup, but stay on the line until I get there."

She couldn't leave. That building held all the artifacts collected over an entire year. And if she got into her car, the dome light might draw attention. Scanning the area, she homed in on a large oak by the edge of the parking lot. Close enough to her car if she needed to get away, and big enough to hide behind. In quick strides, she crossed the field and took cover.

She peered around the tree trunk. The storeroom door opened, and a man dressed all in black emerged with a flashlight in his mouth, carrying a box.

Her stomach dropped. This couldn't be happening.

The guy lumbered around the rear of the building.

A car door slammed, and the sound echoed across the field.

He reappeared and strode back into the storeroom. Seconds turned into minutes. Cold sweat trickled down between her shoulder blades.

She whispered into the phone, "I just saw the burglar. He's carrying boxes out of the building. I don't know how many he's already taken. Oh God, the tribe would be devastated. How far away are you?"

"About ten minutes. What are you still doing there? I told you to leave." Tom's voice rang with concern.

When the thief came out lugging another box, she slapped the phone against her leg to hide the illuminated screen. Ten minutes! He might get away in that time.

The man hesitated. He turned his head and swept the flashlight in his mouth across the field. She held her breath as the beam approached her car.

She dug her nails into the bark of the tree and rolled onto the balls of her feet, ready to run if necessary. A mere foot from her car, the light dimmed.

A long, quiet breath slipped from her lips.

He swung around and trudged behind the building again.

Her mind raced. He appeared to be working alone.

Empty-handed, he returned and went back into the storeroom. A loud noise came from inside.

Crash. Crash. Crash.

She flinched. Each sound punched a direct hit to her gut. He could be destroying artifacts. But they wouldn't be worth anything if he broke them, so it made no sense. She ground her teeth. Time to take matters into her own hands.

Given his size and her lack of a weapon, she shouldn't charge in and try to fight him. She needed to stall him until the police came. Maybe if she wedged something under the door, she could trap him inside until the cops showed up. She shoved the phone in her pocket, dropped to her knees, and ran her hands along the ground to grab a fallen branch.

Feeling the rounded end, she tossed it aside and picked up another. This one had split from the tree to form an angled edge. Perfect.

She took a deep breath and sprinted to the building. Her chest heaved as she flattened against the side. She inched along the wall and crept under the front window. Steam puffed out of her mouth as her warm breath met the cold morning air.

The noise inside the storage unit stopped. Crap.

No turning back now. She groped the cool, metal frame of the door. Her pulse throbbed in her neck.

Silence from within. And then a shuffling. Like feet kicking through debris as they approached the door. Desperation deflated her lungs.

No, no, no, no.

She dove to the ground and fingered the crack under the door. Hands shaking, she stuffed the end of the stick into the space.

Too thick. Damn it.

The steps came closer, and she pressed her lips together. No time to run now.

Wrenching the stick back and forth, she forced it into the crack. Tighter and tighter. Her heart leaped. She had this.

The door handle shook, and she jerked.

Oh God. She gripped the branch with both hands and wedged it harder under the crack.

A thump and grunt came from inside. The door slid open an inch. She threw her weight onto the stick, bracing it against her stomach as she shoved hard.

Not tight enough. The door burst open, knocking her flat on her back.

Her breath left with a *whoosh*. She gasped for air.

A man lurched out of the building and towered over her. Angry eyes glared through the holes of his ski mask. "Bitch."

He was bigger than she was, but she'd go down fighting.

Before she could make a move, he yanked her to her feet and swung a fist.

She dodged her head, but his blow glanced her cheek.

Aiming for his vulnerable spot, she rammed her knee up between his thighs. He twisted his hips, and she missed the mark.

His fingers dug into her arms as he threw her to the ground. Her head smacked against the hard dirt. Searing pain shot through her skull.

She rolled on her side and tried to scramble away. His booted foot stamped down inches from her shoulder.

Blood filled her mouth. Adrenaline spiked through her body, waking her dazed senses. She wobbled to her feet, but stumbled and fell.

Gravel crunched, and the man whipped his head around in the direction of the noise.

Tom, at last.

The thief cursed and ran toward the rear of the building. An engine gunned, followed by the noise of dirt and rocks pelting the concrete wall.

Dizzy, she managed to get up and stagger around the corner of the storeroom.

And then everything went black.

CHAPTER 5

Slumped against a tree, holding an ice pack to her cheek, dread twisted Maddie's stomach. She needed to get a look at the storeroom, but Tom had insisted on calling an ambulance. The EMTs ruled out a concussion and any broken bones. She'd have a nice lump on her head and some bruising, but the real pain wasn't physical. If that burglar had taken enough artifacts, the proposed museum might be in jeopardy, not to mention the huge loss of history.

Two cars approached rapidly and parked in the lot. A Chevy Impala and a police car. Scott jumped out of the Impala. His gaze locked on her, and he jogged across the field. Great, just what she needed.

"Are you okay?" He dropped to one knee and scanned her face.

His proximity warmed the chilly air and made her stomach twist even tighter. Mister Nothing-Personal had no right to be in her personal space, mucking up her emotions.

"Answer me, please. Are you okay?" He reached a hand over hers and pulled the ice pack from her cheek. His eyes hardened as he let go. "I'm going to find who did this to you."

Oh no. He couldn't act all protective and caring now. Not after what he'd said to her. "The EMTs checked me out, to answer your question. And I'm sure the chief will handle the rest."

Chief Lee came up behind Scott. "I'm sorry this happened. Tom filled me in on my ride over. He and Kaitlyn have cleared the scene, and the area is secure. You need anything?"

Maddie pushed off the ground and stood. "Yes. To go inside."

"You can at some point, but you'll have to work that out with Scott."

"Scott? Why?"

Scott stood and glanced at Lee, who cleared his throat. "As the new detective, he's assigned to this case. I'll need you to cooperate with him on the investigation."

Her belly flopped. No. How the hell could she avoid him now? She closed her eyes and sucked in a breath. This day couldn't get any worse.

"Let me check in with Tom and Kaitlyn, and we'll go from there," Scott said. "Just stay put for the moment."

He and Lee walked toward the storage building. She crossed her arms and forced herself to breathe deep and long. What a hot mess.

After what seemed like forever, Scott and Lee came out of the building. Lee headed to the parking lot, and Scott waved a hand for her to approach.

His dark hair gleamed in the rising sun as he stared down at an iPad. Despite the chill in the air, her treacherous body warmed at the sight of him. God, her self-loathing had reached a new level.

She stopped in front of him, and he tapped the iPad. "I've read Tom's notes, but I want to hear what happened from you."

"Can I see the place first?"

"I want to make sure I have everything captured before you go in. Start at the beginning."

Ugh. She'd never get inside at this rate. "I came to work early and saw a beam of light in the building. No one was supposed to be here, so I called the police."

"That was the right thing to do. Then what?"

"I saw a guy taking boxes out of the storeroom. At least two. I don't know how many others. I think he was stealing the artifacts." She set her jaw.

"Go on."

"After he went back into the building the second time, I heard loud noises. Sounded like he was trashing the place."

"Where were you?"

"I was behind that tree." She pointed to the oak.

"Why didn't you leave?"

"He might have gotten away."

"So, instead of leaving, like you were told to, and letting the cops handle things, you chose to stay?"

The way he said it made her sound irresponsible. Heat traveled up her neck. "The police weren't here yet."

He cocked an eyebrow, but let it go. "Continue."

Her gaze stalled on his kissable lips and almost made her forget she wanted to smack that condescending expression from his face. She glanced at the iPad. "I'm sure it's all there. Do I really need to tell this all over again?"

"Indulge me."

Crud. She had deliberately left out a couple of unimportant details when Tom had questioned her about her injured cheek. "Like I told Tom, the guy came out of the building, and we had a scuffle. He ran away when Tom showed up. Now can I go inside?"

"Not so fast." Scott's eyes narrowed. "If you were standing over there"—he pointed to the tree by the parking lot—"how did you get into a scuffle with him?"

A breeze blew a strand of curls across her cheek. She reached both arms up to tuck her hair back into her ponytail holder. Scott's gaze went from her mouth to her chest, and he swallowed hard.

Was he checking her out?

He straightened and returned his attention to the iPad. "I don't see a statement here about you leaving the parking area, so how did you get into a fight?"

Shit. He wasn't going to let it go. "I didn't think it was a good idea to barge in on him, so I tried to lock him in the building."

"Lock him in from the outside? How?"

"I found a branch and tried to wedge it under the door. Only he shoved it open before I could finish."

Scott's eyebrows shot up, and he blinked hard. "You what?"

She nibbled her lower lip and shifted her feet. It had seemed like a good idea at the time. "If I'd had a few more seconds, it *would* have worked."

"Let me get this straight." He closed his eyes and pressed two fingers to his forehead.

She could swear he was counting.

Opening his eyes, he dropped his hand.

Whatever he'd done hadn't worked to calm him because an incredulous expression with a healthy serving of anger lit his face.

He took a step closer and glared down at her. "You approached an active crime scene with no idea how many people were inside or what weapons they might have, with a *stick*?"

Her mouth went dry. It sure sounded idiotic coming from his lips. Which were seriously close to hers. His green eyes sparked, and the chiseled lines of his face deepened. In the past, some of their arguments had turned into hours-long sessions of wild sex. No wonder.

A muscle under his jaw twitched. "You were crazy to do that."

She inched back and placed a hand on her hip. "I only saw one man. I've spent a year on this project. All the artifacts we uncovered are stored in there. I had to do something, and I'd do it again."

"Like hell." He pointed to her cheek. "You're lucky this is all that happened. What if he'd had a gun, or the police had taken longer to get here?"

"I don't know. I wasn't thinking about that."

"Clearly." He stabbed a hand through his hair and took a deep breath. "Okay. Moving on. What happened next?"

"The guy busted the door open and knocked me over. We had a bit of a fight. He took off when the cops showed up."

"Define 'a bit of a fight'," he said through clenched teeth.

"He punched me. I tried to knee him but missed. He threw me to the ground." She touched her scalp. "I guess I hit my head. I don't really remember."

Scott's nostrils flared. "Describe the man."

"He wore a ski mask, so I didn't see his face. A little shorter than you, I'd guess, average build. I know that's not much help."

"Damn it, Maddie. I can't believe you acted so recklessly." He slammed a fist against his outer thigh. "That guy could have killed you."

"I know that now." She crossed her arms. "I had to do something. He was stealing history. I couldn't let him get away with it."

"Well he did, and you got hurt in the process."

He had a point, but she refused to admit it. "Can we finish this, so I can go inside?"

"Fine. Tom said you don't have any information on the vehicle the perpetrator drove away?"

"No. It was too dark." She glanced at the woods to avoid his eyes.

"It's a straight shot a good way before that road bends, so you should have at least seen the tail lights when you rounded the back. Try to think. Were they high like a truck, or lower to the ground?"

"I...don't know. I was kind of dizzy."

"Dizzy?" He swiped the iPad several times. "I don't see anything in here about that."

Uh oh. She trapped her lower lip between her teeth and shrugged. "I'm sorry I don't have more to tell."

"I think maybe you do."

She glanced up. He stared at her mouth and then arched a brow. "What are you hiding?"

"Nothing." Her pulse skittered. He always could tell when she was bluffing.

"Wrong answer. Where exactly were you when the man pulled away?"

"I already told you. I was coming around the back of the building."

"Uh huh." He brought his face closer. "So plenty of time to at least get a glimpse. Why didn't you?"

Busted. She swallowed. "I might have shut my eyes for a couple of seconds."

"What?" His nose wrinkled. "Why would you..."

She scuffed a boot in the dirt and pursed her lips.

"Oh Christ, you passed out, didn't you?"

Damn. Might as well confess. She let out a breath. "Yeah, but it couldn't have been for more than a couple of seconds, because I saw the police car headlights and was awake when Tom came."

"Unbelievable." Scott shook his head. "You lied to an officer."

"No. I told him I didn't see anything, and that was the truth."

Scott held up a finger. "Don't split hairs with me. You know damn well what I'm talking about."

She could almost taste his peppermint breath on her lips. When she ran her tongue across to moisten them, his eyes flashed.

Tom popped his head out from the storeroom entrance. "Scott, do you have…oh…never mind."

Scott lowered his hand, stepped back, and swung around. "What do you need, Tom?"

"It can wait." Tom waved and ducked back inside as if uncomfortable.

She glanced at the door. "Can I go in now?"

"Is there anything else you haven't told me that I need one of your tools to dig out of you?"

Yup. Still angry. Too bad. "No."

"Okay, then." He sighed. "I'm really sorry this happened."

The concern in his tone spread an unwelcome warmth through her chest. She couldn't allow it. A broken heart lived there.

"Follow me, and don't touch anything." He paused before the door. "I hate for you to see this."

Nerves gripped her stomach. She stepped inside. Someone had over-turned the desk. Her stack of reference books had been tossed around the room, and the area maps pinned to the wall torn down.

Scott opened the door to the climate-controlled room, and she entered. A gasp escaped. The shelving units, once filled with clay pots, arrowheads, pipes, carved spoons, and an assortment of other pieces, stood almost empty. A box next to the door held broken pieces of clay and pottery from the newer artifacts prepped to go to the lab. Perfect specimens when she'd catalogued them. Her gaze flew to the shelf where she'd stored the wolf.

Gone.

Her chest caved. No…no…no. Not the wolf! This couldn't be real.

Tom came up beside her and placed his hand on her back. "I'm sorry. I know how much this meant to you."

Kaitlyn, the sole female on the force, glanced up from across the room, where she dusted for fingerprints. With her slim form, sparse makeup, and bobbed, dark hair, she could pass for college age instead of twenty-eight. She tried to put up a tough façade, but a vulnerable soul lurked beneath that Kevlar exterior. Her gaze went to Tom's hand on Maddie.

Shit. Maddie hadn't even seen her at first, she'd been so focused on the devastation.

Kaitlyn had a thing for Tom, but he couldn't have been more oblivious. Maddie kept trying to get him to notice, but right now she had bigger things to worry about.

"There's one box still intact." Scott gestured to the shelf closest to the door.

She made her way across the room, careful not to step on any pieces, and peered inside. A substantial number of arrowheads, flint knives, and other tools. Some of the rarer pieces of beaded jewelry as well. Still, nothing compared to the vast collection missing.

She gulped. "Why would anyone do this?"

"This wasn't just a burglary," Kaitlyn said. "Someone went out of their way to wreck the place."

"Is there anyone who would benefit from discrediting you?" Scott stepped over a broken chair leg. "Maybe a person competing for your job?"

"No. It's not like medical or law school where the competition is cutthroat." Maddie glanced at the bits of torn-up paper on the floor. "Archaeologists love their work. They wouldn't vandalize the place."

She bent down and studied the broken pieces of pottery. "These were whole when we dug them up." She rubbed her forehead and shut her eyes. "This is a disaster." How would she ever break the terrible news to the tribal leaders?

Tom squeezed her shoulder. "We'll find who did this."

"But they have almost all the artifacts. We were storing them here until the museum was built." She glanced at the broken ones on the floor. "What if the thief sells them at auction before we can get them back?"

Kaitlyn maneuvered around a shelving unit to come closer. "We can monitor the online sites and see if any of them pop up for sale."

"I can help with that. I know what to look for." Maddie stood, and Tom let go of her.

Scott frowned. "I think you need to prepare yourself for the possibility we won't recover the artifacts. Whoever stole them will whisk them out on the black market, not through a public auction the police can monitor."

Maddie bristled. "You can't know for sure. We have to try to find them."

"We will, but I want you to have realistic expectations. The first thing we need to do is get the documentation of everything that's missing. Can you compile that?"

"Yeah. It's all on my computer. I'll go home and work on it right now."

"I'll walk you down to your car, and don't worry, we won't give up." Tom rested a hand on her arm. "How about if I make spaghetti for dinner one night this week? My special sauce will cheer you up."

Kaitlyn dropped her duster and then fumbled to pick it up. Her gaze darted to Tom.

Scott stared down at his report as a muscle in his neck bulged.

Maddie nodded, so sick to her stomach that food was the last thing on her mind. "I still can't believe this happened."

Scott pulled a business card out of his wallet and handed it to her. "My email is on here. As soon as you have the files ready, send them over."

His jade eyes had turned cucumber-cool. All business.

Fine by her. That was clearly all he wanted from their relationship. From now on she'd think of him as nothing more than the detective assigned to her case.

CHAPTER 6

VICTOR MOLE FINGERED the scar on his chin, one of several that marred his massive, muscular body. Growing up in the Bronx, knife fights had left a few jagged marks on his flesh. He'd never backed down from a battle. At the first sign of weakness, the sharks circled.

The large bay window behind his desk overlooked the lake and cliffs. Early afternoon, the sun shined in, warming the room. The expansive estate he owned had come complete with tennis courts, a pool, and a sauna. His dictionary didn't contain the word "skimp." Not anymore.

Views like this from his luxury resort would bring in major money if he could ever get a permit to build on the waterfront land. With his Southwest operation shut down, he had to get moving on a new supply of artifacts.

A knock sounded at the door. Must be Eric. He was a loose cannon, but the best connection to the drug dealers that Victor had at the moment. He hit the automatic button to open the door.

Eric slunk into the room, his frame hunched. Wearing torn jeans and a black T-shirt, he reeked of body odor and cigarette smoke.

Victor flicked an ash off the lapel of his designer suit and wrinkled his nose. "Sit the fuck down." He stood to tower over Eric. "I'm starting to think you aren't worth what I'm paying you."

"I'm worth it, man. I'm worth it." Eric wiped his face, leg bouncing.

"You'd better be. Your life depends on it. I can't afford to have a useless sack-of-shit working for me. I expect results."

"Didn't I just bring you a bunch of artifacts from that storeroom this morning?" He wiped his face again. "Good stuff. Worth a lot, I'm sure."

The pieces would buy Victor some time with his clients on the black market. They were antsy over the lack of merchandise for sale since he'd shut down his Southwest operation. The sooner he unloaded his inventory, the better to stay ahead of the cops. "My guys hacked the alarm system so that all you had to do was go in and get the goods. I expected more. What happened?"

Eric squirmed in the chair. "The police showed up when I was trashing the place, and I had to run. Didn't get the last box." He mopped his brow. "Dropped one, but it didn't have much in it. I was careful, super careful."

Fucking useless. "I didn't tell you to trash the place. Why did you do that?"

"So they'd think kids broke in and messed it up for fun." A bead of sweat trickled down the side of his neck. "I destroyed all the records as extra credit, so the cops can't find out what's gone."

Extra credit. He had to be fucking kidding. "I don't pay you to think or change the plans. You do exactly what I tell you."

Eric bobbed his head repeatedly, and Victor curled his lips. "If you'd been focused, you wouldn't have trashed the place until all the artifacts were out."

"I'm focused. I'm focused." Eric bounced his leg faster.

"You're high and wired." Victor propped a hip on the edge of the desk. "Tell me the game plan, because I wonder if your memory works with a head full of crystal."

"Yup. I'm laying the groundwork. When we get the next shipment of meth, you take out the distributor, and we set up operations. Shit's gonna hit the fan when the supply is cut. My people are ready to move in."

"They'd better be, for your sake. And don't tell any of them who you work for. You blow my cover, you're dead."

Eric held up his hands. "I'm not gonna screw up. No one knows anything about you. All they know is I got a supplier. They don't ask who, and I'm not telling."

Victor picked up the cigar clipper. He slid a finger through the round hole. Little prick needed to understand who he was dealing with. "You ever been tortured?"

"No." Eric licked his lips, his gaze on the cutter.

"I wonder if you can keep your mouth shut under torture. I have serious doubts."

Eric's gaze darted to the door and then back to the finger guillotine. "I wouldn't talk for anything."

"I like to be sure about these things. In the past, I've tested my people." Victor spun the clipper around his finger.

"You...don't need to test me. I keep my mouth shut."

"Here's what we're going to do." Victor pushed off the desk.

Eric gripped the arms of his chair, his eyes wide. "Look, you don't need to do—"

"Shut the fuck up. I'm talking." Victor yanked Eric out of the chair and shook him. "You risk my business by being high. Makes me wonder how serious you are about work."

"I'm serious. Dead serious."

"You've got the dead part right. Come back clean tomorrow to go over the final plans."

"I will. I will." Eric took a step toward the door.

"Not so fast." Victor pointed to the desktop. "Empty your wallet."

"What?"

"Your wallet. I want the money in it."

Eric withdrew a worn, scratched-up billfold out of his jeans pocket. He opened it upside down and shook out two hundred-dollar bills onto the desk.

Victor picked up the money and waved it in front of Eric's face. "I know you aren't paying for whatever shit you're using of mine. That ends now. No more of my crystal."

"Okay. Whatever you say." Eric stepped back, his gaze on the cash.

Holding the money against the red tip of his cigar, Victor inhaled a puff. Flames curled up the sides of the bills. An acrid chemical scent permeated the air. He didn't flinch when the fiery ashes fell on his other hand.

But Eric did.

The fucktard beat it out of the room, and Victor returned to his seat.

Heels clicked on the marble hall floor, and he looked up. Gina, dressed in a conservative navy-blue suit, stepped into the room. Clips held her blond hair in a tight bun. As his lawyer and public relations representative, she kept up a professional image at all times. For what he paid her, she was willing to bend some rules and do whatever he needed. At least this bitch could follow instructions and knew her place. If not, she'd be ashes in the wind like the others who'd disappointed him.

She closed the door to his soundproof office and took a seat in front of the huge cherry wood desk.

After easing into the oversize leather chair across from her, he picked up a cigar and wove it between the heavily ringed fingers of his hands. She'd better have some good news. Plans for the construction hadn't been an easy sell in a town with a fetish for history. "What's the latest with the locals?"

"The door-to-door campaign seems to have worked. Once I talked about how much money the tourists would spend in their shops, the owners stopped protesting. Same with the wineries."

"Greed always wins out." One obstacle down. He clipped the end of his cigar. "What's going on with our permit?"

"We've reached another roadblock."

"Now what?" Enough delays. The proposed construction area should hold a veritable gold mine of artifacts according to his research. Once he had the permit, everything on the land would be legally his. He needed the resort to launder his money, if he could ever get the fucking thing built.

Gina waved a hand to the window over the lake. "Because this site is on the shore of a navigable waterway, we need an Army Corps permit prior to construction. With the federal government involved, this land falls under the guidelines of the National Preservation Act."

"Cut to the chase. What does this mean?"

"They require a field survey to determine if there are any finds that need to be analyzed for historic properties."

Another hoop to jump through. He lit his cigar. "What's that involve?"

"An archaeologist has to check out the land and probably dig a portion. If anything significant is found, more surveys could be ordered."

He talked through his teeth, clenching the cigar. "Define significant."

"I don't know. The law is arbitrary."

Fucking feds. Always gumming up the works. Coffee churned in his stomach. He plucked the cigar from his mouth. "You couldn't find a palm to grease with what I'm paying you?"

She shook her head. "This is federal. No way around it."

"How long will this take?"

"It depends. If they uncover valuable artifacts, it raises everything to another level." She frowned. "At the next phase, we'd have to go into consultations with the State and Tribal Officers. Engage the public as well. The process could take a year, maybe more."

"The construction delay has already cost a fortune. Find someone to do the survey. I want it done yesterday." He leaned forward, body taut, and tapped his cigar on the ashtray.

Gina nodded. "I checked. There's only one person listed in the area that does them. Her name is Madeline Cooper."

No fucking way. He had a room full of stolen artifacts that belonged to her. Victor didn't need her snooping around his business. "There's no one else?"

"I called everyone even remotely close." Gina frowned. "It's slim pickings around here with such a small population. We would wait months for someone outside to do the survey, so I scheduled a meeting with Ms. Cooper."

Shit. They were already running behind schedule. He'd just have to be careful around her. No reason to think she'd suspect him of being behind the burglary. "What all do you know about her?"

"She's active with the Seneca Nation tribes. Currently working for Cultural Resources leading an excavation, and she's a teacher's assistant at the university."

Nothing he didn't already know. He sat back in his chair and puffed the cigar. Cooper might be sympathetic to the Indians, but everyone had a price, and time was of the essence. "The field survey has to come up empty. I'll handle the girl. When's the meeting?"

"Tomorrow morning."

"Move it up to today."

Gina clicked her pen. "She said she was fitting us in and had nothing sooner. Do you want me to cancel?"

Fitting them in? Bitch would need to get her priorities straight. He'd see to that. "No, keep the appointment."

"Okay."

After Gina left, he picked up the cigar cutter and ran his thumb along the outer edge.

Tomorrow morning, he'd meet the Cooper bitch and buy her off. If she couldn't be bought, he had other ways of convincing her to cooperate.

CHAPTER 7

Scott rapped his knuckles on Lee's open office door and entered.

Lee glanced up from the computer. "Maddie sure didn't look too happy about having you on her case."

Shutting the door behind him, Scott nodded. "I don't blame her. She did agree to keep my past quiet, though."

"That's a relief. You said there's more you needed to tell me." Lee picked up a glass paperweight etched with the badge number of a fellow cop killed in a drug raid he had worked with Scott. He kept his gaze on the object as he smoothed a thumb across the top. "We've dealt with some heavy shit in our line of work. What happened while you were in Mexico?"

A heaviness settled on Scott's shoulders. He and Lee had done everything by the book, but there was no book when it came to undercover drug raids. Anything could go sideways, and they'd lost a good friend. He sat and turned to face the open window. "This was personal, not job-related. My brother Justin died of a drug overdose when I was away."

"What? When did this happen?"

"Eighteen months ago. He left me a voicemail saying he was in trouble and needed help. I was so deep in the drug cartel cases that I got the message too late."

"Oh man." Lee rubbed his forehead. "I had no idea. I'm really sorry."

"Me, too. I'll never know what he called about. His addiction, debts, or maybe someone was after him. Could be anything."

"I don't understand. Justin never did drugs."

Scott shook his head. "He was clean when he lived at home. Shit, I turned down assignments and stayed in the city to be there for him, like I'd promised my mom. When he left for college, I figured he was good to go." He ran a hand down his face. Maybe if he hadn't been so busy chasing drug lords, he might have visited his brother and seen the signs. "The irony bites. I'm a DEA agent, and my own brother dies of a heroin overdose in a fucking tent in Utah. Didn't even make it to twenty-four. I should have known and stopped him."

"How could you? No one gets personal calls while undercover."

Scott stood and went over to the water cooler. He rested a hand on top. "Anyway, hardly anyone knows about my brother, including Maddie." And he'd keep it that way because if she did, with her big heart, she might forgive him. Much safer for her to stay furious at him. He had to keep as much distance as possible from her and not give Mole a weakness to exploit.

"It might help if you told her now."

"No. It's better this way. I just wanted to let you know the situation. I need to get back to work."

Lee opened the door to the quiet station room.

He had been one of those cops who lived and breathed danger every second on the job. The hairier it got, the higher he rose to the occasion. Scott locked gazes with him. "From what you've said, crimes like this burglary are rare around here. Do you miss it? The action?"

A sad smile formed on Lee's face. He glanced at the framed picture of his wife. "Not as much as I'd miss her."

Scott's heart pressed against his ribs. Lee had chosen his wife over the job, while he had left Maddie dangling in the wind. But they weren't married, and he owed it to his brother to put away the monsters who supplied drugs.

As he stepped out of the office, Lee called, "Hey, Scott?"

"Yeah?" He swung around.

"Your brother's death. It wasn't your fault."

Like hell. If he'd been around to help him, Justin might still be alive. The vise on his lungs squeezed harder. "I'd better get to work."

He headed toward his desk. As always, he'd channel his energy and concentrate on the mission at hand. Whatever it took, he couldn't let Maddie know his feelings for her still ran deep. Chasing the scum of humanity had scarred him. She deserved to be with a whole person. He might need to use every trick he'd learned while undercover to hide his emotions, even if it meant hurting her.

Hurt was better than dead.

CHAPTER 8

FOG HUNG over the cool lake as the morning sun climbed above the trees near Victor's resort site. Maddie stifled a yawn. Once again, she'd been up late, this time working on the files for Scott. She'd sent them in batches so he could start tracking as many artifacts as possible. Now all she could do was wait.

She stopped the car and opened the window. Gazing at the lake, she breathed in the piney scent of the surrounding woods. No wonder the developer wanted to build on the shoreline. The deep, aqua water rivaled the color of the Caribbean. She shielded her eyes to stare up at a bald eagle soaring over the woods. Her injured cheek hurt when she squinted, but she couldn't look away. So majestic and graceful. He flapped his wings and settled on the top of a tree, grabbing a branch with his talons.

A waterfront resort situated across from six vineyards would draw good money. Tourists would boost the economy of the small town as well. But Victor Mole might not be able to build if the area turned up artifacts. When she'd agreed to meet with him, she had no idea her storage building would be burglarized. Now more than ever, the unearthed artifacts needed protection. The tribal members had lost so much.

She still had a full agenda for the next month, though. Finals to grade, the excavation to finish, and now the open police case. A smart woman would walk away from this field survey. But her heart wouldn't let her. The history needed to be preserved.

She drove around the lake to the designated meeting area and parked next to two vehicles, one of them a sleek, black Bentley.

A blonde woman in a business suit, with her hair tied back, got out of a BMW. Lots of money, this group.

"Madeline Cooper?" The lady extended a hand and introduced herself as Gina.

After they shook hands, Gina gestured to an enormous man smoking a cigar, who stood near the cliff overlooking the water. "My boss, Mr. Mole, wishes to speak with you."

"All right."

Bentley flicked an ash to the ground and turned. Dressed in a suit that must have been tailored to fit his bulk, he planted his feet and took another puff, apparently expecting them to come to him. Maddie narrowed her eyes and followed Gina, who picked her way across the sand and rocks in high heels.

The closer they came to him, the larger he loomed. Not a fat man, but massive with broad shoulders, a thick trunk, and huge thighs. He'd make a formidable offensive lineman. Her shoulder blades pinched together.

With slicked-back dark hair, he wore custom Oakley shades despite the foggy conditions. Three of the fingers on the hand holding his cigar sported hefty, gold rings.

Gina stopped in front of him and introduced Maddie. Victor nodded, puffed the cigar, and flicked another glowing ash to the ground.

He waved a hand at Gina. "Wait for me by the car."

As Gina made her way back to the BMW, Victor puffed again on the cigar. "Do you understand the situation here?"

"What do you mean?" Maddie cocked her head.

"Simple. We need to get this project under construction. The sooner, the better. You do your thing; then I can do mine." He flicked more ashes.

"Well, I need to see what the job entails. I'm not sure I'll have the time to do the survey." Or the stomach to deal with such an inconsiderate asshole.

"The job won't take much time."

"I think you're wrong. Native Americans populated this region for thousands of years. This land has a high probability of turning up artifacts. If it does, it will merit further inspection, possibly larger areas to test."

Victor shrugged his enormous shoulders. "Nothing will be found. How much will that result cost?"

Holy shit. He was bribing her. Welcome to the corrupt world of Victor Mole.

He rubbed his chin. "Time is money, girl. Construction delays are pricey. I invest a little up front to make sure we keep on track, and I save money down the road. See how this works?"

Girl? Her blood simmered. Cocky, greedy bastard. If he found someone who could be bought, and those people did exist, he'd forge ahead and demolish everything. She'd seen it happen before. Bulldozers destroying precious relics and nothing could be done to stop them because the laws didn't apply to private property. If this slime ball hadn't needed the Army Corps permit to build, he could have done whatever he wanted with his land. But now there were all kinds of state and federal laws that prevented him from digging until the permit process was completed.

She couldn't risk him hiring someone who would accept a bribe and falsify a survey. Her best shot at saving any possible artifacts was to make sure he hired *her*. Pasting on a fake smile, she nodded. "I do see. What kind of up-front investment are we talking here?"

His shades hid his eyes, but he dipped his head down and back up. Most likely checking out her attire, which consisted of scuffed work boots, worn cargo pants, and an old denim jacket. Probably deciding the minimum bribe someone like her would accept.

He blew out a cloud of smoke and gave her a number in a low tone.

Her heart jumped. Holy crap. He'd have no trouble finding someone on the take for that kind of money. But if she played along, he wouldn't hire another person and would be screwed once she reported a find. She'd never take a cent of his dirty money, and he'd be unable to build.

If only she had proof that he'd tried to bribe her, she could go to the police. But it would be her word against his if he denied it, and he clearly wouldn't lose sleep over lying.

She'd have to find a way to expose him later. Right now, she needed to stop him. Her gaze went to the huge rings on his fingers. The greedy, arrogant jerk had to have low-balled her.

She pursed her lips and nodded her head. "I've seen the plans for this place. We're talking major bucks here. To keep this on track..." She tapped her cheek. "I'll accept your offer."

When a predatory grin split his face, she added, "Provided you add a zero."

The smile disappeared. His eyes turned to slits as he chewed on his cigar.

She must be out of her freaking mind to have asked him for such a huge bribe.

Sweat dripped down her chest.

Black vultures circling overhead caught her eye. She scuffed her boot in the soil. "Well lookie here, I think I see a little something under the surface."

She bent down and scratched her fingers across the sand. Gave her an excuse to hide her very-bad poker face. "Yup. Definitely something."

The crocodile chuckled. A deep, guttural laugh. "You got balls, girl." He waved the cigar at her. "Okay, deal."

All the air left her lungs. She shut her eyes for a second to regain some control, and then rose, dusting her hands on her pants.

He jerked his head at Gina, who stood in front of her car. "She'll work out the details with you."

Maddie nodded, her throat too dry to speak.

After he tossed his still-smoldering cigar on the ground, the sleazebag strode toward his car. He said something to Gina and held his arms out like, "who da man?" Gina bobbed her head and tapped something onto the tablet she held.

Victor lowered himself into the Bentley and gunned the engine. The tires spewed dirt as he executed a U-turn, not bothering to back up and stay on the road.

Irreverent bastard.

Maddie squashed the cigar butt with her shoe and swallowed hard. A chill ran down her spine.

No telling what someone with that much money and power would do when she gave him the middle finger.

CHAPTER 9

ON HER KNEES, digging at the excavation site, Maddie dusted off an arrowhead and placed it with several others in a box. The muscles in her neck bunched. Two hours ago, she'd accepted a bribe of epic proportions from a man with no moral compass, and now she had an empty, unusable storage building wrapped in crime-scene tape. Any artifacts they found had to go straight to the lab.

"Maddie, are you okay?"

She glanced at Kyle, one of her undergrads, who crouched beside her, extracting a new find.

"Just bummed."

"I know. What do you think the chances are of recovering the stolen pieces?"

The hopeful glint in his blue eyes caused her chest to tighten. He'd worked hard on the excavation and was building his own resume. She sighed and rocked back on her heels. "Not good. The police said this morning they had no hits on auctions, and most likely the items had been sold on the black market."

Kyle's freckled nose wrinkled. "Any leads on the burglar?"

"Nope. No fingerprints. He must have worn gloves." Ones that had left a decided bruise on her cheek. She brushed some dirt aside from the area Kyle had been digging. Might as well focus on something positive. "Looks like you're close there."

"I've almost got it." His hands shook as he carefully lifted a long, skinny pipe out of the soil. "I think it's made of bone."

She smiled at the sheer delight on his face. Only another archaeologist could appreciate the excitement of discovery. Despite the heaviness of her heart, she patted him on the back and leaned close to inspect the pipe. "Great job. This one's in perfect condition."

"At least we have these." He placed the piece in the box with the other artifacts.

She glanced at the dark clouds above. "Looks like rain. I think we'd better call it a day."

"Okay." He helped her cover the site with the tarp. "I'll drop the box at the lab on my way home."

"Thanks." She snatched her backpack and headed to her Honda. As she drove through the deep green forest, her tense muscles loosened. Towering hardwoods lined the side of the road, their tangled branches forming canopies. Tiny purple and yellow wildflowers sprinkled color through the flora. Fat raindrops plopped on the windshield. Thank goodness they'd covered the excavation site in time.

The sky opened up. She cranked the wipers to high and eased off the accelerator. Couldn't be a worse road for visibility with its hairpin turns weaving through the hilly forest. From out of nowhere, an animal sprinted across the lane.

She swerved, and her car spun on the rain-slicked road. Adrenaline spiked through her body. She gripped the wheel and cranked it in the opposite direction. Time ground to a halt as trees, blurry from the spinning car, whizzed past her window. The seatbelt cut into her neck as she strained to regain control before the Honda plunged down the steep bank rushing toward her.

Panic gripped her as the vehicle careened toward the precipice. She slammed a foot on the brake pedal. The car slid sideways off the pavement and scraped against a tree. Her body lurched toward the empty passenger seat as the right two wheels of her Honda dropped into the ditch.

Oh God, she prayed it wouldn't roll.

She braced her hands against the ceiling. The car finally stopped.

Mouth dry, eyes squeezed shut, she brought a hand down to her chest and took a deep breath.

She might need a paint job or touch-up, but the car was in one piece. When she could breathe again, she shifted into reverse and hit the accelerator. The wheels spun in the mud. Crap. Now she was stuck. She unbuckled her seatbelt and peered through the rain-streaked window.

A small dog sat hunched under a large oak tree. Light-colored fur molded to the mutt's bony frame. He blinked in the rain, and her heart squeezed. Poor thing. She'd need to call for roadside assistance, but first she'd try to catch the dog before he got scared and ran away.

She opened the door and climbed out. Cold rain stung her face. In a soft voice, she called, "Here, sweetie. Come here."

The puppy raised its nose and sniffed, but didn't run off. She took slow steps toward the animal. He backed away. Burs and pine needles matted the dog's fur. Hard to say how long he'd been on his own. Maybe she could bribe him with some food. She dug a granola bar out of her pocket, opened the wrapper, and broke a piece off in her hand. "Hungry?"

The dog sniffed again, his whiskers twitching from the rain, and took a step forward. A little closer and she could reach him.

Lightning flashed.

Thunder boomed.

With a yelp, the pup bolted down the steep hill, straight toward the swollen, rushing river.

"Stop!" Her pulse skipped as she sprinted after the pup. Branches scratched her face, and rain soaked her fleece jacket. She kept calling, but he continued at a fast clip.

When the puppy reached the rocks at the edge of the river, he tried to stop but slid on the slick mud and tumbled into the water.

Maddie gasped and ran faster. Her chest seized as the current swept him away and his head disappeared beneath the surface.

* * *

Scott drove through the woods on his way to the storage building. The lack of progress in the burglary case made his stomach burn. No leads, no evidence, nothing to trace. He'd take another look at the crime scene to make sure they hadn't missed anything. This wasn't the work of a professional, though. Broken pieces, vandalism, a valuable box of objects left behind. He would suspect Mole, but the man didn't run an operation like this. Had to be someone else.

Almost all of Maddie's artifacts were lost. He flexed his fingers on the steering wheel. Someone would pay when he found the asswipe.

He rounded a curve and passed Maddie's Honda parked sideways in a ditch. His heart jumped to his throat. He slid to a stop and leaped out of the Impala. Rain pelted his head as he yanked her car door open, only to find it empty.

Deeper in the forest, Maddie's panicked voice rang out. What was she doing in the middle of the woods during a storm? He took off in the direction of her call. From the top of the slope, he spotted her racing toward the river.

He called out to her, but whether she heard or not, she kept running. When she reached the shore, she jumped in.

Holy shit.

He scanned the river, wild from the wind and rain. The head of a small dog surfaced.

Christ. Now it made sense.

Maddie swam toward the animal, who struggled to stay afloat while being dragged downstream.

He assessed the current and the surrounding terrain. At the rate Maddie and the dog were moving, his best bet to head them off would be farther south. He traversed the slope diagonally, cursing along the way. Maddie had to be fucking crazy jumping into frigid water.

He glanced back at the river. Thanks to the angle he'd taken, he was ahead of Maddie now. She'd managed to reach the dog, but with one arm around it, in the raging water, she wouldn't be able to swim to shore. Both she and the pup went under and then came back up sputtering.

The river curved ahead. He needed to cut them off there. She had precious few minutes in water that cold before she lost control of her limbs. His legs burned as he pushed to the limit and raced faster.

He stopped at the bend, tore off his suit jacket, and tossed it to the ground. Maddie and the dog continued to bob and go under, but the current was bringing them closer. He plunged into the freezing water and swam in swift, strong strokes toward them.

When he reached her, Maddie's eyes widened, and she spit out his name along with some water. "Sc-Scott. Save the dog, I can't hold him and swim."

He grabbed her shoulders and spun her around to face away from him so he could wrap an arm under her ribs. "You hold the dog. I'll bring you ashore."

For once, Maddie didn't argue. He held her and kicked hard, swimming on his side, her and the dog on his hip. The pup wriggled and churned his legs, frantic to break free. Maddie flailed a hand out and scooped at the water.

He huffed in her ear, "Stop trying to help. Just keep the dog secure. I've got you both."

The mutt whined, and Maddie snatched her arm back to hug him tight. When they reached the shallow bank, Scott let go and sucked in air to catch his breath. He glanced at Maddie. Her entire body shook, and her lips were blue. She still clung to the dog, whose tongue hung out as he panted hard and shivered.

Damn. They were nowhere near out of the woods. First, he had to get them warm, and later he'd light into her about how she'd risked her life with that crazy stunt. The rain continued to pound, and lightning flashed again.

"Where d-did you come from?" Maddie asked.

"No time for talk. We need to get back to the car." He snatched his suit coat from the ground and draped it over her shoulders.

Thunder clapped. The puppy whimpered and wriggled in her arms.

"Give me the dog." He reached over and took the mutt from her. Her eyes were dilated. Not a good sign. "Can you walk okay?"

She attempted a step and stumbled. He caught her with his free hand, thrust the dog back into her arms, and picked her up. "Hold onto him."

Maddie pushed against his chest. "I can d-do—"

"No, you can't." He gripped her tighter and marched up the hill. "You're too cold from jumping into a freezing river. Do as I say, and don't fight me if you want to save this dog."

That did it. She nodded and buried her head into his shoulder, holding the pup against him. He moved faster when she stopped wriggling. With quick strides, he carried her toward the Impala.

He opened the back door, and she slid the dog along the seat.

"Get in and take your clothes off. I'm going to start the car." He popped the trunk release, went to the driver's side, and got in. After turning the key, he cranked the heat. He hopped out and grabbed blankets from the trunk on his way back to Maddie.

The dog had nestled against her breast, both of them still shaking.

"You need to get these wet clothes off. I have blankets." Scott tossed them next to her.

"N-no. I'm fine."

"Like hell you are. Damn, you're stubborn." Didn't she understand how serious the situation was? "Off with the clothes."

Her teeth chattered and her breath was shallow, eyes still dilated.

He shook his head, grabbed one of her feet, and untied the lace of her boot. "We don't have time for this."

The rain continued to pour as he crouched beside the open door and yanked off her boots and socks. The car wouldn't heat up with the wind blowing in, so he slid Maddie across the seat, climbed in next to her, and pulled the door almost closed, careful not to let it latch. The last thing he needed was to be trapped in the back of his police car the first week on the job. "You're shaking. Let me help."

"The dog. He's so cold—"

Typical Maddie, worried about everyone but herself. Scott grabbed a blanket and wrapped it around the whining dog. "He'll be okay. I promise I'll take care of him, but let's get you settled first."

He gently set the dog on the seat beside Maddie and managed to pull off her soaked fleece. Keys jingled in the pocket. Luckily, they hadn't fallen out in the river.

Her breath hitched when he unbuttoned her khaki pants. She tried to grab his hand but shook too hard to stop him.

He glanced up at her as he stripped the sopping pants down her legs.

She blinked a few times as if disoriented, her eyes huge in her ghost-white face.

"Stay with me, Maddie. You hear me?"

She blinked again but said nothing. He grabbed the hem of her polo and pulled the shirt over her head. Her skin, so pale in contrast to the black bra she wore, had no warmth. He snatched up the other blanket and covered her body, pulling it tightly over her.

At last, heat blasted from the vents. She'd be okay. Yet, his heart raced faster than it had on his most dangerous raid. He shivered as well, but with more body mass and less time in the water, he'd recover quicker.

He buckled her seatbelt, picked up the wrapped dog, and placed him on her stomach. She'd have to stay in the back for now, no time to move her. "Hang in there, babe."

Once in the driver's seat, he threw the car in gear and switched on the police lights. Better get her to the hospital.

He kept checking on her in the rearview mirror. She hadn't reacted to him calling her babe. The old endearment had slipped off his tongue.

A few minutes later, she stirred. "Where are we going? Why am I in your car?"

Scott jerked at the sound of her voice. "To the hospital. How are you doing back there?"

"I can feel my face again. Wait. No hospital. I'm fine, now."

Unconvinced, he pulled the car to the side and leaned over the seat. Her breathing seemed normal. She still shivered, but not as much.

He let out a breath. "Recite the alphabet."

"Please. Don't insult me." She rolled her eyes.

"I mean it. Say the alphabet, or we go to the hospital."

"Fine. Z Y X W V U T—"

Smart-ass. His jacked pulse slowed down a notch. He swung back around so she wouldn't see his smile. Wow. It had been a long time since he'd smiled.

"So, what now?"

"I'll take you home."

"What about my car?"

He glanced at her in the rearview mirror. "I'll call a towing service and send Tom to meet them there."

"That's ridiculous. I can drive.'"

Yeah, she was okay. Back to arguing with him over everything. "Not naked. You'd get arrested."

Her jaw dropped, and her eyes narrowed. "Very funny. And we need to talk about that."

"Oh, I intend to talk to you about *all* of this, but right now I need to get you home."

The puppy whined, and Maddie sighed. "Okay."

Scott turned off the police lights and pulled back onto the road. He sure as hell shouldn't have made the naked comment. Didn't need that image. He'd been too worried about her health to pay much attention to what she had on under her clothes when he was focused on getting her warm. Now that the danger had passed...

Damn, Maddie. Lacy black bra and thong?

CHAPTER 10

SEATED in the back of Scott's car, wrapped tightly in a blanket, Maddie tried to wriggle her arms free. The itchy, standard-issue police blanket chafed her bare skin. The puppy, sleeping on her lap, stirred. Poor thing. She stopped moving so she wouldn't wake him. Her toes throbbed with pain as the blood returned to them. Scott kept shooting looks in the rearview mirror. Probably to make sure he didn't need to re-route to the hospital.

God, he'd undressed her and seen her almost naked. Of course, she'd worn her sexy underwear today. She did that once in a while to remind herself she wasn't dead yet. Sad statement about her love life. And really shitty timing.

Her plans to avoid him had sure gone to hell. Now, he probably had reports to write because of her. She'd complicated his life, but not for long.

He answered a call on the radio as she stared at the back of his head. Good thing he'd come along or that dog might not be alive. All rational thoughts had deserted her when he fell into the river. She'd reacted without thinking. But the panic in that furry puppy face fighting to stay above water had demanded immediate action.

She took a deep breath. "How did you end up at the river?"

He met her gaze in the mirror. "I saw your car on the side of the road and heard you calling to the dog."

"Oh." Those gorgeous green eyes of his gave her shivers no warm blanket could stop. He still had that effect on her.

"What the hell were you thinking jumping in like that? You could have drowned." He spoke in a neutral tone, but controlled anger simmered beneath the surface.

"What was I supposed to do? Watch the dog die? What would you have done?"

He turned his attention back to the road. "I would have assessed the situation and found a way to get him out without jeopardizing my life."

Of course, he would. "Well, I haven't been trained like you. I did what I could."

Silence.

She should be thanking him, but the sting of embarrassment that she'd acted rashly and hadn't been able to save the dog on her own put her on the defensive.

"What happened to your car?" He glanced again in the rearview mirror.

"I swerved to avoid the dog and lost control. Only scraped a tree, I think. I was lucky."

"You managed to turn that luck from good to bad quickly."

She counted to ten. Damn if he didn't get under her skin like chiggers in the sand.

He pulled into her complex and parked. When he came around to open her door, she tried to free her arms, but he'd wrapped her in a tight cocoon.

"Don't move. You'll expose yourself to the cold air." He picked up her soggy fleece from the floor and took her keys out of the pocket. "Is one of these to your apartment?"

She nodded.

He reached into the car and plucked her and the dog off the seat as if they weighed nothing. The sky opened up to drop another round of hard rain. It soaked and seeped through the coarse blanket. The puppy burrowed between them.

"Oh my God. You are not carrying me up three flights of stairs to my apartment. Put me down." She struggled to get free, but he once again tightened his grip on her and kicked the car door shut. Strong, muscular biceps held her snug against his rock-hard chest. She swallowed hard and glanced at him. With his chiseled chin, jade eyes, and those sexy lips, she couldn't look away. A dip in the cold river had only served to make him smell like fresh water and pine.

Dangerous.

Good thing her arms were trapped, because despite her resolve, she might not have been able to resist the urge to run her fingers through his hair and kiss him. And set herself up for more self-imposed suffering.

"You are the most stubborn woman I've ever met," he grated out as he ignored her protests and moved to the stairwell. He hunkered over her and the puppy shielding them from some of the rain. "If you keep this up, the dog will fall. I only have two hands."

Crap. He had a point. She leaned closer to wedge the dog between them. Scott's hair dripped with moisture, and the muscles of his wet, cold body twitched. He had to be freezing, although he'd never admit it.

All her fault.

He climbed the flights of stairs without hitching a breath. When he reached her apartment, he tipped back, bringing her face even closer to his, so he could unlock the door. He glanced down, and his gaze dropped to her lips, mere inches away. His eyes darkened.

The dog squirmed in the blanket. Scott snapped his head back and hauled them inside. He maneuvered past the packed boxes to the couch in the living room, where he lowered her. The puppy hopped down to the carpet, and nose to the ground, scampered about exploring.

The poor thing looked emaciated with wet fur sticking to his bones. Judging from his light-colored, medium-length fur, he might be a cross between a golden retriever and a yellow lab. He only came up to Scott's knees and the gangly legs he needed to grow into gave him an awkward, adolescent appearance. His oversize paws made her smile. He loped over to a pile of boxes and sniffed them.

Scott tapped one with his foot. "Moving?"

"Yeah. In a couple of days." She pushed her elbows out and loosened the blanket, at last freeing her arms. "Aren't you freezing? You still have all those wet clothes on."

"I'm fine, but I do need to get dry."

"I think we both need a hot shower."

He froze, his gaze fixed on the box.

Oh God. That had come out wrong. "I mean, if you want to go first, I'll, uh—"

"No." He shook his head. "Listen to me. You have to heat up your core. Drink some tea or coffee, change into some dry clothes, and cover up with layers of blankets. Toss them in the dryer to heat them up first. Can you do that?"

"Geez, I'm not a child. I can figure this out."

He raised an eyebrow. "You told me you needed to take a hot shower, and that's the last thing you're supposed to do when you have hypothermia."

The man knew too much about freaking everything. "Fine. I'll do what you said."

He bent down and placed his hand on her bare shoulder. Her skin tingled under his touch.

"I'm checking to see how cold you are."

Of course. A clinical touch. Her body still ramped up at the contact. These reactions had to stop.

"Considering your skin is warmer than mine, I think you're okay." He glanced at the dog. "This puppy needs attention. Do you have any food for him, maybe a brush?"

"No. I wasn't planning on a canine rescue mission tonight."

Scott frowned. "I'll take him with me and bring him back in a bit." He dropped to a knee and stroked the puppy's snout.

Warmth swirled around her heart. This couldn't be happening. She would not fall for him again. He glanced up and caught her staring at him. Uh oh. Had he asked her something? "What?"

For a second, he seemed lost as well. He took a breath, picked up the dog, and stood. "I'll be back. Do what I told you to, okay?"

"I will." She adjusted the blanket to cover her shoulder. "And Scott?"

"Yeah?"

Holding the puppy in his strong hands, hair still wet from the river and rain, all her resolve to keep her distance dissolved like cocoa powder in hot milk. "Thanks."

His eyes flickered with an emotion she couldn't read before he gave her a curt nod and turned. "I'll be back."

After he closed the door behind him, she quivered. The room seemed empty and cold all of a sudden.

She took a deep breath. Scott's stinging words earlier, about having fun while it lasted, came back a second time.

The drama of the dog rescue had swept her away. She hadn't expected to be up close and personal with Scott again. Surprise and shock had made her vulnerable. He'd already strung her along once, only to leave her behind.

No. Not again.

She glanced at the closed door. When he came back, she'd have her guard up.

* * *

Maddie sat on the couch, sipping her third cup of hot tea as she read a mystery book. Three hours since Scott had left with the dog. God knew what he was doing. Comfortable now, she wore a pink, fluffy robe and rabbit-eared slippers with plastic goo-goo eyes.

Heat the core. Check.

Drink hot fluids. Check.

Guard up. Double-check.

A knock sounded at the door. "It's Scott."

"Come in. It's unlocked."

He opened the door, carrying the dog. As soon as he put him down, the puppy raced around the apartment sniffing again.

"I have some stuff in the car to bring up." Scott closed the door behind him.

A minute later, he re-entered, arms full of supplies. He wore a light jacket and jeans. The room seemed to shrink. He filled every inch of it. The scent of soap and spice filled the air as he breezed by her. She took in the five o'clock shadow he had going on. Sexy as sin.

He dropped a sack of dog food by her feet along with a brown paper bag. His gaze traveled from her slippers to her face. His eyebrows raised, but he didn't say anything. He set another sack on the kitchen counter. "Why was your door unlocked?"

She shrugged. "Most people don't lock them. I'm not in the habit here."

"You're asking for trouble. Considering your storeroom was burglarized, I'd expect you to be more careful." He gave her a stern look.

She stood. "I don't have an apartment full of valuables. I'm sure I'm safe."

"Don't forget you were attacked. That's not safe in my book."

"Only because I got in the way. He wasn't after me, personally." Geez. Scott made her feel so stupid.

"It's an open case. We don't know anything for sure." He went over to the window, checked the latch, and locked it.

Now the man was acting paranoid. She lived on the third floor for God's sake. "I'm sure I'd hear a three-story ladder clink against the side of the building and have plenty of time to grab a pot to clunk someone on the head before they reached the top."

Scott swung around. "Do you think this is a joke? And seriously, that's what you would do? Get a pot?"

Good. She had him riled now. Served him right. "Or a pan. Possibly my meat pounder."

He faced the window and let out a long sigh. Probably counting again. She'd improve his math skills if nothing else. He stepped back to the couch and glanced down at her. "Have you warmed up?"

Near to boiling after his scolding. "Yes. You have a way of spiking my temperature."

Damn, that had come out wrong. She was on a roll tonight.

He smirked.

The puppy nudged him, and he bent to pet the little guy. Good. Maybe he wouldn't notice her burning cheeks.

Scott dug into the bag on the floor. He pulled out two dog bowls, a leash, brush, and bone. "Had to wait for him to thaw out before I could give him a bath."

Maddie's gaze went to the dog. The burrs and pine needles were gone, his fur fluffy. He bit one of Scott's bootlaces and tugged. The corner of Scott's mouth turned up before he cleared his throat and took a step back, as if he regretted the almost-smile.

This wasn't the Scott she knew. The man she'd met two years ago had been laid back and fun. Now, his eyes reflected a deep, sad pain. Almost like he'd lost part of his soul.

"I brought what I thought you might need to get him through a couple of days."

She glanced at the pile on the floor. He'd gone shopping on top of taking care of the puppy, who flopped on the floor beside the couch and closed his eyes. "None of this is your problem. I'm sorry. I didn't mean to—"

"Forget it. The main thing is that you're both safe. Have you eaten?"

"What?"

"Food. Did you have dinner, or do you only use your pots and pans as weapons?"

Smart aleck. She glanced at her refrigerator. "Um. No. I kinda forgot."

"I figured. Brought you some soup. Standard procedure for your condition."

Standard procedure. It sounded like a tactical move instead of an act of kindness when he put it that way. "Thanks, but that wasn't necessary."

Her stomach grumbled.

Crap.

"Clearly, not." He shook his head and unzipped his jacket.

She gazed at the partially visible logo, Marty's Tavern, on his white T-shirt. Her chest tightened. When they were dating, he'd taken her to that bar and bought the shirt on the way out. They'd danced together that night. Molded against him, her head on his shoulder, she'd breathed him in. Maybe he'd worn that shirt to remind her. No. He was a guy. Probably the only clean thing in his drawer.

He cocked his head. "What are you staring at?"

"Nothing."

"Your face is red. Do you have a fever?" He stepped closer and put a hand to her forehead.

She brushed it away. "No, I'm fine."

"Don't get cranky with me." He stabbed his fingers through his hair. "Are you blushing?"

She glanced at his shirt and then away. "No. I just had too much hot tea."

"Bullshit." His gaze dropped to his chest, and he stilled. He took a breath, ran a hand down his face, and muttered, "Fuck me."

"Look, I appreciate everything you've done, but you should go now." Hard to keep her voice neutral when her insides were doing flip-flops.

Scott inched closer. "I remember that night."

The different shades of green in his eyes reflected the light. Her stomach fluttered. She gave a small shrug, too choked up to speak.

"I'm sorry," he whispered.

"For what?" She held her breath.

He didn't answer right away. Only stared at her with what might be regret. Lines formed under his eyes as his face took on an almost tortured expression. He shook his head, took a step back, and zipped his jacket. "You're right. I should go."

She bit the inside of her cheek. He'd closed her off. No way would she cry in front of him. Somehow, he managed to keep getting to her when all her defenses were up. He and his stupid T-shirt could take a one-way trip down memory lane and stay there.

As he headed to the door, reality kicked back in. She asked, "Can I borrow your phone? I need to call for a tow truck, and my cell is drying out in a bag of rice. I guess I'll find out tomorrow if that trick really works."

He paused. "If your car's only scratched, you won't need to tow it. I'll grab Tom, and we can pick it up for you."

"I hate to bother him." Maddie frowned.

"He's on duty anyway. Give me your key, and we'll drop your car off." Scott took a step back toward her.

"No need. Tom has one."

Scott froze. "What?"

"Tom has a spare key. He can use that."

"To your car? You don't lock your doors, and you hand out keys to your car?"

He had a lot of nerve to question her. "No, as a matter of fact, I don't. Only one, to Tom, who's a cop."

"I see." His eyes turned to flint.

"What's that look for?" Maddie stomped over to him. "I know you're not jealous, so what's your problem?"

"Nothing, Maddie," he said in a weary voice. He strode to the door and opened it. "You have a right to do whatever you want with your life and your keys. Lock up behind me."

He left, sucking all the energy out of the room with him.

She stood planted in place. The man was infuriating. She hadn't kept her guard up. The chemistry between them had blown away her resolve.

And his face. All those painful emotions that had played across his features. Whatever secrets he had made him look horribly sad, like he didn't think he had the right to even smile.

He'd sure gone cold at the mention of Tom. If she hadn't locked her keys inside so many times, Tom wouldn't need to carry a spare.

If Scott was jealous, he had no right to be. Not a peep from him in two years. He'd made himself clear about how little she'd meant to him. Thank God, nothing had happened today. She'd have to keep her libido in check, which shouldn't be hard since she had no plans to spend time with him.

The scent of chicken soup came from the bag he'd left on the counter. The puppy jumped up, looked around, and sniffed the path Scott had taken on his way out. She glanced at the stash of goodies he had brought. He'd thought of everything.

The pup stopped in front of the door and whined. Maddie dropped to her knees and hugged him. Tears blurred her eyes as the mutt licked her face and burrowed against her. "I know, buddy."

Even when she was pissed at Scott, she yearned for him.

Damn that man.

CHAPTER 11

SCOTT PARKED his car along the property line of Mole's proposed new resort.

He rubbed the back of his neck. He'd tossed and turned all night over what had happened at Maddie's apartment. The woman drove him crazy. She turned his blood hot even in bunny slippers and a ridiculous pink, fluffy robe. She'd stood in front of him, hair a wild mess, and he'd itched to thread his hands through it and kiss her. Couldn't blame it on the adrenaline rush from the rescue. He'd taken three hours to shop, bathe the dog, and shower. Plenty of time to recover.

Thank God he'd stopped before he made a fool of himself. The last thing he needed was trouble with Tom. He carried a key to her freaking car, and who knew what else. Scott clenched his teeth. He had no right to be jealous. She owed him nothing. Small town or not, he had to keep his distance, or he'd go nuts.

At least he wasn't alone in his misery. He hadn't counted on drama, but he'd bet the house Kaitlyn, for all her toughness, had a soft spot for Tom.

Scott shook his head and grabbed the folder Lee had given him with the construction area information. Time to check out the perimeter for some vantage points to set up surveillance. The DEA had advanced tools, and he'd make the most of them.

He got out of the car and trudged across the sandy-colored clay soil, his gaze on the tree line. The forest provided ample places to mount hidden cameras. If Mole tried to dig up artifacts here, at least the place was small enough to monitor. Not like the Southwest, where he'd had a field day with its vast tracts of unpoliced land.

Hands on his hips, Scott scanned the area. His gaze dropped down the steep, rocky cliff overlooking the lake. The resort would sit above the rise. They'd have to put up a fence, or some drunken idiot could come out for the view and topple to his death.

He hiked along the bluff, assessing more of the property. When he rounded a bend, he stopped at the sight of a man in the distance with his back to him. Not Mole. Too small in stature, which could be said of most men in comparison. Scott stole his way to the forest and stood in the shade between two trees for a better look.

A medium-built, dark-haired man with a shovel was digging a hole near a Coming Soon sign splashed with pictures of the proposed luxury resort.

The man brushed away some dirt and then glanced around as if nervous someone might be watching. Scott jogged through the woods and came up behind the man without making a sound.

"Find anything?"

The guy jumped, tripped over the shovel, and then fell on his ass.

Suspicious as hell, this one.

"What the fuck? Who are you and what do you want?" The man pushed off the ground to stand.

Scott pulled his suit coat back to expose the badge and gun hanging on his belt. "I'm a police officer."

The man's mud-colored eyes widened. "What now? I didn't go anywhere near her. She's a lying bitch if she says I did."

No idea who he was talking about. With guilt written all over his face, he wouldn't last a second in a police interrogation. Scott let his jacket slip back into place. First things first. "What's your name?"

"Eric Wilson." He scratched his chin. "Wait. If you don't know my name, then you aren't here to arrest me."

"Should I be?"

"I'm not doing nothing illegal. I work here." He glanced over Scott's shoulder. "Where did you come from?"

"Not your business. What are you doing here?"

Eric avoided eye contact. "Putting up a sign. No law against that, is there?"

"Watch the attitude." Scott waved at the hole in the ground. "What's this about?"

"I'm uh...moving that sign." Eric pointed to it with a shaking hand.

Not a good liar. With the twitchy movements, darting eyes, and yellow-toned skin, he had the look of a tweaker. Mole had used those meth heads to do his looting in the Southwest because they had drug-induced focus and energy to dig for nights on end. Stood to reason he would use them again. Scott crossed his arms and stared Eric down. "You have some ID?"

"I'm telling you, I work for the owner." Eric dug out a license. He cocked his head as he handed it over. "This is private property. You got a warrant? My boss wouldn't like you snooping around."

This guy was all over the place. Paranoid, evasive, defensive, and now defiant. "Why? He have something to hide?"

Eric snickered. "Like to see you ask him that."

"Think I will." Scott kept his face impassive as he handed the license back. "Right after we discuss the tunnel you're digging to China."

Eric's gaze dropped to the hole. He wiped a hand across his mouth. "Just doing what I'm told."

If Mole had ordered Eric to dig for artifacts, it wouldn't be in broad daylight. He needed the cover of darkness to sneak out the relics. Mole must have lowered his standards if he'd added this cockroach to his payroll. Or maybe there weren't enough kids in town for him to hook on drugs and then put to use.

Eric picked up his shovel and kicked some dirt into the hole. "I gotta go."

Time to plant the might-be-a-crooked-cop seed. "I'll be seeing you around. I'm new here." Scott tapped the shovel with his foot. "And I play by my own rules."

He waited until Eric drove away and then bent to study the hole. If he had to guess, the guy was probably digging to see if he could find anything valuable. Stupid ass. Mole would kill Eric if he stole from him.

* * *

Victor picked up his coffee mug and chugged some caffeine. At eight a.m., he was on his fourth cup. He'd sold and shipped all the artifacts Eric had stolen within two days. Well worth the lost sleep.

A new buyer with deep pockets and an interest in Native American pieces had popped up on the black market. The fool would pay fortunes for old clay pots. Victor needed to get his hands on more.

Time wasted while he waited for that archaeologist bitch to fit him into her tight schedule. He couldn't dig up the resort property without the building permit, which required a clean field survey. His land might be off limits, but he could turn his workers loose on other places ripe for the picking. All he needed were the tweakers.

Fucking DEA. He'd had the perfect operation in the Four Corners until they'd gotten too close. If it weren't for the snitches, Victor would still be in business. Instead, it was amateur hour in New York with the stoner, Eric. He had better have found some tweakers to get to work.

Addicts would do anything for their fix. Victor's own parents were a prime example. He grimaced. Pathetic crackheads. A mother who sold her own body to feed their habit, and a husband who let her.

Victor rubbed his arm, tracing the scar he'd gotten at age twelve when his mother decided she'd whore him out as well. If not for the rough neighborhood, he wouldn't have kept a switchblade on him. Before then, he'd only flashed the blade as a warning to kids who might want to screw with him. But that day, he'd used the knife to slice the throat of the pervert. The cocksucker fought back, but was too high to do more than leave his mark.

Victor had learned two things. First, the rush that came when life drained from his victim's eyes, and second, he would never use drugs. Much better to sell them to people who would do what he wanted in exchange for more. He'd cracked the code on how to get ahead. Target kids. Start them on weed, lace it with the heavier stuff, and in no time, they were his puppets. It all came down to power. Whoever controlled the drugs held the power.

Footsteps sounded in the hall, and Victor spun his chair around. Eric shuffled into the room and took a seat. The hoodie and jeans he wore were clean this time. No need to fumigate after he left. Victor searched Eric's eyes. Not glassy or red. He'd live another day.

He shifted in the chair. "I came back today like you said to."

"Where do we stand with the diggers?" Victor placed his mug on the desk and lit a cigar.

"I'm working on it."

"That's your answer to fucking everything. What's that mean?"

Eric scratched his head. "I found a guy, and he says he knows a couple others."

Victor took a drag of the cigar and shook his head. "One guy. That's it? I don't think I'm getting through to you. We're at a dead stop right now. We need workers."

"I know. I know. It's not easy. This town is small. I had to go outside the limits to find them."

"You told me you had connections." Victor leaned forward. "This is simple. Come up with a group for me, or you're done."

"I'm on it. I have a meeting with a guy tonight. Already found a place for everyone to camp that's not in town." Eric wiped his brow, slick with sweat. "I promise I'll have a team soon."

Victor blew out a cloud of smoke. "You'd better, because I'm out of patience." He waved a hand at the door. "Go. I expect a report after your meeting."

Eric jumped to his feet and nodded like a bobble-head doll before leaving the room.

Victor eased back in his chair. Nothing but one roadblock after another. First the permit, now the lack of workers. Time for action. If Eric didn't come through with a team, Victor would kill him off same as that snitch in Utah. No one questioned it when druggies died of overdoses.

CHAPTER 12

MADDIE OPENED the door to the apartment complex office and entered. The manager, a middle-aged woman with glasses and graying hair, looked up. "Can I help you?"

"Yes. I came for the keys to my apartment. I move in tomorrow."

The thin, pale-faced girl, to whom Maddie had given her deposit check the other night, emerged from the bathroom in the hall. She glanced at Maddie and went over to a computer on a small station near the window.

"Name and unit?" the manager asked. She flipped through a folder after Maddie gave her the information.

Tom entered the office. "Hey, Maddie. What are you doing here?"

"Getting my keys. You all set to help me move tomorrow?"

"Yup. Schedule's clear." He smiled and placed a check on the manager's desk. "Monthly rent for Unit 201."

"Thanks." The woman didn't look up, a frown on her face. "I'm sorry, Ms. Cooper. When we didn't receive your deposit, I rented the apartment to someone else."

Maddie blinked, and her stomach knotted. With her old lease up, she had to move out tomorrow. This couldn't be happening. "What do you mean? I dropped the check off three days ago."

The girl at the computer spun her chair around. "I made the deposit."

"When?" The manager eyed her.

"Umm. Before lunch, Tuesday. Didn't it go through?" Sweat glistened on the girl's forehead.

The manager stood. "Why didn't you deposit it that night, or at least leave me a note the payment had been made? I had no idea."

The girl twisted a ring on her finger. "I…didn't know that's what I was supposed to do."

"We went over this before. This is unacceptable. There aren't any more units and this one is rented now."

Tears filled the girl's eyes. "I'm sorry." She turned to Maddie. "I'm so sorry; this is all my fault. I'm new. I didn't realize—"

"Hold on. Let me look into this." The manager sat and typed on her computer. She leaned close to the monitor. "Yes. I see the payment here." She glanced up. "I'm very sorry, but I have a newly signed lease, and the unit is no longer available. I will refund your payment, obviously."

Maddie's mouth went dry. "But I need this apartment. My old lease is up, and I have to move. You're the only ones who rent monthly. I paid on time."

The manager raised an eyebrow. "Technically. You just made the grace period."

"What grace period? I was told the rent was due by Monday, and I got it here by then," said Maddie.

Tom cleared his throat and put a hand on Maddie's shoulder. "Legally, they violated the lease. You could take them to court."

The young girl clamped a hand to her mouth and then let it fall. "Court? Oh no. Please—"

"I do apologize." The manager approached Maddie. "Trust me; this won't happen again." She gave the girl a stern look and then faced Maddie. "I can put you on the top of the waiting list. Since we rent monthly, apartments do turn over."

Hell. Maddie gritted her teeth. She didn't want the kid to lose her job.

"Since this was our fault, I'll knock off a hundred dollars from your first month's rent if we can work this out."

Maddie sighed. "Okay. Put me on the list."

The girl wiped a tear and gave Maddie a weak smile.

"I'll call as soon as a unit is available. Thanks for your understanding," the manager said.

Tom opened the door for Maddie, and they stepped outside. She stopped by her car. Now what could she do? "Well, this really sucks."

"That was nice of you in there. She might have gotten fired."

"Heck. Did you see her? She's like all of sixteen or something. Probably her first job."

"You have any place to go?" Tom asked.

Maddie closed her eyes. "No. I don't want to sign a year's lease, because I'm not sure I'll stay here that long. I haven't decided yet. Damn it." She checked her watch. "I'd better get going. I'll figure something out."

When she took a step away, Tom placed a hand on her arm. "Wait. I have a spare room. Why don't you move in with me?"

Whoa. Red flag.

Every fiber in her body screamed "no." Sure, she'd had the *just friends* talk with him, and he'd never crossed the line, but she sensed he'd like to. She glanced at her arm, and he let go, stuffing his hands in his pockets.

"I don't know, Tom."

"Think about it. You could stay until something opens up." He fished keys out of his pocket. "I've got to get to work. Give me a call later."

"You're a good friend. Thanks, I will."

She got into her car and drove toward the coffee shop. When she passed the police station, her heart tripped. She'd dreamed about Scott all night. Those piercing green eyes and the way he'd carried her up the stairs nestled against his chest. When she'd awakened, the faint scent of his cologne had still lingered the air.

No.

No time to ruminate over what would never be. She had more pressing matters at hand, like finding a place to live. And yet, she still scanned the lot searching for his Impala.

Her phone rang, and her sister's name came up. Maddie hit speaker and answered. "Sarah?"

"Hey there. Just checking to see how you're doing. Any luck finding that thug?"

"No leads. It's a little crazy right now. How are you feeling?" She stopped at a light. Hard to believe in two months she'd be an aunt. And she was a year *older* than Sarah. She swallowed and tamped down the tiny ache that rose from her stomach. Her career had always been the priority, but approaching thirty, if she wanted kids, she'd have to open her heart again soon to someone. And damn that Scott, he still held it prisoner.

"I'm fine," Sarah said. "But I can tell from your voice that something's wrong. What?"

Maddie never could hide her feelings. "I just lost my apartment, and Tom invited me to stay with him until another opened up."

"Oh no. I'm sorry. But you guys are good friends, so it might work out."

"Yeah. He has night shift a lot, so we wouldn't be together much. I just don't know if it would bother Kaitlyn. She has a thing for him." Maddie turned at the light and parked in front of the coffee shop.

"Ask her. No offense, but you're usually pretty direct."

Right enough on that count. Maybe she could feel Kaitlyn out. They'd never openly discussed the topic. "True. I'm hoping to catch her. We usually get our caffeine fix around the same time. How's Bruce been lately? Still doting on you?"

"Hand and foot. He's making me crazy. Thank God I'm at the dance studio teaching most of the day, or I might kill him."

Maddie stifled a laugh. Bruce, the tough former Navy SEAL, pampering his wife. "Hey, he almost lost you to that crazy stalker. Cut him some slack. He earned the right to be protective."

"Well, he's got that down." Sarah let out a breath. "Have you seen Scott much?"

Maddie's smile melted from her cheeks. "More than I care to. It's a small town, and I'm still involved in the burglary investigation."

"Has he ever explained what happened the last two years? I mean, even Bruce still doesn't know, and they're close."

"Nope. He's shut tighter than a sarcophagus, and I'm done trying to crack him open."

"Maybe—"

"I love you, sis, but I don't want to talk about him."

"All right. Anne and I have just been worried."

Maddie grimaced. She owed Anne a call. Their older sister fretted over both of them. At least she and Sarah both lived in Maryland and could see each other. Traveling and living in New York made it hard for Maddie to get together with them. "Everything okay with her? She's been quiet."

"I was going to talk to you about this. She's not herself. Last time I saw her, I asked what was wrong, and she blamed it on year-end teaching stuff. Busy and all that. I'm not buying it, though."

"Hmm. Well, she always has tried to protect us and not burden us with her problems. I'm worried now."

Sarah sighed. "Me too. I'll let you know if I find out anything."

"Okay. I miss you guys. I have to go, though. I'll let you know what happens with moving."

"Okay. Love you."

"You, too. Take care of that baby."

Maddie hung up and stroked her chin. They were all adults now. Anne didn't need to keep playing the oldest sister role. If she was upset over something, it might help to talk. She dialed Anne's number, but it went straight to voice mail. Her spirits sank.

Everyone seemed to be holding back information. Especially Scott. She'd have better luck uncovering the lost temples of Alexandria than digging out his secrets.

She got out of the car as Kaitlyn opened the door from the coffee shop. Good timing.

Kaitlyn stopped on the sidewalk. "Hey, Maddie. How's it going?"

Might as well cut to the chase and get it over with one way or another. "I have a problem."

"What?" Kaitlyn cocked her head.

"I lost my apartment lease, and Tom offered to let me room with him until I find another place."

Kaitlyn blinked. "You don't have anywhere to go?"

"No. And it was nice of Tom, but I wanted to run it past you before—"

"Why would you need to do that?"

Well, hell, now her guard was up. She shouldn't have asked. "Never mind. I'll figure something else out."

"No need." Kaitlyn shrugged and glanced away. "I'm...seeing someone, so it's not a problem."

This was news. "You are?"

"Yup."

"Since when?" Not that Maddie knew everything about Kaitlyn's private life, but gossip traveled fast in this town, and no one had mentioned anything.

"It's recent." Kaitlyn straightened and checked her watch. "I really need to get to work, though. Catch you later?"

"Sure."

Kaitlyn raised her coffee cup in a goodbye gesture and strode toward her police cruiser.

Maddie frowned. Something didn't feel right. The sudden boyfriend seemed like a convenient way to avoid the whole topic of Tom and let Maddie off the hook. Maybe she should try to find a place outside of town and commute. She didn't have time to look for one, though. Either way, she'd need to rent a storage unit and get her stuff out of her current apartment.

She entered the coffee shop, jingling the bells over the door.

Nikki came out from the back. "Hey, Maddie. You just missed Kaitlyn."

"Nope. I ran into her out front."

Nikki grabbed a cup and filled it from the pot. She leaned over the counter and said in a hushed voice, "Some guy was in here with her earlier. Never seen him before."

"Oh?" Maddie's radar went up.

"Yeah. A tall, skinny, dude in a business suit. Very polite. He gave me a nice tip."

"Huh." He must be the guy Kaitlyn had mentioned. That being the case, it made the decision to move in with Tom easier. Still not the best solution, but she needed a temporary fix. She would call him later and take him up on his offer. And good for Kaitlyn. She'd mooned over Tom long enough and deserved to be with someone nice.

Nikki slid the coffee cup across the counter. The sleeve of her shirt hitched up, revealing a dark bruise on her forearm.

A slow burn ignited in Maddie's stomach. Son of a bitch. "Are you okay?"

"Yeah." Nikki bobbed her head, swinging her pink-streaked ponytail, and turned away from Maddie to grab the coffee pot.

"I know it's none of my business, but I can't stand to see you hurt. Why do you stay with Eric?"

Nikki filled the carafe with water and glanced at her. "We're fine. He just has a temper sometimes when he drinks."

She talked a good story, but her hand shook as she placed the pot back on the burner. Maddie dug her nails into her palm and drew her lips together. "You don't need to put up with this. People like him don't change. You deserve better."

Nikki busied herself with refilling the sugar container, her back to Maddie. "It's hard. With my parents dead, and my brother in jail, Eric's all I have. He...loves me."

"Look, I don't mean to overstep, but if you ever need anything. I mean, if he—"

"Thanks, but I'm good." Nikki raised her chin.

The stubborn set of Nikki's jaw kept Maddie from pressing harder. She paid for the coffee, picked up her cup, and headed to the door. She glanced back at Nikki, who tugged the bottom of her sleeve down.

Eric. That asshole.

Outside the coffee shop, Maddie dialed Tom's number. She needed to make sure he knew her moving in with him was short-term and completely platonic. He answered on the first ring.

"Hey, Tom. Looks like I'm going to take you up on your offer. But it's just as friends, and I insist on paying rent. Hopefully, a unit will turn over and it won't be for long."

"Understood. We'll discuss the rent. I'll get the spare room ready after my shift. Can't talk now, but thanks for letting me know. This is great."

He hung up.

Her stomach twisted into a what-have-I-gotten-myself-into knot. He'd sounded way too excited. What a mess.

Shit.

She'd forgotten to ask him about the dog.

CHAPTER 13

SCOTT DROPPED a box on the floor of his new apartment. Not owning much made for quick work. The move into the detective's office at the station had been harder.

While Kaitlyn and the others were respectful, they still held back, understandably annoyed at him for taking Tom's promotion. Scott couldn't expect anything less in a small town where ties held tight. The local civilians were more open in their disdain. He'd caught their looks when he'd gone to O'Leary's to pick up carryout.

A dog barked in the outside stairwell.

"Shush. Let's not start trouble." A woman's voice echoed against the concrete walls.

Maddie? No, Scott had her on the brain. It couldn't be.

Another yelp, this one closer. He stepped onto the cement landing. Maddie and the puppy they'd rescued scampered up the stairs to the third floor.

"Hey, Maddie." Tom's voice rang out. "Whoa. What's this?"

Tom stood in the open door of the apartment directly above. Scott's blood pressure spiked. Un-fucking-believable.

"This is the dog I told you about. Didn't you get my message?" Maddie asked.

"What message?"

"The one I left last night."

Tom rubbed his eyes. "No. I worked the late shift and went right to bed."

"Shoot. I didn't want to spring this on you. He's a stray. Is it going to be a problem if I keep him here until I can find a home for him?" She yanked on the leash and tried to shush the barking mutt.

Scott tensed. Maddie moving in with Tom right above him. What a nightmare this would be. Hard to avoid someone when they lived in the same building.

Tom reached out and stroked her arm. "No. I'm sorry. I'm allergic."

"You are?"

The dog raised his nose in the air and sniffed. He ran to the stairwell, barked at Scott, and raced down the stairs. Maddie's arm jerked and she slipped. She let go of the leash and fell on her butt.

Tom dashed to her and put an arm under her shoulder to help her up. "You okay?"

The pup hopped on his back feet and clawed on Scott's legs, whining like he'd found a long-lost friend. The tight armor around Scott's heart loosened. The little guy remembered him. He reached a hand down to try to calm the dog, who licked him with renewed vigor, tail whipping back and forth like a live electric wire.

"Scott? What are you doing here?" Maddie's eyes widened.

"Moving in."

She gave a small shake of her head and pointed to the door of his apartment. "Wait. You're moving into that unit?"

The dog, even more frantic, pawed at Scott's jeans. He bent and scratched a hand up and down the mutt's side. "Yeah."

Maddie's nostrils flared. She shot a look at Tom, who raised an eyebrow.

They clearly weren't any happier than Scott was about the situation. He glanced at Tom's arm still around Maddie. "I'd better get back to moving."

"Wait a minute." Maddie stomped down the steps, picked up the dog's leash, and pointed to Scott's door. "That was supposed to be my apartment."

"What do you mean, your apartment? I've been on a waiting list. The office called me. I signed the lease, and they gave me the keys."

Tom came down the steps. "It's not his fault, Maddie. The office manager told us they'd messed up the deposit."

Scott glanced at Tom, not missing the *told us*.

Maddie looked up at Tom and then back to Scott. "Isn't there anywhere else you can go?"

The agitation in her voice grated on him. Too damn bad if the honeymooners didn't want to share the complex. "As a matter of fact, no. This town doesn't have much in the way of rentals. Looks like *you* have to move somewhere else."

"I am." She took a step closer to Tom. "In with him."

Perfect. He'd driven her right into Tom's lair.

Tom shifted and faced her. "Let's focus on the problem at hand. What can we do about the dog?"

The puppy nudged Scott's leg and whined again. When Maddie tugged on the leash, he tried to back out of the collar.

"Oh my God. Really?" She huffed out a breath. "I saved your life."

Scott could argue that he'd played a big part in the rescue, but the look in Maddie's eyes kept his words at bay. She'd been the one to jump in the freezing water to try to save the dog. And if she hadn't been there, who knows what would have happened?

She nibbled her lower lip and leaned down to pet the puppy. "I can't take him to the pound. He's been through so much already. I put up signs, but no one's called."

Scott gazed at the puppy's big, brown eyes. The poor thing was nothing but skin and bones. He bumped his head against Scott's leg.

Man, he'd regret this. Never volunteer. *Never* volunteer. But the words left his mouth, anyway. "He can stay with me until you find a home for him."

Maddie's head snapped up. "You?"

"Well, he obviously likes me."

"But he's my dog." Maddie stood and crossed her arms, the leash clutched in her hand.

She was pissed. First her apartment, now her dog. He'd almost feel bad, but she was so in his face about it, like he'd planned a coup. Her eyes shot daggers at him as her cheeks flushed pink. Something stirred in him, low and primal.

Shit.

"Fine. Just trying to help. He's all yours." He shrugged and took a step back, but the dog leaped and stood next to him, tugging the leash away from Maddie.

Tom placed a hand on the small of her back. "It seems like a good temporary solution. Maybe Scott could give us a key, and you could walk the dog and help take care of him." He faced Scott. "I mean, unless you aren't comfortable?"

Scott frowned. *Us* again. He glanced at Tom's hand on Maddie. He sure took every opportunity to touch her.

As far as the key went, Scott trusted a cop with it. But Maddie would be in his personal space. Her sweet scent would linger in his home to torture and remind him of what he couldn't have. She'd take the dog on walks with Tom. They'd go to the park and throw a ball, maybe steal a kiss while the puppy chased after it. Pressure built in Scott's chest, squeezing his lungs.

Tom said, "Sorry. Didn't mean to put you on the spot."

Scott blew out a breath. "It's not a bad idea. I don't know what time I'll get home some nights."

Maddie frowned, and her shoulders slumped. "Fine. I'll bring you his food and stuff."

Scott nodded and led the dog into his apartment, shutting the door behind. He unleashed the pup and opened a box to unpack. A few minutes later, a rap sounded at the door. When he opened it, Maddie marched in with the sack of dog food and the items he'd bought for her the other night. She placed them on the floor. The mutt ran to her, wagging his tail.

"Sure, now you want me." She gave a sad smile and bent down to scratch him behind the ears.

Scott went to the counter and plucked up a key. "They gave me two. You can have this one. I don't mind walking the dog, but there may be times I can't. Does he have a name?"

She glanced up at him. "Yeah, Taken."

Scott snorted. "Come on. Seriously?"

Her gaze lowered to the dog, and a sad pout formed on her face. She ruffled the fur on his head and said in a soft voice, "Name him what you want. He answers to you."

She bent and hugged the puppy close. Held him for a long moment. "You know, he helped save you. So be good."

Great. Way to make him feel like a dick. None of this was his fault. But she had her pride, and that pitiful look on her face when she'd stroked the dog ate at him.

"Let me know if he needs anything." She gave the puppy a backwards glance that ripped Scott's heart out. And then she was gone.

He forced himself to finish unpacking. After he emptied the last box, a noise sounded from above.

Thump.

Thump.

He closed his eyes. Front row seats to the Tom-and-Maddie show. X-rated and they could be doing it right now. His fingers dug into his palms.

He couldn't give Maddie what Tom could. Sunset strolls and ice cream cones by the lake. Movie nights and dinners out. That's what she deserved. She needed someone normal. Not someone who'd seen the darkest side of humanity and fought with the devil.

The woman had passion and fire. A bright light in a black world. No way he'd let himself get close enough to put out her flame.

Thump.

He grabbed the leash. Time to get the hell out before he went batshit crazy.

Maddie had his key. He had her apartment and dog.

Tom had the world.

CHAPTER 14

MADDIE'S PHONE chimed as she entered Tom's apartment. A text from Scott. He was running late and asked if she could feed and walk the dog. She typed back an answer and ignored the sinking of her heart that he'd texted instead of called.

Ridiculous.

She didn't want to talk to him anyway. Nope. Not at all.

After snatching the key to his apartment from a drawer, she made her way down the flight of steps and unlocked his door. The dog stood from his bed, slunk over to her, and whined when she bent to pet his furry face.

"What's wrong?" She sniffed. Something stank. Her gaze traveled to a pile of puke on the carpet near the sofa, and she gagged. Yet another spot under the window next to the television. Oh no. All over Scott's new apartment.

"Are you sick, boy?" The pup nudged her hand and burped in her face. Blah, doggie puke breath.

"It's a good thing you're so cute." She patted his snout, clipped a leash to his collar, and took him outside.

When they got back, she called the vet and made an appointment. In the meantime, he instructed her to feed the dog beef and rice, mixing it with a little kibble. Her already-full schedule just got busier. With a sigh, she smoothed the fur down on the puppy's head. Sad, brown eyes gazed at her.

"Don't worry. I'll take care of you, no matter what."

The dog snuggled back down on his bed while she tended to the mess. Wet stains soiled the new beige carpet. Maybe Scott had some detergent in a bottom kitchen cabinet, where she stored hers.

He sure kept everything neat. Not a dish in the sink or a crumb on the counter. Nothing had changed from the time they'd spent together.

With any luck, she could clean up and get out before he came home. The dog ran to his bowl and looked up at her. If he was hungry, it might be a good sign.

"Sorry, guy. The vet said we have to ration the kibble." She frowned. If she put chemicals on the carpet, she couldn't leave the dog alone while she cooked upstairs. She'd have to make his dinner at Scott's. She scratched the puppy behind his ears. "I'll be right back. I know you're hungry, but don't eat the furniture."

She hurried upstairs to Tom's apartment. The shower was running. Good; she wouldn't have to explain the whole thing to him. Frozen beef in hand, along with a box of rice and a bottle of carpet cleaner, she bounded down the steps.

Maddie let herself back into Scott's unit. She opened a window for some fresh air and sprayed foam stain remover on the spots. As much as she hated to dig around in his cabinets, she did until she found a skillet and pot. After she cooked the food, she set it out to cool. Wearing a pair of rubber gloves she'd found under the sink, she knelt to work on the spots.

She had to figure out what she was she going to do about Scott. Sharing the dog meant she'd have to interact with Mr. Aloof. As much as he'd hurt her, she should be over him. Only she wasn't. Not even close. Too many memories still flooded her. Sure, her temper flared around him, but once it passed, the ache in her chest returned. An empty, hollow spot he'd once filled.

The pup left his bed to lick her face and jump around her, clearly excited to have someone down on his level. Maddie laughed as she nudged him aside with her elbow and scrubbed the carpet with a sponge. Her smile fell. Once, she and Scott had donated towels and treats to a shelter, checked out the dogs, and talked about the kinds they liked. Now they had one together. Not the way she'd pictured it. "You know, puppy, I really need to leave soon. No matter how mad I am at him, he still gets to me."

"What are you doing?" Scott's voice came from the doorway.

Maddie jumped. He probably heard her talking to the dog. "You scared the crap out of me."

The pup raced over to him, yapping. From her position on the floor, Maddie gazed up at Scott as he crossed the room to place a pizza box on the table. Dressed in his suit again. So hot. Damn him.

He glanced around the kitchen, where dirty pots filled the sink, and steam rose from the plates of ground beef and rice on the counter. "What's going on here?"

Maddie eased back on her knees and used her arm to brush back a strand of hair from her face. She gestured with a rubber-gloved hand to the spot she'd been scrubbing. "The dog got sick, and I'm cleaning up the stains."

He caught her gaze, and even from across the room, his sea-green eyes lit a fire in her belly, and then a little lower. She swallowed, despite the lump forming in her throat. "I'm sorry about the mess."

He shook his head. "You didn't have to go to all this trouble. I would have cleaned it. Tom's off tonight. Go home."

"What?"

"I parked next to him."

"So? What does his schedule have to do with me?" She drew her brows together and then it hit her. Scott thought they were a couple. "Wait, do you think Tom and I—?"

"You moved in with him."

She huffed out a breath. "Because you stole my apartment, and I didn't have anywhere to go."

"For the millionth time, I did not steal your place. And on the other count, I'm glad things worked out for you and Tom." Scott bent to scratch under the dog's chin.

"There's nothing between us. We're just friends, and this is temporary."

He stopped petting the pup. The tight lines in his face smoothed out. He straightened and rolled his shoulders. "I see. Regardless, you don't need to worry about my carpet."

His tone had lightened. Almost like relief. If he had been jealous of Tom, it made no sense. She'd never figure Scott out. He didn't want her, but he didn't want her to be with anyone else, either. Time to get a move on. "If you didn't have my dog, this wouldn't have happened. It's my problem." She went back to scrubbing. "I'm almost done."

His shoes came into her line of vision. The man moved without making a sound. She glanced up along the muscles stretching the fabric of his pants, to his narrowed waist, and right past his broad shoulders to his face. "What?"

"I can't say I don't like you in this position, but please stop. I got it."

She dropped her jaw and sprang to her feet. "I can't believe you—"

"Figured that would get your attention." The corners of his mouth twitched.

She pursed her lips and narrowed her eyes. "Very funny. I should report you for harassment."

"I'm off duty. Sorry." His gaze dropped to her lips and then back to her eyes.

The room shrank as waves of heat came off his body. Gold flecks in his eyes sparked at hers. He placed a hand on her arm, and she shivered. Hard to stay pissed when her body betrayed her.

He tugged at one of her gloves. "I'll finish."

The mutt barked and wedged himself between them. Scott looked down at him. "Okay, okay. I see you."

Maddie took a step back and peeled off the other glove. Her pulse fought to return to a normal rate. "I'm finished. The spots just need to dry."

"What's up with all this?" Scott waved a hand at the kitchen.

"Oh, the vet said the dog has to get used to the kibble. Sometimes they throw up with new food, and we don't know what he ate before. We're supposed to give him rice and beef mixed with a small amount of dog food and gradually increase the ratio of kibble."

He rubbed his chin. "Guess I can do that."

"I made a lot, so you don't have to keep cooking it. This should last a few days." She moved to the counter. "And I'm sorry about the pots; I'll wash them. I needed to cook here so I didn't leave the dog with the carpet chemicals on the floor."

"It's fine. Don't worry about it."

"No. It's not fine. I made the mess. I'll clean it." She took a step toward the sink, but he tugged her arm.

"Do you have to argue with me about everything?"

She glanced up at him. "I don't like being bossed around."

"Don't I know it." He kept his hand on her arm. "But I'll take care of the pans. It's my apartment."

"Don't I know it," she muttered.

He snorted and let go of her. "Your smart-ass attitude is going to get you in trouble one day."

If he only knew. The same brashness had caused her to ask Victor for a staggering amount of money. "I'm way ahead of you."

"What's that mean?" Scott tilted his head.

"Nothing." Victor was her problem. Maybe if she'd worn a wire and recorded his bribe, she'd have proof of his corruption. But she'd had no idea he'd offer one. As it stood, she had nothing, so for now, she'd keep the police out of it.

She caught a whiff of pepperoni, and her stomach grumbled.

Scott frowned. "I bet you didn't eat yet with all this cleaning and cooking."

"Not this discussion again. Why are you always so concerned about me missing meals? Do I look like a twig or something?"

His gaze wandered down her body and back to her face. "Absolutely not."

Heat crept up the back of her neck. She'd set herself up for that.

The dog barked twice and ran back to his bowl. Maddie cleared her throat. She needed to take care of the puppy and get the heck out. "I think this is cool enough for him to eat now. Where do you keep the dog food?"

Scott stepped around her and opened a pantry door in the kitchen. A dustpan, broom, vacuum, and ironing board all filled the small, organized closet. She bit into a grin. Only he would find a way to fit them in with space to spare.

He dragged out a large bag of dog food. The puppy raced to the sack so fast he couldn't stop. He skidded across the linoleum right into it. Maddie burst out laughing. "He's such a goof."

Scott smiled and grabbed the dog's collar to keep him away from the open top. "Can you get his bowl?"

"Sure." She brought it over, and Scott scooped out a small amount. His bicep bulged under his suit coat. "How much did the vet say to mix?"

"That looks good." Only she didn't mean the food. She took the bowl after he dumped the contents in and added the cooked beef and rice. The dog abandoned Scott to follow her. "Now who does he like more?"

"Ha. He'd go with Satan into hell if he led with a biscuit."

"Way to stroke my ego, Detective."

Scott folded the top of the bag down, slid it back into the pantry, and shut the door.

She picked up the key to his apartment from the counter. "I'd better get going, if you insist on doing those pots."

"I insist." Scott loosened his tie.

Her thighs tightened. He made such a casual move look damn sexy. Once, he'd slipped off his tie and used it to fasten her hands to the headboard. She'd given herself up to him completely that night. Warmth spread to her face. God, enough already. Time to leave.

"Why don't you stay and have some pizza? You already cooked once tonight." He undid the top button of his shirt.

She should go. Run fast and far. But her gaze lingered on his chest, and the pizza called to her like the Holy Grail to Indiana Jones.

The puppy lapped up water and then stood at her feet, drooling over her boots. "I don't know—"

"He needs to go out after eating. Do me a favor and take him while I change? I don't want to get pizza grease on my shirt." He headed to the hall without waiting for an answer.

Bossy man, but her mouth watered. Like he'd spill anything. Probably carried a spot remover in his holster. She clipped the leash on the dog and took him out.

The cool air hit her face, and she sucked in a deep breath. As the puppy sniffed around, she firmed her resolve to leave. Much easier to do when Scott wasn't inches from her smelling so damn edible.

When she reentered the apartment, he stood in the kitchen slicing vegetables. In jeans and a snug black T-shirt with a Wounded Warrior emblem on it, he expertly wielded the large knife. Something about a man cooking stirred her insides. So much for her resolve.

"There's beer"—he glanced up at her—"I mean, iced tea in the fridge if you'd like some."

"Water's fine." Odd that he'd offered her a beer and then retracted it. Maybe it smacked too much of the old times when they'd have a couple over pizza and talk about their day. He probably didn't want to give her the wrong idea.

He brought two bowls of salad to the table along with a couple of plates. "Have a seat."

"I'll get the drinks. Where are your glasses?"

"I got it." He yanked out a chair. "Sit."

Bossy. Rather than searching the cabinets for cups, she sat.

He filled two glasses with water and brought them to the table.

She placed a slice of pizza on both of their plates. A quick meal and she'd be out the door.

After snagging ranch dressing from the refrigerator, Scott opened a cabinet and grabbed bottles of olive oil and vinegar. He set them beside her salad and took a seat. "Sorry, I don't have balsamic vinaigrette. Is this okay?"

Maddie stared at the bottles by her plate. He'd remembered the salad dressing she liked. "It's fine, thanks." She raised her gaze to his, and the warmth in his eyes caused her heart to thump. Oh no, she wouldn't go there. Had to keep it light. "I appreciate this. I'll admit I might have had to take some of the dog's beef and rice home for my dinner."

"Stubborn woman." Scott took a bite and snapped his fingers at the pup, who had raised his nose as high as he could to try to reach the table. "Sit."

Great. She shared the same commands as the dog. The mutt stole off to his bed. Maybe he could sense Scott's authority and the futility of a mutiny as well as she could.

She took a bite of pizza and pieces of sausage fell off and landed on the floor. The dog leaped up and raced to the droppings. Oh no. He might puke again if he ate them. She dove under the table and shoved his head away as she scooped up the bits with the other hand. The pup churned his legs and stretched out his snout to try to get the meat.

Scott circled the table and grabbed the dog's collar. "No."

Maddie scooched back and tried to stand but misjudged the distance and whacked her head hard on the edge of the table. "Shit."

Searing pain shot through her skull. She grabbed her head with one hand, the other still fisted around the greasy sausage.

Scott dragged the dog away. "Are you okay?"

She squeezed her eyes shut tight and took a deep breath. "Holy cripes, that hurt."

He reached down to help her up. "Let me check you out. Come to the sink where it's brighter."

"What if the dog—"

"He's fine. For once, can you do what I ask?" He put an arm around her and guided her under the light in the kitchen. "Where's it hurt?"

She patted the spot, and he gently put his fingers through her hair. His breath tickled the top of her head as she inhaled the musky scent coming off his chest. "Am I bleeding?"

"Who the hell knows with this mess of red hair?"

"Mess?" She bristled.

"Calm down. Bad word choice. I just mean you have a lot of it, and the color isn't helping right now."

"I'll inform my parents of their inconvenient genes."

He snickered. "You have a nice lump forming, but I don't see any blood. We need to get some ice on this."

"Can I clean up first? I have a hand full of sausage."

"Huh. I don't feel a thing."

She snapped her head back. "What?"

He gazed down at her, a mischievous smile on his face. "Just making sure you're lucid."

"God, Scott. That was..." A laugh bubbled in her throat. "Really bad."

He turned on the water. "I don't know what you're talking about. Clean up, dirty girl."

She glanced at him, and his eyes twinkled with humor. This was the Scott she remembered. His entire face transformed when he smiled. Her heart did a somersault, and she cursed it.

While she washed the grease off her hand, Scott got a bag of frozen peas from the freezer. He held them to the sore spot on her head, lacing his fingers through her hair to hold them in place.

Odd sensation. His warmth and the cold pack at the same time. "I can do this." She put her hand over his on the peas and tipped her head back. "Thanks."

He didn't let go. "Let me help. No need to freeze your hand."

"What about you?"

"I'm plenty hot right now."

She stared up at his smoking eyes, and all the air left the room. Breathe. She had to breathe. "What happened to you? To us? We were good together."

Shit. She'd said that aloud. Her pulse skipped.

Scott froze. He shut his eyes for a moment. When he opened them, they were emotionless. He drew his hand back and stepped away. "I'm sorry. For everything."

Maddie tossed the peas into the sink. "I don't want an apology. I want an answer. And don't give me that 'it was fun' crap. I deserve better."

"Yes, you do. This won't happen again." His Adam's apple bobbed. "I forgot myself. It was a mistake. Go home, Maddie."

Something had happened to make him shut down. She'd had him back. Her Scott, the one she still dreamed about, and just like that, he'd flipped the switch and gone dark again. She wasn't sticking around for another slap. He wanted her to go home. Fine.

She plucked the key to his apartment off the counter and stomped to the door. The dog trotted after her.

"Lucky, come," Scott called.

Maddie stopped. She swung around. "Lucky? Why'd you name him that?"

Scott dropped his gaze to the dog. "Because he was lucky you came along to save him."

Twist the knife deeper. He said things like that, but then pushed her away. Chest heavy, she fumbled with the handle and hurried outside, letting the door slam behind her.

CHAPTER 15

RAIN PELTED the barred window of the prison where Scott stood staring out at the dark sky. He needed to get his head straight before he talked to the man he hoped to enlist as an informant. Sleep, which he'd been getting very little of lately, might help. After Maddie had left last night, he hadn't been able to shut his eyes.

All the resolutions he'd made to keep her at a distance had dissipated. A huge weight had lifted when he'd found out she and Tom were just friends. He'd flirted with her, made suggestive comments, and invited her to stay for dinner. He'd let go and had fun with her.

A big mistake. He'd been a selfish son of a bitch to drop his guard and allow himself to feel again. To laugh. To get a rise out of Maddie and enjoy her reaction. Her passion was addictive, but she had no place in the dark abyss of his world.

Life had thrown him a hard curveball and caused him to change paths because of it. He wasn't working in Mexico anymore. His enemy had set up camp in Maddie's freaking town. Mole, a brutal man, did unthinkable things to those who incurred his wrath, and Scott intended to do that.

Time to compartmentalize. Maddie belonged in the past. For her safety, that's where he needed to keep her. He couldn't risk losing his focus. His job was to put away the drug dealers, for Justin and all the others like him.

An image of his brother's lifeless body flashed in his mind. A bolt of lightning sizzled across the sky, jerking him from his thoughts. Angry thunder rumbled and reverberated the rain-drenched glass. Time to get to work.

He shook off the ghosts with a roll of his shoulders and crossed the stark room to a scratched metal table with two hardback chairs. He took a seat in front of his open computer. A mug shot of twenty-four-year-old Zachary Gordon filled the screen. Collar-length dark hair with some small scars on his cheek and a slightly crooked nose. He bore no resemblance to his pink-haired sister, Nikki, the waitress from the coffee shop.

The records showed that until he'd been incarcerated four years ago for possession of drugs and illegal weapons, he only had a short list of minor juvenile offenses followed by a clean record from ages sixteen to twenty. The kid had managed to pay off all the medical bills from his mother's cancer treatments and keep him and his sister afloat until his arrest.

Scott's chest tightened. He knew how hard it was to have no father around, bury a mom, and take care of a sibling.

Apparently, getting custody of Nikki hadn't been easy for Zachary, who was nineteen and Nikki only fourteen then. He had to know he would lose her if he got into trouble. Not worth the risk. Something didn't click.

Metal on metal squeaked, and Scott glanced up. A guard escorted Zachary into the room. He wore an orange jumpsuit. Not an ounce of fat on the guy, and the bulging veins in his arms meant he worked out. He slid into the wooden chair across the table. Honest brown eyes, the same shape and color as Justin's, met Scott's gaze straight on.

His stomach churned. He hadn't caught the similarity on the computer screen shot.

The guard uncuffed Zachary and glanced at Scott. "I'll be waiting outside."

Scott nodded and willed his gut to calm down. "Thanks. I'll let you know when we're done."

The guard left, the thick metal door slamming behind him.

Zachary rubbed his wrists and then stared at Scott, unmoving.

Patience. A good trait. "I'm the new detective in Tuckerton." Scott tapped his badge. "I've been looking over your record. You took the high road for a while, kept your nose clean. What happened?"

"I made a big mistake. It cost me everything."

"If I told you there might be a way out of here, would you be interested?"

Zachary blinked. Hope lit his eyes before they narrowed. "I'd need to know more."

Scott nodded. Hard time made a person cynical. "I might be able to work a deal to get you out. Depends on this conversation. I want to hear your story." He clicked the computer to bring up a mug shot and then angled the screen so Zachary could see it. "What was your relationship with this punk? He has a rap sheet a mile long."

"Gerry Roberts?"

"Yeah. Roberts."

"I knew him from high school. Lost track of him when he started doing hard drugs. Couple years later, he got a job at the auto parts store where I worked." Zachary glanced at the computer image. "He told me he wasn't using anymore and needed a place to crash for a couple of nights. He begged and promised he was clean, so I agreed to help him out."

"But he brought weapons and drugs to your apartment?"

"Yeah, because I forgot the number one rule."

"What's that?"

"Never trust an addict. They'll do or say anything to get what they want." Zachary blew out a breath. "I was dumb, and I risked my sister's life. I deserve to be in here."

"Not if you're innocent." An inmate who didn't accuse the system of screwing him? He'd have to check the sky for flying pigs.

Zachary shrugged. "It's shit I'm in here. Every second of every day is shit, but what if that fucknut, Gerry, had killed my sister?" He shook his head. "I acted like a sappy pussy buying his line about how he'd cleaned up. Like I didn't have enough crap to deal with trying to keep a roof over our heads. As if I...of all people...could help anyone."

Scott kept his face neutral and let him talk.

"The fucking gym bag." Zachary snorted. "I should have realized from the way he carried it, something was up. Too heavy to be clothes. He crashed on the couch, and I went to check it out." He fisted a hand. "Gerry woke up and saw me with the duffel opened. He pulled a knife out just when Nikki came from her bedroom. She started screaming."

Zachary's face contorted. "He grabbed her. Held the blade to her throat. I froze. I fucking froze because if I charged him, he might kill her. That's when the FBI pounded at the door."

Scott tapped his thumbs together. So far, everything Zachary said tracked with the report.

"When I didn't open the door, they kicked it in. Gerry shoved Nikki at the agents and tried to run, but there were three of them with guns. They grabbed all of us. Nikki was bleeding." His nostrils flared. "That douchebag cut her when the FBI stormed in. She kept crying, but cuffed, I couldn't do anything but watch. Watch her bleed because of me. I fucked up big time."

Scott sank back in his chair. His gut said Zachary was telling the truth. "Well, you're right about not trusting a drug addict."

"You know what burns the worst?" Zachary's mouth twisted. "The FBI saved Nikki's life. I sure as hell didn't. She went into the foster system." His eyes filled with raw anguish. "She was...abused by a man at the last home. Then she moved in with some asshole."

The perverts preyed on the vulnerable. It had to kill Zachary, after all he'd done to gain custody of her. "Too many times the system fails."

Zachary's knuckles turned white on his still-clenched fist. "Every day, I live with the fact I let my sister down. I was all she had. Do you have any idea how that eats away at me?"

Preaching to the choir. Scott dug his heels into the tile floor. This guy deserved a second chance. "I'll bet. I might be able to work a deal for you if you're willing to be an informant. I'm working a case and need an insider."

"That's how I'd get out?"

"If you cooperate."

Zachary bobbed his head. "I'll do it. Anything, so I can help Nikki."

"Not so fast." Scott held up a hand. "This is dangerous. I can't guarantee your safety. You need to know that going in. The man I'm after has no conscience. He's killed people. Uses children to do his dirty work. We don't have enough evidence to convict him. That's where you'd come in." Scott stood and sauntered to the window, keeping Zachary in his line of sight. "Think about it if before you answer."

After a pause, Zachary asked, "I'll be out of jail if I do this?"

"That's the deal I'm working."

"Then I'll take my chances. What would I need to do?"

Scott came back to the table and clicked the computer mouse to bring up a picture of Victor Mole. "Well, for starters, get on his team." He gestured to the screen. "He hires meth heads. You might have to deal with them. Is that a problem?"

"No. After being in here, I can handle anything."

"Mole doesn't dirty his own hands." Scott rubbed his chin. "I want to find out who his distributor is. Based on what he did in the Southwest, I think he's setting up operations to launder money here through a resort he's building."

Zachary's gaze rested on the laptop screen. He nodded slowly.

"I'll work out the details and get back in touch." Scott held out a hand. "Deal, Zachary?"

They shook on it. "Zach. My friends call me Zach."

Scott's heart pinched as he gazed into Zach's hopeful eyes. A heavy weight settled on Scott's shoulders. Couldn't help but like the kid. He had spunk and cared more about his sister than about himself. If anything happened to him, Nikki would have no family. And damn it, everyone knew Maddie and Nikki were friends. Maddie would hate Scott even more than she already did.

But nowhere near as much as he'd hate himself.

CHAPTER 16

THE MOUTH-WATERING SCENT of garlic and basil wafted from the kitchen to where Maddie sat at her computer.

"Dinner's ready," Tom called.

She rolled her tired shoulders, logged off, and stood.

When she reached the kitchen, Tom handed her a full plate and poured two glasses of merlot.

"This smells like heaven. Thanks for cooking on my last night here. You spoil me."

Tom set the wine bottle on the table. "I'm just glad you didn't have to wait long for an apartment to open up. You ready to go tomorrow?"

"Yup. I appreciate your help." She took a seat and cut the sauce-drenched pasta into manageable pieces. Her taste buds danced with joy.

Tom pointed a fork at her across the table. "I should take that food away from you for slicing spaghetti. It's a crime."

"Arrest me, officer." She raised an eyebrow and continued cutting. "It's America. I can chop up my pasta if I want."

"They'd kick you out of a real Italian restaurant."

She scoffed. "They'd kick me out for twenty other reasons way before that."

"You're a fiery one." He swirled noodles onto a fork against a large spoon. "You've had a tough week. You okay?"

"Yeah, well, I'm still alive and kicking."

"Thank God." He held up his glass of wine in a salute.

She tapped her glass to his. "Are you going bowling tonight?"

"Yup." He glanced at her. "Are you sure you'll be okay here alone? I don't have to go."

"I'm fine. Why wouldn't I be?"

"I don't know. Like I said, I know it's been a crazy week. Thought I'd offer you company."

"Absolutely not." No way she'd ruin his night. And she couldn't stand to be coddled. Besides, a warm bath called to her, and she wouldn't feel right hogging the bathroom if he stayed home. When they finished eating, he stood and took his plate to the sink.

"Leave the dishes." She got up from the table. "You cooked. I clean. That's our deal."

"I don't want you to—"

"Stop it. I'm fine. Now go." Crap. That had come out harsh.

His expression sank as he set his plate in the sink. "All right, then."

Geez. Now she'd upset him. "Hey."

He looked up.

"I'm sorry. I really appreciate the dinner. It's just been a long week, and I want to help out since you were nice enough to make this."

"I understand. Don't worry about it."

The doorbell rang.

"You expecting anyone?" he asked.

"Not yet."

He strode to the door and peered through the peephole. "It's Kaitlyn."

When he let her in, she handed him a folder. "Scott asked me to drop this off to you." She breezed by him dressed in a black mini-skirt, cream-colored clingy sweater, and spiked heels.

Tom's jaw dropped. He blinked and then glanced at the folder. "Thanks. I need to make a couple of calls on this...but they could have waited until morning. Sorry to inconvenience you."

Kaitlyn shrugged. "I stopped at the station, and he tossed this at me and said it was urgent." She sighed. "You were on our way, anyhow."

Tom remained frozen in place by the door, his gaze fixed on Kaitlyn as if seeing her for the first time.

"Wow, you look great." Maddie patted Kaitlyn's arm.

"Hey, girl. How's the cheek?" Kaitlyn eyed Maddie's bruise. "Looks green now. Still there."

"I know. I'm okay, though. Where are you going all dressed up?"

Kailyn glanced at the bottle of wine on the table. She straightened. "Sorry, I interrupted you guys."

"You didn't." Maddie shook her head. "We're finished eating. Tom's on his way out. What about you?"

Kaitlyn smoothed back her hair. "Going to dinner with someone. He's waiting in the car, so I should get back to him."

"Have fun tonight."

"Where are you going to dinner?" Tom seemed to have found his voice.

Kaitlyn halted in front of him. "Anthony's. Why?"

Body rigid, he stared down at her. After a pause, he shrugged. "Just curious."

"Mm-hmm. Well, have a good night." Kaitlyn strolled out the door.

"Pretty pricey, that place," he muttered as he stepped onto the landing.

Maddie joined him. He crossed his arms and watched a tall, dark-haired man get out of a BMW and open the passenger door.

"Nice wheels." Maddie whistled.

"That's the new model seven-fifty." Tom kept his gaze on the car until it disappeared from view. "Expensive restaurants, fancy cars. Who is this guy?"

"I don't know. But Kaitlyn seems happy." Maddie went back inside so Tom wouldn't see her smirk. Score one for Kaitlyn.

He followed but remained oddly silent. No banter or chitchat. Maybe he was brooding about Kaitlyn on a date. About time he opened his eyes.

"I'd better get going. See you later." He picked up his bowling ball bag and left.

Maddie sighed. Poor Tom. He really was a great guy. She stared at the dishes on the table. Screw it. They could wait. What she needed was a relaxing bath and no one fussing over her.

While running the water, she added some peach-scented bubble bath, and sank down into the warm suds. Her mind still ran in overdrive, reliving the events of the past week.

She'd swear Scott had been about to kiss her in his apartment the other day. The tenderness in his expression had almost given her hope. But that was Scott. Hot one minute, cold the next. Impossible to figure out. He pushed all her buttons and then stepped away. Like she needed that shit.

She sunk deeper into the tub, closed her eyes, and forced her body to relax.

The doorbell rang, and she jerked. She blinked a couple of times and sat up. The bath water had turned cold. She must have fallen asleep.

After toweling off, she threw on a short-sleeved terry-cloth robe and stuffed her feet into the bunny slippers. When the doorbell rang again, she called out, "Hold on, I'm coming."

She traipsed down the hall, through the living room, and peeked out the hole.

Scott.

Her heart leaped. Damn his effect on her. Just because he lived below didn't mean he could knock at all times of the night. She glanced at the clock. Huh, it was only eight.

She opened the door, ready to protest. One whiff of his cologne caught the words in her throat. The forest-green T-shirt he wore molded to his ripped abs and pecs. And yeah, she stared at them.

A chilly breeze blew in. She stepped aside and cinched her robe tighter. "Come in, before I freeze."

Scott entered and closed the door behind him.

She lifted her arm to push back her wet hair. "What do you—?"

"Damn. I never saw this." He sucked in a breath and leaned down to inspect the bruise on her arm, courtesy of the thief. When he raised his head, fury burned in his eyes.

He reached for her other arm and gently checked the matching bruise. "I *will* find this bastard."

Her skin warmed under his hand. "I'm okay."

"Like hell." He touched one of her sopping curls. Wound it around his finger. "I promise, he'll pay for hurting you."

She shivered from the cool air and his proximity. "Why are you here? Is Lucky okay?"

"Yes. I came to give you back your flash drive and show you our updated file on the case." He kept his gaze on the curl around his finger as if mesmerized.

Maybe he remembered the way he used to play with her curls when they watched movies together.

She cinched her robe tighter. If another cold drip ran down her neck, she'd turn to ice. "I need to change and get this mop of mine under control. That'll take a few minutes."

His voice broke, causing her heart to do the same. "I remember." He let go and took a step back. "No rush."

"The computer's on the coffee table if you want to pop that in." She headed down the hall but stopped halfway to the bathroom. "Hey." She turned. "What was up with Kaitlyn and that folder? Tom said he didn't need it tonight."

Scott shrugged. "I know. It's all I had."

"What do you mean?" Maddie wrinkled her brow.

He slid the flash drive into the computer and kept his gaze on the screen. "Sometimes you have to improvise. Tom needed to see her in that skirt. I found a way."

Damn it. Maybe Scott thought Kaitlyn was hot. She'd sure caught Tom's attention. "Why did he need to see her?"

Scott glanced up and raised an eyebrow. "Do you really have to ask?"

Relief washed over her. He'd been playing matchmaker. She bit her cheek to stop a grin. "So, were you—?"

"Stop interrogating me and go change." A smile tugged at the corner of his lips, and he turned his attention back to the screen.

Warmth filled her chest. There he was again. The old Scott. Mischievous, fun, caring about other people. Hell, he hadn't been in town a full week and had figured out how Kaitlyn felt about Tom. And in one smart move had gotten Tom to notice her, when Maddie hadn't managed to in over a year.

For a second, she let herself stare at Scott. The angles of his face illuminated by the light of the screen. She'd memorized every curve and line before he'd left for his assignment. Kissed his full, sexy lips and laced her fingers through his wavy hair.

Her eyes misted. She swung around to hurry down the hall. Away from him.

After changing into sweats, she came back out of the bedroom.

Scott stood near the kitchen, one hand on his hip, a deep frown on his face. His gaze rested on the table still set with the wine bottle and empty glasses. First Kaitlyn, now him. The last time she checked, it wasn't a crime to eat spaghetti with her roommate. She'd told him she and Tom were just friends. For that matter, Scott had no right to be jealous even if they weren't.

She crossed her arms. "Something wrong?"

"Red wine gives you headaches. Considering how many bangs yours has taken in the last couple of days, do you really think you should risk drinking it?" He waved to the wine bottle.

Her blood pressure shot up. "Excuse me? For your information, I had a glass of wine with a full meal. What are you gonna do, arrest me for it?"

"I'm just saying—"

"I took a bath, too. Maybe that was risky as well. Could have drowned, with a recent head injury and all. Where do you draw the line with all my reckless behavior?"

He took a step closer and scowled down at her. "Damn good question. There isn't a line you won't cross. Fighting off a thug to protect your artifacts, jumping in the river to save a dog. Where does it stop?"

His lips pressed into a disapproving line as his eyes darkened. This close, the spicy fragrance of his soap, likely from a fresh shower, filled her nostrils. She smacked away the temptation to bury her head in his shirt and breathe him in.

"Why do you feel the need to save the world?" he asked.

Pissed at herself for being turned on by him, she shot back, "Someone has to. Lucky would be dead if not for me."

Scott's eyes softened. "Who takes care of you, Maddie? I won't always be here." The corners of his mouth turned down.

The words punched a small hole in her heart. If only she could capture this moment and freeze in time the caring expression on his face. "I wish you would be."

God, she hadn't meant to say that aloud. Damn her lack of filter.

He took a step back. "No, you don't."

She held his gaze and her breath. "Maybe I do."

"No." He slowly shook his head. "You need someone nice."

"Nice?"

The blank expression returned to his face. He spoke as if lecturing a science class on the properties of matter. "Yes. Nice. Reliable. Safe. That's what you need."

She brought her hands to her hips. "You're unbelievable."

"I need to go. You can check out the data on the computer. We're done here."

"Oh no, no." She poked a finger in his chest. "You don't drop that on me and then waltz out of here. You think I need 'nice'?"

He hitched an eyebrow. "Yeah. Someone like Tom. Not him, because of Kaitlyn, but someone like him."

"So, a guy who cooks meals for me, carries around a backup key to my car, and gives me a lift if I need one? You think that's what I want?"

Scott glanced at the table. "I'm leaving."

"No, you're not. Your arrogance is unbelievable. What right do you have to tell me what I want? To even assume you *know*?"

He stared down at her, his face still impassive. "I know what's best for you, even if you don't."

Her ears burned. Like hell. "Well, maybe I don't want someone who apologizes to me when I get angry and backs down." She took a step closer. "Or treats me like I'm fragile and can break. Do you know what happens when I date nice guys?"

Scott held his hands up, a pained look on his face. "I have no idea and don't want to."

"Too bad." She didn't stop her rant. He'd earned it, telling her what to do. "I walk all over them. I don't mean to. And I feel horrible afterward. Like I kicked a puppy or something. That's why I never dated Tom. He's too damn nice." She took a breath. "I hurt his feelings because I told him to leave after he'd spent the night cooking for me."

She paced the room. "I need someone with a thicker shell. Someone who can take a little fire. Someone who isn't so sensitive I have to tiptoe around them and watch what I say so I don't hurt them. Or push them away because they're smothering me with kindness."

"Well, if you could control that temper of yours—"

"Don't you dare tell me how to act. What am I supposed to do, pretend things don't get under my skin? Hold it all inside for fear of driving someone away? That means changing who I am, and I won't do that for anyone."

"Well, maybe you should." He moved to stand in front of her. "Maybe if you had someone to keep you in line, you'd stop acting like you have a death wish and live a little longer."

She huffed. "To what point? I don't want to conform. I want to feel, to live, either alone or with someone who can take me for what I am. I don't want to spend my life worrying about what I say or do." She waved a hand. "What if I want to get wild in bed? Try something different? I can't do that if the nice guy I'm with might not approve."

"For God's sake, Maddie." Heat spiked in his jade eyes.

Her chest heaved as she gazed up at him. "What? You don't want to hear about my sex life? How the last man I kissed was you? How I haven't gone out with anyone in two years because I don't want to kiss someone who can't kiss me back like...like..."

Fuck it.

She wrapped her arms around his neck and yanked his mouth down to hers.

He didn't pull away.

She dug her fingers into the back of his neck and kissed him. He tasted of mint. Sweet arousal flooded her body, and he crushed her against his chest.

His hungry mouth possessed hers as his tongue flicked against her teeth.

She opened for him and moaned.

He took the kiss deeper, slanting his mouth to cover hers.

She stood on tiptoe, reached up to go deeper. God, the man could kiss. Their tongues danced as he ran one hand down her side and the other through her hair. She rocked against his growing erection, and he groaned, a deep, guttural sound that vibrated through her soul.

When he dragged his mouth away and shifted back, she leaned into him and almost fell over. She tugged at his neck to bring him back down. "Scott—"

"No." He pushed her away.

Her breath ragged, body revved, she reached again for him. "Don't stop."

"I'm sorry. I can't do this." His eyes blazed with torment. He brushed past her and out the door, shutting it soundly behind him.

She blinked and stared at the closed door. Her aching heart still pounded. He'd kissed her back and then walked away. The same as he had two years ago. Unlike her, he could shut it down.

Hot tears filled her eyes. She covered her face with her hands and let them fall. All the craziness of the last few days washed out as she cried. Not for long, but enough to leave her in an exhausted puddle. She dabbed a tissue on her wet cheeks and took a long, shaky breath. No more. She'd move, take her dog back, and keep Scott out of her life as much as possible.

When her phone rang, she jumped. Maybe it was him. She mentally cursed to herself at the spark of hope after she'd just been burned. Seriously?

The caller had blocked his number. "Hello?"

"I'm done waiting," Victor said. "Maybe I need to clear out your storage room again so that you have more time to work on my survey. I expect you to be at the lot tomorrow. Tell the police and the first officer who asks questions won't be around long enough to hear the answer."

The line went dead. Maddie's mouth went dry, and she froze. Victor had been behind the burglary. He hadn't attacked her, so he must have hired someone. She touched the still tender lump on the back of her head. The man at the storeroom had beaten her up and might have killed her. What kind of a monster was Victor?

She paced the room as blood roared in her ears. That bastard. He'd jeopardized everything she'd worked for in one fell swoop by stealing the Native Americans' artifacts. If he thought she'd be his puppet, he couldn't be more wrong. And now he'd threatened her friends on the force. She slammed a fist on the counter and squeezed her eyes shut.

She'd burn the son of a bitch. Shut him down. He wanted her at the lot tomorrow. He'd get her, but only for half the day because she was moving in the afternoon. Too bad.

Once she started Victor's survey, she wouldn't stop digging until she uncovered something significant to put in his damn field survey report. Didn't matter if it took weeks. He would never be able to build his resort if she found enough. Once she saw to that, she'd go to cops and tell them everything.

Screw Victor.

CHAPTER 17

THE SUN PEEKED over the treetops as Maddie drove to the field survey site. She tried to focus on anything other than Scott.

She'd made an absolute fool of herself last night. He had to think she was desperate after she'd mouthed off about how she wanted to get wild in bed and hadn't had sex in two years. He'd always pushed her buttons so badly she lost all sense and said things she normally wouldn't.

The worst part was how incredible the kiss had been. Every nerve in her body had sparked when he'd kissed her back. And that hadn't been his gun pressed hard against her belly. He could push her away, but he wanted her, for whatever good that did.

Now, she'd have to face him when he brought Lucky to her new apartment. Heat burned her cheeks. She had her pride and didn't throw herself at men, Scott being the obvious exception.

She parked in the dirt by the proposed development and hopped out of the car. A cool breeze blew across the lake and rustled the trees. Specs of yellow pollen swirled in the air, tickling her nose. A group of ducks flew across the water and skidded to a landing. They quacked and tipped their butts up as they ate plants in the shallows.

Maddie smiled and took in a deep breath. She never expected to fall in love with the Finger Lakes. Once winter released its grip on the world and the trees turned green, sprouting new life, songbirds migrated to the area. She had joined some of the tourists who flocked to the lake with binoculars to view them in quiet amazement.

Sure, the winters were brutal, but the town grew quiet with the absence of fair-weather visitors. The locals stuck together when blankets of snow buried their world. Neighbors brewed coffee and blew out the driveways of those who only had shovels, or for the elderly with no family to help them. They took care of one another and had accepted Maddie into the fold.

Yeah. She'd found a little bit of heaven in the small township and even bonded with the folks. But she'd have to move on. People raised their families here, willed their land and homes to their children. Maddie had a rental apartment and no ties. The complex plowed her parking lot, so no sharing coffee and laughing as the snow accumulation reached the top of yardsticks.

She didn't belong. Maybe Scott would fit in and become a beloved member of the community like Tom and Kaitlyn. Marry someone and raise a family. Images filled her head of Scott flipping burgers on a grill while his kids chased a puppy around the yard. A loving, perfect wife bringing him a beer and planting a kiss on his lips. A fist squeezed her empty heart, and she shut her eyes. She couldn't stay and watch that happen. Best she focus on her career and follow where it took her.

After walking the area for a visual survey, she fetched her tool kit, camera, and composition book from the trunk. From her research, she picked an area with the highest probability of containing artifacts and measured it. For the next three hours, she staked it out and set up strings to prep for the dig.

Her phone rang.

"It's Gina. I'm checking to see if you made it to the site this morning."

"Yes. I'm setting things up."

"Excellent. I'll inform Mr. Mole. How long do you expect this to take?"

Until Victor's balls turned blue and fell off. "Hard to say until I get started. There's a lot of prep work involved, and I can only work half the day."

Gina's voice turned firm. "I don't need to remind you time is of the essence."

"I got that. Loud and clear."

"Excuse me?"

Maybe Gina didn't know about Victor's threats. "Nothing."

"I'll check in later for an update."

The line went dead. Maddie tucked the phone into her coat pocket. Of course, Victor didn't expect her to do things by the book. Probably figured she'd dig a couple of holes and lie her ass off on paper. Even if that had been her plan, to make it look right, she'd still have to follow procedure. A proper excavation required considerable setup to keep track of the depths and exact location of the finds. Which she *would* uncover.

As she sketched a site map on graph paper, the wind gusted, carrying with it the scent of cigarette smoke. She stilled. The small hairs on the back of her neck stood up. She glanced around the tree-lined shore in the direction of where the breeze had come from. A figure lurked along the edge. She held a hand up to shade her eyes and peer into the forest.

If size were any judge, the person was a man, but too small to be Victor. Dressed in black, the guy blended in with the dark woods. He stepped deeper into the shadows and out of sight. Victor might have hired someone to spy on her. A shiver climbed her spine. She shook it off and went back to work.

The sooner she finished her survey, the quicker Victor would leave. If she found and reported significant cultural artifacts, his construction would be tied up for so long he'd have to find another place to build. Not like he could use his scare tactics on the Army Corps and Seneca Nation tribes to get his way. He'd be done.

She wiped her brow and rocked back on her heels. If all went well, tomorrow she should have a chance to actually dig and get her hands dirty. She checked the time. Better get back to the apartment complex. Tom only had an hour to help move the heavy stuff, and then Kaitlyn had offered to pitch in after her shift ended.

Maddie glared at the ground. If Victor did anything to hurt either of them, or any of the others, she'd make sure he got what he deserved—a jail cell and a prison full of boyfriends.

After packing up, she drove to the complex and waved to Tom, who stood beside a small rental moving truck in the lot. She hopped out of the car. "I hope you haven't been waiting long."

"Nope. Just got here." He opened the back doors of the truck. For the next hour, they moved furniture up three flights of steps to her new apartment. She took a side of a headboard. Her arms burned from exertion when they reached the top landing. Tom set his end down, and she let hers clunk to the ground.

She mopped her brow and gazed at the engraved flowers in the wood. More than once that headboard had knocked against the wall while Scott had made love to her. Damn. Why did he have to jump into her brain all the time?

Below them, he rounded the corner of the building carrying a box.

God. He would show up when she had the headboard in her hands. The one he'd tied her to and ravaged her body, driving her wild.

Dressed in a suit, with mirrored shades on, he made her insides quiver.

"I brought Lucky's stuff." He glanced up.

Her heart skipped a beat. *She* shouldn't be nervous. He was the one who had run out after their kiss.

He climbed the steps to where she and Tom stood.

"You okay, Maddie? Your face is red," Tom said.

"I'm good. We're almost done, and I know you have to get back to work."

Scott took off his sunglasses and tucked them in his pocket. "Let me help with the headboard. You take the box."

"No." She shook her head. "I don't need your help."

Tom made no move to pick his side back up. "You're flushed. Why don't you let Scott handle this one? It's heavy."

"I said I'm fine." Great. That came out bitchy. She blew out a breath. "Sorry, guys. I just want to get this done."

Scott thrust the box at her and lifted her side of the headboard.

She frowned. As usual, he figured he could waltz on over and bark out orders. She didn't need or want his help with moving or with anything else. "I told you I had it."

"Just bring the box in," he said over his shoulder as he and Tom carried the piece into the bedroom.

She stomped in behind them and placed the box on the kitchen counter. Tom came out of the bedroom with Scott and gestured to the open front door. "I'll get the last chair."

"Thanks, Tom," Maddie said.

Scott fixed his gaze on her.

She had to look a mess. Sweaty, in a ratty T-shirt and her oldest, worn jeans. She shouldn't care, except her stomach flipped from one look into his green eyes.

She glanced at the box. "I can pop over to get Lucky. Save you the trip."

"Maddie," Scott said quietly.

She rifled through the box. "Hmm?"

"I'm sorry about last night."

Holding a bottle of pills, she stared at the label as though reading all the drug facts thoroughly. "I don't want to talk about it."

"Well, I owe you an apology. I wish I could explain—"

"There's no point. Believe me, it won't happen again." She tapped the bottle in her hand. "What are these?"

"Maddie, please." He touched her arm. "At least look at me."

She'd rather skin a snake, but she had her pride. When she raised her gaze to his, the clear regret on his face gave her pause. Only she didn't know if he was sorry he'd left or sorry he'd kissed her back. Either way, it didn't matter. She was done.

He sighed. "My life is complicated right now."

"You know, I'm pretty busy myself. So, forget about it. Nothing happened as far as I'm concerned. Let's move on." She brushed his hand off and held up the bottle. "Now, what are these pills?"

He stared down at her for a long moment.

She broke eye contact and shook the bottle. Anything to stop the torture of his intense scrutiny. "Are you going to tell me or what?"

He exhaled. "Omega oil supplements. The vet said it would help keep Lucky's coat shiny." He dug around in the box to retrieve a can of spray cheese. "You have to cover the pill with this. Lucky can eat all around the med, even lick the bowl clean, and leave it in the middle."

Clever. Both the dog and Scott.

"Also, he sometimes gobbles his food so fast he chokes and then pukes it all back up. Mix a little water in and give the kibbles to him in two servings."

She nodded. Lucky had been in good hands.

Scott placed the cheese back in the box. "And if you take him to the park by the lake, don't let him go near the big bush by the restrooms. He tried to nose around in there and got thorns in his face. Took me forever to get them out, poor guy."

A lump formed in Maddie's throat. Obviously, he'd felt bad for the dog's injury, maybe even responsible.

Tom carried a kitchen chair through the door and set it by the table. "Truck's empty."

"I can't thank you enough." Maddie patted his back.

"This where the party is?" Kaitlyn stepped into the room. "Oh, hi, Scott. Didn't expect to see you."

He tapped the box. "Dropping off some dog stuff."

Kaitlyn smoothed her hair back. "Umm, well, since we're all here I might as well tell you the news."

Maddie glanced at Tom, who raised his eyebrows and shrugged. His gaze shifted to Kaitlyn.

"I got a new job. Looks like they'll need to hire someone to replace me."

"What job? What are you talking about?" Tom stepped closer to her.

"I applied for a position in Shamong."

"Wait. You what?" Tom stared at her, his mouth open.

Kaitlyn squared her shoulders. "I probably won't even move, since it's so close. Time for me to branch out."

"But their force isn't any bigger than ours. I don't get it. You never said anything to me about this." Tom shook his head.

"Did you accept the offer?" Maddie asked. Tom might lose his chance with Kaitlyn if she wasn't working with him or ended up moving after all.

"Not yet, but I probably will."

Scott headed to the door. "I gotta go get Lucky. Great news for you, Kaitlyn." He stopped and turned around. "Oh, and you might want to tell your cousin to lighten up his lead foot. I let him go when I realized he was related to you. That new BMW is a lot of car to handle."

Maddie blinked. *Cousin?*

Tom's jaw dropped even further. He glanced at the open doorway, but Scott had left.

Kaitlyn blushed and waved a hand around the room. "So, what needs to get done?"

Tom covered his eyes for a second. He took in a deep breath and blew it out. "Hold on. The guy you went to dinner with the other night was your cousin?"

Maddie stifled a smile. Holy crap. Scott sure dropped a bomb with that one. She had to give him credit. Tom was beyond flustered between the news of Kaitlyn's job and the "date" with her cousin.

Kaitlyn rubbed her neck. "Yeah. He works here now, so I was showing him around. What's the big deal?"

Tom placed his hands on his hips. "But you never said he was your cousin. Why?"

"I—"

"Can you step outside with me for a minute?" Tom puffed his chest out and pointed to the door.

Maddie lowered her gaze to the box so she could hide the grin on her face. What she wouldn't give to hear what Tom had to say. He looked ready to explode. Very un-Tom-like.

After they left, Maddie rummaged around in the box. Tug toys, balls, biscuits, a spare collar; Scott had spared no expense.

The clitter-clatter of claws on the steps came from the stairwell, and then Lucky bounced into the room with Scott close behind. The dog raced over to Maddie and licked her sweaty arm.

Scott unclipped the leash and shut the door. He glanced around. "Where did Tom and Kaitlyn go?"

"They weren't out there?" Maddie knelt down and bent her head to the side so Lucky could slobber doggie kisses up her neck.

"No." The corners of his mouth turned up. "Guess they went somewhere to have a little chat?"

"You can wipe the shit-eating grin off your face. I know you did that on purpose."

"Did what?" He dropped the leash into the box.

She stood. "Casually mentioned Kaitlyn's cousin in front of Tom."

"Did it work?" He arched an eyebrow. His eyes twinkled, and Maddie's chest fluttered.

"I guess we'll find out soon enough."

Lucky barked, and Scott bent to pet him. "I gotta get going, guy. You be a good boy. Don't eat the furniture or puke on the carpet. You're living with a lady, now. Behave yourself."

Lucky licked Scott's face, tail wagging hard.

When he stood and took a step toward the door, Lucky followed. Maddie swallowed. Damn it. She might as well wear a black gown and ride on a broom for taking the dog back. Lucky adored Scott. But he was *her* dog. Technically, anyway.

Scott bent again by the door. He hugged Lucky and patted his side. "I'll see you around, mug-face."

"Wait." Maddie's eyes misted. She couldn't do this. "If you want to keep him—"

"No." Scott shook his head and straightened. "He's yours. I'm going to be busy. He needs to live with you."

"Well, he clearly likes you better."

"Only because he hasn't spent much time with you." He patted the puppy's head. "You're going to be one lucky dog."

Scott left and shut the door.

Lucky whined and sniffed at the crack.

Maddie swiped at an overflowing tear. Scott kept wrenching her heart out. She couldn't take any more.

At the swift knock on the door, Maddie opened it, and Kaitlyn bustled in.

Maddie grabbed Lucky's collar. "I got him."

Kaitlyn shut the door behind her and then rubbed her hands together. Pink-cheeked and breathless, she bubbled with what appeared to be nervous energy. "Tom's taking the truck back on his way to work. We can fit the smaller stuff in our cars."

Maddie picked up Lucky's bowl and filled it with water. "Sure. Is everything okay with you and Tom?"

When Kaitlyn didn't answer, Maddie turned from the sink. Kaitlyn's hand was over her mouth, but a giggle escaped. She never giggled.

Maddie placed the bowl on the floor and hurried across the room. "What are you trying so hard not to laugh at?"

Kaitlyn let her hand drop, and a huge grin spread across her face. "He asked me out."

"Hallelujah, girl!" Maddie high-fived her.

"Oh God, but he was so pissed. I've never seen him like that." Kaitlyn shook with laughter. "He tried so hard to hold it in, but he was on fire."

"What did he say?" Maddie pulled out a chair and patted the seat.

"I'm too wired to sit." Kaitlyn waved a hand in the air. "He read me the riot act. First for keeping the job a secret, and second for misleading him. But I didn't lie."

Maddie narrowed her eyes. "Maybe not to him, but you did to me. You said you were seeing someone."

"Well, I knew you wouldn't move in with Tom if I didn't come up with something. It sorta just came out." She rubbed Maddie's shoulder. "Can you forgive me?"

"Of course. It was worth it to see the look on Tom's face when you showed up in that skirt. He couldn't form words." Maddie smiled.

"I have to admit that was kinda fun. I mean, the guy never looked at me like I was a woman, you know?"

"He did that night. Anyway, are you really going to take this other job?"

"Eh." Kaitlyn shrugged. "It's only twenty minutes from here. If things do work out with Tom, it would be better for us not to be on the job together."

"Yeah. Could be a bit much."

Kaitlyn nodded. "I honestly applied there to get away from Tom. I mean, when you like someone so much it hurts, after a while, you can't take being around them anymore. You know?"

"I can imagine." No matter how hard Maddie tried to shut down her feelings for Scott, every time she ran into him her heart ached. When all she wanted was to move on, he did something to remind her of how caring he could be. He'd plucked thorns from Lucky's face, pushed Tom to make a move on Kaitlyn, and given back the dog he obviously cared so much about.

She glanced at Lucky, who had fallen asleep in front of the door. Nose to the crack. No doubt waiting for Scott, the one he loved, to return. She squeezed her eyes shut.

Been there. Done that.

CHAPTER 18

VICTOR TAPPED HIS CIGAR. An ash fell to the ground and glowed red before disappearing into the dirt. He scraped mud from the sole of his glossy black shoe onto a wooden stake holding string that marked the corner of the excavation site.

The sun had been up for over an hour, and Cooper still hadn't made an appearance. He'd come to personally have a chat with the procrastinating bitch. She obviously needed more persuasion than the nudges he'd given her.

Finally, Cooper's cheap Honda pulled up, and she parked next to his Bentley. She got out and glanced in his direction. Her eyes widened.

He tapped his watch and frowned. Clearly, she hadn't spent the morning on her appearance. Even pulled back in a ponytail, her wild hair refused to be constrained. Stray curls fell around her forehead. In cargo pants and a worn denim jacket with multiple pockets, she'd come dressed to play in the dirt.

At least she'd come, for once.

She opened the trunk and yanked out a tool caddy. He puffed on a cigar and blew out smoke circles in the calm, misty air. The complete opposite of the angry storm brewing inside of him.

Shoulders back, head held high, she approached him with long strides, her breasts bouncing. He had a thing for redheads with big racks. Maybe he'd have another use for her once she'd finished the survey. But the girl had an attitude. If she didn't check it, she'd get more than she bargained for out of their deal.

She dropped her bag at the perimeter of the site. "I didn't expect anyone to be here."

"We had an agreement, and you're not holding up your end."

She waved a hand at the staked area. "What do you call this?"

"Late."

"I've been busy working at the other site. We have a lot of missing pieces to try to replace. And you never set a time frame for this." Her eyes flashed with anger.

"You should have been here." He took a few steps along the side to come closer. "I'm not sure you're getting the message. I don't see any results."

Her nostrils flared. "I got the message. I'm doing the job."

Snarky bitch. He stepped nearer, using his height to intimidate her. He could twist her pale neck and snap it like a twig. "If you want your money, I expect this to be done soon, or there will be consequences."

"Let me clue you in. I'm the only archaeologist within a hundred miles who's qualified to do this survey. If you want it to stand up to scrutiny, then I need to do it." She thrust her chin out. "And your threats are as unnecessary as your presence here. Push me, and I'll quit."

Bitch had balls of steel. His hand itched to smack that insolent face of hers. He held her gaze and chewed on the end of his cigar. Dominating her would be a challenge, and she needed taming, but business first. He glanced at the staked site. "Why so big an area?"

"I have to follow procedure, and everything has to be done by the book so no questions come up. I have a career to protect, and you don't want any official attention. This is the proper size for the amount of land."

He didn't need anyone nosing around the survey results. "How much longer before you write the report?"

She cocked her head. "I have to finish prepping, dig, document, and then write it up. I'd say a minimum of four days, maybe longer."

"That's as fast as you can do it?"

"If you don't want questions asked, yes."

"I expect you to call and update Gina at the end of each day until this is done." He puffed again on the cigar. "If there are any delays, I want to know immediately."

"Understood. Now I should get to work." She bent to pick up a ball of string from the toolkit.

He checked out her ass. "You should have been here earlier. The sun's been up for over an hour." He rubbed his jaw. "Maybe that dog of yours is taking too much of your time. I'd hate to have to clear more things from your schedule."

Her head snapped up, and her eyes grew wide. Bright red patches stained her cheeks as her breath hitched.

That was more like it. Bitch needed to know who was in charge. "I don't play games, and I don't waste my time. You'd fucking better not, either. Understand?"

She nodded, her whole face red now.

He smiled. "I see you're chummy with the police force."

She squeezed the ball of string. Her chest heaved.

Victor dropped his gaze to her breasts, and his groin tightened. "I keep tabs on my people. Tell me, are you cozy with the whole police force or just the men?"

"What?" She flinched.

"Living with one, and all the help moving. You do get around. Our business had better not become pillow talk."

As shock registered on her face, he leaned in. "Make sure you get around to *this*." He knocked the ball of string out of her hand and strode toward his car.

Yeah. Now he fucking had her attention.

* * *

Maddie's keys jingled as she unlocked her apartment door. The scamper of Lucky's feet and an impatient whine from the other side slowed her racing pulse. Damn Victor for threatening her sweet puppy. She entered and dropped to the floor to give the dog a hug. He nuzzled her face and licked her cheeks.

God, Victor knew about Tom and Scott helping her move. He could be watching her right now. The sick bastard could have hired someone to follow her. She might be in deeper than she thought, working for this guy. After a glance at the open blinds, she hurried over to lower them.

Lucky wagged his tail and barked by the door.

"Okay, boy. I'll take you out." She hated the sliver of fear sitting in her belly. Someone could follow them on the walk. Best to stay away from the woods just in case.

Victor's arrogance was unbelievable. Bad enough she'd been seething over the theft of her artifacts, but when he'd threatened her dog, he'd taken the game to a whole new level. She'd held it together. Barely. Not easy for her, but she'd kept the big picture in mind.

She brought Lucky out to his usual place to do his business. If anyone was watching her, it wouldn't be Victor. That pompous prick wouldn't dirty his own hands. He'd hire someone else like he did to burglarize the storeroom. She needed to keep her eyes and ears open. Maybe invest in some pepper spray and give the guy a face full of chemicals the next time he jacked with her.

"Come on, Lucky. You have to be hungry." She tugged on the leash and took Lucky back inside. After she fed him, she opened the refrigerator and stared at her empty shelves. Guess it would be carryout until she had a chance to food shop. Eight o'clock and she still hadn't had dinner.

Her cell rang.

Nikki.

Maddie frowned. Nikki usually texted, not called.

"Maddie. I—I need a favor." Nikki sniffed, her voice nervous.

"What's wrong?" Oh no. Victor hadn't mentioned Nikki in any threats, but he had eyes everywhere, apparently. What if he knew they were friends and had done something to scare or hurt her as another *message*?

"Can you give me a ride?"

"Where are you?" Maddie's pulse quickened as she grabbed her purse and keys.

"In the parking lot behind the coffee shop. I can't go home. I'm not safe there anymore."

"Why aren't you safe? Are you hurt?"

"Not bad. I need a lift to my friend's dorm."

"Stay put. I'll be right there." *Not bad* didn't tell her much.

Ten minutes later, when she pulled into the parking lot, Nikki emerged from the woods by the dumpster, the hood of her jacket covering most of her face. She dropped into the passenger seat.

"Thanks for coming. I didn't know who else to call." Her hand shook as she pulled the door shut.

The hood slipped back when she turned to face Maddie. A bloody lip, bruised cheek, and a cut over her eyebrow marred her face.

The blood in Maddie's veins turned to molten lava. "Did Eric do this to you?"

"Yeah." Nikki tugged a tissue out of her pocket and dabbed at her lip.

That jerkoff asshole. "We need to get you to the hospital."

"No. I'm okay. It's not the first time, but it's the last."

"At least let me take you to the police station."

Nikki's eyes widened, and she shook her head hard. "If I report him, he'll come after me. Do something worse."

"Worse than this? Come on, Nikki. You can get a restraining order or something."

"Like that would stop him. Please, can you take me to the university?" Her eyes pleaded. "I can stay at the dorm with my friend for a few nights."

Maddie huffed. "That dick needs to get locked up."

"You're right. I don't know what he's capable of." She glanced at the woods. "Please, can we get out of here?"

"Okay." Maddie put the car in drive and pulled out of the lot. "What do you mean by you don't know what he's capable of?"

"He's into drugs now."

"I take it you don't mean a little pot on the weekends?"

Nikki leaned her head back. "I found meth in the apartment, and he came home and saw me with the bag. He was high. All wired and jumpy. Glazed eyes. I've noticed a difference in him the last few months, but I guess I didn't want to admit it."

She swiped away a tear. "Yesterday, he wasn't high. I thought maybe he'd quit. Nope. Tonight, he started yelling at me and calling me a meddling bitch. I...I told him no drugs, or I was done."

Maddie glanced at Nikki. "Then what?"

Nikki looked out the window. A tear slid down her cheek.

"Nikki?"

"He grabbed my purse and opened my wallet. Took my tip money. Said it wasn't enough." She drew in a shaky breath. "He told me I was nothing but a pitiful leeching whore and smacked me. Said I didn't contribute shit and...hit me again."

Son of a bitch. Maddie gripped the steering wheel tighter, turning her knuckles white.

Nikki covered her eyes with a hand. "I didn't fight him. I just wanted to get away."

Maddie reached over to pat Nikki's leg. "It's okay. You're gonna be okay. Do you have any family you can stay with?"

"No. With Zach in jail, that's kinda it."

Maddie stopped at a red light in front of O'Leary's. Nikki gasped and then ducked down. Maddie glanced at the parking lot. Good-for-nothing Eric was getting out of his truck.

Nikki shrank lower in the seat.

That asshole had balls. Beat up his girlfriend and then go for a beer to celebrate. Maddie's blood pressure skyrocketed.

"Please don't tell anyone about this. I'm done with him. I promise."

The light turned green, and Nikki directed Maddie through the university to the right dorm lot. She stopped in front of the building entrance. "Are you going to be safe here?"

"Yeah. He said he was done with me as long as I kept my mouth shut. No one can get in the building here without swiping, anyway, and he doesn't know where I am."

"Okay." Maddie leaned over to hug Nikki. "I'm glad you called me."

Nikki squeezed her tight, and a tear dampened Maddie's shirt. "Thanks."

When Nikki let go, Maddie held her gaze. "Promise me if you hear anything from that prick, you'll call the police."

"I will."

The events of the last week played through Maddie's mind. Damn it, she was tired of being bullied. And now, Nikki, too?

She waited until Nikki was securely in the dorm and then gunned the car and headed to O'Leary's.

* * *

Maddie glared at Eric's black truck parked under a lamppost in the lot. That putrid piece-of-shit excuse for a man. At least Nikki had left him. But that could be temporary. She didn't talk much about her past. Something must have scarred her enough to make her settle for that jackass.

Maddie would call her later and try to convince her to go to the police. Eric belonged behind bars. Maybe he'd get scared if he thought Nikki might press charges.

After cutting the engine, she grabbed her purse and climbed out of her car. She kicked the oversize tire of Eric's truck on her way past, fighting against the urge to key the side. The last week had been just short of hell. The stolen artifacts, assault, threats from Victor, and now Nikki. Enough. Someone needed to put these assholes in their place.

After a last glance at the beast-mobile, she marched into the pub and scanned the room. A few of the regulars called out and waved to her. No time for chitchat.

Eric stood by the bar, his arm draped around the back of the bottle-blonde known in town for her easy hook-ups. Blood roared in Maddie's ears. She strode across the room and tapped Eric on the shoulder. He turned around, and the stale scent of cigarette smoke wafted her way.

His red-rimmed eyes narrowed to slits. "What do you want?"

"To tell you to keep your hands off of Nikki. You touch her again, and you'll go to jail."

"What'd she do, run crying to you?" He held up a hand and fluttered his fingers. "Oh, look, I'm shaking."

Maddie's heart pounded against her rib cage. Dickhead. "You should be. I mean it. Stay away from her. And you"—she pointed to the blonde—"should quit while you're ahead. He beats up his girlfriends."

The blonde curled her lips in obvious disgust. She shook off his arm and stepped away. "Don't need that shit."

Eric's gaze followed her. He turned back to Maddie. "You keep the fuck out of my business."

"I will if you keep your filthy paws off of my friend. You want to beat someone up? Pick a fight with a man, you coward." She pivoted on her heel.

Eric whipped a hand out and grabbed her arm, yanking her back. "Shut your mouth, bitch. I'll do what I want. And if Nikki goes to the cops, I'll tell them the truth." He leaned down and sneered. His fingers dug into her still-sore bruise. "She likes it rough. What about you?"

Maddie sucked in a breath as a red haze blurred her vision. She cranked her arm back, fisted a hand, and punched Eric in the face. Blood spurted out of his nose as his head whipped to the side. He crashed against the bar, knocking glasses to the ground, where they shattered.

The room went silent.

Eric pushed off the counter and whirled around. Like a rabid dog, he bared his teeth, let out an angry snarl, and lunged for her.

CHAPTER 19

SCOTT'S FISHING lure plopped as it landed on the smooth surface of the lake, sending out circular ripples in the water. He stood along the rocky shore under a large oak and reeled his line back in rhythmic jerks. The sun dipped lower behind the tree line. Another hour until sunset. Zach was due to show up any minute.

The deal to free Zach and enlist his help as an informant hadn't come easily, but Scott had refused to give up until he'd convinced the chain of command that he needed someone on the inside. The sooner he locked Mole away, the better. No one was safe with him walking the streets. Scott flicked his wrist to cast again.

Maddie could never know the scope of his undercover work or the dangers involved. She had a right to be pissed after that kiss last night. He'd lost control and kissed her back. Couldn't help himself. She'd ignited an inferno when her tongue had slid into his mouth.

She'd been the last woman he'd kissed, and that had been a hell of a long time ago. His body had reacted before his mind engaged. He couldn't let that happen again. The pain on her face when he'd broken their kiss haunted him. She probably thought he was playing games with her, messing with her head and heart. Guilt gnawed at him, but what mattered most was protecting her.

His line tugged, and he yanked his rod. The lure and empty hook broke the water surface.

Missed it. Too eager. He needed to be more patient. At many things.

Footsteps rustled through the brush behind him, and Zach emerged from the woods, fishing pole in hand. His gaze darted around the perimeter of the lake. "Hey, Scott."

Scott nodded. "It's okay. No one's around. That's why I picked this place." He tapped a Styrofoam cup of worms with his foot. "Try some live bait. I'm using a lure. One way or another, we'll set a hook."

Zach raised an eyebrow. A hint of a smile teased the corners of his lips. Out of the orange jumpsuit, in jeans and a T-shirt, he could almost pass for relaxed. But Scott knew too well the telltale signs of a person on high alert.

After picking up the cup, Zach pulled out a worm and struggled to bait the hook. He whipped the rod, plunking the bait a couple of feet out.

Clearly, he hadn't been fishing much.

He cast again. "I think I have an in with this guy, Eric, who works for Mole. He's looking for someone to boost crystal sales. I convinced him I had connections. Eric said he was going to talk to his boss about me. Thinks it might impress him that he found someone to bring in on the operation."

"It might. This town is small. Not a lot of criminals to recruit." Scott reeled in his line. "Did you meet Eric or just talk to him?"

"We met." Zach shook his head. "He's a fuck-up. I'm guessing he uses. The guy couldn't focus on anything."

Sounded familiar. "What's Eric's last name?"

"He never said."

Scott yanked some green, slimy weeds off his lure and cast again. "I ran into an Eric at the development site. Probably the same guy. Can't lie for his life, and is jumpier than a grasshopper in a birdcage?"

Zach snorted. "Yup. Gotta be him."

"Must be slim pickings if Mole's using Wilson in his operation."

"Wilson?" Zach's hand froze on the rod. He slapped a palm to his forehead. "Are you shitting me? Eric Wilson? This is the asshole Nikki's living with?"

"Whoa. What?" Scott whipped his head around to face Zach. "Your sister is involved with Eric?"

Zach lowered his hand. His nostrils flared. "She told me his name once, but I never met the guy since I was in prison. They've been together for a while. I had no idea the jerk was a meth head. What the hell, Nikki?"

This threw a wrench into things. Scott plucked his line out of the water and set the handle of the rod on the ground. He rubbed his jaw. "If this is too complicated, I'll understand your need to bail."

"Fuck." Zach reeled his line in fast and then cast it out hard. "No, I'll handle it. I just can't believe she's with him. I left her in the lurch, and this is what she ended up with. She doesn't do drugs and never hung around anyone who did. I don't get it."

Scott checked his lure and tossed the line back out. "I take it Eric doesn't know you're Nikki's brother?"

"No. Last time we discussed Eric, she admitted she never told him about me. I figured she was embarrassed to have a brother in jail. Now, I wonder if it's because she never wanted us to meet."

"This is a small town. Eventually, Eric's gonna find out she's your sister."

Zach turned to Scott and looked him in the eyes. "I won't let it affect what I have to do. Nikki doesn't know I'm out yet. I'll talk to her and make sure she keeps her distance from me. I'd planned to anyway, for her own safety."

The guy was a straight shooter. Nothing but honesty and determination on his face. "All right. I'll let you handle the situation."

"I won't let you down." Zach went back to cranking his reel.

Scott nodded. "In the meantime, I'm working an angle to make Mole think I could be on the take. If anything comes up about me, jump on it. In fact, if anyone does see us here together, it could corroborate that idea."

"Okay."

"Anything else we need to discuss?" Scott kept his gaze on the lake.

"No. Except I...uh...wanted to thank you."

"Hey, you're earning this. You don't need to thank me." Shit. The kid deserved the break.

"Yeah, well, you coulda left me to fend for myself finding a place to live. The condo I'm in rocks."

Warmth spread through Scott's chest. Zach was easy to like. Scott had arranged with the owner to pay a portion of the rent without Zach knowing about it. He thought the police were picking up part of the tab while he acted as an informant.

Things might have been different for Justin if someone had stepped up to help him. Maybe he'd been in a tough spot, like Zach. Arrested and no one around to bail him out. Scott was tired of holding everyone at a distance, but he couldn't afford to be Zach's friend. He had to keep it professional. Mole used friends of his enemies as leverage.

Scott shrugged. "You have to look legit. If you were slumming, they wouldn't buy you had money or connections."

"Makes sense." Zach's bait surfaced, and he cast again. "I'm going to do whatever it takes to help you nail Mole. Then, I'll work on getting Nikki away from Eric. She needs me. I failed her once. Not again, ya know?"

"Yeah, I do." Scott's gut clenched. Zach's tortured eyes haunted him. Like looking into his own soul. Only Zach had lived with his guilt for four years and had plenty of downtime to think about it.

At least Scott had been immersed in cartel cases. If he'd had to stare at a cell wall and face his failure to save his brother every day, he'd have gone crazy. Zach was one tough dude. He'd need to be for what lay ahead. Tension squeezed Scott's ribs. He'd better not fuck this up and get him hurt.

Zach's rod bowed, and the reel spun fast, taking line with it. "Holy shit. What do I do?"

Scott pointed to the reel. "Turn the knob to tighten the drag. When the fish stops pulling, crank fast and keep the rod tip up."

A quick study, Zach reeled when the line slackened and held steady when it went taut. At last, the fish surfaced with a frothy splash, and Zach landed it on the bank. It flopped wildly on the sand and rocks.

"Whoa. He's huge." Wide-eyed, he stared down at the fish.

Scott stabbed a couple of fingers behind the gill plate to hold it up. "It's a lake trout. Biggest one I've ever seen."

Zach grinned. The sheer joy and excitement that lit his face ripped right through Scott's heart. Took him back to the first time he'd fished with Justin, and he'd caught a largemouth bass. Same as Zach, Justin had followed his instructions. He had hooted when Scott netted the fish and brought him in the boat. Now, Zach stood beside Scott with the same look on his face.

"We make a good team." Zach continued to admire the fish.

"You work well under pressure."

A trickle of blood dripped from where the hook caught under the gill. Zach's smile fell. "You gonna let him go? I mean, I don't want to cook him or anything."

The guy had a soft spot. He'd have to be careful not to show it. Scott nodded, removed the hook, and bent to gently place the fish back in the water. When he let go, the trout's tail thrashed as it swam away.

Scott wiped his hands on his jeans and faced Zach. "When we catch the one we're after, we won't be letting him off the hook. You with me?"

Zach's eyes steeled. "Damn straight."

"It'll be dark soon. Better pack it up." Scott picked up his rod and the cup of worms. "Let me know when you hear from Eric."

"I will." Zach took the worm off the hook and tossed it into the water. "Thanks again. For…everything. This sure beats the shit out of sitting in a dark cell." He glanced at the sky. The first streaks of orange and pink laced the clouds. "Think I'll hang here for a few more minutes. I'll be in touch."

"Will do." Scott made his way through the woods and back to his car. His stomach growled, and he couldn't help but smile. No fish for dinner tonight. Looked like it would be carryout from O'Leary's. He called in an order and headed to the pub.

When he pulled into the lot, he spotted Maddie's car. Of course. Just his luck. Put a pickle next to his shit sandwich and serve it up. Maybe she'd be at a table in the back, and he could grab his order at the bar and leave without seeing her.

He opened the door to an eerie silence. His senses went on high alert as his gaze shot around the room. Everyone stared at the bar where Maddie stood in front of Eric, who had a hand to his face covered in blood.

He lunged at Maddie. She dodged him.

A man at a nearby table stood and took a step toward Eric.

Scott shouted, "Police. Nobody move!"

The crowd turned as one to stare at him. Except Eric. He lunged for Maddie again, who dodged out of the way.

Scott sprinted across the room and grabbed Eric's arm, pinned it behind his back, and put him in a chokehold. He flexed his bicep against Eric's throat causing him to gasp for air. "I said freeze."

Wheezing and spitting blood, Eric waved at Maddie, who stood with her hands on her hips glaring at him. He rasped, "I'm fucking pressing charges. Bitch punched me."

Scott clenched his jaw. Zach had every reason to be concerned about this asshole living with his sister. Now what-the-fuck trouble had Maddie gotten herself into? "We're going outside." Scott pointed to her. "You stay here. I'll be back."

Eric tried to wriggle out of his grasp. "I got rights. I'm coming after you, whore. I'll kill—"

"Threatening her in front of an officer is a really bad idea." Scott manhandled him through the bar and out the front door. He shoved him against the brick wall and kicked his legs out, spread-eagled.

Scott patted him down and snagged a bag of weed out of Eric's back pocket. "Your night just got worse."

"Hey, that's not enough for you to do crap with. Why aren't you arresting the bitch in there? She's the one who started this."

"I'll wait to hear her side of the story. I know what I just saw." Scott ground his molars. The first time he'd met Eric, the guy had mouthed off about some bitch lying. Now he'd threatened Maddie. What Scott wouldn't give to be able to deck the prick right there. He spun Eric around.

Blood oozed from his nose. He ran his sleeve along it.

"Remember when I told you I make up my own rules?" Scott leaned in.

Eric swallowed.

Good. He'd intimidated him. Now, instead of going full out Angel-of-Death on the guy, he had to keep his end game in the crosshairs. Even though he could have killed the maggot ten different ways with a stir-ring straw in the bar, he needed to keep his cover as a small-town cop, and a corruptible one. He forced himself to stay in DEA mode. Detach from emotion. Handle the situation and keep Maddie safe at the same time.

"Here's the deal. You go after Maddie or any other woman, and I'll have this police force so far up your ass you won't shit for a month." He shook Eric. "You understand? Because I'm betting your boss doesn't want a lot of police attention."

Eric gave a jerky nod.

Scott held up the bag of weed. "And this?" He glanced around as if to make sure no one was looking. "It's gonna cost you fifty for me to forget I found it."

Eric's eyebrows shot up. "Wait. You saying—"

"I'm not fucking saying anything. And you'd better not either." Scott rubbed his fingers together, making the universal signal for money. "I'm waiting."

Eric wiped his mouth, reached into his pocket, and pulled out three twenties. He slipped them into Scott's hand and cocked his head.

Scott snickered. "I don't make change. Now get the fuck out of my sight."

Eric took a few steps toward the parking lot and looked back. Scott placed his hands on his hips, stance wide. He waited for Eric to drive away and then heaved a sigh.

Good thing Scott had shown up when he did. He might not have been able to control himself if that dickhead had hurt Maddie. Zach would have his hands full hiding his anger while he dealt with Eric. The guy could infuriate Mother Teresa.

And Maddie kept ending up in dangerous situations. How she'd survived this long was a mystery.

The woman made him crazy and had added more to his already-long day. Hungry and tired, he'd now need to write up a report on the incident. At least about what had happened inside. His discussion with Eric would stay off the record.

Scott went back inside the pub. Maddie squatted on her hands and knees in front of the bar, blotting the floor with cocktail napkins. The place quieted as people turned to look at him. Like it or not, he had to act like he was there to do his job. That meant following procedure.

The bartender came out from the kitchen with a mop. "I told you I had this, Maddie."

"Well, I caused the mess, so—"

"I need to speak with you, Ms. Cooper. Outside, please," Scott said.

Maddie grimaced and stood. "Can't we talk in here?"

The last strand of his patience snapped. "No." He pointed to the door. "Outside. Now."

She blew out a breath, but marched to the exit. After the door closed behind them, he turned to her. "What the hell were you thinking in there?"

Maddie jutted her chin up. "Aren't you going to ask what happened, Detective Fisher, since we're going by last names now?"

Damn, she smacked the head of the rattlesnake in him. "You're on thin ice. Drop the attitude."

She pressed her lips together and tapped her foot on the concrete.

"Why'd you punch Eric?"

She met his gaze. "The bastard beat up Nikki. She has no one to stand up for her."

Scott's shoulders stiffened. They needed a special hell for men who hit women. "Is she okay?"

"I think so. Bruised and bleeding, but refused to go to the hospital."

Shit. Zach might not handle this well when he found out. Scott would make damn sure Eric paid for laying his hands on that sweet girl. He was right up there with Mole now. "Why didn't she call the police?"

"She's scared of Eric. Thought he'd come after her."

"So, you decided it was up to you to take him on?"

She shrugged. "I made him bleed."

Scott placed his hands on her shoulders to get her attention. Now she was fucking with Mole's guy, playing too close to the fire. "This isn't a joke, Maddie. He could have really hurt you."

"No kidding. You should see Nikki's face."

Defiant, strong, full of passion. Maddie never backed down. Her cheeks flushed. The sweet scent of apples wafted up from her hair. His hands turned hot over the thin fabric of her blouse. He warred with himself over whether to lock her up for her own safety or kiss her senseless. Before he did either, he let go and took a step back.

She wouldn't listen to reason in her current state. At the same time, he couldn't fault her for defending a friend. He sighed. "Go home. I have work to do."

"Go home? Again?" She crossed her arms. "That's all you seem to tell me to do. Don't I need a lawyer or something?"

"No. I'll handle it."

"I don't want you to do me any favors. I'll—"

"Damn it, Maddie. I said I'd handle it. Now, go home."

She closed her mouth and glared at him.

He'd had enough for one day. He held up his hands. "I know. You don't like to be told what to do. Too bad. Please, leave, so I can finish up here."

He strode to the door, yanked it open, and left Maddie in the lot.

The room went quiet once again when he walked in.

"Can I have your attention, please?" He waited a beat until all eyes were on him. "Did anyone see anything tonight they'd like to go on record and report?" As he ambled through the room, people shook their heads and looked away. He waved a hand. "Okay, then. Thanks."

As he went to the bar to pick up his carryout order, some of the regulars nodded at him. The air in the room changed. Gone were the hostile looks. The noise level returned to normal.

The bartender disappeared into the kitchen and came back with a box. Scott reached for his wallet, but the server held up a hand and smiled. "This one's on the house."

Yeah, the climate sure had changed. Scott thanked him and took the food. He'd planned to stop over at Maddie's to get his spare key back, but that could wait. She'd still be pissed at him for telling her to go home. In their current states, one of them might burst into flames if they got together.

Tomorrow would be soon enough to have words with her about her actions.

And she'd damn well better listen.

CHAPTER 20

MADDIE CLOSED her eyes and let the warm shower wash away all the dust, dirt, and angst of the day. Eight hours of digging and no finds. Of course, she had plenty of area left to excavate, but she'd hoped to hit pay dirt on the first try. She scoffed as she rinsed the shampoo from her hair. Pay dirt. How appropriate.

As she toweled off, the events of the previous night played in her head. Damn that Eric. He belonged in jail. The situation did get out of control at the bar, though. If anyone else had gotten hurt, she'd have been to blame.

Scott had a point. She didn't think things through sometimes. Still, he didn't need to be such a know-it-all. And yet, how he'd taken control had been impressive. Hot, even. The way he'd swept in like a ninja, all business, with eyes of steel and a body to match. If she hadn't been dodging blows, she might have enjoyed a well-earned gawk.

Scott's iron grip around Eric's throat had been worth the price of admission. Asshole deserved it and more. So far, she hadn't heard anything about Eric pressing charges, but he could have grounds. Even though he'd grabbed her first, she'd punched him in the face in front of a bar full of witnesses.

After she dried her hair, she slipped on a pair of yoga pants and a soft, purple T-shirt. Better. Human again.

Her phone dinged with a text. She tapped it to zoom in on a picture. A screenshot of Sarah's ultrasound. *It's a girl!*

Maddie broke into a grin and typed back, *Congratulations. Wanna bet Bruce polishes his gun in front of her first date? LOL.*

Oh God. You're so right!

I'm just messing with you. Seriously stoked!

Thanks. I'm already picking out ballet shoe stencils for the nursery.

A knock sounded at the door. Lucky jumped up from his bed and raced across the room barking.

Maddie set the phone aside and peeked through the peephole.

Scott.

Uh oh. Maybe she was in trouble after all. She opened the door. Lucky's tail thumped fast like the wings of a hummingbird at the sight of his best friend. He whined and frantically licked Scott's hand.

"Are you here to arrest me?" She crossed her arms over her chest and glared at him.

"Why does every word out of your mouth have to be confrontational?"

"Why does every encounter with you bring that out in me?"

His T-shirt stretched taut over bulging biceps, and his hair was damp as if he'd also just showered. Maybe they'd been in the stalls, naked, at the same time. The spot between her legs tingled. God, she needed to get a grip.

He hadn't shaved. She refused to think about how the sexy stubble might feel against her face—or anywhere else for that matter.

"I stopped by to get my spare key." He pulled a biscuit out of his jeans pocket and gave it to the dog. Lucky ran away to gobble it on the kitchen tile.

Unbelievable. He'd come armed with cookies. Her gaze dropped to his jeans. Yeah, once she'd been lucky enough to enjoy the treats he had in his pants. She bit her cheek. If she had access to a hammer, she'd smack herself in the head with it. Maybe that meat pounder would do the trick.

He gave her a strange look. "You okay?"

"Yeah." She opened the door wider. "Come in for a sec?"

He hitched an eyebrow. "Into the lion's den? You have a pack of hyenas in there waiting to rip me apart?"

"Please. I'm not that bad."

Scott snorted as he passed her and glanced at the kitchen. "Something smells good."

A whiff of soap and spice met her nose. She wouldn't argue. "I had Pronto's seafood marinara tonight. To die for."

"Haven't eaten there yet."

Maddie opened the kitchen drawer and plucked his key out. "Oh my God. Better than sex. You gotta try—"

"Why do you say things like that?" Scott's eyes flashed.

Good question. Maybe because when she was around him all she thought about was sex. She sure didn't say that stuff to Tom. Enough already. She would not make a fool of herself again. Scott had to go, but not until she talked to him about Nikki. She held the key out. "I don't know. Here."

He took it and stepped toward the door.

She placed a hand on his arm. "Wait. Do you have a minute? It's about Nikki."

Scott stopped. "Yeah. What's going on?"

"Sit for a minute?" She waved to the couch.

He followed her, took a seat at the end, and angled sideways to face her, propping a knee up as he leaned against the armrest. Her gaze dropped to his lap. When they'd been together, she'd crawled over and sat on those hard, muscular thighs. He'd stroked her hair and kissed her head as they'd settled in together to watch a movie. Her heart twisted.

Scott tapped his leg, irritation in his voice. "What are you looking at?"

"Wh-what?" She glanced up. Nibbled her lip.

His gaze went to her mouth and lingered. He shifted in the seat and cleared his throat. "What about Nikki?"

Maddie frowned. Right. Her friend. This was important. "I called her at the dorm where I left her."

"How is she?"

"Okay, I guess." Maddie shook her head, and then rubbed her throat. "I couldn't convince her to call the police, and trust me, I tried."

"You have quite the arsenal and are used to getting your way. If you couldn't steamroll her into it, no one could."

She pursed her lips. "I don't steamroll anybody."

"Really? You think you just go with the flow?"

"What's that supposed to mean? Just because I care about people—"

"Don't play that card with me." Scott stood. "You don't think before you act. You let yourself get beat up over artifacts. Pieces of clay, not even alive."

"The Seneca Nation tribal members they belong to are." She pushed to her feet and glared up at him. "And stop talking to me like I'm a child. I know damn well what I'm doing."

"Well, you're certainly not acting like a mature adult. You run around half-cocked. Look at you." He dragged her by the arm to the hall mirror. "I mean it. Take a good look."

He had a lot of nerve, hauling her around like some caveman. She sputtered, "Let go of me."

"Not until you look in the mirror."

"What are you trying to prove?" She glanced at her reflection. The bruise on her cheek from the attack a week ago had turned an ugly yellowish-green. A new scrape flanked the other side of her face, but damn if she had any idea how she'd gotten it. Maybe from a flying shard of glass at the bar. She swallowed and glanced up at Scott. "Nikki looks worse."

His eyes were fierce as his mouth drew into a hard line. "Eric will pay."

She took a breath. "At least I gave him a taste of his own medicine."

"Damn, you're infuriating. Did it ever occur to you, if Nikki wouldn't go to the police because she was scared of Eric, you telling him to keep his hands off her means he knows she confided in you?"

The realization formed a knot in her stomach. She'd never considered that, just let her anger take control. If Eric found out where Nikki was, he might go after her. If not now, later. She couldn't hide forever. "You're right. I have to warn her."

"Eric won't bother her."

"You don't know that. He's a meth head. If anything happens to her—"

"Calm down." Scott shook his head. "Nothing will happen. I had words with Eric. He won't dare touch Nikki."

"But I put her in jeopardy. I wasn't thinking. I'm the worst friend ever." She closed her eyes and put a hand to her mouth.

"No, you're not." He gave her a gentle shake. "Hey, look at me."

She couldn't. If she did, she might give in to the desire to bury her face in his broad chest. He'd made it clear he didn't want that. Yet, his hands were on her. Warm and reassuring. She had to get him to leave before she caved, only to have him toy with her again. "Go. You're right. I'm too impulsive. I don't think things through. I'm a shitty friend. You win, okay?"

"Not okay." He squeezed her arm.

When she turned her head away, he sighed. "Listen, I'm sorry. I never meant to make you feel like a bad friend, but you scare the shit out of me sometimes." He raised her chin with a fingertip. "Do you want to know what I really think about you?"

She gazed into his eyes. Gorgeous green like the soft moss under a mighty oak. Unable to look away, she gave a slow nod.

"I've spent enough time with you to know you're loyal and caring. You're strong and fierce when it comes to protecting your friends." The corners of his mouth turned down. "It makes me crazy when you take on the world, because sometimes it bites back."

He stroked a finger beside the scrape on her cheek, and tears sprung to her eyes.

She couldn't let him see her cry. Her shoulders shook as she fought for control. "Y-you should go."

"I'm not leaving you like this. You're a good friend. Why do you think Nikki called *you*?"

She gave a slight shake of her head. "I failed her." A sob escaped as the emotions of the last week broke the floodgates. Hot tears streamed down her cheeks, and she shut her eyes.

Scott wrapped his arms around her. She soaked his shirt as pain and frustration poured out. He rubbed her back. "Let it go. I got you."

Solid, strong, a lifeboat in the rocky sea, she clung to him. When the tears were finally spent, she swiped at her cheek and muttered into his shirt. "I don't usually cry."

"Me either."

"It's embarrassing." She hiccupped.

"Hey, we all cry at some point."

"When's the last time you did?"

His arms tensed around her, and he didn't answer.

She sniffled and gazed up at him. "Tell me. I know something happened to you. You're different."

He brushed a damp curl from her cheek. His brow furrowed, and sadness crept into his eyes. For a long moment, he stared at her, a clear debate raging in his head. Whatever he was keeping from her had to be big. She held her breath and willed him to share the secret.

At last, he said quietly, "When I was in Mexico, I lost my brother."

"What?" Justin was younger than Scott, and healthy as far as she'd known. She reached up to rest a hand on his jaw. "I'm so sorry. Was he sick?"

He closed his eyes. "A drug overdose. I wasn't there for him."

She blinked, trying to process the devastation Scott must have felt. So that was why he'd changed from the carefree, laid-back guy she'd met two years ago into this hardened shell of a person who never let himself go and didn't make room for fun. The guilt had to be eating him up. She caressed his chin. The stubble was rough under her fingers, like so many times before. "It's not your fault. You were undercover, trying to put away the bad guys."

He opened his eyes. "Years ago, when my mother was dying, I promised her I'd take care of Justin. I let them both down."

The raw pain in his expression tore at her. Her vision blurred with new tears. "You can't be responsible for what he did as an adult." She threaded her fingers though his, brought his hand to her chest, and squeezed. "I'm so sorry. I didn't know. You should have told me."

"I'm making you cry again." He wiped a tear from her cheek. His gaze fell to their entwined hands, nestled between her breasts. He took a sharp breath. "I need to go."

She squeezed his hand again, holding it to her heart when he tried to pull back.

No. Not now. Not after he'd finally opened up and let her in. At last, she understood his reason for closing himself off. No wonder he hadn't called her in two years. He'd been mourning his brother, feeling responsible for his death. Scott wouldn't have wanted to burden anyone with his grief. Sad as she was for him, a huge weight lifted. It had never been her.

She slipped her free hand up through his hair. "Please, don't go."

A war waged behind his eyes, the battle palpable. He stared down at her. Through her. His body tensed. Time seemed to stand still. The chirping birds outside her window and all other sounds faded into the background.

She leaned into him and raised her chin. If he couldn't see the unmasked emotions swirling through her, then he might be truly lost. She had nothing else to give. Her lips trembled, and she slid her hand to his cheek. "It's not too late. I-I understand now."

He took a deep breath. Once again, she held hers, sure he would push her away as usual, but hoping beyond hope that he'd let her in. And then he brought his face down closer. Held it a mere inch away from her mouth. "I'm a selfish SOB."

"Why?" she asked, her pulse skittering.

"Because I can't resist you."

He lowered his lips to hers.

Yes, oh God, yes. Her heart leaped into her throat. She melted against him and slid her arms around his neck.

He deepened the kiss. Their tongues tangled as the taste of spearmint and the scent of his spicy cologne filled her senses. Scott. Finally letting go. She pressed her body to his and met his passion with a fury. The kiss turned into something so primal she couldn't draw a breath. He fisted a hand in her hair and dragged his mouth away to look into her eyes.

"Maddie." His voice, rough and deep, sent shock waves through her. The intensity of his gaze mirrored her own floodgate of emotions. "I can't stop."

"Don't." She tugged at his shirt. He broke contact to whip it over his head before kissing her again. And hell yes, he could kiss. She'd missed this. She'd missed him. She'd missed the way he, and only he, could set her body on fire with just a kiss.

Urgent. Hot now, she craved skin-on-skin contact. He unbuttoned her blouse and yanked it off. The bra came next. She ran her hands over his pecs and pressed her breasts to his chest.

He unsnapped the button of her jeans as he explored her mouth with his tongue. The ache between her legs begged to be filled. He unzipped her jeans, slipped his hand inside, and traced circles with his finger around the sensitive nub.

Oh God, yes. They were going to do this. Heat came from him in waves. She rubbed the straining bulge in his jeans, and he sucked in a breath. "Condom. Do you have one?"

She shook her head. Damn it. And then he was kissing her again. Backed her up against the wall and slid a finger inside her. She nipped at his lip and tried to undo his pants button, but he trapped her arm between them and continued to work magic with his mouth and fingers. Waves of pleasure built as he brought her closer and closer.

No one had ever made her so crazy with need. Every fiber in her body sang for him. Scott. At last, Scott. A whimper escaped as she surrendered.

"That's it. Come for me, Maddie." His hot breath on her neck and the sweet sound of her name from his lips hurled her over the edge. He brought his mouth back to hers and swallowed her cry as her body rhythmically squeezed his fingers.

With a shudder, she opened her eyes and met his scorching gaze. Aroused, Scott was beyond sexy. Reminded her of the time they'd made love in a cove. Hair tousled and his heart thumping against her flattened palm. Only then he'd been wet, and the cool water had dripped from his hair, tickling her breasts as he'd drawn her back into him. Nothing had changed. When Scott made love to her, she lost track of the world. All that existed was the two of them and the crazy, heightened sensations of her body reacting to him. She grasped his neck and kissed him hard, one hand attempting to free him from his jeans.

His phone rang.

No. She tightened her grip on his neck, but he stilled and took a deep breath. "I have to take this. It's the work ringtone."

She sighed. He shot one last look at her, his eyes still raging with raw desire, before he unclipped the phone from his belt and stepped into the kitchen.

Goosebumps formed on Maddie's arms as she waited. She crossed them over her bare breasts.

When Scott hung up, he frowned. "I'm sorry. I have to go."

Not again. Her stomach dropped. Not after he'd just...

Quickly crossing the room, he stopped in front of her, cupped her face in his hands, and kissed her. "Do you want me to come back?"

Her soul soared. God, yes. She nodded, too choked up to form words. He wasn't ditching her again.

"I shouldn't, Maddie. I know I shouldn't." He kissed her. "But I can't help it." He snatched his shirt from the floor and tugged it on while she fetched her bra and blouse.

She slipped her arms into her sleeves, and he opened the door. "I don't know how long I'll be. If it's too late, I'll—"

"Be waiting for you." Look at that. She'd found her voice. "Hey, Detective?"

"What?"

She dropped her gaze to his crotch. "Stop at a drugstore."

"Now who's being bossy?" He grinned and left.

CHAPTER 21

SCOTT SWITCHED on his police lights and headed toward the address Kaitlyn had called in for backup. A domestic dispute case. Those could get ugly. Maybe they could resolve things quickly so he could get back to Maddie.

So much for his will to stay away from her. He couldn't do it. Even when she made him mad, he wanted her. Her fire and spunk kept him off-balance. Half the time he was torn between the urge to throttle her and the desire to throw her on the bed and make wild love to her.

He'd fought to keep his distance, but her tears had undone him. One look in those sad hazel eyes, brimming with concern for her friend, and he'd caved. Noble intentions to hell, once she'd cried herself out, he'd lost control. Her fingers in his hair, her soft lips, the way she'd trembled under his touch before finally surrendering.

He had to be insane to go back to her apartment later. The list of reasons why grew by the minute. Even if they managed a relationship while he worked in town, it wouldn't last. As soon as he put Mole away, Scott's work would take him somewhere else.

And Maddie had mentioned traveling on digs again. Add the danger of his case with Mole into the mix, and the result was a ticking bomb waiting to explode. Abort mission. He needed to walk away.

Except he wanted her. More than anything in his life.

Beyond wanted.

Needed.

Craved.

Consumed with a yearning so deep and primal it robbed him of his ability to think or sleep.

No, he wouldn't give up. He'd find a way to keep her safe and separate from the darkness of his job. For the first time in years, a spark of hope lit inside and warmed him. God help him because like it or not, he was going to fan those embers and start a fire.

Tom beeped on the radio.

"I talked to Kaitlyn. Turns out the DD was just a couple arguing loudly. She has it under control and won't need backup."

Scott's chest lightened. He could get back to Maddie now. "Okay."

He whipped into the drug store and bought a pack of condoms. In the car, he opened the box and slipped a couple into his wallet. Couldn't remember the last time he'd carried around protection of the non-weapon kind.

The radio beeped again, and he frowned.

Tom.

"I got a call about some suspicious activity over at the excavation site near the storage building. I'm heading there now and could use some backup."

Maddie's site. Nothing should be going on at ten o'clock at night. Scott made a U-turn. "Meet you there."

When he arrived, Tom's police SUV sat in the lot. A flashlight beam bobbed in the open field past the storeroom building. Scott picked up the two-way radio.

"On the scene, Tom. What do you have?"

"Apprehended one suspect. The others ran off. Looks like they were digging up artifacts."

"Be right there." Shit. Maddie would go nuts. Bad enough her finds were stolen; now the assholes were raping the land. He fisted a hand against his thigh. No point calling her until he assessed the situation. Maybe it wasn't as bad as it sounded.

He aimed his flashlight on the ground ahead and jogged toward Tom.

Like walking on the moon, he jumped over craters. So much for hoping for minimal damage. Empty soda cans and candy wrappers littered the area. Same as in the Southwest. The tweakers, who rarely slept, high on meth, would eat while they dug and leave their trash all over the place. Of course, it could be teenagers, but this setup mirrored what he'd come across out west—and stank of Victor Mole.

Scott's heart pumped faster. If Victor had his druggies digging at Maddie's site, it meant he probably was behind the burglary as well. But it made no sense for him to destroy the storeroom. That piece didn't fit, which is why he'd flown under Scott's radar. The police were looking in the wrong direction. Damn the bastard.

Scott stopped in front of Tom, who snapped cuffs on none other than Eric. Scott shined the light on his face. "You're worse than a bad penny."

"Fuck off. You can't arrest me. I didn't do anything."

Tom flashed a beam on a hole in the ground. "They're all over the place. When I showed up, people ran into the woods. Don't know how many, more than three anyway. No surprise Eric here is involved. He spends more time at the police station than we do."

"Did you see anyone digging?" Scott asked.

"No. When I pulled up, everyone scattered like cockroaches when the light hits them."

A car engine roared to life in the distance. Scott glanced at the woods. "See if you can find any of them. I'll take care of this asshole."

Tom nodded and dodged his way through the dark to the forest. Scott turned back to Eric. Much as he'd love to bust the sniveling shithead, he had bigger fish to catch. Eric might be his ticket into Victor's operations. The meth king would go down for this.

Scott's plan to keep Maddie and his work separate imploded. His gut wrenched. They wouldn't be making love tonight, or anytime soon. He'd have to keep away from Maddie if Victor had a hand in this burglary. Way too close to home.

Scott had lost focus tonight. Dared to dream. His world didn't have happy endings. A coldness settled around his heart.

When Tom disappeared into the woods, Scott swept his light across the area. Time to play the corrupt cop role. Maddie would hate him for it, but hopefully, she'd understand once he put Mole away and had a chance to explain.

"Did you find anything?" he asked Eric.

"Don't know what you're talking about."

He grabbed the front of Eric's shirt and yanked him closer. "Don't bullshit me. I'm not a fucking idiot. Start talking before he comes back."

Eric shook his head. "You got nothing on me."

"Trespassing and digging on federal property. That's illegal." Scott leaned in and lowered his voice. He hated the next words he had to utter to keep up the act. "I honestly don't give a shit, but if you want me to look the other way and keep your little operation going, you'll have to pay up."

Eric cocked his head. "What do you mean?"

"I can shut you down, or you can grease the skids." Scott shrugged. "Going free right now will cost you five hundred bucks."

"Five hundred? I don't have—"

"Too bad. Looks like you're going to spend your day finding it. Meet me behind the bank tomorrow night at seven with the cash. If you don't show, I'll find and arrest you." He gave him a shake. "And tell your boss if he wants the police to stay out of his business, he's gonna pay for it."

Eric's mouth twisted. "I'll get the money, but you're crazy if you think my boss is gonna be bullied by you."

"If he's smart, he'll see it as the cost of doing business in my town." Scott let go. "If not, I'll personally follow you and your meth heads around. Next time you'll all be arrested."

"You're fucked up, man."

"Yeah, and you're just fucked." Scott unlocked the cuffs and shoved Eric. "Now get the hell out of here."

Eric took a few quick steps toward the forest and stumbled to the ground. He got up and picked his way to the tree line.

Asshole.

Scott sighed. He needed to call Maddie. Just hearing her voice would tear a hole in his chest. He hated to hurt her. She expected him to come back and make love to her, not call her on police business. Shit. No choice. Until he put Mole away, he couldn't be with her.

CHAPTER 22

MADDIE RAN a finger over her lips. Her body still buzzed from Scott's touch, but the most amazing part of the night had been when he'd opened up to her. At last, he'd let her in. Shared a dark place in his heart. Hers had warmed when he'd smiled up at her later, his eyes sparking with heat and promise. She'd put that grin on his face. The guilt and pain he carried shouldn't rule his life. He deserved happiness, and she'd work to make him believe it.

But then what? She didn't do long-term, serious relationships. Scott's scars were deep. Casual, fun dating wouldn't be an option. And she couldn't make a commitment when her work took her all around the world. She ran the risk of letting someone else control her life decisions if she let him in, and her independence had always been a top priority.

Logic aside, she couldn't deny the feelings he stirred in her. She'd never allowed herself to get close to anyone in the past, but all bets were off with Scott. He matched her passion and challenged her. No one had ever done that, and it made her want him all the more. She ached for him to walk back through the door and make love to her.

Yeah. She was screwed. As crazy as the ride might be, she'd take it with him.

Her phone rang with Kyle's ringtone. Why was he calling so late?

"Hey, Kyle."

"Sorry to bother you, but I wanted to let you know there's something going on at the excavation site. I was passing by and saw lights out in the field, so I called the police."

"What?" Maddie's heart jumped, and she gripped the phone tighter.

"After what happened to you, I didn't want to take any chances. I parked on the road past the site and saw the cops drive by."

"Okay. I'm going out there. Go home. I'll call you if I find out anything."

"I was just on my way over there to see what was—"

"No. Go home. I promise I'll let you know what's happening." She tugged on her boots as she cradled the phone to her ear.

"All right. I don't know what anyone could be doing."

"Me neither. I'll be in touch."

She hung up and grabbed her coat. Prickly heat burned the back of her neck. Scott hadn't told her the work call he took was about her excavation site. He'd left with a smile on his face. Did her job mean so little to him that getting laid was more important than telling her? Probably afraid he'd kill the mood.

Keys in hand, she stormed out the door. She scrambled down the steps and climbed into her car. When she reached the site, she found Tom's police SUV and Scott's Impala parked in the lot. All hope sank that maybe he'd been called to another scene.

She switched on her flashlight and got out of the car. Someone was out in the field shining theirs. Must be Tom or Scott. As she trudged toward the person, she maneuvered around huge potholes.

Her stomach twisted into a bigger knot with each step. Clearly, the place had been looted. The size of the holes meant whoever dug them had used shovels. Probably damaged whatever they might have found. Idiots. Nothing like this had ever happened on the federal properties in town. The Seneca Nation tribal members and her team would be devastated for a second time.

Someone in the field shined a flashlight on her. She squinted and stopped in her path.

A groan echoed in the night.

Scott.

And yeah, one sound and she knew it was him. Not like the groan from earlier, laced with lust, primal to the core. This was the *oh-shit* kind of groan. The *I'm-not-getting-laid-tonight-after-all* kind.

Damn right.

"Can you stop blinding me?" She held a hand up to shield her eyes.

A figure emerged from the woods shining a light. She flashed hers on the person carrying it.

Tom.

She marched over to Scott. "What's going on here, and why didn't you tell me about this?" Her breath came out in steamy clouds from the cold air, or it could be she was fuming inside.

He held up a hand. "Calm down. I didn't—"

"Where's Eric?" Tom stopped next to Scott.

"I let him go."

"What?"

Maddie froze. "Eric? What's he have to do with anything?"

"Why didn't you take him to the station?" Tom frowned.

Scott shined his flashlight on a pair of gloves on the ground next to a shovel. "We don't have anything to keep him on. He wore those, so no fingerprints."

Tom said, "We don't know for sure, and we should have at least taken him in for questioning. Try to find out who else he had out here. I don't—"

"I made the call. Let it go." Scott squared his shoulders.

Maddie stamped a foot on the ground. "Are you telling me you found that scumbag out here digging and let him walk away?"

"This is a police matter. Someone would have called you once we had things under control."

Someone. An hour ago, he'd had his hand down her pants, and now he couldn't be bothered to make a simple call. She glared at him. "This is my site. I deserve to know what's going on, and I sure as hell don't think you have this under control. Even Tom doesn't think so."

Tom's cheeks puffed as he let out a long breath and looked to the sky.

Scott turned to him. "I assume you didn't find anyone out there in the woods."

"No." Tom shook his head. "And in the short time I had Eric in custody, he didn't talk."

The two men stared at each other. Maddie's ears burned. That bastard, Eric, had desecrated the place, and Scott hadn't even bothered to take him in. Never mind the incident with Nikki. He might as well have slapped her in the face.

She tapped him on the shoulder. "You know, I don't expect special treatment after what we…" She glanced at Tom, who shifted and scraped a boot on the ground. "Forget it. What's the point? It's pretty clear where I stand with you."

Scott's chest rose and then fell. In a monotone, he said, "Go home, Maddie. There's nothing more you can do here."

Tendrils of betrayal coiled around her lungs, forcing the breath out of them. Those words were no accident. He knew how much she hated it when he told her what to do and treated her like a child. He *meant* to piss her off. She was done with his sick game of cat-and-mouse. Her body shook as, for once, she was at a loss for words.

Tom slung an arm around her and squeezed her shoulder. "I'm sorry, Maddie. We can come back tomorrow in the light of day and check it out if you want."

Beside Tom, Scott stood rigid. Impassive. His gaze averted.

She'd wasted enough of her time with him. Waiting for him, pining over him, finally letting him in, only to be tossed aside. She sure as hell didn't need Mr. Bipolar.

Tom released her, and she faced him. "Thank you for always being so *nice*."

She turned on her heel and took a step toward the parking lot. "Oh, and Detective?" She swung around. "You won't need to make that stop on your way home. I've been screwed enough for one night."

CHAPTER 23

VICTOR SLAMMED his cell phone on the desk. That prick, Eric, hadn't checked in or answered his phone. It was after midnight. By now, he should have reported back with the results from the loot at Cooper's excavation site. Black market buyers were waiting in the wings for new artifacts. He paced his office, a slow burn starting in his chest, and snatched the phone to dial Eric again.

"Hey, boss."

"What took you so long to answer? I've been calling you for the last half-hour."

"I…uh…ran into a little problem." Eric's voice wavered.

Fuck. Of course. "What?"

"The cops showed up. They grabbed me, but they didn't get anyone else."

Stupid shit. He would be the only one caught. "Where are you?"

"At the camp with the team."

"Why weren't you arrested?" Something didn't add up.

"That dirty cop let me go. He—"

"What about the artifacts? Did you get any?"

Eric cleared his throat. "Yeah. The tweakers had already gotten away with some before the cops came."

"Send me pictures of what you have, and then haul your sorry ass over here." Victor hung up. He'd get the rest of the story in person from the little dick. Make him sweat blood.

A few minutes later, Victor's phone beeped. He opened a picture message. Boxes of broken pottery. He zoomed in and swiped the screen. All pieces like someone had taken a sledgehammer to them. Worthless. Not a single item intact. His blood pressure ratcheted.

"Stupid useless fuck!" He slammed a fist on the desk. The twitchy jerk had messed up everything, netted nothing of value, and now had the police on his tail.

* * *

An hour later, a knock rattled through the empty mansion.

Victor answered the door and dragged Eric by the scruff of his filthy jacket into the office. He grabbed his throat and squeezed.

Eric's eyes bulged. He gasped for air and tried to talk, but nothing came out.

Victor pressed harder. The pulse in Eric's neck throbbed under the pressure. His face turned red, and he clawed to loosen the grip.

"You've fucked up again." Victor brought his face closer and squeezed harder. The urge to kill coursed through his veins. A quick snap of the neck or another few moments of strangling, his preferred method, and it would all be over. Nothing like watching a person's face contort as panic and helplessness registered. No one deserved it more than Eric, but the asshat had information Victor still needed. He released his death grip.

Eric sucked in a deep breath, coughing and struggling for air. He doubled over and dropped to his knees, one hand on his thigh, the other on his throat.

"Get your shit together. You have some explaining to do." Victor jerked his desk chair out and sat. He fixed his gaze on Eric, still on the floor wheezing.

Eric managed to hoist himself onto a chair and sniffed. Sweat dripped down the side of his grimy face. He wiped it and jerked his head up. "Wh-what do you want to know?"

"For starters, what happened with the artifacts your guys dug up tonight? They're in pieces."

"The diggers used shovels." Eric coughed and rasped, "Might have damaged some of the goods."

Victor's lungs threatened to explode. "Whose fault is that? You were in charge of giving them the right equipment. They got shit. I can't sell any of it. I'm done with you."

"No." Eric jumped to his feet and then quickly sat. "I mean, this is fixable. Those artifacts I stole from the storeroom last week, they were worth something, right?"

"They were worth something because the archaeologists had dug them up, not your bulldozer-in-the-sandbox tweakers. You aren't capable of running this end of the operation."

Eric's gaze darted to the door, his body shaking. He licked his lips and touched the red marks on his throat. "But I found someone good to bring in. Already met with him. He's a real badass and has connections. We could double the crystal sales. You need me to, you know, get him onboard. We can work together."

Just another ploy to try to save his miserable ass. "You're full of shit. If someone like that existed, I would have found him. Besides, if he's a friend of yours, I'm sure he's a fuck-up, too."

"We aren't friends. I got a lead on him. He just got out of prison and knows the business. His name's Zach Gordon. Turns out I was dating his sister, only neither of us knew it at the time. I got nothing to do with her anymore." Eric plucked his phone from the pocket of his jacket. "I'll call him in so you can see for yourself he's the real deal."

"Not so fast. What do you mean, you dated his sister and neither of you knew it?" Victor narrowed his eyes.

Eric shrugged. "She never told me she had a brother. Guess she was embarrassed because he was in jail. I don't know. I figured it out from the last name. Doesn't matter. It's all over. He only cares about the money."

Victor stroked his chin. Convicts were a good source to tap for worthwhile contacts, but anyone Eric brought to the table needed checking. And the whole sister thing added another layer. Yet…worth looking into.

"I can get him here tomorrow for you to meet. I'm telling you, he's good."

Victor picked up his cigar and lit it. "I'll check him out first and let you know. Now, give me an update on the survey. What did Cooper do today?"

"She dug most of the day. That's all I could see from the woods."

Victor nodded. Digging at last. One step closer to the final report. "All right, tell me more about this crooked cop."

Eric gripped the armrests of his chair and rocked. "The new detective's on the take. I need five hundred dollars for him to look the other way and let us do our thing. We'll be right back in business."

"What are you talking about?"

"I paid him off once before already. He wants more for tonight."

Victor shook his head and puffed out smoke. "I told you to stay out of trouble. What the fuck do you mean by 'before'?"

Eric blanched. "That Maddie bitch sucker-punched me in a bar the other night. The detective let me go."

Victor snorted. The girl had some guts. He didn't even want to know why she'd slugged Eric. "What part of dumb-fuck-stupid logic am I missing here? If she punched you, why were *you* going to be arrested?"

"The detective, uhh…he's a hard ass. You know, just wants to bust everyone."

Victor squinted. He had work to do, and Eric might not live if he didn't get the fuck out. Which wouldn't be a bad thing, but this Gordon guy might be worth looking at. "Wait for my call tomorrow. And don't do anything. Maybe you can do absolutely nothing without fucking that up."

"But what about the cop? He wants the five hundred by seven tomorrow night."

Victor reached into his pocket and tugged out his money clip. He unfolded five hundred-dollar bills and tossed them on the desk. "Pay off the cop. This comes out of your payroll plus an extra hundred for interest. Got it?"

"Yeah." Eric snatched the money, rubbed a hand over his throat, and slunk out of the room.

* * *

Victor's doorbell rang exactly at noon. For once, fuck-up Eric was on time. Victor had spent the morning getting the lowdown on Zach Gordon. Showed promise, but he'd judge for himself. On paper, anyone could look good.

He eyed Zach as he entered the room with Eric. Squared shoulders, with a confident stride, Zach met his gaze head on. This was no sniveling meth head. Victor waved to the chairs across the desk. "Sit."

He tapped his lit cigar on the ashtray. "I checked you out. Not much on you."

"I fly under the radar, and so do the people I work with."

Victor nodded. "Only a dumb fuck gets caught with drugs and weapons."

Zach kept his face neutral in spite of the insult. Good. A man who could control his emotions.

"I trusted someone I shouldn't have. I've learned since then. That won't happen again."

Victor took a puff of his cigar and stared at Zach, who held his gaze. "How's your sister? I understand she came to visit you quite a bit in jail."

Zach twisted his mouth. "Yeah, when she needed money or wanted to bitch about her boyfriend, who turned out to be him." He jerked a thumb in Eric's direction. "She blames me because she had to go into the system. Shit, she only spent three years in foster care. I did four in a cage with a rat. My sister liked to visit so she could remind me how I fucked up her life and then hit me up for cash. I got no use for her."

"Blood's not thicker than water?"

"Hey, I got no respect for whiners. I made my way. She can make hers. People in this business are ruthless. They use family as leverage. Me?" Zach brushed his hands against each other in the universal dismissive gesture. "I'm free and clear."

Eric mimicked Zach's hand brushing. "Me, too. I got rid of the bitch. Taught her a lesson."

Victor shot a glance at Zach, who didn't so much as flinch. Either he really didn't give a shit about his sister, or he had one hell of a poker face. Something like that could come in handy. Victor turned his gaze to Eric. "Shut the fuck up. Unless I ask you a question, keep your mouth closed." He swiveled around to Zach and pointed to Eric. "You don't have a problem with him?"

Zach shrugged. "Sounds like they're done, but her love life is none of my business. Neither is his."

Victor eased back in his chair and took another puff of the cigar as he studied Zach. So far, he'd cut it. Enough about the sister. Time to talk shop. "Eric said you can double our sales."

"I have connections. Looking to use them here and make some money now I'm out."

Eric bobbed his head. "See? Like I told you. He's got connections."

"What part of 'shut the fuck up' did you not understand?" Victor gave Eric a caustic glare, causing him to shrink back in his seat. Reaching into the top drawer of the desk, Victor drew out a small plastic bag filled with crystal meth. He slid it across the table. "This is quality stuff. I only deal with the best. Test it."

Zach glanced at the bag and shook his head. "I'm a businessman. I don't use. Need to keep my head clear and not smoke up the profits."

Finally, someone who go it. "I think we might be able to work together. I'll be in touch."

Zach stood. "I'll wait to hear from you."

Eric rose as Zach strode out of the room.

"Sit down. I'm not done with you." Victor snuffed out his cigar, and Eric dropped back into the chair.

He fingered his bruised neck. "What's wrong? You like him, right?"

"We'll see. I'm not letting him in on too much yet. So keep your mouth shut about the tweakers and the digs." Victor would keep Zach in the dark about the black-market business until he'd proven himself. The sooner, the better. Eric had to go.

"I didn't tell him nothing about that."

"If you fuck up and get caught again, you're dead. Understand?"

Eric swallowed.

Victor leaned across the desk. "You get the right tools for the job and make sure the finds aren't destroyed next time. Now get lost."

Eric all but ran out of the room. Victor rubbed his chin. Zach was cool and had all the right answers. The complete opposite of fuck-up Eric. Maybe with the crooked cop on board, they could move things along.

But first, Zach would have to pass a test.

CHAPTER 24

MADDIE SNAGGED her coffee cup and stuffed a tip into the jar on the counter. The bruise on Nikki's face from two days ago had a green tint to it now. Huh. They both had battle scars. At least Nikki was back to work.

Bringing the steaming cup to her nose, Maddie inhaled deeply. She didn't like to drink coffee at night, but she had to finish grading final papers and after a long day of digging, she needed the fix.

Damn that Scott. Since he'd showed up in town, her caffeine intake had doubled. He never failed to agitate her, leaving her either hot and bothered or royally pissed. Between that and the coffee, she tossed and turned all night.

Maddie glanced around the empty shop before asking Nikki, "How are you?"

"Okay, I guess. I'm kinda worried about my brother, though."

"What's up with Zach?"

Nikki shrugged. "He's out of jail and—"

"What? When did this happen?"

"A couple of days ago. He got out early, but he wouldn't tell me why." She frowned. "He met me outside of town to give me money for rent until I can get my finances together. I'm not supposed to tell anyone I saw him, but I trust you."

"Well, it's nice he's helping you out, but why all the secrecy?" Maddie set her cup back on the counter.

"He said he's working a dangerous job, and I shouldn't come anywhere near him. What if he's doing something illegal?"

Maddie cocked her head. "That doesn't sound like him. He never even committed the crime he went to jail for. I think you need to trust him."

"I don't really have a choice. I hope he doesn't go after Eric." Nikki touched her bruise. "Zach saw my face, and I've never seen him so angry. Thought he was going to pull a Maddie. You know, find Eric and punch him out."

Maddie pursed her lips. It hadn't been her finest moment. "I didn't plan to, but he deserved it."

"Eric might not see it coming. I didn't want to share anything about my family with him, so I never mentioned Zach. Guess the fact I didn't want Eric to even know about my brother should have been a clue we weren't going to last."

"At least you know it now and aren't with the asshole anymore."

"I just hope Zach lets it go. He can't afford to get into trouble, and I don't want to be the reason he ends up back in jail."

Nikki would be crushed. Maddie tapped her cheek with a finger. "If he got out early, maybe he ratted on someone and worked a deal. He could be trying to protect you because those guys have friends on the outside."

"Anything's possible. I wish I knew."

The front door opened, and a couple entered the shop. Maddie picked up her coffee. "I'd better get going. I'm glad he's out, anyway. Keep me posted, and let me know if you need any help with your new place."

"Thanks." Nikki waved a hand. "I'm all set for now."

Maddie slipped past the customers, stopped in the doorway, and frowned. Eric, that degenerate loser, cruised past in his truck, turned into the bank entrance across the street, and drove around the back.

Probably depositing money from the sale of the artifacts he'd dug up. Her pulse spiked. Scott should have at least interrogated him. Maybe he could have found out where the thieves had stashed the goods. By now, whatever Eric had dug up would be sold and gone like everything stolen from her storeroom.

Speak of the devil, Scott drove by and also turned into the bank lot. He continued around to the back of the building. Maddie cocked her head. Eric's truck hadn't come out the other side yet. The ATM machine was in the front. It was seven o'clock, and the bank closed at six.

She opened the café door and strolled down the sidewalk past her car. Nerves jittered in her gut. Something wasn't right. Stopping behind a large oak, she peered at the far corner of the parking lot across the street. Her breath caught at the sight of Eric's pickup parked next to Scott's Impala.

Eric stepped out of his truck, a shoe box in hand, and glanced around. He scurried over to Scott's car. The driver's side window lowered, and Eric leaned down. He opened the box lid a few inches, as if to show Scott what was inside.

Scott took the box, and Eric stood back, a satisfied smile on his face that quickly fell. His shoulders slumped, and he shook his head. After a moment, he shoved a hand into his pocket and drew out a wad of cash. Lips pressed together tight, he thrust the money through the open car window.

The little bit of coffee in Maddie's stomach threatened to come up. Scott on the take. No way. He had let Eric go last night, but the man she knew would never accept a bribe. Yeah, not any more than he'd turn her to putty in his hands, make promises, and then leave her cold.

Again.

She could figure out Stonehenge easier than him. Much as she'd like to march over and smash both their heads together, she held back. Maybe all the time Scott had spent working with criminals had rubbed off and he'd turned dirty. It went against every fiber of her being to believe it, but hard to deny the proof right in front of her. She broke out in a cold sweat.

Eric got into his truck and drove away. Maddie strode down the sidewalk to her car and yanked the door open. She set the coffee in the cup holder and took a deep breath. Sure, Scott had changed since his stint in

Mexico, but she'd chalked it up to grief and guilt over the loss of his brother. This was a whole new side of him. She clearly didn't know Scott anymore and owed him nothing. He'd compromised the illegal digging at her site by letting Eric go, and he sure as hell had played her yet again. To think she'd almost slept with him last night.

Maybe she should turn him into Chief Lee. The tribal leaders would want answers.

First things first. She still had Victor to deal with, and the field survey needed to produce some finds. What could have been in the box? She shook her head and started the engine. Too many questions.

When she got to her apartment and opened the door, Lucky went wild, chasing his tail as he turned in circles. "I know how you feel, buddy. I've been chasing mine all day, too."

At least this guy in her life was consistent and genuine. She took him around the back of the building to do his business, her mind on Scott. His betrayal cut to her core. As much as she'd like to go to the chief, she needed to hear the words from Scott. Let him lie to her face. If he could do that, she'd turn him in.

She rounded the building, unclipped Lucky's leash, and stopped cold.

Scott stood in front of her door, dressed in jeans and a black T-shirt, holding what appeared to be the same box Eric had given him.

Lucky bounded up the steps and whined, leaning against Scott's legs.

No denying the dog loved him.

Same as her, despite everything, damn it all.

Scott knelt and gave the mutt a one-armed hug as Lucky frantically licked his face.

Maddie climbed the stairs, her heart beating double-time as always when around Scott. He straightened when she reached the top of the steps. "Can I come in for a minute?"

She eyed the closed box and unlocked the door. Too angry to speak, she entered the apartment and waved a hand for him to follow. After a deep breath, she turned to face him, her insides quivering. Even as pissed as she was at his betrayal, she wanted him, and hated herself for it.

He handed her the box. "I'm really sorry about the looting. I'm not sure if any of these are salvageable, but I was able to recover them."

She set the box on the table and opened the lid. Inside were pieces of clay pots, broken arrowheads, and bone shards. Her spirits sank. For dating, they might have significance, but nothing was fit for display at the proposed museum. Hard to say what condition they might have been in prior to being dug up, but based on her excavation results, she'd bet some of them had been intact.

"Where did you get these?" She swung around and thrust her hands on her hips.

He met her gaze with a cool, steady one. "This is an ongoing investigation, so I can't divulge that, but I wanted you to have them."

"Nope. Not acceptable. Give me an answer." The man was good. Not a trace of guilt on his face. No wonder he'd stayed alive undercover.

"I'm sorry. I can't." He took a step toward the door. "I only came to drop them off."

"Like hell." She grabbed his arm. "Don't you dare leave. Not until you tell me the truth."

"Let it go, Maddie." His eyes darkened.

"Like you did Eric?"

Scott shook his head. "We're not having this conversation."

"Why, Scott? Because you're in bed with him?" She moved closer, so she was right in his face. "I guess if I hadn't shown up at the site, you could have screwed me over twice. First by giving Eric a get-out-of-jail pass, and then by coming here to literally do it. Do you even have a moral code anymore?"

"Stop it. You don't know what you're talking about."

"Then tell me the goddamned truth." Tears burned her eyes.

A vein on Scott's forehead pulsated. He stared down at her, his mouth shut tight like a closed gate to stop any words he might utter.

She waited him out. Refused to look away. Truth or lie, she wouldn't give in until he talked. "I want an answer. Why did you let Eric go?"

"I can't tell you. You need to trust me on this."

"Trust you? You've got to be shitting me." She jerked her hand away from his arm. "I'm done. You don't have the balls to tell me the truth, so

I'm turning you in to the chief. Citizen's arrest or whatever the hell you call it."

Scott jerked his head back. "What are you talking about?"

"You, Eric, I saw the whole thing. This box, the money he gave you at the bank." She shoved his chest. "You make me sick. To think I believed in you while you were running around behind my back taking bribes from looters."

Fuck. Scott exhaled a long breath. "It's not what you think."

"Well, then, you'd better explain because nothing could be worse than what I think, and don't you dare lie. I've had it."

"Sit?" He gestured to the couch.

Maddie sat, back rigid. "Talk."

He took a seat beside her. "I shouldn't be telling you this, but you leave me no choice. I'm not a dirty cop. I'm not even a cop. I'm still a DEA agent working undercover."

"What? I don't understand."

"It's complicated. I'm on a DEA case, and I have to play this role. Obviously, no one can know." He scraped a hand across his chin. "We're on the same team. Nothing made me sicker than letting that asshole go last night, and I know I hurt you, but I was trying to protect you. Keep you out of all of this."

He wasn't on the take. A huge weight lifted. So that's why he'd gone cold on her. "Does anyone know about this besides me?"

"Only Lee." He placed a hand over hers. "It's why I was so insistent on keeping my past quiet."

"I wish you would have told me. We could have saved a lot of—"

"I don't make the rules. People die if things get fucked up. It's not a game."

She swallowed. "Of course not. But with Eric, why are you pretending—"

"Anything more I tell you can put you at risk. Please, trust me?"

All along, he'd been looking out for her. That explained the brush-offs. He couldn't allow himself to get close. Everyone knew Eric was a meth head, so Scott was probably trying to follow the drug trail and would have lost his lead if he'd busted Eric. It made sense.

She met Scott's gaze. His eyes were wide open and honest.

He squeezed her hand. "I'm sorry about your artifacts. I promise, Eric will be arrested and charged for the crime, but not yet. I still need him. The looters destroyed or threw away anything else they dug up. The asshole gave me this box and said it was all he had left. He tried to convince me it was worth something."

"It is, but not much." She took a deep breath. Finally, the truth. "Thank you for trusting me. I won't tell anyone."

"I shouldn't be talking to you about this, but if you'd gone to the chief, he'd have to report it to the DEA. With the operation compromised, I'd be reassigned. Everything my team has worked for would be lost."

"Really? Just because I know you're still DEA?" Maddie shook her head.

"Yes. This case is high-profile and extremely sensitive. What you know paints a target on your back. I'm serious, Maddie. Don't underestimate it." He squeezed her hand again.

He'd risked his career confiding in her. "I...don't know what to say."

"There's nothing to say. You had every reason to doubt me." His sad half-smile made her chest ache.

"So the other night, you were really going to come back to me?"

He stiffened. "Yes, but it was a bad idea. This is too dangerous now. You're too close to the fire with Eric involved."

"I'm not afraid of him, and it wasn't a bad idea." The Scott she'd fallen in love with two years ago sat beside her, and she wouldn't let him go. Noble, selfless, fighting to stop the evils of the world. He'd sacrificed so much. She slid closer and placed a hand on his chest. His heart thumped hard beneath her fingertips. "Don't leave me hanging again."

He brushed back a strand of her hair and traced a finger along her cheek.

Her body shivered at his touch. "One night. You're here. Nothing's going to happen to me." She took his hand in hers. "God, I've missed you so much. Go back to your job tomorrow, but if you want me anywhere near as much as I want you..."

There. She'd said it. The next move was his. And time had never moved slower as she waited for his response.

The heat in his eyes ignited a slow burn inside her. She knew that look. She loved that look. She craved that look. The look that made her feel like she was a hot fudge sundae in the hands of a starving man.

His finger, still on her cheek, sent a tingle of awareness through her body. His gaze held her captive as ever so slowly, he lowered his head and mere inches from her mouth, whispered, "Just for tonight."

"Yes." The breath she'd been holding whooshed out. God, yes.

He drew her onto his lap, and his hot mouth took hers. She crushed herself to him, lacing her fingers through his hair. At last, together. Both wanting the same thing.

He groaned and deepened the kiss, tasting of peppermint and promise.

His tongue explored her mouth while he tugged at the hem of her shirt. He broke the kiss to yank the T-shirt over her head, and then trailed hot kisses from the base of her neck to the tip of her bra. Thank God she'd worn the lacy, black one today. Every fiber of her being yearned for him, and only him. He'd trusted her, opened up at last, and she wouldn't hold anything back.

His warm breath brought goosebumps to her flesh as he muttered, "Your skin's as smooth as I remembered."

When he sucked a nipple through the thin fabric of her bra, she arched her back and whimpered. Leaving the bra on, he slid the lace down to expose a breast and tugged at the peak gently with his teeth. She writhed in aching need as her sex grew damp. It might have been years since they'd done this, but he knew exactly where to touch, how to stroke her, and what turned her on. And selfish as it sounded, she reveled in the fact that neither of them had been with anyone else since he'd left. They belonged to each other.

Scott undid the button and zipper on her jeans and slid a hand inside. He found her sweet spot with this finger, and she sucked in a breath.

Oh yes. Right there.

"Too many clothes." He lifted her off the couch and stripped her jeans off. "We need to take this to the bedroom."

He picked her up, carried her to the bed, and set her down on the side. "Take your bra and panties off. I want to watch."

This kind of bossiness she didn't mind. His eyes followed her every movement as she slowly slipped them off. He took a deep breath, pulled a condom out from his wallet, and tossed it on the nightstand.

She glanced up. "Wait. Aren't we going to—"

"Not yet. You deserve more." He eased her shoulders back. His gaze traveled over her naked body. "You're so beautiful. Even more than I remembered, and believe me, I remember a lot."

"You do?"

"Yes." He slid onto the bed next to her. "Memories of you got me through the hard times." He brushed back a stray curl from her cheek. "No matter what happened, no one could take those away."

A lump formed in her throat. He hadn't forgotten her or what they'd shared.

"But I don't want to talk about Mexico." He threaded his fingers through her hair. "In fact, I don't want to talk at all."

He covered her mouth with his. A small moan escaped from somewhere deep inside, and he brought the kiss to the next level when she opened her mouth for him. His warm, hard chest pressed against the side of her breast. She explored the contours with her hand, kneading the strong muscles. So hard, so fit. From his broad shoulders to his lean waist and lower, she had her own living, breathing statue of David.

He ran a finger down her stomach, stopping just short of where she ached for him to touch. Her body quivered in response. This was Scott. Adoring her. Worshiping her. Putting his own needs aside, which were obvious from the bulge in his jeans.

She reached down between them and unsnapped his pants, breaking the kiss. Breathless, she tugged at the waistband. "Take these off. I want to feel all of you."

"Won't have to ask twice." He shifted back and yanked the pants off.

He sprang free, and she bit her lip. She'd forgotten that every aspect of Scott was larger than life. Well, not forgotten, but chosen not to remember. When she reached a hand out to stroke him, he captured it and brought her fingers to his lips. "Not yet."

Eyes intent on hers, one by one, he took each finger in his mouth and sucked it. She swallowed hard. The tease of his hot tongue against her fingertip made her long for him to lick other places. As if he'd read her mind, he released her hand and kissed her shoulder, working his way up her neck to her ear. With a featherlight touch, he smoothed a hand down the side of her body. Her nipples puckered, begging for attention.

"You, Maddie. It's always been you." His warm breath tickled her ear, causing another round of goosebumps. And her name from his lips, spoken so reverently, floated through her body, a soothing balm. Her entire being hummed for him. They'd declared this to be a *one-night thing*, but her heart had other ideas, and come tomorrow, she might regret it, but tonight she would take in all that was Scott.

He brought his hand up to cup her breast and shifted positions to suckle the other one in his mouth. Flicking his tongue over the taut peak, he teased and tugged first one, and then the other until she trembled under the assault.

Her legs shook, and her body tensed. He'd brought her to the brink with his words, his touch, and those eyes that bored into her soul. Remembered every nuance of her.

"Now, Scott, now." She gripped his shoulders.

"Yes." He grabbed the condom from the nightstand, sheathed himself, and climbed back onto the bed. Braced on his elbows, he hovered above her, the tip of his hard length pressed against her entrance.

She spread her legs wide and reached for him, cupping his ass. Eyes wide open, he held her gaze when he entered her. Inch by inch he filled her. Scott inside her, where he belonged, where they fit each other perfectly. Her body welcomed him, wet and ready as he pushed in and out, deeper and faster.

She dug her fingernails into his back and squeezed her eyes shut. He pumped harder, thrust after thrust as their hips moved in rhythm, bringing her closer and closer to the edge. She let the last wave take her over and cried out as he stiffened with his own release.

A floodgate of emotions poured through her body. How she'd missed him. Dreamed and waited for him, and now she was in his arms again. He rolled to the side and slid an arm under her neck. She cuddled against him, her cheek pressed to his hard, slick chest.

"You make me crazy, Maddie."

She raised her head to gaze up at him. No words came to mind because none existed to describe the feelings he evoked. And the tender look in his eyes melted her heart. She nuzzled his neck and sighed, content for the first time in two years.

He brushed her hair back and kissed the top of her head. His soft caress meant more than the hot sex, if that was possible. If she never had to move again, she'd be happy. He stroked her back, and she wallowed in the soft sensation. Whatever happened tomorrow, tonight she had her dream.

CHAPTER 25

VICTOR BUZZED Gina into his office, darkening his computer screen before she entered. "What's the status on the field survey?"

"Nothing new to report. Cooper's been digging for several days, and so far, nothing has turned up. When I spoke to her yesterday, she said she needed more time."

The bitch was pushing her luck. Maybe she thought she could milk him for more money by taking longer to finish. "She's had enough time. Get her on the phone."

Gina glanced at her watch. "It's seven-thirty, and she starts early in the morning. If she's at the lot, she won't pick up. She told me yesterday if you want her to finish this job, she couldn't keep taking calls asking about the status. I usually have to leave a message."

"What? We're supposed to be her fucking priority." He slammed his fist on the desk.

"I'll try her again." Gina's high heels clicked on the hardwood floor as she hastened out of the room.

Victor brought up the stats for his black-market sales. With no artifacts to sell, his buyers would spend their money elsewhere while he sat on a veritable gold mine waiting for the stamp of approval from that bitch archaeologist.

He ran his tongue across his teeth, picked up his metal handgrips, and squeezed off a round of twenty. Gina beeped him on the intercom.

"No answer from Cooper. Zach is here to see you."

The fucking bitch had blown him off again. He'd had enough of her, but first things first. Time to see if Zach passed the test Victor had set up. Last night he had given the drug buyer a higher price than he'd told Zach to collect. If Zach kept the difference, he couldn't be trusted. "Send him in."

Victor set the handgrip next to the computer and leaned back in his chair. Zach entered the room wearing jeans and a navy-blue hoodie. He shut the door behind him and strode to the desk. "I made the drop last night."

"Good."

Zach reached into the front pocket of his sweatshirt, drew out a fat envelope, and slid it across the desk to Victor. "Here's the cash. Your buyer tested the meth. Percentages were good."

Victor opened the envelope and thumbed through the bills inside. Exactly the amount he'd told Zach to collect, not the higher price he'd agreed to with his distributor.

Zach had failed.

"It's all here." Victor stood and crossed the room to open the cabinet with a safe behind it. He punched the code in and placed the envelope inside. Too bad. He could have used an ex-con in the business. Someone seasoned and tough, unlike crystal-head Eric, but he had to be able to trust Zach.

"Not sure what you want to do with the extra," Zach said.

Victor stilled. Maybe Zach hadn't failed. Victor shut the safe.

Zach held out a wad of money. "Can't account for this."

"What's that?"

"No idea." Zach shrugged. "He overpaid."

Victor took the cash and counted it. He raised an eyebrow and met Zach's steady gaze.

Zach waved a hand at the bills. "Hey, I'm a businessman in for the long haul. Not looking to make a quick buck or an enemy by screwing anyone. This is your customer, your money, your call."

No shit, this kid got it. Cool head and didn't take the first chance at some easy cash. He'd earned his way in. Victor nodded. "Nice doing business with you. I'll be in touch about the next deal."

Zach nodded and exited the room.

Victor paced to the window. He needed to find out what was going on with Cooper on the property. If he hadn't been so preoccupied with the drug cartel and his meth manufacturers, he'd have gone back to the lot and checked it out himself. Relying on Eric to keep tabs on Cooper was like asking a baby to guard the house.

Once again, Gina's voice sounded over the intercom announcing Eric.

Eric, awake and functioning before eight, remained to be seen. Victor sat and picked up the handgrip. He squeezed off another twenty as Eric shuffled into the office and dropped into a chair. Eric's gaze darted to the metal grip. He swallowed hard.

"Give me a status report. When's the last time you were at the lot?" Victor switched the grip to the other hand.

Eric cleared his throat. "Yesterday. She's still digging."

Fucking rocket scientist, this one. "No shit. Has she found any artifacts?"

"I don't think so. Not while I was there."

If he hadn't been too high to notice. Victor tapped the grip on the desk. "Do you have anything useful to report?"

Eric leaned forward and bobbed his head. "Yeah, that dirty cop, he might have something for me."

"What do you mean?" So far, all Eric had done was pad the guy's paycheck. Detective Scott Fisher. Victor had checked him out. Some beat cop from the city. Rumors about some missing evidence and money swirled around his name, but nothing had ever been proven. He'd transferred out to Tuckerton on the heels of the scandal. Made sense he'd be on the take, coming from Hell's Kitchen. Nobody left that place without a few scars.

"When I met with him yesterday and gave the box—"

"What box? I thought you were paying him five hundred dollars." Victor narrowed his eyes.

Eric licked his lips. "The box...with the money, I mean."

"What box?" The guy couldn't lie for his life. What fast one was he pulling now?

"I was trying to work a deal. Figured he might take some of the broken artifacts instead of the money." Eric's leg shook as he quickly added, "You told me to throw them out, but I wanted to get some cash for them if I could."

Unbelievable. Victor shook his head. "Did the detective go for it?"

Eric slunk back in the chair. "Well, no."

"But I bet he took them, right?"

"Yeah. I mean, you said they weren't worth shit, so I didn't think you'd care." Eric licked his lips. "Right?"

Victor stood and smashed the handgrip on the desk. "You stupid motherfucker, you handed a cop physical evidence of a looting?"

Eric jumped. "It's cool. It's cool. He doesn't give a shit about the artifacts. Just wants money. I told you, he might have a lead for me."

"You have two seconds to tell me something that might save your miserable life." Victor itched to throw this junkie through the fucking window and end both of their misery. Only, now he was intrigued. He rounded the desk and towered over Eric.

Eyes wide, Eric gripped the armrest. "He...uh...said he might be interested in some cash for leaking information to me on where they keep some rare artifacts."

"Locally?"

"I think so. He didn't say. I'm supposed to talk to him again."

Victor stroked his chin. He needed to get his hands on some relics and the security in town was laughable. Eric might actually be onto something.

"There's more." Eric let go of the armrests and rubbed his hands together. "I'm doing good, right? You wanna know more?"

If Eric were a bug, Victor would grind him under his shoe. But the druggie was bringing some useful information. Every time Victor wanted to off the damn idiot, he came up with something worthwhile and bought another chance at life. "Keep talking."

"I went to spy on Maddie, and I saw the detective go into her apartment."

"Yeah, and?"

Eric grinned and raised his eyebrows. "I saw their silhouettes through the curtains. He was frisking her all right."

Fisher and the archaeologist. That was something to chew on. Both into money over morals. If the detective was sleeping with Cooper, he might know where she kept those rare artifacts. Maybe using her. Then again, she could be in on the whole thing, providing him the information for her own cut. "Find out more about them and report back."

Eric leaped up, went to the door, and opened it. "You got it, boss."

Gina stood in the entrance. "I left another message, but Cooper's still not answering."

Fucking bitch. Blood roared in Victor's ears. He grabbed Eric's arm and yanked him back. "Don't go yet. I have another job for you."

CHAPTER 26

Scott opened his eyes but didn't move. Maddie, snuggled against him, stirred a morning wake-up call he hadn't experienced in a long time. She shifted as his cock came to life and nudged the leg she had nestled against his thigh.

They'd made love four times last night. Insatiable, after years of wanting her so much, he'd lost all control. Rough, tender, crazed, they'd done it all. To be fair, she'd given right back.

He pressed his lips to her forehead and the sweet scent of her lilac perfume filled his nostrils. His heart squeezed. He never thought he could fall more in love with her, and yet he had. Now what the hell could he do?

One night, she'd said.

Right.

Like that would ever be enough.

She sighed and turned over. Her shapely ass pressed against his erection, causing him to catch his breath. But if he made love to her again, he might never leave. He'd hold on to this memory, but now he had a job to do. One that could endanger her life.

He eased out of the bed and tucked the blanket around her. Fighting the urge to crawl back under the covers with her, he forced himself to take a step away. A smile tugged at the corners of his mouth. Maddie slept like the dead. The woman didn't do anything halfway.

Pillow against her cheek, lips slightly parted, she wasn't as vulnerable as she appeared in her sleep, but his protective instincts kicked in anyway. He wouldn't let anyone hurt her again. Mole had dug up her land and stolen her artifacts. If Scott wanted to help her, he had to get back to the business of putting the man away.

He didn't want to wake her, so he dressed quietly and slipped out of the bedroom. With the sun not even up yet, Lucky snored on his bed in a dark corner of the living room. Scott paused by the front door. Maybe he should leave a note.

Even if he could find a pen and paper, he'd be sure to get the dog all excited when he switched on a light. No point. Maddie knew the deal. One mutually-agreed-upon night of mind-blowing sex. That was all.

He eased the door open, locked the handle as he stepped into the stairwell, and pulled it shut.

Leaving his heart behind.

* * *

When Scott entered the station, Lee sat behind his desk in the chief's office. Scott crossed the room and gave a quick rap on the door. "Hey, Chief."

Lee glanced up from reading a file. "Oh, I lost track of time. Are we all set to video conference with Zach?"

"We have a few minutes." Zach couldn't be seen at the station, so they'd have to talk over the computer.

"Let's step out. I need some fresh air." Lee stood and went over to the coffee machine by the window. "You want a cup?"

Scott eyed the black brew. "Is it too thick to pour?"

"Smart-ass. Yes or no?"

"Yeah. I'm not gonna live forever."

Lee filled two mugs, handed one to Scott, and led the way outside. Nine o'clock and still a nip in the morning air. Sure was different from the city where the buildings blocked the wind and heat stagnated. They stopped under a tall oak.

Lee looked up as a squirrel scampered across a branch, sure-footed as a tightrope walker. "Ever been shit on by one of them?"

Scott followed his gaze. "No. Is that a problem around here?"

"Only if it happens to you." Lee grinned and took a chug of coffee.

"Pretty quiet at the station this morning." Scott glanced at the empty building.

"Tom just left my office." Lee sighed. "He's a damn good cop. Didn't exactly rat you out, but he's not happy with you letting Eric go."

"He should be pissed. I'd have complained to you if the roles were reversed."

"I smoothed it out as best I could, but you ruffled some feathers around here." Lee gestured to the station with his mug.

Scott nodded. "I'm sure. Not much I can do about it. Goes with the territory when you're undercover."

"Mostly, he was upset for Maddie and the damage the looters did digging up her site."

"Understandable." Scott took a swig of coffee. Wouldn't be long before his body revved to life with that brew. Considering he'd spent half the night making love to Maddie, he could use the caffeine kick.

"What's the latest with Eric?"

Right. Time to get his head back in the game and forget the last twelve hours. "Stupid shit. He tried to give me the broken artifacts instead of the bribe. Probably planned to screw Mole over by keeping the money, assuming that's where it came from."

"He's predictable at least."

"I told him for the right price I'd let him know where some rare artifacts were being stored. Mole has to be jonesing with his black-market sales shut down. They didn't get anything worthwhile from the digging, so I figure he might take a chance at stealing more."

"Of course, he'll give that job to Eric."

"Because he's done so well in the past." Scott snorted and leaned against the tree.

"If they steal the relics and sell them to our black-market man—"

"I've been talking to him. He let Mole know he wants Native American artifacts and money's no object. If we can get some into Mole's hands, he'll sell all right, and then we can trace the transaction through the goods."

"We'll have proof this time, and hopefully, Zach can tie the money to the drug cartel."

"That's the plan, but with one small problem." Scott scratched his head. "We don't have any rare artifacts."

"Yeah, it's not likely anyone's going to hand over valuable pieces to us."

Too bad Scott couldn't employ Maddie's help. She was tight with the Seneca Nation tribal leaders and worked for Cultural Resources. It would make the job easier, but no way would he get her involved. He'd found another solution. "Actually, I'm making some progress. I met in private with the State Historic Preservation Officer, and he's working with the DEA to provide us some relics for replication."

Lee frowned. "You think Mole will believe they're real?"

"I'm banking on it. He had to be behind the theft at Maddie's site. No reason for him to think he's not stealing more authentic artifacts."

"It's a risk, but I guess it's one we'll have to take." Lee checked his watch. "We'd better go inside and set up the conference with Zach."

At least Zach wouldn't be compromised if things went south with the fake pieces. So far, he hadn't been involved with any of the artifacts, but that could change. Scott followed Lee back inside the building. Kaitlyn glanced up from her desk and then quickly back to her monitor as if uncomfortable. Tom must have told her about the whole Eric thing. Kaitlyn was probably pissed, too. Go figure.

Lee shut the door behind Scott in his office.

"What's the latest with Zach?" Lee asked as they both took a seat.

"Guess we'll find out. He had a job last night for Mole." Scott's shoulders tensed. If anything happened to Zach, it would be his fault for bringing him onboard.

Lee eased back in the chair. "What? Something's eating at you."

Scott never could hide anything from Lee. Not after all their time together. But this was personal. He's the one who needed to separate Zach from his brother, Justin. Yeah, right. "It's nothing. Zach can take care of himself. I mean, four years in jail. The guy's seen it all."

"Well, I haven't met him, but it sounds like he's tough enough. Let's talk to him." Lee initiated the video call and swiveled the monitor into Scott's line of vision.

Zach's face came to life on the screen. "You guys see me?"

Wearing a blue hoodie, brown eyes staring back at them, he reached out to adjust something on his end. "There, that's better. Hey."

Lee blinked twice and then turned to face Scott. He scrubbed a hand across his chin. "Shit on a stick. Now I get it."

Scott glanced at Lee. "What?"

"He doesn't remind you of someone?" Lee hitched an eyebrow.

Scott shifted in his seat.

"Did I miss something?" Zach asked.

"No." Scott cleared his throat and jerked his head in Lee's direction. "This is Chief Davis. Can you bring him up to speed?"

"Sure. I made the drop last night, and I think Mole set up a test for me."

Lee cocked his head. "What kind of test?"

"The dealer overpaid me. I gave the extra money to Mole. Played the honest businessman card. Think I sold him on it. He said he'd have more work coming my way."

Scott nodded. Of course, Mole would want to make sure he could trust Zach. "Good job. We're working on an angle to get Mole to steal some fake artifacts so we can trace them. Would he ask you or Eric to do that?"

Zach rubbed his chin. After a second, he shook his head. "Eric's a total fuck-up, but for some reason, Mole hasn't fired him. I think he intends to keep me on the drug end of the business, where most of the money is right now. So far, he hasn't shared any information about the artifacts. Only Eric works that side. Mole probably figures he's expendable."

"Makes sense." Lee picked up his mug and took a sip of coffee. "More than likely, he has someone on the inside who would snuff Eric if he went to jail and tried to talk his way into a deal."

"Eric wouldn't last a second behind bars. The inmates would eat him alive," Zach said.

Scott folded his hands and tapped his thumbs together. "We can't risk taking in Eric. As big a maggot as he is, we need him to work Mole."

"I'll make sure numb-nuts gets released if he's picked up by one of the other cops, unless he really fucks up and kills somebody or something," Lee said.

Scott leaned closer to the monitor. "What I have in mind is a meeting with Mole away from any watchful eyes. Someplace where you and he can discuss the drug transactions."

Zach nodded. "That will work because he needs to keep up appearances as an upstanding citizen and businessman. He mentioned we should meet somewhere else next time, not at his house. I'm thinking his new construction site might work."

"You read my mind," Scott said.

Lee turned to Scott. "Have you installed the surveillance cameras around the perimeter yet?"

"Yup. I know a good spot deeper in the woods where we can use a long-range parabolic dish microphone to record the conversation. I don't want to risk Zach wearing a wire. I'll be there to listen to the whole thing from a discreet distance. I can intervene if things go sideways. You okay so far, Zach?"

"I'm good."

"I'll be there, Zach, but we both know things can happen fast." Scott grimaced. "I can't make promises about your safety."

"I know what I signed up for. I'm in."

Zach had nerves of steel to keep a calm demeanor. One mistake and Mole could take him out. Scott waved a hand to Lee. "Did I miss anything?"

"I think we're covered." Lee faced the monitor. "Let us know when Mole contacts you."

"Will do. I'll be in touch."

Lee ended the session and let out a long breath. "You never mentioned the resemblance. Same age, even. You okay?"

"Yeah." Scott stood and went over to the coffee pot to pour another cup. "I've been thinking about Justin and still don't understand some things."

"Like what?"

"I did some checking, and Justin had two arrests for meth possession the year before his death. Don't know much else. The police said his tent-mate took off when Justin died."

"You make anything of that?"

"I don't know." Scott turned to face him. "What's bothering me is Justin died of a heroin overdose, but there's no record of any possession or priors for it."

"All our years in narcotics, you know what it's like with drugs." Lee frowned. "People start on one and then try another."

Nothing Scott could do anymore to help Justin, but he could look out for Zach. "I guess. I just want to nail this bastard and keep Zach safe in the process."

"You can't control everything. There's always a risk." Lee joined Scott at the coffee machine. "It's not too late to pull him out."

Scott filled Lee's cup. "No. He's earned Mole's trust. It's our best shot. My gut's telling me Zach can handle himself."

"We've survived before following those instincts. I have the same feeling."

"I sure as hell hope I'm right." Scott stepped to the window and gazed out at the morning sun filtering through the bright, green leaves of an oak tree. "I can't take losing anyone else."

CHAPTER 27

THE ALARM next to Maddie's bed went off, and she rubbed her eyes. Six o'clock. Time to get moving. She slammed her mouth shut halfway through a yawn when she smelled Scott's aftershave. The scent clung to her skin the same as he had all night. On top of her, underneath her, all over her. She shuddered. The man was thorough.

She stroked the cool sheets on the empty side of the bed. Disappointment sliced her heart. She shouldn't have expected anything more. They'd agreed to one night. Only she'd hoped he wouldn't be able to walk away.

She already missed him. Everything she'd longed for the last two years, he'd given her and then some. When he'd made love to her with his eyes open, he'd bared his soul, and they'd connected on a level beyond physical.

And now, the emptiness in the room suffocated her. When she slept in this bed again, she'd yearn for his caress. Even if his case ended soon, he hadn't made any promises for the future. Not this time.

He'd made it clear he had an agenda that didn't include her, for her own safety, as if she couldn't take care of herself. For God's sake, she had everything under control. Eric was no threat to her. If he'd wanted revenge for the incident in the bar, he would have done something by now. The idiot was like any other addict, looking for stuff to sell to feed his habit, so he'd dug up her site. Nothing personal. He would move on to the next target. Scott was worrying about nothing.

The scamper of Lucky's paws on the hardwood floor sounded from the hall as he raced around the corner, sliding to a stop by the side of her bed.

Too small to reach the top, he whined and hopped. Maddie scooted to the edge and bent to scratch his ears. "Hey, guy. Gimme a second and I'll take you out."

When she reached the kitchen, she glanced at the counter. No note. Her hopes sank. Of course, he wouldn't have left one. He probably didn't want to wake the dog by turning on lights. She shook her head. One night with Scott could never be enough.

In her tennis shoes, robe hugging her body and hair a wild mess, Maddie followed Lucky across the dewy grass. After he did his business, she took him back inside, fed him, and let out a long sigh. If Scott stayed in town, she would die a slow death every time she ran into him. They'd come too far for her to dial back the heat. Now that she'd fallen in love with him again, the only way to survive would be for her to leave. Hell, she'd planned to at some point, anyway. Her teaching assistant job had ended with the semester, so she had nothing to keep her in town. She'd look at the job openings out west and line one up for after she finished Victor's field survey.

Lucky slurped water from his bowl and then gazed up at her, drool dripping from his mouth. She gave him a sad smile. "Not sure I can take you overseas." She fluffed the fur on his head. "It's okay, pup. There are plenty of places out west I can work. I've never been to that part of the country. You and I have to stick together."

* * *

Maddie focused on the piece she'd partially uncovered at Victor's site. Sweat trickled down the back of her neck as she leaned close to the ground and peered at the tip of a hard, gray object. Thin and sharp, this could be a weapon. Her pulse jumped. Careful not to damage the artifact, she took her time with the hand brush and dental pick to loosen it from the earth, taking pictures to document every step of the process.

The more sand she brushed away from the artifact, the faster her heart raced. It could be a Clovis blade, one of the first stone tools used by man. To the untrained eye, the blade would appear to be nothing more than a large arrowhead, except these were longer and could pierce the hide of a mastodon. Thirteen thousand years ago, a hunter of the Paleo-Indian culture had sharpened stones and fashioned them into spears.

This was huge. Many archaeologists believed these weapons once belonged to America's first human inhabitants. Of course, she'd seen Clovis points in museums and read about others found in the west, but this one was right under her nose. It might even be the first ever discovered in New York. If so, she'd hit the jackpot. The tribal members would be stoked. A spark of hope after the devastating losses. The weight on her shoulders lifted.

On a personal level, this could help repair the damage to her career. With this on her resume, she might re-earn the respect of her peers and be able to get another job. Scott could stay in Tuckerton as long as he wanted. This would be her ticket out.

After she'd brushed the piece free, she picked it up and held it in her gloved hand. A perfect specimen with the signature flaking on both front and back. Her fingers trembled as she measured the artifact. Eleven centimeters long, three wide, and shaped like a mini-surfboard, this little gem would be more than enough to merit further investigation. Without a doubt, she'd uncover more. If she found enough, it might be just what they needed to put the area on the maps and supply enough pieces to get the museum built. Wait until she told Kyle and the other undergraduates. They would go nuts. "Sorry, Victor. Looks like your resort isn't going up anytime soon, if ever."

She filled a Ziploc bag with dirt and nestled the blade inside. Almost dinner time, she had to take care of Lucky. Still plenty of daylight to come back later. She carried the box to her car, drove to the lab, and dropped it off for dating. Next stop was home.

When she entered her apartment, Lucky greeted her with his usual excitement, tail thumping the wall like a maniacal metronome. Damn if the scent of Scott's aftershave didn't still linger. She closed her eyes and breathed it in. He didn't even need to be in the same room to have that effect on her.

All day, she'd been focused on the dig, and then the find, but now her body craved him worse than a drug. The month before he'd left for Mexico, they'd exchanged keys, and more than once she'd come home to find him cooking dinner or working on the computer at her kitchen table. What she wouldn't give for that now. Many meals had turned cold because they'd jumped each other. Priorities.

He hadn't called or texted her all day. Obviously, one night together was all he intended to have with her. That's what she'd offered. Only she'd hoped he would want more. With a sigh, she put Lucky's collar on him and took him out back to his usual spot. When the leash jerked, she glanced at Lucky, who had found a half-eaten hamburger and was trying to wolf it down before she could yank him away. "No. Bad dog."

Lucky continued to chomp, eyes apologizing while his jaws moved fast. Oh hell, a dog couldn't resist a hamburger. The community barbecue grill at the back of the apartment building meant people sometimes dropped food, but she always kept a careful eye out. "Guess you got a treat because my mind is on a man."

She'd swear he grinned, although he pulled it off as panting. "Uh huh. Come on, time to go back in. We'll take a walk later. I need to dig while it's still light."

She let him inside and went to her computer to check email. Nothing from Scott. Silence. She lowered her head into her hands. So been there, done that.

Hell-bent on protecting her, he wouldn't let her back in. At least this time she understood why. Didn't make it any easier. She wanted him more than anything in her life. In some ways, it had worked better to think he'd moved on. Well, this time *she* would move on because she couldn't stand the torture of living so close to him.

The dog made a gagging noise. Panting, he walked stiffly to the kitchen and vomited. He shook his head twice and paced on uneven steps around the room like a drunk.

"Lucky? What's wrong?" Her nerves jumped. The dog whined and moved like he'd forgotten how to walk. Something wasn't right. She checked her watch. The vet was closed.

Scott's words rattled in her head. *You always run off half-cocked.* She took a deep breath. Not this time. Okay, so Lucky might be reacting to the hamburger, but that shouldn't make him stumble around. He'd eaten beef before. There had to be an emergency vet somewhere in the area. She grabbed her phone and looked it up. Nothing closer than thirty miles. Her stomach balled into a hard knot as Lucky continued to bump into the furniture and pant.

She dialed the number with shaking hands.

"Veterinary Hospital, how can I help you?"

"My dog is acting strangely. He ate a hamburger outside and threw up. He's stumbling and can't catch his breath. What should I do?"

"Bring him right in along with a sample of whatever he threw up. We'll need to run tests. This could be serious. It sounds like he ate some- thing bad. If it's chemicals, time is of the essence."

Chemicals? That sounded way worse than rotten meat. A whimper escaped her lips. "I'll get him there as fast as I can."

She grabbed the sample. Keys in hand, she picked up Lucky and carried him out to the car. "You're going to be okay. I got this," she said more to herself than him.

Lucky struggled to breathe as she drove to the clinic. She kept glancing at him to make sure he was still alive while cold sweat soaked her shirt. What kind of chemicals could he have gotten into?

Thank God, the GPS brought her to the right place. She parked the car, hefted Lucky into her arms along with the sample, and ran inside. The woman behind the counter glanced up. "Are you the one who called about a sick dog?"

"Yes. Something is very wrong." Tears sprung to her eyes. For someone who could count on one hand the number of times she'd cried in the last three years, she was breaking all sorts of records lately.

A couple of vet techs emerged from a back room. They whisked Lucky and the sample through a set of swinging doors behind the desk. Maddie's heart wrenched at the separation.

The receptionist gave her a polite smile. "I'll need a credit card before we can run any tests or treat the dog."

"What? This is an emergency."

"I'm sorry. It's our—"

"Never mind. Okay." She dug out her wallet and handed over her Visa card.

"Thank you. Depending on what's wrong with him, this could be a substantial amount. Are you able to cover the expenses should they become considerable?" The receptionist gave her a sad smile that Maddie knew meant others had said no, they couldn't afford it. Those poor people and their dogs.

"Whatever it takes. My credit is good." She'd eat peanut butter and jelly sandwiches the rest of her life if she had to as long as Lucky would be all right.

Once the card cleared, the receptionist hurried into the back, no doubt to let the techs know they could commence treatment because the cost would be covered. At least Maddie had a credit card with no balance and a respectable limit. Veterinary care, like anything else, was a business. Not that the people didn't care, but bottom line, it came down to money. Maddie shut her eyes and tried not to think about the pets who were turned away.

She took a seat in the waiting room. Scott probably would have handled the situation better. Noticed sooner or driven faster. No. She slapped down the thought. She'd reacted quickly and responsibly. Besides, Scott wasn't there, and wouldn't be there. She and Lucky would be fine.

One of the vet techs rounded the corner and approached. "Apparently, your dog ate rat poison. It was in the hamburger. Good thing you brought him right in because strychnine can be fatal if not treated immediately, especially in a puppy."

Maddie stared at the woman. "What? Why would a poisoned burger be on the ground behind my apartment?"

The tech shook her head. "It's sad. Some people don't like dogs, and they do things like this."

"Will"—Maddie choked on the words—"will Lucky be okay?"

"Yes. Thanks to your quick response, he should be. He's getting an IV and needs to stay overnight so we can monitor him, but he's young and healthy. You did everything right. Saved his life."

Saved his life. The tension in Maddie's body eased. She hadn't let Lucky down. "Can I see him?"

"He's knocked out right now. It really would be better to come by in the morning." The tech placed a hand on her arm. "I promise, we'll take good care of him. I'm here all night. He won't be alone."

"Okay." Maddie took a deep breath. "Thanks. I'll come back tomorrow."

The receptionist waved her over and printed out a receipt. "If you could sign here, please, for the charges tonight, we'll be all set."

Maddie cringed at the costs for tests, overnight care, and the IV, but at least Lucky was going to be okay. Her dog. The one she'd saved. By herself, this time.

She drove back to her apartment. Not enough daylight left to dig even if she had the energy. She climbed the stairs and dug out her keys. Someone had stuck a red sticky note on the front of her door.

I warned you. Finish the job.

The blood drained from her body, and ice ran through her veins. Victor!

He'd poisoned her dog. She whipped her head around, searching the parking lot for anyone lurking. Whoever did this knew enough to place the hamburger where she took her puppy to pee, which meant someone had been watching her. The sick bastard would go to any length to get what he wanted. She jerked the door open and entered, slamming it shut behind her. Her knees buckled, and she sank to the floor. Fisted her hands in her hair. He'd almost killed an innocent puppy.

Her foot bumped Lucky's treat ball. She glanced at his empty bed, and her chest caved. Poor dog, in a cage with an IV dripping life into him.

She pushed up and headed to her computer. Screw that heartless monster. She had what she needed to shut him down.

CHAPTER 28

SCOTT FIRED up his computer and went to the kitchen to brew some coffee. He'd managed not to call, text, or show up at Maddie's door for an entire day. Barely. Hard as it had been to leave her yesterday morning, the torture of passing her apartment last night had been worse. He'd wanted to knock on the door, whisk her back to the bedroom, and pick up where they'd left off.

He craved her touch. Her soft lips, the way she'd moaned and writhed under him, everything about their night had been freaking unbelievable. If only he could tell her how much he loved her and wanted to wake up every morning with her cuddled against his body. But he didn't dare contact her. The sound of her voice alone might be enough to shatter his resolve.

He scooped some coffee and dumped half into the filter. The rest sprinkled on the counter. Shit. Grabbing a paper towel, he wet it and wiped up the grinds. At least this mess cleaned up easily. The one with Maddie, not so much.

She was a bright light in his world of darkness with her caring, giving nature. The complete opposite of criminals like Mole.

His chest grew heavy. If he found a way to stay and work in New

York, Maddie might not even want him. She'd fallen for the man he used to be. The new version had wounds that left scars. Drug lords were brutal. The things Scott had seen couldn't be erased and would forever alter his view on life. Yet, Maddie kept coming back to him. He was the one pushing her away.

Undercover so long, he didn't know anything else, but if it meant a chance with her, maybe he should consider other options. He could use his DEA experience in a different capacity. Lee seemed to be managing with his change from narcotics, but Scott could never walk away from his obligation to help those like Justin. He'd have to find a path that allowed him to fulfill the debt.

He poured some coffee and then took the mug with him to the computer. Last night, he'd installed surveillance cameras on the property where Mole intended to build. With a right click, he brought up the live feed. He had checked before going to bed, but the area remained dark and showed no signs of life. Maybe in the light of day he could figure out what was going on with the staked-out section he'd come across while setting up. It looked as if an excavation was underway, but that made no sense, because Mole didn't have any permits. Nine o'clock and nothing but birds flitted in and out of view.

One of the cameras panned and then stopped. Right along with Scott's heart.

"What the hell?"

He gaped at the image of Maddie, bent over in the staked-out area, more than halfway dug up. She'd been at this for a while. Holy shit. What was she doing there? He'd done everything humanly possible to keep her out of harm's way, and here she was right smack in the fucking middle of it. He broke out in a cold sweat as Maddie hunched down with some sort of pick in her hand.

Scott leaped out of his chair, grabbed his jacket, and raced to his car. He dialed Maddie, but she didn't answer. He had to think. While he drove to the site, his entire body stiff with tension, he sorted through the possible reasons for her to be there. Maybe Mole hired her to dig up artifacts so he could sell them on the black market. She would never do that. Why hadn't she mentioned this?

The other night, she hadn't exactly been chatty in bed. Maybe if they'd spent more time talking than fighting or making love, she would have told him what she was up to. He turned onto the gravel path that led to the lot, his tires flinging gravel.

At last, he reached the site. Maddie sat back on her haunches, a sieve in hand, and whipped her head around in his direction.

Thank God, she was safe. He got out of the car. In swift, long strides, he approached her. He stopped at the edge of the rectangular pit and glared down at her, his heart rate still spiked.

When she first met his gaze, he could swear hope lit in her eyes before they quickly became guarded.

"What are you doing?" he asked through clenched teeth.

She thrust her chin out, but blinked several times, her nervous tell. "My job."

"Pack up your stuff. You're coming with me. We'll talk about this in the car."

She crossed her arms, still holding onto the tool. "Excuse me? I'm not going anywhere."

"I'm not kidding, Maddie." Hot blood coursed through his veins. "If you don't come right now, I'll drag your ass out of here."

"Like hell you will. I'm not breaking the law." She bit her lip and stared up at him.

Another tell. She was hiding something. He had to find out what, but not on Mole's property where he or Eric could show up at any time. Every second she spent arguing with him put her safety in jeopardy. "Last chance."

"Unless you have a warrant—"

"And you blew it." He bent, wrapped an arm under her thighs, put a hand on her ass, and slung her over his shoulder. She kicked her feet and smacked his back cursing the whole way to his car.

He opened the back door and plopped her inside. The automatic lock secured her after it slammed shut. When he slid onto the driver's side, she yelled from the rear, "How dare you? Let me out of here."

"Soon enough." He threw the car in gear. A vein in his forehead throbbed as he drove several miles through the woods. He found a clearing with enough space to park off-road and stopped the car.

He got out and climbed into the back next to her where she fumed, arms crossed, lips in a thin white line. The pink in her cheeks and the fire in her eyes wrenched his heart. He'd done everything possible to keep her far from Mole. And now, she'd endangered her life. "Let's start from the top. What are you doing on that property?"

"For the record, the only reason I'm talking to you is because I need to get back to my job." She angled to face him. "I'm so pissed right now. I could—"

"Duly noted. And back at you." He spiked a hand through his hair. "Tell me right now what's going on."

She tapped her boot on the floor and explained her role in the field survey. Scott's throat constricted. Of course, he knew building permits would be needed, but the whole Army Corps requirements were news to him.

"Hold on a second." He sucked in a breath and let it out. "Are you saying if you report any significant finds from this survey you're doing, the builder can't proceed?"

"Well, not necessarily, but it stops everything cold and launches a sequence of events that could take years to resolve."

Shit. Mole would go ballistic if he didn't get his resort built. Maddie couldn't be the reason why. Her gorgeous hazel eyes sparked, warming him at the same time icy fingers of fear shivered down his spine. "I want you off this survey. Now. They can find someone else to do it."

"No way. It's too far along, and I'm too invested." She straightened, back rigid. "Why do you care? What's this got to do with the DEA?"

Fuck.

He'd have to tell her the truth. She was in deep, and if she didn't know how dangerous Mole could be, she might do something rash.

Maddie nudged him with her elbow. "What? Why are you so upset?"

"Because I didn't want to have this discussion with you." He huffed out a breath. "The developer, Mole, is the guy I'm after. He's a drug lord who intends to use this resort he's building to launder his money."

She gasped. "A drug lord? I thought he was just a greedy SOB who wanted to dig up all the artifacts on the land."

"He's way more dangerous. You don't understand who you're dealing with. He thinks nothing of torturing or killing people. This is serious shit, and I want you the hell away from it."

"T-torturing people?" Her eyes grew wide.

"I'm telling you, he's brutal, and I want you out of this."

"Well, I can't stop now. He tried to bribe me to falsify this report. If I quit, he'll find someone who will. Once he has his permit, he'll ravage the land."

That bastard. No surprise. He'd use any means to get his way. If she screwed him over, he'd kill her. "Tell me you didn't take the money."

"No." She rubbed her hand across her chin, leaving a smear of dirt. "But, he thinks I will once I fake the report, which I have no intention of doing."

Holy shit. The whole time Scott had been in town, she'd been dealing with the devil, and he'd had no fucking idea. A burning sensation rose from his stomach to the back of his throat. "Damn straight you aren't faking a report. That's it. You're off the survey as of right now."

She snorted. "Just because we slept together doesn't mean you can order me around. I'm going to finish this job. I've already uncovered a piece that will put this place on the maps."

"What?" Hell, no. She'd be signing her own death warrant.

"Yup. A Clovis blade. It's being dated as we speak. I called in a favor from my professor at the university, and they're rushing it."

"Listen to me. You can't report this." He reached out to shake her shoulder. "This isn't a game. Mole is dangerous."

She swallowed. "I know, but I'm not walking away."

"God fucking dammit, Maddie." He stormed out of the car. As he paced, the chilly breeze did nothing to cool his hot skin. Maddie working for Mole. Scott's worst nightmare come true. Bad enough he had Zach to watch out for, but now Maddie. He couldn't be everywhere to protect them both.

Maddie got out and stood beside the car.

He rounded on her. "Why didn't you tell me about this?"

She scraped a boot over a gnarled tree root. "Until the other night, we weren't sharing much." Hurt shone in her eyes. She let out a long sigh. "I don't want to fight with you, but I need to get back to work."

Worry fogged his brain. Scott shut his eyes for a second. When he opened them, Maddie gazed up at him, her mouth drawn in a determined line. Stubborn. She had a point. He couldn't keep her from going back unless he kidnapped her. Not out of the realm of possibilities, but he had to figure out a realistic plan to move forward. "Let me catch up here. Does Mole know you found this Clovis-thing?"

"No, and it's not a thing. It's a major artifact."

Scott paced again. She should be safe if Mole thought she had nothing to report. He wouldn't hurt the person working to get his permit. And if the artifact she'd found was so valuable, maybe the DEA could make a replica to be used in their sting with Eric. "The blade you dug up. Is it someplace where I could take a picture of it?"

Maddie cocked her head. "What? I mean, yeah, it's at the university, but I have a ton of pictures, and I use a 3D camera, so they're very good."

"Do you think I could have a copy of them along with any measurements you might have made?"

"I guess. But why?" When he hesitated, she puffed out her cheeks. "Never mind. I know you're going to say you can't tell me."

"You have to keep the artifact a secret from Mole. Do you understand?"

"I'm not going to tell him. I want to finish this already."

"If for any reason you think he's found out—"

"He won't. You and the professor are the only two people who know."

Scott nodded. He didn't like it, but she might be in more danger if she backed off right now. Mole must expect her to finish soon, and he'd no doubt make her pay if she kept him waiting. "Can you email me the photos and some snapshots of your data from the lot?"

"Yeah."

"Okay. I'll take you back. But I mean it: if you think for a second Mole has any idea you found something, call me, and get the hell out of there. In fact, come straight to the station, so you're protected." He rested a hand on her shoulder. "Promise me."

She nibbled her lip and then nodded. "Okay. Fair enough." She blushed, and her expression softened. "Hey, about the other night…"

Oh no. They weren't going there. He had to shut that right down. "I shouldn't have let myself get carried away. I meant what I said about one night." He pulled his hand back. "You can't be near me, Maddie. I'm sorry. It's for your own safety."

The light left her eyes. She pushed off the car. "Take me back, so I can finish my job. The sooner I'm out of here, the better."

He closed the car door to shut her in. His stomach churned. Did she mean she would leave town? He didn't ask because it wouldn't change anything. Until he convicted Mole, the best place for her was far away.

CHAPTER 29

MADDIE'S PULSE quickened as she clicked the mouse to bring up the report for the Clovis blade. In the last day, she'd uncovered two more, along with scrapers, drills, and needles. The Clovis point was part of a generalized toolkit—the Leatherman of the ancient world, and she had a whole set right in her hands. Well, in the hands of the university anyway.

Yesterday had been long and stressful. Each time she'd found a piece, she'd sweated, unsure if Victor would show up and see it.

She inched closer to the screen. The test results indicated the blade went back at least thirteen thousand years. She pumped a fist in the air and let out a *whoop* causing Lucky to jump up from his bed.

"Sorry, little guy." She patted his head. Thank God, he'd recovered from the poisoning. And Victor Mole would pay for hurting her pup. Now, she could shut down his operation and launch the field survey into the next phase. He'd never get his resort built.

Scott's warnings about Victor echoed in her head. *He's tortured and killed people.* Her shoulders pinched together. Once she filed the report, he'd have no recourse. He couldn't deny the evidence of historic treasures on the land. To protect herself, she needed to get out of town.

She logged into her email and found a message concerning a job she'd applied for in Colorado. They were offering her a position. Not as a lead, but a job was a job. She could bring the dog, and the project started next week. If she wrote up the real field survey and booked her flights, she could be out before Victor even knew she was packing.

Her phone rang with Sarah's tone. Ugh, Maddie wouldn't be around to see the new baby. She'd be that long-distance relative who sent cards and gifts. Her stomach tightened. With her current situation, she had to do what she needed. Maybe something would change down the road.

She answered the call. "Hey, Sarah. How ya doing?"

"Great. Up to my eyeballs in pink stuff."

"I bet. That's the fun part, right?"

"Yup. I wanted to check on you. The last time we talked, you and Scott were—"

"Yeah, that didn't work out." Maddie's heart sunk. She'd told Sarah about them sleeping together. "A lot has happened in the last couple of days."

"Like what? I was so excited that you two were together again."

"I was...hoping for more...but it's not meant to be." Maddie glanced at the computer. "In fact, I'm going to take a job in Colorado."

"What? This is sudden. Why? You just moved into your new place."

"Well, they rent by the month here, so I'll only be out a couple of weeks." Maddie rubbed her eyes and spoke matter-of-factly, "I'm going to give my furniture to Nikki because she has a new place and not much money. It's all for the best."

"Hold on. What the hell happened that I missed? The last time we talked—"

"I was a fool to think we had a chance at anything. Scott made it clear his job is too dangerous for us to have a relationship." And the guilt over his brother's death kept him duty-bound to put away the drug lords. Maddie came second. The truth squeezed the air from her lungs. "I have to leave, Sarah. It hurts too much to be around him."

"Oh, Maddie." Sarah sighed. "I'm so sorry. Are you sure?"

"Yeah. My finals are graded, and the excavation I've worked on for the last year is finished. There's nothing left to keep me in town."

Except the man she loved.

"I don't understand how Scott can pick his job over you. He's done nothing but jerk you around from day one," Sarah said in a I-wanna-kick-his-butt tone.

"Can't argue that, but I opened myself up to it. And things are kinda complicated." Damn, despite the hurt, she couldn't stop herself from defending him. Sarah didn't know about his brother or Victor.

"Doesn't sound like it to me. He's never going to find anyone like you. He'll—"

"I should go, Sarah. There's a ton I need to do if I'm going to move. I'll keep in touch."

"All right. I'll stop ranting. I'm just so disappointed. Anne and I were hoping to see you soon and have a sisters day before the baby comes."

Maddie's throat swelled. It could be a while before she came back. "I'm sorry."

"I know. Call if you want to talk or if you want me to send Bruce out there to—"

"Not necessary, but thanks."

"Okay. Talk to you later."

Maddie hung up and scooted off the chair to hug Lucky. He licked her face and whined as if he understood her pain.

"It's okay, boy. I did it before, and I'll do it again." She rubbed his furry belly and blinked hard. Back to the old days where she packed light and lived frugally. A box for a coffee table, a canteen to fill with water, and most everything else was fluff.

She used to love living rough with only the necessities, but something had changed. Just like he had two years ago, Scott made her long for a home where they shared dinners together. One night in bed with him and she couldn't erase the warm feeling of his body against hers. What she wouldn't give to wake up in his arms every morning. She sniffled, squeezed Lucky one last time, and stood. Enough wallowing. Scott didn't have room for her in his life.

Time to move on.

* * *

Scott stood in front of the computer and stretched. Excruciating didn't come close to describing the last twenty-four hours. Between phone calls with Zach and watching Maddie extract piece after piece from the field survey site, his nerves were fried. Now that she had packed up and left for the day, he switched off the live feed.

His stomach grumbled. He went to the refrigerator, opened the door, and frowned at its paltry contents. Beer, water, a packet of mini carrots, and a jar of salsa. He could dip the carrots in the salsa and call it a meal if he were a bone-thin supermodel. That kind of woman did nothing for him. Not like Maddie—damn. Back to her. She had nothing but sexy curves, all too ready to press against him. And that spunky attitude of hers that made him stay on top of his game, he loved everything about her.

Unfortunately, he couldn't do a thing until he nailed Mole. But he should have enough evidence to arrest him soon. After, Scott's life would be his own, and he'd find a way to be with Maddie.

Right now, he had to meet with Eric and tell him where the fake artifact the DEA had constructed was hidden. What a complete dickface. He had it coming big-time for hurting Nikki and doing Mole's dirty work. Dinner would have to wait. Scott grabbed the carrots. Better than nothing.

He headed to his car, drove to the meeting place, and parked by a hiking trail next to Eric's empty truck. Scott made his way up the path to the first marker. Eric, his back to Scott, stood in front of a wooden plaque with pictures and descriptions of the local vegetation.

Scott silently approached. "Learn anything?"

Eric jumped. "Why the fuck do you do that?"

"Because I can." Anything to scare the little prick. "Did you bring the money?"

"Yeah, but the boss wasn't too happy about it. Said this lead better pan out." Eric tugged out a wad of bills and handed it to Scott.

"All I'm doing is telling you where the artifact is. What happens after, I don't want to know." Scott had asked for three grand this time. Chump change for Mole, but Scott needed to act like a cop who would think that was a lot of money. He counted the cash.

"It's all there." Eric glanced around. "Put it away before someone sees us."

Stupid dipshit. Didn't even realize Scott was the one who would be at risk if caught in the act. He glanced at Eric's other jeans pocket. Unless Eric was excited to see him, he had something in it. One guess what. "Gimme the rest."

Eric shifted his feet as his gaze darted around the woods. "Don't know what you're talking about. That's the amount you asked for."

Scott snorted. "You're a dumb fuck. Empty the other pocket."

"Why? You got what you came for." He slid a hand over the denim as if to hide the lump.

The smell of sweat and fear wafted off him. Scott took a step closer. "Don't fuck with me, or I'll tell your boss you tried to cheat him."

Eric's eyes widened. "You don't know nothin'."

"You willing to risk that? What do you think he does to people who cross him?"

The color drained from Eric's face. With a curse, he shoved a hand into his pocket and whipped out another wad of bills. "This is my money."

"Yeah, right. And I'm the Pope." Scott snagged the cash and shook his head as he counted. A thousand dollars. Eric must have told Mole that Scott wanted four thousand, intending to keep the rest himself. He could have died over a measly grand if Mole knew.

"I need to go. Where you got that thing hidden?" Eric asked.

"In a refrigerator at the storeroom." No one used the place since repairs were underway and the climate control system didn't work. Scott had put a small padlock on the outside. Eric would at least think he was breaking in again. A nail clipper probably could cut through the tiny bolt.

Eric raised an eyebrow. "Why would she keep it there after the place was already busted into?"

Huh. The asswipe still had some brain cells. Scott shrugged. "How do I know?"

"Yeah, whatever. I gotta go." Eric yanked his keys out and dropped them. They fell into a pile of vines under a tree. He snatched them up and took off down the trail.

Nothing like a good case of poison ivy.

Scott smiled to himself and headed down the trail to his car.

Even though Maddie shouldn't have a reason to be at the storeroom, he had to make sure she didn't go there. With his luck, she'd stop in to check on the progress and bump into Eric. Not likely, since Eric shouldn't be stupid enough to break in before dark. Still, Scott wouldn't put anything past the loser.

After he got in the car, he dialed Maddie. The phone rang four times and then went to voicemail. He left a message for her to call. Shit. She might be avoiding him. If he could have given her some sort of promise, he would have, but Mole had slipped through the DEA's fingers before. Until Scott had him for sure, all bets were off with Maddie.

He drove out of the lot and tried her number again. No luck.

Damn it.

Now he'd have to find her.

CHAPTER 30

MADDIE HOVERED her fingers over the computer keyboard and took a deep breath. Once she pressed enter, her life would change. She'd be on a plane to the Rockies in two days. New job, new place, new people. Wouldn't be the first time she'd picked up and moved. But this time the excitement of a new adventure didn't bubble inside as it usually did. More like a heaviness in her chest. She'd be leaving the man she loved. Probably never see him again.

He wouldn't change, though. And she had no hold over him. She hit enter, snatched the flight itinerary off the printer, and set it on the table. Her head spun with everything she had to do in the short time before she left.

Lucky brought his treat ball over and dropped it by her feet. Her stomach knotted. Poor guy. Ever since the night of IVs, he'd been starved. "I promise, I'll make Victor pay, puppy."

She went to the kitchen and filled his toy with treats. He nosed it around the floor as they trickled out, gobbling them up. Maddie sat back down and pulled up the blank field survey report. An idea formed. A way she could help nail the son of a bitch. She needed to talk to Scott.

Her bell rang. After peering through the peephole, she yanked the door open to Scott, standing on the other side with a sour expression on his face.

"Why didn't you answer your phone?"

Her heart skidded sideways. Maybe he'd changed his mind. He'd wrap his arms around her and say he wanted another shot. The most she'd be out was airfare. No. She mentally whacked herself. The grim line of his mouth told it all. "What? It never rang."

"I've been calling you for the last half-hour." He stepped into the room.

She glanced around for her phone. "I guess I left it in the car."

Lucky ran over and did his usual hero worship dance. Scott stroked the dog's ears. "I wish you'd keep track of it, because I needed to talk to you."

Considering he hadn't called in two days, he had a lot of nerve getting pissy when she didn't answer on the first ring. She kicked the door shut. "Well, you're here now, and as it turns out, I want to talk to you, too."

"About what?" He paused from his love fest with Lucky and glanced at the slammed door.

"You go first."

"I need you to stay away from the storeroom. I have something going on, and I don't want you anywhere near."

His dark hair fell just above his gorgeous green eyes, and parts below her waist squeezed. Damn him. "Can you be more specific?"

"I'm setting up a sting."

Huh. He'd shared information. Not exactly a wheelbarrow full, but at least something. "What kind of sting, and how does my storeroom fit in?"

He shook his head. "It's really best if you trust I'm doing what I can to get Mole. Can you please promise me you won't go anywhere near the place for the next couple of days?"

She sighed. Some of her anger dissipated. Of course, he wouldn't be at liberty to discuss the details of his operation. Even though they came at it from different angles, they both wanted to put Victor away. Whatever she could do to make that happen, she would. "Fine. I'm busy anyway. And this leads right into what I wanted to talk to you about."

"What?"

"I have an idea how to help you."

Scott raised a suspicious eyebrow. "What are you talking about?"

Maddie paced. "The bribe Victor is trying to give me? I think I can record a conversation about it. You can put him away for that, right? Some sort of federal crime, since it's the Army Corps he's trying to screw?"

"Oh hell no." He shook his head. "Don't you even *go* there. You keep away from him, understand?" Eyes firm as steel bored into hers. "Don't mess with him. Don't go near him. This is no joke, Maddie. Are we clear?"

She held her head high. "It's a good plan. I can get a recording and you can—"

"I said no." The words came out in a clipped, guttural growl.

"Why? Why can't I do something to help? He…he poisoned Lucky. He's gotta pay."

"What?" Scott's gaze dashed to the dog and back to her.

She pressed her lips together. "Lucky almost died. Victor left a note on my door telling me to finish the survey."

Scott's face turned red. His nostrils flared, and she half-expected steam to come out of his ears. "Why didn't you tell me about this?"

"What's the point? It's over and done with. I want this bastard behind bars. Let me help." She grabbed the front of Scott's button-down shirt. "I can do this."

The heat of his body, the soft cloth under her fingers, and the longing to make him trust and believe in her was too much. "Scott, please…"

"Dammit, no way, Maddie." He pushed her hands away and pounded a fist on the table right on top of her travel itinerary.

He froze.

She caught her breath as he stared down at the sheet. He raised an icy gaze to her and asked in a too-calm voice, "You're leaving?"

"Why do you care? You've made it clear there's no room for me in your life." Pain sliced through her entire body. If he had any thoughts of ever getting back together, now was his last chance to talk her out of going. The one-way ticket receipt had to make her intentions clear.

"I'm sorry. You know my priorities."

"So you keep telling me. Just leave. It's what you're best at." The words scorched her soul with the truth.

He blew out a breath and crossed his arms. "Not until you promise me you won't go near the storeroom."

Of course, his sting, which was the only reason he stood in front of her. "Fine. You got it."

"All right, then." He strode to the door. Lucky followed and whined at his feet. Scott closed his eyes tight for a second and bent to hug the dog.

The muscles in his broad shoulders flexed when he embraced Lucky. A lump formed in Maddie's throat. She had to be the biggest loser on earth to try again, but if she didn't, this might be the last time she set eyes on Scott. And even with all that had happened, she yearned for another chance.

Despite the quake of emotions churning inside, she managed a steady, calm tone. "If you walk out the door, we're done. Don't ever contact me again. I mean it."

He gave her a slow nod and reached for the handle. "Don't go anywhere near the storeroom or Mole. Get on that flight."

She held her breath until he stepped into the hall and shut the door. After it closed, she covered her face with her hands.

Fool.

She had to stop begging him to change his mind. Lucky whined at her feet.

She sucked in a long breath and fluffed the dog's head. Enough of her pity party. Scott didn't love her. Work ranked above her and always would. So be it.

Time to take care of her own priorities. She had the means to bring down that bastard looter dog-poisoner, and Scott wouldn't let her help him. Like hell she'd walk away. Sure, she'd leave, but not before she got her pound of Victor's flesh. She snatched a ponytail holder from the counter and twisted her hair into an angry knot. If Scott wouldn't work with her, she'd find her own way.

First thing tomorrow, she'd hand-deliver Victor's survey and record their conversation about the bribe on her phone.

And then, she'd take it to the chief at the police station.

* * *

Maddie announced her name into the shiny silver intercom, and the white iron gates to Victor's mansion slid open. She drove through and parked next to the five-car garage. The opulence he'd purchased at the price of the Native Americans' ancestry made her stomach roil.

Obviously, she should have asked for more money to fake the survey. Didn't matter. She never intended to take it anyway. Scott may not want her help, but if she recorded Victor admitting to the bribe, that might be enough for the police to put him away. Maybe then, Scott could move on with his life and at last be free of the guilt he carried over his brother's death. No matter what, she loved him enough to want that for him.

She glanced at Gina's car parked nearby. In broad daylight, with other people around, Maddie should be safe enough. Victor wouldn't have any reason to suspect her. After a deep breath, she turned on the recording app and stuffed her phone in her pocket. She snatched a folder from the passenger seat, opened the door, and got out.

A chilly breeze blew the morning mist from the lake. Swans floated in the turquoise water, and the scent of pine laced the air. Such beauty amidst the ugliness of Victor.

Tugging her light jacket shut, she climbed the concrete stairs to ring the bell. Gina opened the door. Dressed in a dark suit with matching pumps, she gave Maddie a nod. "Mr. Mole is expecting you. Follow me."

Gina led Maddie through the expansive hall with a humongous crystal chandelier and gold framed landscape paintings that looked like Renoir's work. Hell, they probably were originals. Gina's heels clicked on the marble floor as Maddie scuffed along in her boots. With any luck, she'd leave nasty mud marks. Her pulse picked up its pace as they ventured further into the massive mansion.

When Gina pushed open an office door, Maddie entered. Victor sat behind a desk, talking on the phone. He didn't bother to stand or acknowledge her presence. In a spacious room, he still filled the place, dwarfing the oversize furniture.

Gina gestured to the chair across from him. Maddie took a seat as Victor waved Gina away like a pesky fly. She left, closing the door behind her. Whatever the jerk paid her must be a fortune for her to put up with him. Arrogant prick.

Victor hung up, folded his arms on the desk, and leaned forward. "Have you finally brought me what I've been waiting for?"

His dark eyes bored into hers, harsh lines wrinkled at the corners. He reeked of some high-end cologne. So unlike Scott's clean, fresh scent. God, stay focused. She slid the folder to him.

He opened it and read the counterfeit report.

Maddie's palms sweated. "This satisfies my end of the bargain. I've falsified the report. Now, the money you promised?"

Victor's gaze shot up. He rounded the desk and yanked her out of the chair.

"You think you can play me?" he sneered, as he ripped her jacket off and shook it. Her cell phone flew out of the pocket and crashed to the floor.

Panic gripped her throat. She glanced down. The screen was cracked and blank. Was it still recording?

Victor brought his face closer and narrowed his eyes. "You'd better hope you come up clean." His sneer turned into a vicious smile. "I might enjoy this."

"I don't know what you—"

"Shut the fuck up." He released her and took a step back. "Take off the shirt and pants."

Her mouth went dry. "Excuse me?"

"I wanna make sure you're not wearing a wire. Strip." He crossed his arms and planted his feet wide.

Goosebumps popped up on her arms. "I'm not wearing a wire. I need this money. Why would I double-cross you and risk losing it?"

"I'm not taking any chances."

She glanced at the door. Would Gina do anything if she screamed?

He snorted. "This is a soundproof room. No one's coming." His lecherous gaze traveled down her body. "At least not yet."

A wave of nausea rolled in her stomach. She never should have come alone.

"Do it, or I'll do it for you."

She had no choice. Forcing herself to remain impassive, she whipped off her T-shirt and slid out of her jeans. Her face burned as he came closer and peered down her bra. His foul coffee and cigar breath all but choked her.

Her insides trembled, but she bit down on her molars and kept from shaking. He could do anything he wanted, and no one would hear.

He stroked a fat finger from the middle of her cleavage up to the bottom of her chin and tilted her head up. His ugly cow tongue came out and slid over his top lip. "Looks like your lucky day."

She struggled to find her voice. "Are you done?"

"For now." He flicked her chin and went back to sit behind the desk.

Relief flooded her body. She snagged her clothes and took her time putting them on as if being strip-searched was nothing new.

Someone knocked.

"It's unlocked," Victor called.

Gina came in. She glanced at the cell phone and jacket on the floor but didn't say anything. Maddie picked them both up.

"The Army Corps has affirmed receipt of the field survey report," Gina said. "Anything else you need?"

Victor grabbed the folder Maddie had given him and handed it to Gina. "Make sure the one they received matches this."

Gina nodded and left, once again shutting the door behind her. Thank God, Maddie had sent the fake survey over. She'd told her friend at the Corps this preliminary report would be followed by another. He trusted her enough not to ask questions.

Maddie's heart pounded. She wasn't out of the woods yet. Victor would expect her to demand her money. Otherwise, he'd be suspicious. She folded her jacket over her arm. "Now that I've done my part, when do I get paid?"

Victor rolled back his chair and opened a drawer to extract a cigar. He lit the end and took a puff. "Come back tomorrow."

Shit. What would he expect her to say? She frowned and met his gaze head on. "Why not now?"

"I don't keep cash here. You made me wait; now it's your turn."

She raised her chin. "If you come up short, I can always file a revised survey."

He stood, stuffed the cigar on the ashtray, and advanced to tower over her. "That would be a fatal mistake."

No doubt he meant it.

She locked her knees to keep them from buckling. "As long as I get paid, we're square."

"Tomorrow at ten." His lips twisted into a sardonic smile. "I'll even throw in an extra grand for the peep show today."

It would serve him right if she barfed up the coffee swirling in her stomach. "Okay. I'll be back tomorrow."

Gina opened the door. "The surveys match."

Victor nodded. "Good fucking thing."

While Gina led her to the front, Maddie fought to hold back tears. She forced herself to walk at a normal pace to her car. Damned if she'd run. He probably was watching her on a surveillance camera.

At least this would be the last time she ever saw the monster. Like hell, she'd return for the bribe money.

She drove through the gates and back onto the winding road. Her heart rate slowed with every mile she put between herself and Victor. She pulled off to the side of the road and checked her phone. When she played back the partial recording, it ended before Victor said anything incriminating.

Crap. She had no evidence to give the police. Her body shook from the pent-up terror she'd held in check while with Victor. She crossed her arms over her breasts where he'd run his nasty finger.

She'd survived. Come out of the lion's den in one piece and even given the bastard a bit of lip. But she'd failed to get the recording. If only she could help Scott find the closure and peace he sought. But she'd played her card and lost.

Her phone rang. Guess it still worked for calls.

Nikki.

Maddie cleared her throat and answered. "Hey, Nikki. What's going on?"

"I've made a decision," Nikki said, her voice firm.

This tone was new. Maddie straightened. "About what?"

"Wait. Are you okay? You sound upset."

Maddie dragged in a breath and steadied her voice. "I'm fine. Just some allergies acting up. What's going on?"

"Eric. I keep bumping into him, and he creeps me out. Even has the nerve to come to the coffee shop, after everything he did."

Prick. He would. Fresh from her own experience, Maddie's ears turned hot. She pulled back onto the road and put Nikki on speakerphone. "I hope you don't serve him."

"I can't exactly cause a scene at work."

How demeaning. Maddie hit the brakes as a squirrel darted across the road. "So, what are you going to do?"

"I'm filing for a restraining order." Satisfaction rang in Nikki's tone.

"Good. You deserve to live your life without him bothering you."

"Well, I figured this way if he does come around, I can get him arrested. I'm tired of hiding and worrying."

Maddie checked the rearview mirror. Nikki wasn't the only one with bad men popping up out of nowhere. "Why stop at the restraining order? You still have the bruises to prove you were assaulted."

"Do you think it's too late to press charges?"

"I don't know. I could ask Sco...um...Kaitlyn, I mean." Conversations with Scott were over.

"No. I'll find out myself."

Huh. This wasn't the same Nikki who had cowered under a hoodie and hid for several days. "What made you change your mind about going to the police?"

Nikki sighed. "Hope."

"What do you mean?"

"My brother. Now that he's out of jail, I have family around. I'm not alone anymore."

"Didn't Zach tell you to stay away from him?" Maddie slowed as she approached her apartment complex.

"Yes, but he sent me more money. I'm gonna pay him back—"

"I know you will. What else did he say?"

"He said to hang in there because he thought soon we could spend time together again. Maybe even share an apartment. I'm so excited. I've missed him so much."

Maddie parked and turned off the engine. Nikki had made a breakthrough. Finally, she was taking control of her life. "I'm so happy and proud of you, girl. It's about time you stuck up for yourself."

"Well, I'm not as strong as you, but I'm trying."

Nikki wouldn't think Maddie was so strong if she'd seen her shaking a few minutes ago. "What you're doing takes guts. Let me know what the police say."

"I will. Thanks."

Maddie hung up and rolled her shoulders. She might not have a recording, but she had the real field survey. Nikki would stick it to Eric as Maddie sent Victor packing.

Time for the women to dish out some payback.

CHAPTER 31

VICTOR STARED at the now-empty parking spot vacated by Cooper's car. He'd been tempted to bend her over the desk and fuck her senseless. Show that belligerent bitch who was in charge. Only he had more pressing matters at hand.

She wasn't in the same league as him. Like he'd be stupid enough to admit to a bribe. The way she'd questioned him had set off warning signals. Comical and pitiful. The strip search had been fun, mostly because it humiliated the whore and put her in her place.

She'd dared to threaten him with a revised alternate survey. What bullshit. His blood heated. Time to eliminate her. No loose ends.

He hit the intercom. "Is Eric here yet?"

"Yes. I'll send him in," Gina said.

He placed the cigar on the ashtray and sat. Eric sidled in, hands in his faded jeans pockets. His gaze dashed around the room. "I did good last night, right? Got that expensive piece for you that the cop told me about?"

"You're still alive, aren't you?" Victor picked up the cigar. The blade Eric had stolen was already shipped to the new buyer on the black market, who had coughed up a huge chunk of money for the object. Once Victor held the finalized building permit, he could dig on his property and get back in the business for real. First, he had to clean up shop. "I have another job for you."

Eric cocked his head and sat. "What?"

"I need you to arrange a fatal accident."

"What?" Eric's jaw dropped. "You mean like I gotta kill someone?"

"Yes. I don't care how, but it needs to look like an accident."

Eric's face paled. He shook his head. "No, no, man. I never killed no one before."

Pussy. Not surprising. "If you set it up right, you won't even be there when it happens."

Eric squinted. "Wait. No shooting or knifing someone?"

"That sure as shit wouldn't appear to be an accident." Stupid fuck. Victor blew out a puff of smoke.

"I might be able to do that." Eric rubbed his hands together. "Yeah, yeah, I got it now. A mollytok cocktail right through the bedroom window. Bam."

Mollytok. He must mean Molotov. Victor's teeth hurt from grinding. He slammed a fist on the table.

Eric jumped and blinked.

Victor huffed out a breath and leaned forward. "How would a flaming bottle thrown through a window look like a fucking accident?"

Eric blinked again and clasped his hands together. "Right. I gotta maybe make a toaster catch fire, or a faulty wire or something. That's a better plan?"

Halle-fucking-luja. He'd seen the light. "Yes. I don't need details, just results."

"Who is the person? I mean the one I gotta…take care of."

"Maddie Cooper."

"Whoa." Eric jumped to his feet and paced. "She's a bitch, but I don't know about killing her."

"Well, I do, because now I've got another problem." Victor picked up his letter opener and tapped it against his palm.

"What?"

"Now that you know, you're a liability." He pointed the sharp end at Eric. "A risk. A loose end."

Eric stopped pacing and held up his hands. "Oh no. I wouldn't tell anyone what you said. You don't have to worry about me."

"I agree. You won't be able to say a thing." That was the goddamned truth. Just give him an excuse to off the asshole.

The last bit of color left Eric's face. Victor opened a drawer and drew out a wad of bills. He shoved them across the desk. "For last night, and part of tonight's work."

Eric snatched the money, eyes wide at the stack of hundred-dollar-bills.

Always so eager when it came to cash. This would be a true test. Victor drew out two more stacks and slapped them on the desk. "Twice this tomorrow when the job's done."

"Holy shit." Eric's eyes bulged.

Yeah. Fucking right. Victor flipped the edges of the bills like a stack of cards.

"I'll do it." Eric bobbed his head. "If I'm not there, I don't gotta see any blood, right?"

"Whatever, but it has to be done tonight. Got it?"

"Tonight?" Eric gulped. "Doesn't give me much time."

"Then why are you still here?" Victor tossed the money packs at Eric, who caught them.

Licking his lips, Eric rubbed the top bills. "Hey, you really hate her, right?"

"What's your point?"

Eric's eyes squinted to narrow slits. "If I find a way to, you know, do it that hurts, too. Would that be worth more?"

Mind-boggling. Victor kicked his chair back and pointed to the door. "Get the fuck out of here."

"Right, boss." Eric turned tail, stuffed the money in his pockets, and hurried out.

Victor stubbed his cigar out.

Mollytok? Fuckin' A.

CHAPTER 32

SCOTT TOSSED a sandwich wrapper into the trashcan by the police station door. Sitting outside in the fresh air to eat lunch had done nothing to change his mood. Maddie would leave soon for Colorado, and he'd probably never see her again. Didn't matter that he loved her and only wanted to keep her safe. His heart constricted. She'd had enough. He'd snuffed out the last glimmer of hope in her eyes. For good.

At least she would be far away from Victor. She could finally file her survey once they arrested him. It shouldn't be long. Eric had taken the bait and stolen the fake Clovis blade. The plans were coming together. Scott glanced at his watch. He had another video chat set up with Zach in ten minutes.

Scott headed to Lee's office. Lee sat at his desk, a hand over his eyes, head down with the phone to his ear. He glanced up when Scott entered and gave him a shit-doesn't-get-worse-than-this look.

Lee waved to the seat across from him and spoke into the phone, "Hold on; I'll put you on speaker. Scott's here."

Since Lee hadn't addressed Scott as Detective, the call must be personal. Scott slid into the seat and leaned forward.

Lee took a deep breath. "Bill Keeler's on the phone."

Bill worked for the DEA in Utah where Justin had died. Scott had flown out and met him. Decent guy. But he never came up with anything other than an overdose as the cause of death.

"Bill, how about filling Scott in?"

Bill's voice came across the speakerphone. "Scott, I have some new information on your brother's death."

"I'm listening." Scott inched closer to the phone, his pulse ratcheting.

"Justin's tent-mate came back to town. His name is Nathan Griffin. He went to the police and said Justin was murdered, by one of Mole's guys."

Scott's breath caught in his throat. "What?"

"Apparently, Justin had cleaned up and tried to snitch on Mole. Thought he was working with a DEA agent, but Mole had his own undercover fake operatives. He sniffed Justin out and ordered a hit on him."

Scott's world spun out of focus. Mole had killed his brother. "I don't understand. Justin died of a heroin overdose."

"Yes, but we now believe it was forced on him. Griffin said he was coming back from taking a piss and heard someone threatening Justin inside the tent. The guy told Justin he'd messed with the wrong man, and Mole made snitches pay."

Lee picked up the paperweight and closed a fist around it. "Did Griffin see anything?"

Bill sighed. "No. He said it happened fast. Before he could think what to do, the man came out, and Griffin took off. It was too late for Justin."

Scott's ears burned. "Let me get this straight. You're saying Justin had cleaned up and thought he was working with an undercover DEA agent, but he turned out to be one of Mole's men?"

"Yeah. That explains why we didn't know he was an informant. Justin wanted to help put Mole away."

"Why did Griffin disappear?" Scott pressed his fingers to his forehead.

"He was worried they'd come after him, thinking he knew something. He's pretty torn up over the whole thing. Justin had gotten through to Griffin enough to convince him to stop doing drugs, and then guilt ate him up for running away."

"Is he willing to testify against Mole?" Lee asked.

Bill cleared his throat. "Yes. That's one of the reasons he came back. Said he wanted to do what he could to make Mole pay for killing Justin. But Griffin admits he was high at the time, and let's face it, we don't have any physical evidence. Not an overwhelmingly convincing witness."

Scott glanced at Lee, who shook his head and said, "Still, it's another piece we can add to our case."

"Yes. I'll proceed on this end. Keep me posted on yours. And Scott?"

"Yeah?"

"I'm really sorry," Bill said.

"Thanks."

Lee hung up. "Are you okay?"

"No." Scott stood and went to the window. He fisted a hand. "Mole killed my brother. Justin was trying to do the right thing and paid for it with his life."

"We're going to get that son of a bitch."

The relief over finding out that Justin had been clean was overpowered by the rage at Mole for killing him. Scott closed his eyes for a second before stepping to the door. "I need a minute."

"I understand."

He strode outside, sat on a bench under a tall oak, and buried his face in his hands. Justin must have suspected something and called Scott for help. His gut had been right. Justin never did heroin. Mole had to figure no one would suspect a drug overdose to be murder. Not in an area full of tweakers.

This went beyond personal now. A heaviness settled on his shoulders. Whatever it took, he'd put Mole away forever.

He stood, brushed his hands together, and headed back to the station. Lee glanced up when he entered the office. "Anything I can do?"

"Yeah. Start the conference. Time to nail that piece of shit."

Lee held Scott's gaze. "We're going to get him."

"Damn right."

Zach's face appeared on the screen.

As always, his resemblance to Justin punched a hole in Scott's heart. Especially this time.

"What's the latest?" Lee asked.

"I have a meeting set up tomorrow night at eight with Mole on the property like we talked about."

Scott slid his chair a few inches for a better angle. "What do you expect from it?"

Zach shifted his attention to Scott. "He's supposed to bring me a gun. Insisted I keep one on me if I wanted to work with him. It's his way of making sure I stay his bitch. An ex-con can't carry, and he knows it. My fingerprints on a weapon would land me back in jail."

"What did you say about it?" Scott asked.

"I tried to argue at first, to make it look legit, but in the end, I agreed. He said it was his business, and he wouldn't keep anyone on who didn't have the means to protect his interests."

Zach was one cool customer. He always came up with the right answers. Scott clicked his pen top. "Nice work."

"He said he'd give me the address and instructions for the next meth shipment." Zach's face filled the screen as he leaned closer. "This one is major. He hasn't trusted me with anything big until now."

Lee drummed his fingers on the desk. "We'll record him giving you the information and then bust the place. It should be all over at that point."

Unless something went wrong. And things did. Zach could end up dead like Justin. Scott squeezed the pen. "Listen, Zach. I told you before we couldn't make promises about your safety. Are you sure you're in on this?"

Zach's eyes held steady. "No way I'm backing off. I want this prick as badly as you do."

Impossible, but Scott just nodded. "Okay. I'll be monitoring from the woods. If you have any suspicion he's onto you, say, 'I think we're being watched.' Then point to the surveillance camera in the tree. It will buy you some time and convince him you aren't in on it."

"Not a bad idea. Worst case, we abort the meeting and set up for another place and time." Zach sat back.

"No, Zach. Worst case, he shoots you," Scott said.

"I can handle myself." Zach's face hardened.

Invincible youth. Men Zach's age thought they were indestructible. It's why they weren't afraid to enlist in the army and go to war.

Lee shifted in his seat. "Let us know if anything changes. Otherwise, we're on."

"You got it. Later, guys."

The screen went blank. Someone knocked on the door, and Scott opened it.

Nikki stood on the threshold, pale, but with a determined look in her eyes. The bruises on her face had turned yellow and faded, but the marks were still there.

Soon, very soon, Eric would pay for everything he'd done. Scott shot a glance at Lee. No way Nikki could have overheard their conversation outside the soundproofed room.

Lee gave a quick shake of his head. He crossed to her. "Hi, Nikki. What brings you here?"

"I came to file an application for a restraining order against Eric."

Scott stiffened. Not now. They needed Eric to reel in Mole.

Lee propped a hip on top of the desk and waved at the seat Scott had vacated. She slid into it and clutched her purse in her lap.

"What's Eric doing?" Lee asked.

"He keeps harassing me, and I'm tired of it." She fidgeted with the strap of her bag. "Maddie says I should charge him with assault."

Scott gritted his teeth. Maddie would be in the middle of things. Damn. Nikki was finally standing up for herself, and now they would have to stall her. Scott couldn't arrest Eric for assault when they were so close to nailing him and Mole for the drugs and black-market trade.

Lee pushed off the desk. "I'll get this started in a second. Scott, a word?"

"Sure, Chief." He followed Lee outside the office to the far corner of the station.

"This throws a wrench in things." Lee shook his head.

Scott spoke in a low tone. "We have to follow through for Nikki, but now's not the time to put Eric in jail."

Lee nodded. "What do you suggest?"

Scott blew out a breath. They couldn't risk Nikki's safety by dragging their feet. "The judge is gonna need probable cause for the restraining order, which should go hand in hand with the assault charge. Both require us to investigate before we file. What's the best way to process this?"

"I'm golfing with the judge tomorrow. I'll talk to him on the side. I think I can get him to issue the restraining order based on Nikki's testimony and some supporting statements from others. Doesn't hurt that Eric already has a record." Lee glanced at his office.

"If things go as planned, we should have what we need on Mole within the next day or so. I'll start the assault charge paperwork, but hold off picking Eric up," Scott said.

Lee rubbed his neck. "Makes sense."

"Mainly, we need to protect Nikki from the asshole. If the judge cooperates, this will work."

"I'm with you."

They returned to the office, and Lee brought some forms up on the computer screen. "Let's get the request for the restraining order in place and start the paperwork for the assault charge. That will take a little time to process."

Scott glanced at Nikki's hands clamped tight on her purse. Poor kid.

"You got this, Chief?" Scott picked a folder up from the table.

"Yeah, go ahead. I'll be here. Stop back in a bit."

"Will do." Scott touched Nikki on the shoulder. "You're doing the right thing. Hang in there, and if Eric bothers you, call us."

"Thanks, I will." She gave him a weak smile.

He headed to the station door. So much evil from anyone who worked for Mole. Now, more than ever, Scott burned to finish what Justin had started and paid for with his life.

He gazed at the bright blue sky when he stepped out of the building. A bird sang and a light breeze blew the sweet scent of blossoming apple trees across his face. Nothing but beauty surrounded him.

Nothing but pain and anger lived inside.

CHAPTER 33

PACKED boxes lined the wall of Maddie's apartment. The sooner she got away from Victor, the better. Still shaken from her earlier encounter, she couldn't keep her mind from the humiliating strip search. He'd meant to take her down a notch, and it had worked. Much as she hated to admit it, Scott was right. She had underestimated Victor's evil streak. If he'd caught her recording him, she might not be alive. She rubbed her arms to warm the chill that ran through her. Tomorrow, she'd be gone. Good riddance to the monster.

She snatched her list from the counter and headed for the door. Someone knocked, causing her to jump. She checked the peephole.

Nikki.

Maddie yanked the door open. "I thought you were going to the station to talk to the police?"

"I did. Can I come in?"

"Of course." Maddie stepped back.

Nikki entered, face taut, her shoulders hitched with tension.

"What's wrong?" Maddie pulled out a kitchen chair and took Nikki's hand to guide her to sit. "Did you file the assault charge?"

"Yeah, I guess. I mean, I filled out some paperwork, but they said it would take time. They asked me questions to get the restraining order in process."

True it would take time, but the assault charge should support the restraining order. Scott might not want to arrest Eric until he had Mole. Poor Nikki caught in the middle, but a hard spot for the police as well.

"I'm so scared. I don't know what to do." Nikki pressed her fingers to her lips.

That asshole better not have hurt her again. "Did Eric—"

"No, not Eric." She waved a hand. "Zach."

"Oh?" Maddie dropped into a chair next to Nikki. "What about Zach?"

"Here's the thing. I passed him the other day pulling into the driveway of that hotshot developer's mansion, Mole. What do you know about him?"

Maddie blinked. God, more than she ever cared to share. The room of doom popped into her head. "Is Zach okay? Victor Mole is bad news, to say the least."

Wrinkles creased over Nikki's forehead. "I knew it. And he lied to me."

"What do you mean? Who lied? About what?"

"Zach." Nikki leaned back in the chair and looked up at the ceiling. "I called him because, I don't know, I thought maybe he got a job cutting the lawn or something." She ran a hand through her bright-pink hair and dropped her gaze to Maddie. "He denied being there. Said I was wrong."

"Well, could you have been?" Maddie's gut told her otherwise.

"No. I saw my brother behind the wheel. He lied to me."

Maddie waited, not sure what to say.

Nikki hugged her arms across her body. "We've always been honest with each other. No matter how bad things got...he shot it straight."

Maybe Zach's time in jail had turned him into a real criminal. He'd been surrounded by them. How horrible if he'd hooked up with Mole.

"Maddie?"

"What? Sorry, I was just thinking. Go on."

"My conversation with Zach didn't go well." Nikki shook her head. "I kept asking questions, and the more upset I got, the more he clammed up. He told me not to worry and he had things under control. Said what he was doing would buy his freedom. It would be over soon and that I should trust him."

Maddie tilted her head. Zach's early release, him telling Nikki to stay away, and now the connection with Mole. He had to be working as an informant to buy his freedom. Otherwise, he wouldn't deny a legitimate job with Mole.

A tear slipped down Nikki's cheek. "He said if anything happened to him I'd be okay because he has accounts set up for me."

"Oh, Nikki." Maddie moved from the chair to kneel next to her. Lucky jumped from his bed, trotted over, and leaned into the hug, whining as if he understood.

Nikki sobbed into her hands. "I don't want money. I want my brother. He's all I ha-have."

Tears blurred Maddie's eyes. She slung an arm around Nikki, who cried on her shoulder.

Nikki sniffled, raised her head, and dabbed at her eyes with a tissue. "I think he's working as a snitch for the police. When he got out, he hinted about his new job being dangerous. I can't lose him. Why is he doing this? He was safer in jail than whatever he's gotten into."

If she only knew. There had to be someone else the police could find to plant as a snitch besides Nikki's only living relative. Cops trained for this stuff. Zach's time in jail might have made him street smart, but it wouldn't prepare him for undercover work.

Nikki hiccupped. "All I can do is wait and hope my brother doesn't die. God, I can't stand it."

"I'm so sorry. This has to be hard. Can I help in any way?"

"Maybe...I mean...it's obvious you and Scott are close. Would he listen if you asked him to let Zach out of whatever deal he made? He has to be working for them. Nothing else makes sense." Hope lit in her eyes.

Maddie's throat tightened. "Scott and I are done. Even if I tried to talk to him, he'd never listen to me."

"It's worth a try. He might be able to convince Zach to walk away. Or...work out some other deal. Anything is better than nothing." She let out a shaky breath. "I...I don't know what else to do."

Damn it. After telling Scott not to contact her again, Maddie didn't want to be the one to start a conversation, but Nikki was desperate. Now more than ever, Maddie understood how dangerous Mole could be.

As if sensing her hesitation, Nikki placed a hand on her arm and squeezed. "Please, I'm so scared for him."

Well, crap. She couldn't say no. "I'll try, but I really don't expect much to come from it."

"Thank you. Thank you so much." Nikki grabbed a napkin from the table and blew her nose. "I'm sorry about you and Scott. I thought—"

"It's okay. I'm moving on." Maddie rolled her shoulders and glanced away.

"You leave tomorrow night, right?"

"Yeah, and I have a lot to do, so I'd better get down to the station now if I want to catch Scott." Maddie stood.

"I hope he listens to you. I really appreciate this."

"Don't get your hopes up. Try to remember: no matter what, your brother is tough. If anyone's going to be okay, it's him." Maddie led Nikki to the door.

"Wish I knew for sure. Please call me as soon as you find out anything."

"I will." Maddie gave a quick hug. "And I'm proud of you for standing up to Eric."

Nikki half-smiled. "At least there's that."

Maddie shut the door and closed her eyes. Nikki had been through enough and needed Zach in her life.

Damn it all. Time to have a conversation with Scott.

* * *

Maddie parked next to Scott's Impala. Perfect. Face-to-face would be better than a phone call, which he might or might not have answered given their last exchange. She pushed the car door open, slung her purse over her shoulder, and marched into the police station. The outer area was empty, but voices came from Chief Lee's office.

She strode across the room and rapped on the partially open door. The chief and Scott glanced up. Scott's eyes widened. He leaped to his feet. His gaze raked her body as if looking for injuries. "You okay?"

"Yes." She had injuries all right, but not the visible kind. The kind that made her traitorous heart compress at the sight of him.

Forget it. This was about her friend.

"Why are you here?" Scott asked.

She thrust a hip out. "Nikki came by today very upset. What's going on with her brother? And don't bullshit me. I know he's working with you."

Scott raised an eyebrow and crossed his arms. "Thought we were done communicating."

"Yeah, well, I'm making an exception."

He stepped past her to a nearby desk, shrugged his suit coat off, and draped it on the back of a chair. "No need. You have a plane to catch, and I have things to do."

"Oh, you've made that abundantly clear." She followed him. "I know your priorities." Wait, he was trying to throw her off. Get into a fight about their relationship to avoid her question.

Nice try.

She straightened. "You're right. I'm leaving tomorrow, and this has nothing to do with us. I want to know why you are letting Zach, Nikki's only living family member, put himself in danger."

Scott gave her a cool look. "This is police business and none of yours."

Those jade eyes of his could frost an inferno. Well, he had one right in front of him. "Police business, huh? Is this where you make the rules and everyone follows them?" She threw her purse on the chair. "You think your rules are going to keep anyone safe from that bastard? He's a... beast, and you can't let Zach anywhere near him."

Damn her voice and body for shaking.

Scott's eyes narrowed. "I've been telling you this all along, yet you insisted on doing that goddamn survey for him right under his nose. And now... Hold on. Why do you suddenly believe me?"

Her nerves fired, still raw from her earlier encounter with Victor. The stench of his cigar breath as he'd scraped his ugly finger up her neck still lingered in her nostrils. She shook her head and cursed the blur that came to her eyes. "Because I've seen the bastard in action, okay?"

Scott tensed. "What do you mean?"

"Nothing. This isn't about me." She blinked hard to force the tears away.

"Like hell. Tell me what happened to change your mind."

She sucked in a breath and huffed it out. "I took Victor's precious, fake survey to him and tried to get a tape of his confession about the bribe."

Scott flinched and his eyes grew wide. "You what?"

"Well, you wouldn't let me use your special"—she waved her hand in the air—"DEA stuff, so I tried to record him on my phone."

"Your phone?" His voice amplified. "What the hell were you thinking?"

"I was thinking someone needs to stop him, and I had the perfect opportunity."

Scott pinched the bridge of his nose. "The DEA has devoted two years of undercover investigations with multiple agents, here, in the Southwest, and Mexico to nail this bastard." He lowered his hand to glare at her. "But what we failed to realize was all we needed was you, singlehandedly, with a cell phone recording, to take him down?"

"It could have worked."

"Damn it, Maddie." He paced the room. "Even if you got a full confession, there are so many reasons why that recording would be useless. You have no idea how the law works. Do you think..." He stopped next to her and took a deep breath. "Never mind. Just tell me what happened."

Her insides vibrated, boiled again over Victor's violation. "He didn't catch me recording him, and he didn't say anything incriminating before he...he..."

"He what?" Scott's asked, his voice dangerously low.

The humiliation of standing in front of Victor in her bra and underwear flooded back. Hot blood raced to her face. She swallowed. "I guess he got suspicious when I asked him about the bribe money for the fake survey. So, he st-strip searched me."

"What?" Scott gripped the back of a chair, raw fury in his eyes. "He's fucking dead." In a low tone, between gritted teeth, he asked, "What exactly did he do to you?"

Jittery energy pulsed through her, and she couldn't control the tremble of her lip. "He tore off my coat and shook it. My phone screen cracked when it hit the ground, so he didn't know I was recording."

The tips of Scott's ears turned bright red. His gaze intensified.

Her throat dry, Maddie croaked out, "He made me take off my clothes while he watched, and then he searched me for a wire."

Scott's chest heaved as his face darkened. She'd seen him angry before, but this went beyond. His fingers turned white from his grip on the edge of the chair, and a vein in his forehead bulged. He picked up the chair and whacked it down. A broken leg skittered across the floor, as he stormed out of the station.

Lee appeared in his doorway and frowned. Maddie reached for the chair to set it back up on its remaining three legs. Scott had never been violent before. Not in her presence. Steamed, yes. Pissed, sure. But never violent.

"Just leave it." Lee picked up the two pieces.

Well, angry or not, she still had to convince Scott to get Zach off the case. She grabbed her purse and headed to the door.

"Maddie?" Lee waved the chair leg at the station entrance. "I'd leave him alone, too."

She shook her head. "He's not the only one who's upset."

Outside, Scott stood with his back to the building, hands fisted against his hips. She stalked up behind him. "We're not finished with this conversation."

He held up a hand without turning. "Don't push me right now."

God, his voice. So hostile. She dug her heels in. "I'm not leaving until you tell me you can get Zach out of whatever he signed up for."

Scott swung around and faced her. "You are done meddling. Understand?" He took a step closer. "Don't you go near Mole again. Stay away from him and get on that fucking plane tomorrow night. Are we clear?"

Telling her what to do again. "No. I want to know Zach is going to be okay. He's not trained like you guys. Victor—"

"Stop it. Zach's a grown man who makes his own decisions. Now butt out and leave." He raised a bloodied hand and gestured to her car in the lot. "Now."

She gazed at his scraped knuckles. They looked like he'd punched a tree or something. God. Her stomach lurched. The man he used to be was gone. Lost in a world of darkness and pain. Damn it, she wanted her Scott back.

"Look what this man has driven you to." She snatched his wrist and gazed at the bloody scratches. "He's a maniac, and you've lost all sense of reason. You'll stop at nothing to get him. It's consumed you."

In one swift motion, Scott pulled out of her grip. "I'm telling you for the last time: stay out of my business."

As soon as he promised not to drag Nikki's brother into the vortex. "You've given up your life, but Zach hasn't, and Nikki needs him."

Scott's eyes flared as he rocked on his heels like a volcano ready to explode. "I won't discuss this with you."

"Really, because I would think you, of all people, would know what it means to lose your only family. Look what it's done to you." She waved at his bloodied hand. "You might be breathing, but you're not alive. From what I've seen, you died right along with your brother."

Scott stilled.

Oh God. She slapped a hand to her mouth.

A deep, primal pain radiated from his eyes.

Too late to take back the words. She'd pulled the scab off his deepest wound. Regret wrenched her gut. "Scott, I—"

"Save it." He held up both hands. "You're right. I'm a callous bastard."

"No, I'm sorry. I didn't mean it." She reached for his arm, but his eyes flashed a warning, and she jerked back.

She'd gone too far in bringing up Justin. The pain on Scott's face made her heart bleed.

His expression went cold. "You said if I walked out your door we'd never communicate again. I wish you'd kept your end of the bargain."

He pivoted on his heel and strode to his car without a backward glance.

A small sob escaped her lips. What a mess. She'd let Nikki down by failing to keep Zach out of danger.

And to Scott...just like his family, Maddie was dead to him.

CHAPTER 34

MADDIE OPENED HER APARTMENT DOOR. Lucky cantered over and whined.

"What's wrong, guy?" He didn't chase his tail like usual or lick her frantically. Maybe he was sick again. A few hours ago, when she'd returned from the station, he'd gobbled his dinner down like always. She crouched to check his eyes. Clear and normal. He might need to pee. She'd been gone for most of the night running errands and buying boxes for the move.

She grabbed his leash and took him out, careful to inspect the ground for any suspicious meat. God, her life had come to this.

Lucky finished doing his business, and she walked him around the building. Kaitlyn approached from the parking lot, dressed in her police uniform. "Hey, Maddie."

"Hi, Kaitlyn. What are you doing here? It's late."

Lucky yipped and begged to be petted. Kaitlyn scratched under his chin. "Lee asked me to stop by and check on you."

Huh. He had to have overheard her telling Scott about the strip search and Victor. Maybe even witnessed her argument with Scott outside the station. Not like Scott was going to swing by to make sure she slept well. Not after what she'd said to him. He'd never forgive her, and she couldn't blame him. The sooner she left, the happier he'd be.

Kaitlyn frowned. "What's wrong?"

"Nothing. Come on up for a minute. I've had a shitty day and need a glass of wine." And a little company to distract her from thoughts of Scott. She glanced at Kaitlyn's uniform shirt. "You're on duty, though, right?"

"Just getting off."

"Good. Wanna join me?"

"Sure."

They climbed the steps as the sun sank behind the surrounding woods. When they got inside, Lucky dashed around the room sniffing the ground.

"Oh, wow. You got rid of most of your furniture." Kaitlyn glanced around the room.

"Yeah. Nikki's friend came over with a truck. She doesn't have money to buy stuff for her apartment, and I'm happy to help. She didn't need a desk and already had a couch and table, so Goodwill is coming for them tomorrow."

"That was really nice of you to give her so much." Kailyn's gaze went to the dog, who kept circling the room. "What's Lucky doing?"

"I don't know. He's been acting strange ever since I got home." Maddie grabbed a bottle of wine from the refrigerator and poured two glasses. She handed one to Kaitlyn. A gust of wind blew in through the open window and the papers on her desk scattered about. Maddie went over to collect the printed-out copies of the real survey. She'd send that in before bed and pack up her computer and files. The report would take at least a day to process and by then, she'd be on her plane.

"Maddie?"

She glanced over at Kaitlyn, who raised an eyebrow. "You seem kind of out of it. Is something wrong?"

Too many things to name. "No. I'm just thinking about what I need to do before I leave tomorrow night."

"Want me to stop by and help you pack? I'm working the late shift."

Maddie shook her head. "No. All I have left is a few drawers in the kitchen to box up." She pointed to her wine glass. "Grab that for me and come sit down?"

"Sure." Kaitlyn brought the drinks over, took a seat, and sipped hers.

"I don't mean to pry or anything, but Scott was strung tight when I saw him. Is everything okay?"

Kaitlyn and Tom had been around them enough to know Scott and Maddie had something going, but she'd never openly talked about it. "I really can't say. We aren't on speaking terms right now, and with me moving..." She shrugged and took a swig of the wine. "I don't suppose he, uh, said anything about me?"

"No. In fact, when Lee asked me to stop by, Scott..." Kaitlyn grimaced. "Never mind. I know relationships are tough."

Scott had what? Maybe glared at Lee, or cursed under his breath, or threw darts at a picture of Maddie he'd hung on the station wall. Stupid of her to even ask the question. She took another healthy sip of wine.

"We're sure going to miss you around here," Kaitlyn said.

Maddie glanced around the almost-empty room. Same story as always—on the move again. "Yeah, I'll miss you guys, too. Am I leaving Tom in good hands?"

A blush crept up Kaitlyn's neck. Her phone rang before she could answer. She glanced at the screen. Her face turned scarlet red. "Um, it's Tom. Do you mind if I—"

"Of course not. Answer the man." Maddie stood and strolled to the kitchen to give Kaitlyn some privacy, although ten feet didn't provide much. She opened drawers to check what she needed to pack up in the morning, as Kaitlyn spoke in low tones that still carried across the room.

"I'm sorry, I have to cancel. Lee asked me to—"

"Kaitlyn?" Maddie hurried from the kitchen.

Kaitlyn looked up. "Let me call you back, Tom." She pulled the phone away from her ear. "What?"

"I didn't mean to eavesdrop, but are you canceling a date because Lee told you to hang out here with me?"

"I enjoy spending time with you. It's not like that."

Maddie sighed. "I don't doubt it, but there's no reason for you to change your plans. I'm going to bed soon anyway."

"I don't know. He seemed worried about you."

Lee was a good guy. "Well, I'm fine." She ran a hand through her hair. "Honestly, I'm dead tired and have a long day ahead of me tomorrow. I appreciate you stopping in, but I'm headed to bed. Please call Tom back and go out with him."

Kaitlyn cocked her head. "Are you sure?"

"Positive."

"Okay, then." A smile tugged at the corners of her mouth. "We did sorta have…special plans tonight."

If Kaitlyn's face got any redder, she'd burst into flames. Holy shit, they were going to have sex, and judging from her reaction, maybe for the first time. Maddie grinned. "You'd better keep your *date*, then."

"What?" Kaitlyn giggled.

Yeah, they were going to do the nasty. "Get out of here. Tom's waited long enough for this."

"Him? What about me?" Kaitlyn stood and brought her glass over to the sink.

"Amen to that." Maddie laughed and then glanced down. It would be a very long time before she ever had sex again. Someone should.

Kaitlyn picked up her purse and stopped in front of Maddie. "I'm going to miss you."

Tears burned in the back of Maddie's eyes. She moved around so much that she never made close friends. Over a year in Tuckerton was the longest she'd stayed anywhere, and she'd grown close to the people in town. She could only imagine what it would be like to settle down, see someone's kids grow up, and share barbecues. Not in the cards for her.

"Back at ya. Now, go change clothes, and then get it."

"What makes you think I'm going to change?" A mischievous light twinkled in Kaitlyn's eyes.

Maddie snorted. "Oh God. TMI."

Kaitlyn gave her a hug, and warmth curved around Maddie's heart. Tough-as-nails Kaitlyn wasn't a hugger. She stepped away, ruffled Lucky's head as she passed his bed, and left.

Maddie swallowed. Leaving friends was hard. Best to keep traveling. Another gust of cool air chilled the room. She strode to the window and closed it, pulling the blinds down. Her gaze dropped to the printed survey. An image of Victor's beady eyes as he'd stared at her near naked body popped into her head. Bile rose in her throat.

She sat and brought up the new survey on the computer. Victor might have been bent on intimidating her today, but she'd get the last word.

With one click of a button, maybe she'd crash his world.

She hit send.

"My work is done here." She shut off the computer and then tucked it into a case along with her files. Time to move on.

After taking Lucky out one last time, she crawled into bed. Doubtful she'd sleep with the image of Scott's tortured eyes etched in her brain. She'd said horrible things to him. The subject of his brother was off-limits, and she'd gone there anyway. No taking it back. She'd dug herself in deep.

CHAPTER 35

MADDIE STARED up at Victor from the bottom of a huge pit. Nothing but dirt all around her and no way to climb out. Desperation clawed her chest.

Eric's pasty face appeared over the edge of the hole as he stood beside Victor.

"Bury her alive." Victor's mouth twisted with a cruel smile.

The sound of a spade scooping dirt, and then earth rained down on her. She sputtered and coughed as Eric shoveled load after load into the hole. The soil filled her mouth and nostrils.

Lucky barked in the distance. Oh no. She had to get out. Her lungs burned as she breathed in clay dust that smelled like ashes. Clawing with renewed vigor, she dug her fingernails into the walls to try to climb out. The dog's barking grew louder and more insistent.

Victor's deep laugh crackled through the air and then changed to an ear-piercing screech.

Something wet and warm swiped her cheek. She opened her eyes. Lucky, front paws on the edge of her bed, barked in her face and tugged on the sleeve of her gown.

A nightmare.

She coughed and sat up. Smoke filled the room as the fire alarm screeched. Oh God. A real, live nightmare. Adrenaline spiked through her body. She sprang out of bed.

A glance at the door, and her insides quaked. Black smoke entered the hall between the kitchen and her bedroom. She'd have to pass through it to get to the front door or the fire escape in the living room. Shouldn't the sprinkler system have gone off?

Lucky whimpered and barked frantically at her feet. She dropped to her hands and knees. That's what she was supposed to do. Stop, drop, and roll. Only she shouldn't roll. Not until her clothes caught on fire.

Her brain must have frozen. She was thinking crazy shit when she needed to get the hell out.

She crawled to the bathroom and yanked a hand towel off the rack. More coughs wracked her lungs as she turned on the faucet, wet the cloth, and held it over her nose and mouth. No freaking idea if that was what she was supposed to do, but she'd seen it once on a TV show she and Scott had watched together.

Scott…she might never see him again. Pain sliced her heart.

Sweat dripped into her already blurry eyes. Lucky yapped and cried by her side as she made her way to the open bedroom door. A wave of nausea rolled up from her stomach. Pitch-black smoke filled the hall. She'd have to go into it blind, even on all fours.

When she moved toward the hall, Lucky backed away, whining, but she grabbed his collar and yanked him along with her, dropping the wet rag in the process. "Don't fight me. I have to get us out."

Her nightshirt kept catching under her knees as she tried to hurry. It stuck to her sweaty body. She dug her fingers into the shag carpet fibers to pull herself along. The smoke got thicker, and bits of lacy, red ash flew around. Tiny pricks of pain stabbed at her back and neck as embers burned through her nightshirt. At any second the fabric could ignite and burn her alive.

If she died right here, she'd never see Scott again. Never get to tell him how godawful sorry she was for everything she'd said. And that she loved him. Always had, and always would, no matter what he did to push her away.

Someone whimpered.

Had to be her.

Lucky stiffened his front legs and tried to back out of his collar. She clenched tighter and threaded her fingers through his fur. If she let go, he'd run away and never make it out. "Come on, boy. I got you."

Her high-pitched voice had to make the dog think she had no control. Almost to the living room.

A round of coughs stopped her in place. She yanked her nightshirt over her nose while attempting a deep breath. She couldn't get enough air into her lungs. The smell of burnt hair mixed with the noxious fumes from the carpet and wood.

She shot a glance at Lucky. The fur on his back was smoldering. No! She spit on the spot as best she could with a dry, parched throat. She smothered the embers, blistering her palm. "I'm sorry. Stay with me, boy. Stay with me."

A crash sounded, and flames shot from the kitchen. A gasp escaped, followed by more coughing. Her gaze went to the bright yellow streaks licking the wall as they climbed to the ceiling. The roof could cave. She had to hurry. Alarms blared in the neighboring apartments, but still no sign of help.

With the kitchen table ablaze, she couldn't get to the front door. She gulped. The fire escape was her only way out.

Another coughing fit kept her from moving. Precious time she didn't have ticked away as face against the floor, she wheezed and fought for air. Pushing back up to her knees, she scrambled and dragged Lucky with her. He buried his nose against her nightshirt and let her lead him.

As she approached the couch, a section of burning ceiling tile fell. She cried out and yanked the dog back. The afghan caught fire and flames spread along the sofa.

Lucky bucked and yelped, pulling hard against the collar to be free.

"No, Lucky. Come. You have to come with me. I won't lose you. I promise. We're in this together." She had to shout over the din of the flames devouring her apartment.

Hurry. She had to hurry.

Through the narrow passageway between the couch and the kitchen, she kept the dog close to her side and muscled her way past the blazing sofa. Her skin warmed, and her unruly curls wavered in front of her face, moved by the wind from the fire. If her hair caught, would she die fast or bubble and melt like a marshmallow on a stick?

No time for these thoughts. She had to keep moving.

Around the corner, with the window in sight, hope fought with hysteria.

If Scott were there, he'd tell her to focus. He always kept his cool under pressure. Never panicked.

Her heart jackhammered. Almost there. Three more feet and she'd be at the escape window. The raging heat from the kitchen seared her bare legs.

Lucky barked in absolute panic. His eyes bulged, and she had to double-lock her fingers through his collar to keep him close. "I got you. I got you."

She sucked another cough-laden breath of heavy smoke into her lungs as they threatened to give out. She gripped him tighter, lunged for the window, and tried to yank it up.

Didn't budge.

She had to release the dog to use two hands and fight with the window. With the inferno closing in on them, he'd stay by her side.

Unlocked, it still wouldn't open.

Lucky whined and clawed at the glass. She let out a whine of her own and wrenched the frame up with all her weight.

Nothing.

She'd have to break it.

With a frantic glance over her shoulder, she gasped. The fire had spread across the carpet, growing stronger as it consumed the floor and walls.

She grabbed her desk chair, the only thing within reach.

CHAPTER 36

SCOTT SAT on a park bench next to the police station and flipped through a file. Nothing more to do. Every aspect of the upcoming meeting with Mole was covered. Yet, he couldn't quite bring himself to go back to his apartment and see Maddie's car in the lot. She would probably be in her place packing up last-minute things to take on her one-way ticket out of his life.

Sure, she'd stung him with her words, but only because they rang true. Nothing he hadn't known all along. It was the reason he'd avoided her. She wanted the old Scott, not the new, tortured version. And she had a point. He was obsessed and would continue to be until he put Mole away. Especially now. That bastard had killed Justin.

Scott glanced at his grazed knuckles. Stupid. Hitting a tree. But the thought of the strip search…he fisted his hand. Mole would pay.

His stomach knotted. He sat straighter and cocked his head. A weird sense something was wrong made his insides tighten. He glanced at his phone. No messages or calls. Yet, he couldn't shake the feeling. Like someone was trying to get his attention.

No. It had just been a long day with a lot of bad news. He took a deep breath.

But there it was again. A gut punch that told him he needed to do something. With a frown, he shut his folder and stood. He'd always trusted his instincts, and right now, they told him to go home.

He headed to his car. The image of Maddie pleading for forgiveness stuck in his brain. She'd never meant to hurt him. He knew that. And she didn't know about the devastating news he'd gotten about Justin. But he had enough on his plate without her tossing in guilt over what might happen to Zach.

Yeah, he was fucking *aware* of the danger. It made him sick. Woke him up in the middle of the night with scenarios of what could go wrong and how it would be his fault if anything happened to the guy.

Scott flexed his fingers on the wheel. At this point, they were all in too deep. And Maddie needed to be out. Get on that goddamned plane and fly far away from Mole before he did more than play mind games with her in his office.

As Scott drove, his mood darkened. It all came down to tomorrow night. If everything went as planned, they'd get Mole. Griffin's testimony would be another nail in the coffin.

Sirens wailed in the distance. He glanced in his rearview mirror. Nothing. He pulled into the apartment complex and his heart skidded to a halt. People huddled outside the building and pointed to smoke billowing up into the sky.

From Maddie's building.

His gaze shot to the top level where flames danced in the windows. Adrenaline spiked as he slammed on the brakes, threw the gearshift into park, and jumped from the car. He scanned the crowd.

No sign of Maddie.

An iron fist closed around his heart. She had to be out.

He raced to the stairwell, dodging through people, and took the steps three at a time. When he reached her entrance, the heat blasted from within. He touched the door and tried the knob.

Blazing hot and locked.

He bounded back down the steps. Fire trucks and police cars roared into the lot.

If Maddie was still in the apartment...

He shoved back the thought. Refused to accept it. She was probably standing somewhere out of the way with Lucky.

Only the gut feeling that never served him wrong told him otherwise.

The fire escape. If she couldn't get out her front door, she'd have to use it. He cut around the corner of the building and sprinted to the back. So much smoke. More people died of smoke inhalation than the fire itself.

Great. No time for recalling morbid facts.

He halted below her apartment and looked up at her window.

Closed, with nothing but dark smoke clouding the glass.

She could still be inside. Every muscle in his body stood at the ready. Regret for all the things he'd held back from her flooded his mind. He should have told her he loved her. Accepted her apology. Wrapped her in his arms and explained why he'd been such an asshole the whole time he'd been in town. Now, he might never get the chance.

Mole had to be behind this fire. Murdering son of a bitch.

A movement from behind the window caught Scott's attention. He strained to see through the smoke. His breath caught as Maddie appeared on the other side. Time stood still as his stomach plummeted to his feet.

Fuck.

Her frantic attempts to open the window failed.

He tore to the fire escape. His legs pumped as he charged up the steps, the roar of the fire in his ears, and the stench of burnt wood in his nostrils.

One landing. Two.

"Hold on, Maddie. Almost there."

He finally reached the top and bent down to yank open the window. Stuck or locked. He'd have to break it.

His heart pounded triple-time. He stripped off his suit coat and wrapped it around his arm.

The window shattered as the legs of a chair busted through. Maddie's panicked face appeared behind the jagged glass.

"Stand back," he yelled.

With his shoe, he kicked in the shards. Smoke poured out and blurred his vision. Lucky leaped onto the landing. He whined and cried as Maddie climbed out.

Christ, the flames had singed the edge of her nightshirt. She coughed and sputtered on her hands and knees. He whisked her into his arms. "I got you, babe. I got you."

She gasped for air. "Sc-Scott."

He carried her down the fire escape as firefighters rounded the corner with hoses.

When they reached the bottom, an EMT rushed to him. He asked Maddie if anyone else was in the apartment.

She wiped her eyes and coughed again. "No one but my dog. Is my dog…"

Lucky barked at Scott's feet. Maddie sighed, and her body went limp.

CHAPTER 37

THE SCENT of freshly brewed coffee stirred Maddie to open her eyes. She blinked and rubbed her crusty lashes. Probably from the soot she couldn't wash out. Damn, she'd come close to being roasted.

She sat up and gazed around at the unfamiliar surroundings. At least she wasn't in the hospital. They'd released her last night after checking her lungs and burns. She wriggled her toes against the bandages on her feet. Still tender, but doing better.

Her mucky brain strained to recall the events of the previous night. That's right. Scott had driven her back to his place. Now she wore his T-shirt, which thankfully was long enough to cover her bare ass. Her nightgown had been destroyed by the smoke. Probably all of her clothes, for that matter.

Huh. She'd finally made it into Scott's bed, only without any sex involved.

Lucky hopped by the side of the mattress and licked her arm. He whined, and she stroked under his chin, careful to avoid the singed spots on his body. "Sorry, guy. You okay?"

He lifted his snout and leaned into the rub.

"Hey, you." Scott entered the room.

The clean scent of spicy soap filled the space. Her own hair still smelled of smoke, even after she'd washed it last night.

"Hey, yourself."

He approached the bed, leaned down, and brushed his lips against hers. Soft and gentle, he placed a hand along the side of her face. "We need to talk."

Lucky wedged his head between Scott's knee and the bed. Scott smiled. "Hold on. I ran out this morning to buy him food and picked up a bone. I think it'll keep him occupied. I'll be right back."

He'd thought of everything. When he called for Lucky, the dog high-tailed it out of the room. Maddie sucked in a breath. Her lips tingled from the unexpected kiss.

We need to talk.

The four words that could strike fear into the bravest gladiator.

Butterflies flitted around in her stomach. Oddly enough, being blinded by smoke had opened her eyes. She and Scott belonged together. She loved him. His strength, his touch, even the way he called her out on some of her "stunts."

After a close brush with death, she wasn't about to lose a chance for a life with him. The urge to keep on the move no longer drove her. There were plenty of jobs in her field that didn't require travel. She could find one on her career path and be with Scott, if he wanted her.

He returned and took a seat on the bed. She sat cross-legged, her back against the headboard to make more room for him. "So, what did you want to talk about?"

For a few seconds, he just stared at her. His gorgeous green eyes traveled over every inch of her face as if memorizing it.

"I thought I'd never see you again. When I looked up and saw the roof on fire, and there was no sign of you, I..." He swallowed hard.

Oh God. So much emotion. This was new. Her own throat tightened. "I know. I—"

"Wait. Let me finish. This is important." He rested a hand on her knee. "There's so much I haven't told you. Mostly for your own protection, but also because it was too painful to discuss."

"And now?" she asked softly.

He rubbed her leg. "Now I have to, or I may lose you for good, and I couldn't live with that."

The room turned warm, or maybe it came from within. Was he saying what she thought?

"I did everything I could to make you angry at me and send you packing."

"I won't argue."

"It killed me to do it, but I thought it would keep you safe. Hell, I figured you would be better off without me in your life."

"So…" She fiddled with the hem of her shirt. "What are you saying?"

"I don't ever want to feel the way I did last night when I thought I'd lost you." He took her hand, twined his fingers through hers, and brought them to his lips. "I'm saying I love you. Please don't leave."

She blinked and took in the words. Her heart soaked them up like a dry sponge, filling her chest. His eyes were wide open, clear, and full of hope.

He ran a thumb along her chin, and then leaned closer. "Tell me you'll stay."

Too choked up to speak, she nodded.

He exhaled and touched his forehead to hers. "I thought a lot last night about what you said. Me dying along with my family."

"I'm so sorry. I never should have—"

"But it was true." He leaned back and stiffened. "Part of me did die. I've been in a dark place for a long time, and I need to change that. Live again."

She swallowed. Nodded. Waited for him to continue.

"I have some ideas about what I want to do, and they all include you. If you'll give me another chance."

Every cell in her body danced. He loved her. He wanted a life together.

Still rigid, he eyed her as if bracing for the rejection.

"Oh, Scott." She launched herself into his arms and planted a kiss on his warm neck. "Yes. I love you. I always have."

His body relaxed at the same time he squeezed her tight. His voice, rough with emotion, reverberated against her ear. "I don't deserve you, but I'll take it."

She clung to him as he rocked her in his lap. He stroked her hair while his strong arms held her close. Burying her head into his chest, she took comfort in the steady beat of his heart against her cheek.

He kissed her on the temple. "I don't have all the answers, but you've given me hope for the first time in so long. I've missed you so much."

She shifted to look up at him. "All I ever wanted was for you to come back. I dreamed about it every night. I never stopped loving you."

"Keep saying those words until they sink in." He grazed the side of her face with the inside of his hand.

"As many times as you need to hear them."

"Yeah?" He nibbled her neck and slid a hand behind her back to pull her closer.

"Mm-hm." What he was doing made it hard to think. His warm breath sent shivers along the sensitive skin above her collarbone.

He nudged her shoulder down until she was lying beneath him, and then he pulled back and traced a thumb over her lips. "There's more for us to talk about, but it can wait. I want to make love to you. Feel you. Know you're alive, but I don't want to push you."

His beautiful eyes stared into hers, radiating a light of hope she hadn't seen since he'd come back. Her soul melted at the love he let shine through. She pressed her palm to his cheek. Push her? Not possible. Like him, she needed the reassurance they'd survived and craved that connection at the most intimate level.

She raised her head to touch her lips to his. "I love you. Fill me, Scott."

He kissed her tenderly, and then did exactly what she'd asked. Filled her body and her heart.

* * *

Scott placed two mugs of coffee on the kitchen table and took a seat beside Maddie.

After stirring in a generous amount of milk, she sat back in the chair, the hem of Scott's T-shirt the only thing between her naked butt and the hard wood. She really needed to get some panties.

Or not.

Scott tapped his thumb on the table and kept his gaze on his phone, reading something. He reached across to take her hand and squeezed it. The simple gesture sent a wave of warmth through her body.

All morning, he'd been caring and attentive. Held her close in bed and told her again how much he loved her. At last, everything she wanted from him he gave her in spades. But now, he was avoiding eye contact. She scooched closer. "What's wrong?"

He glanced up. "I don't want any more secrets between us."

"Agreed."

Worry lines etched the side of his face.

He let go of her hand and leaned back. "There's some serious shit going down tonight, and I need to have my head in the game."

A little piece of her winced. The "I love you" conversations were over. "I understand."

"Not all of it." He frowned and picked up his coffee. His knuckles turned white as he gripped the mug, not taking a sip.

"What?" She leaned close and set a hand on his shoulder. "Talk to me."

He blew out a breath and shut his eyes. "I found out yesterday that Mole had my brother killed for snitching."

Shock squeezed the breath from her lungs. Mole had murdered Justin? No wonder Scott had been so upset at the station. She grabbed his hand. "Oh my God—"

He raised his gaze. Cold, calculated, and focused. "I'm going to nail the bastard. We're close. If everything goes right today, I should have enough evidence to put him away for life."

Maddie leaped to her feet and paced. "Wait. I...I'm confused. You said Mole *had* him killed. What does that mean?"

Scott shook his head. Raw fury simmered in his eyes. "He ordered a hit on him."

Her mouth went dry. Knowing Mole was behind Justin's death must have put Scott over the top. And she'd shown up and added insult to injury, hounding him about Zach. That was why he'd punched a tree and tried so hard to get her to leave town. "I'm so sorry. This is worse than anything I'd ever imagined. He—"

"I'm just glad you're okay." Scott stood, pulled her into his arms, and held her tight.

She shuddered. That monster stopped at nothing. How many people with no conscience were on his payroll?

Scott eased back. "Everything with Mole is risky. You were right about Zach's involvement, but he's critical to the operation, and we'll get Mole."

Shit. Nikki's biggest fear. Maddie bit her lower lip. "I know you'll do your best to keep him safe."

Scott gave a quick nod, stepped to the table, and picked up his coffee mug. "Nothing's guaranteed."

Her stomach flipped. But he was being honest. Open and upfront. What she'd always wanted. "How can I help?"

"By staying out of it." He took a swig of coffee and set the cup back down. "This fire was no accident. Mole obviously didn't intend to pay the bribe. I figure he decided to get rid of any loose ends."

Maddie glanced at Lucky, sleeping on his bed, burned patches on his fur. Her poor, sweet puppy. They both could have died. From the start, she'd underestimated Mole. "Maybe he found out about the real survey I sent in."

Scott blinked. "What survey?"

"The…ah…real one that documented the Clovis blades and all the findings." She rubbed her arms. If one of the darts shooting from Scott's eyes hit her, it would leave a mark.

"You filed the real survey? We talked about this. You said you'd sit on it."

"I was leaving town, remember?" And he'd wanted her on that damn flight as soon as possible. Besides, Victor shouldn't have found out about the report so fast.

"Christ, Maddie." Scott squeezed his eyes shut and rubbed his temples. "You issued your own death warrant by thumbing your nose at him. No wonder he torched your apartment."

She picked at a fingernail. "If you take him down tonight, he can't really do anything else, right? Besides, I didn't file that report until right before I went to bed, but someone had to have been in the house earlier.

Lucky was so freaked out when I came home. I don't think this had anything to do with the survey."

Scott rubbed a hand across his jaw. "Well, whoever set the fire is still out there. I want you under police protection until this is over. I'll call Kaitlyn to watch you." He raised a hand and gave her a do-not-argue-with-me glare.

She bit back the objection on her lips, a knee-jerk reaction to being babysat. He had a point. Her feet still burned, and Lucky had patches of singed fur. It had been too close. She'd taken too many risks. From now on, she'd think hard before she put herself or anyone else in harm's way. "Okay. But if Kaitlyn's coming, ask her to bring me some underwear."

He sighed and stared at her. At last, the corners of his mouth turned up. "What am I going to do with you? Not what I expected you to say, and the answer is no. Not police business. Totally unprofessional." He gave her a mock stern look.

She smirked, and he closed the distance between them to wrap her in his arms again. He held her tight and kissed her forehead. "Seriously, though, I have to go to work. When I get home tonight, and this is all done, can we talk about our future?"

Their future.

Her heart jumped to her throat. "Try to stop me."

CHAPTER 38

VICTOR PASSED by Gina's desk on the way to his office. She glanced up from reading the newspaper, her eyes wide. Pictures of the apartment fire splashed the front page. She fumbled to tuck the paper away.

His phone rang, and Eric's number scrolled across the screen. Of course, he'd fucked up and botched the hit. He'd messed up for the last time. Victor entered his office and shut the door. He answered the call. "Get your sorry ass over here."

"Sure. Okay...but it wasn't my fault. She should have died. I nailed the window shut, but she busted it with a chair."

Always an excuse. If Victor had used any one of his men from the Southwest, the bitch wouldn't be breathing. They knew how to do a job right. "I don't want to hear it."

"I...I can fix this. I already came up with another plan. And there's more. I found something really important when I was in the apartment. At least, I think it is."

His whiny tone grated. "I don't wanna hear—"

"But I saw a report on her desk, and it listed all this shit she'd uncovered. Cloves or something. Blades. I don't know, but it looked all official and was pretty long."

Victor gripped the phone tight. An alternate report. The bitch couldn't be stupid enough to have actually filed one. She had to know she wouldn't get her bribe if she did that. He was supposed to have the money for her this morning. She might still show up unless she'd figured the fire wasn't an accident.

"Boss? This is important, right? Worth something?"

"Just get over here." Victor hung up.

If Maddie had double-crossed him, she'd pay. Big-time. He had a reputation to uphold.

Gina buzzed him, her strained voice sounded over the speaker, "Do you have a minute?"

Something was up with cool-as-a-cucumber Gina. So far, she'd been his puppet on a string for the right price, but she'd only worked on press, office business, and legal issues. Maybe she'd figured out he was behind the apartment fire. Big fucking revelation. He picked up his cigar. "Come in."

Gina entered. Dressed as usual in a suit and heels, her hair pinned back, she averted her gaze and smoothed down her skirt, fingers twitching. "I need to ask for a leave of absence. For personal reasons."

Victor lit his cigar and leaned back in the chair. Well, well. Another useless bitch. Happy enough to take the exorbitant salary he paid her as long as she could look the other way. Maybe she'd grown a conscience. If he'd underestimated her moral code, too bad for her.

He puffed on the cigar. "Personal reasons. Like what? For what I pay you, you shouldn't have a personal life."

She wrung her hands. "It's my mother…she's sick. I need to take care of her."

The smoke in Victor's lungs turned acrid. He knew the look of a liar, and she screamed bullshit. Her mother had died years ago. He'd checked out Gina's history before hiring her. She was done. He'd play nice to get what he wanted out of her, but she wouldn't be coming back. "All right, but I'll need a complete business report of all my accounts and transactions before you leave. Got it?"

She heaved a sigh and visibly relaxed. "Of course. I'll work on it right now. No problem, and…thank you for understanding."

Oh, he understood. Understood she'd just screwed the pooch.

Her phone rang, and she glanced at the screen. "It's the Army Corps."

"Answer them."

Gina's face paled as she listened to whatever the person on the other end of the line said. She swallowed, eyes wide. "But the survey was already filed. What do you mean, another one? Is that even permissible?"

Victor's gut balled into a hard knot. No. No fucking way.

Gina hung up and took a small step back. "It's over. Cooper filed another survey, and there's more than enough evidence of artifacts with historical significance to launch this into the next phase. It could take a very long time, if ever, to sort out."

A vein in Victor's forehead throbbed. He stood and faced Gina. "What recourse do we have?"

Gina shook her head. "None. With the new findings on record…I mean, you can't un-ring that bell."

Victor kicked the door shut, tore the phone from her hand, and threw it across the room. It shattered against the window, leaving a spider crack.

Gina cowered and flattened her back against the wall.

His face burned with rage as he closed in on her. "You were supposed to keep tabs on all this survey shit. I paid you to stay informed."

She sputtered, "I-I didn't have any control over—"

"Shut up." He punched the wall, inches from her head.

Whimpering, she brought a hand to her chest. Tears streamed from her eyes.

So much for his tough, professional assistant. Nothing but a useless pussy.

His voice boomed. "Generate that status report and then get the hell out of here. I'm done with you." He sucked in a long breath and flared his nostrils. "And don't think of leaving until I have it."

Gina nodded. Trembling, she slunk along the wall to the door. She opened it and called over her shoulder as she left, "Yes. I'll do it right now."

Victor's blood pumped hard in his veins. She'd pay just like the other incompetent people before her. She knew too much about his business, and he sure as shit wouldn't keep someone who lied to him.

White spots appeared before his eyes, and his breath burned his lungs. Blood trickled between his fingers from where his rings had sliced the flesh when he'd pounded the wall. But it was nothing compared to the eruption going on inside.

Fuck her. And fuck Cooper, that arrogant archaeologist double-crossing bitch. He picked up the trashcan and hurled it against the wall.

She'd devastated his world with one report. No resort to launder the drug money. No land to rape for artifacts. He'd worked long and hard to set up the perfect operation, and the bitch had blindsided him. The transportation system, the drug connections, everything he'd established—useless. A bleeding heart with a hard-on for history had compromised his entire operation.

His hands itched to grip Cooper's neck and squeeze the life out of her. This was personal, now. He'd do the job himself. Nobody got away with screwing him.

* * *

Two hours later, his intercom buzzed.

"Eric's here," Gina announced in a small voice. "And I emailed you the file with all the stats."

"Good. Send Eric in and then leave." He had to clear the place so he could finish Cooper off in private.

"Okay."

Eric slipped into the room and took his usual seat across from Victor. The little shit had taken his time getting there, but just as well. Victor had kept plenty busy.

He didn't need Eric anymore. The only useful thing he had done was work with the dirty cop to get the Clovis blade, which had netted a hefty sum on the black market. Good thing, because that money would fund this last drug deal.

After the call from the Army Corps, Victor had run through multiple scenarios. If his operation was going to be shut down, he needed to empty the pipeline; liquidate his drugs so he would have cash to move on. He ran his tongue over his front teeth and picked up the cigar cutter from his desk.

Eric sniveled. "So, umm...you wanted to see me?"

Victor tapped the cutter against his palm. He couldn't be in two places at one time, and this was the perfect opportunity to get rid of Eric. "I need you to meet with Zach at the survey field tonight."

He slid a piece of paper across the desk and yanked open a drawer. Reaching inside, he grabbed a pistol in a plastic bag and wads of money. "Give Zach this address, the gun, and the cash. He's going to get the latest crystal shipment."

Eric nodded. "You got it."

Victor thumped a stack of money. "I know how much is here. One dollar off and you're dead. Understand?"

Eric's Adam's apple bobbed. "Yup. Deliver this stuff. That's all I'll do."

Victor swung his chair around to face the window. "Good. Because I've lost my patience with incompetent people."

An explosive boom shook the room, and flames burst from the road beneath the cliffs.

Eric jumped to his feet. "What the hell?"

Victor sneered and turned to Eric. "Gina fucked up this morning. Make sure you don't."

CHAPTER 39

MADDIE OPENED the door to Kaitlyn.

Dressed in her uniform, she bent to pet Lucky and handed Maddie a bag. She shot a glance down the stairs. "I passed Scott on the way up. I brought you some clothes that I hope fit. Had to guess at the sizes."

"Thanks. It's not awkward at all to be standing here in nothing but Scott's shirt." The attempt at levity fell a bit short. Her gaze lowered to the gun in Kaitlyn's holster. A reminder of the danger at hand. Maddie tugged at her earlobe and glanced at the curtained window. Sure would be nice to go back to a normal life where she didn't have to worry about stalkers or arson.

The lack of clothing hadn't bothered her around Scott, where she felt safe. Now, all she wanted was to cover up. "Just need a second to change."

She hurried down the hall and then slipped into the shorts, underwear, and a T-shirt. Better. If something unexpected happened, at least she'd be dressed. When she came back to the foyer, Lucky had managed to coax a full belly rub out of Kaitlyn.

Kaitlyn glanced up. "Good thing we like each other, because I'm going to be stuck to you like glue."

"I know you're pulling a double shift to do this. I really appreciate it."

"It's not worth taking a chance." Kaitlyn straightened. "The fire wasn't an accident. Apparently, the window to the escape was nailed shut from the outside. Someone tried to kill you."

Maddie broke out in a cold sweat. "I won't lie. It kinda freaks me out to think about it."

"Well, I'm here now and under strict orders not to leave you alone. If you have to pee, I'm supposed to go with you."

"What? That's—"

"I'm kidding." Kaitlyn placed a hand on Maddie's arm. "But seriously, we stick together. Scott told me if you gave me any grief to call him right away. He's pretty intense today."

No doubt, with all he had going on. She wouldn't add to his worries. "I promise to listen."

"Good." Kaitlyn checked her watch. "Did you eat dinner yet?"

"No. I haven't been hungry." Zach's meeting with Victor was in an hour. Her stomach knotted.

Kaitlyn slid a chair out from the kitchen table. "How about sitting down? You don't look so hot."

Maddie slouched onto the seat. "I'm worried about tonight."

"I know." Kaitlyn eased down on the chair beside Maddie. "Scott's not a rookie. He can handle himself and whatever comes up."

"It's just that now I've fallen…" Ugh. What was she babbling about?

"You can say it, you know." The corners of Kaitlyn's mouth curved. "In love. I'm really happy for you two."

Maddie stood and went to the refrigerator. "Well, we still have to talk about the future, but yeah, we'll find a way to be together." She glanced over her shoulder. "Speaking of which, how are things with Tom?"

Kaitlyn blushed. "Going well. But I think it's a good thing I'll soon be working in another town. It's kinda hard to focus…"

"When you're hot and bothered, right?" Maddie laughed. Some of the tension left her body. This was what she needed, some normal conversation.

"I didn't say that." Kaitlyn's face turned crimson.

Maddie waved a hand. "Oh, please. You don't have to worry with me." She opened the refrigerator. "Leftover pizza?"

"Sure. I'd rather not have anything delivered."

Right. Safer to stay in and limit exposure to strangers who might have been hired to kill her. The muscles in her neck bunched. She opened the cabinet to pull out two plates, and her phone rang.

Scott.

His ringtone alone caused her pulse to race. Anything could go wrong. "Hey, Scott."

"I passed Kaitlyn on my way out. Everything okay?"

"Yes." Hearing his deep, smooth voice took the edge off her nerves.

"Good. You're still in the apartment, right?"

"Yes." She opened the refrigerator and pulled out a pizza box.

"And you know to stay in?"

Well, now he was making her jumpy again. She tapped a foot on the floor. "Did you call just to grill me?"

"No. I called to say I love you."

The words wrapped around her heart like a warm blanket. She closed her eyes and smiled. "Thanks. I love you, too. And I'm worried sick."

Kaitlyn moved to the other room.

Scott spoke in a soft tone. "It's gonna be okay. Soon this will all be nothing but a bad memory."

"I hope you're right."

"I am. Trust me. I can't wait to come home to you."

She pressed her lips together as tears threatened. For so long she'd yearned to hear him talk like this. "Promise me you won't take any risks."

"I'll do all I can."

Which wasn't the same, but she couldn't expect much more. "Okay. Call me when it's over. I…need to know you're safe."

"Will do. Stick with Kaitlyn. No flying solo."

"Yes, sir."

"And Maddie?"

"Yeah?"

"Did Kaitlyn bring you panties?"

Maddie grinned. "A complete outfit."

"Damn that woman. Can't follow a direct order to save her life. When I get there, I want you dressed the way I left you."

"Just make sure you get here." Her throat tightened.

"I'm properly motivated. See you soon."

She hung up and brought a hand to her forehead. He'd be all right. They hadn't come this far to lose it all.

Kaitlyn popped around the corner. "How about watching Bruce Willis kick some ass to kill time? I found a *Die Hard* movie."

"Sure." Maddie brought the pizza, took a seat on the couch, and plopped down beside Kaitlyn. Time dragged as they ate, her nerves on high alert.

She glanced at her watch. Almost eight. Scott was probably setting up for the meeting. Her frayed nerves stretched tighter.

Lucky pawed at the door to go out. Maddie stood. "I usually walk him about now."

Kaitlyn shook her head. "Not tonight. Can you put some newspapers down for him to pee on?"

"No." Maddie scratched her head. "He won't randomly pee in the house because I put down a paper."

Lucky whined at the door as if to emphasize her point.

Kaitlyn got up. "Poor dog. He doesn't understand. Okay. I'll take him out with you, but no walk. Scott wants us inside."

"I hate this, but you're right." Maddie plucked Lucky's leash from a hook. He yipped and chased his tail. Damn Victor for making her feel like a prisoner. She tucked her cell phone in the front pocket of her cargo pants and bent to ruffle the fur on Lucky's head.

When she unlocked the door, Kaitlyn reached out and placed a hand on the knob. "Wait for me to check it out."

"Okay, but I wish—"

"I have my orders. Please don't make this harder than it has to be."

"I'm sorry. Of course." Maddie sighed. "I'm pissed at Victor and taking it out on the wrong person."

"I understand, but let me do a quick sweep."

Maddie waited until Kaitlyn called from the bottom of the steps, "All clear."

They walked to the back of the apartment complex. Tonight, Maddie wouldn't mind having some people around, but the place was empty. She unsnapped Lucky's leash. Kaitlyn stood alert beside Maddie, her gaze on the woods as Lucky sniffed the ground.

He didn't trot to his regular spot by the edge of the forest. Instead, he kept sniffing around like he couldn't find a place to go. He raised his head, and the whiskers on his snout twitched fast as if he'd caught a scent in the wind.

"He's not used to you being here. Anything different disrupts his routine." Maddie crossed her arms.

At last, Lucky made it to his spot. Maddie took a step toward the dog, but Kaitlyn grabbed her arm. "Stay here. I'll pick it up."

Kaitlyn jogged across the yard and stopped by Lucky.

A massive figure, dressed all in black, emerged from the forest.

Maddie's stomach dropped to her feet as terror sparked every nerve in her body. She didn't need to see his face. She knew the outline of his hideous body.

Victor. Holding a gun.

Kaitlyn had her back to him.

Maddie pointed and called out, "Behind you!"

While reaching for her weapon, Kaitlyn whirled around. A shot rang out as Victor fired point-blank at Kaitlyn's chest. Her body flew back and landed with a *thud* on the ground, her head whacking hard against the cement slab of the grill area. Blood seeped from under her hair onto the concrete.

Someone screamed from an open apartment window above. "Oh my God. A shooter!"

Maddie's knees buckled, and her heart seized. "Help. Help!"

Her gaze darted from Kaitlyn's motionless form to the building.

Lucky's ears flattened, and he bent his hind legs. He growled and barked as Victor quickly approached Maddie, a sneer on his evil face. "Save your breath. No one can help you now."

He stopped in front of her, pointing the gun at her head. His cold, dead eyes stared down at her.

Panic welled inside her. He could kill her right there. Someone had heard him shoot Kaitlyn, but no one was rushing to the rescue. Without a weapon, Maddie didn't stand a chance against him. Somehow she had to help Kaitlyn.

He moved behind her and clamped a hand over her mouth, pinning the back of her head to his chest. The cold metal tip of his gun pressed against her temple. "Enough yelling, bitch. You're coming with me."

"No." She clawed at his iron grip and tried to grab the gun.

Lucky's deep growl turned fierce. He charged Victor, who gave him a vicious kick. The dog yelped and flew across the yard to land in the grass with a *thump*. He didn't get up.

A raging surge of adrenaline spurred Maddie. She tried to jerk her jaw loose and bite Victor's hand, but he held it too tightly over her mouth. His clunky, gold rings mashed her lips against her teeth. Coppery blood seeped onto her tongue.

If she broke free, Victor would have to chase her away from Kaitlyn and the dog. The maniac might shoot again if either of them moved. She fought to wriggle loose but to no avail.

As he dragged her body into the woods, she glanced at Kaitlyn's limp form not far from Lucky's. Her heart split into pieces.

Victor shoved his gun into a pocket and grunted as he manhandled her through the trees. Thorns scratched her arms and legs. Limbs slapped her face. She was no match for his strength, but she still grasped for the trees and kicked her feet at his shins.

He stopped and squeezed her so hard she lost her breath.

"Fight all you want. I'm enjoying this. You won't escape."

His hot breath in her ear caused a wave of nausea to roll up from her stomach. Someone had to have called the police. It would be her fault if Kaitlyn died. She never would have been in the position to take a bullet if Maddie hadn't double-crossed Victor.

On the move again, Victor hauled her deeper into the thick of the woods.

He was supposed to be at the meeting with Zach. Scott's plan could be in jeopardy, and she had no way to warn him. Her gut heaved.

Again, Victor's hot breath blasted in her ear. "You fucked with me. Now I'm gonna fuck with you."

Sweat poured down her neck, soaked the back of her shirt, and mixed with the bastard's sickening stench of overpriced cologne as they finally came to an opening where his Bentley sat.

He shoved her against the passenger side and pressed his body to hers, forcing the air out of her lungs. A wonder he hadn't cracked her ribs.

Yet.

She fought to suck in a breath as he crushed her from behind. Scott said the beast had tortured and killed people. She had to be on the top of his hate list.

He yanked the door open, grabbed something from the seat, and wrenched her head back.

After stuffing a gag in her mouth, he slapped tape across her face. It pinched her cheeks. More blood pooled in her throat. She tried to cough, but the rag gagged her. If she barfed, she could die choking. Her stomach gurgled in response.

Victor roped her hands tightly behind her and shoved her into the back of the car.

"This should keep you quiet while I take care of business." He slammed the door, got in the driver's seat, and glanced back at her, a vicious gleam in his eyes that made her insides quake.

CHAPTER 40

From his hiding place in the woods, Scott peered through binoculars. Zach paced at the tree line of the field survey site.

Lee, huddled beside Scott, held a parabolic dish recorder. As the local police chief, he'd offered his help, but the DEA ran this show with Scott as the lead. Which meant if anything happened to Zach, it would be Scott's fault.

Scott spoke into his Bluetooth. "Can you hear me, Zach?"

"Loud and clear." Zach paused his pacing to glance in the direction where Scott was staked.

Scott turned to Lee. "Looks like the earpiece is working. All we need is Mole."

A tactical team of DEA agents stood by at the police station. Once Mole gave Zach the location of the drugs, they'd storm the place and get the evidence to arrest the son of a bitch. At the very least, Mole would be taken in for questioning. The police had been looking for him after one of his employees had died in an explosion not far from the mansion earlier.

Zach bent as if to brush dirt off his jeans. "Car approaching."

Scott's nerves stretched tight. He swung the binoculars to where dust kicked up from the dirt road. Eric's truck lumbered down the path. "What's Eric doing here? Did he bring Mole?"

Lee shook his head. "Never good when things are switched up."

"Fuck," Zach said under his breath. "Eric's driving."

"Keep your cool, Zach. Mole might be with him." Anxiety coiled a grip around Scott's throat. He'd expected Mole to be at this meeting. Now he could be anywhere.

Lee placed a hand on his shoulder. "I know what you're thinking, but Maddie's protected."

Scott nodded, his jaw clenched. If anything happened to her…

Eric got out of the truck holding a black gym bag and sauntered over to Zach.

"Where's Mole?" Zach asked.

Eric dropped the bag on the ground. "Change of plans. You deal with me now."

"Since when?" Zach planted his hands on his hips.

"Since Victor told me to meet with you. He's busy."

Scott's heart jolted. But he couldn't leave now. He was in charge. He forced himself to focus. "See what he has to say, Zach. Ask about the drug money."

Zach waved a hand at Eric. "Get on with it, then. You bring the cash?"

"Yeah." Eric fished a piece of paper out of his jeans pocket. "I'm supposed to give you this address."

Zach read aloud. "The warehouse at 1725 2nd street?"

Scott pointed to Lee, who snatched his radio and called the station with the information.

"You sure this is right?" Zach asked.

Eric shrugged. "He told me to give you this address, the money, and a gun." He bent to unzip the sack and drew out a pistol in a plastic bag. "Guess he thinks you need one. I don't."

Scott's chest tightened. He needed to talk to Maddie. Make sure she was okay. "We got what we wanted, Zach. Lose Eric, and let's get out of here."

Eric pulled a phone out of his jeans pocket and typed a message. "Mole told me to text him when I got here."

Scott froze. What the hell game was this? He raised the binoculars back to his eyes.

Seconds later, Zach's cell rang.

"Victor. I don't like this change in plans. What's going on?" Zach asked. "Okay, I'll put you on speaker."

Mole's voice came across the line. "Did Eric give you everything?"

Eric shoved the gun toward Zach, who took it.

"I have cash, an address, and a gun. Is that everything?"

"Yes, good. He finally did something right. Now, shoot him," Mole said.

Scott flinched.

Christ, if Zach killed Eric, Mole would have all he needed to keep Zach under his thumb.

Eric gasped, and his eyes bugged out. He gave a nervous laugh. "You're kidding, right? Tell Zach you're kidding. It's not my fault the broad escaped the fire."

So, Eric had set the fire. Scott's pulse throbbed in his neck. This was spiraling out of control.

Mole said, "You wish, you worthless sack of shit. You've fucked up for the last time. Did you really think I'd let you live?"

Scott spoke into the mic, "You can't shoot him, Zach. Act casual about it. Make Mole think you'll do it, no problem."

Eric took a step backward. "But I—"

"Shut the fuck up, Eric," Mole said. "I'm done with you. Zach, this is your final test. You want to move on in the business with me, you take care of Eric. Got it?"

Lee tapped Scott's shoulder. "Time to intervene?"

Scott inhaled sharply. If they blew their cover, Mole might have time to warn the drug dealer before the DEA got there, and then they wouldn't have the evidence they needed. Despite Mole not showing up, the operation was still going as planned. Eric didn't appear to have a gun, and Mole couldn't do much to Zach over the phone. But Zach could actually shoot Eric. He had more than enough reasons to want to kill the little shit. Sweat dripped down the side of Scott's neck.

He shook his head at Lee and spoke to Zach. "Mole wants your fingerprints on that gun so he has you as his bitch. Play along."

Zach cleared his throat. "I'm in. Where do you want me to shoot him?"

As Zach unzipped the plastic bag and drew out the gun, Eric began to shake. "No. You don't have to—"

"Right there," Mole said.

"No, I mean what part of the body?" Zach pointed the gun from Eric's head to his stomach and then to the family jewels. Eric's jaw dropped and he followed the motion, bringing his hands up to cover the different parts.

Lee blew out a breath. "Jesus, I'd swear Zach's having *fun* down there."

Scott's pulse raced, but he had to give it to Zach. He was keeping his cool.

"I don't give a fuck as long as you kill him," Mole said.

Zach shrugged. "All right. I might go for the gut. Those are the worst."

Eric's chest rose and fell faster than a kid on a pogo stick. Good chance he'd pass out from hyperventilation or die of a heart attack before Zach could shoot him.

"Just do it. I want to hear the shot."

Sick bastard.

Eric tried to run but stumbled and fell.

Scott said, "Grab Eric and make him understand he has to keep his mouth shut."

"All right." Zach placed the pistol and phone on the ground, yanked Eric by the collar, and clapped a hand over his mouth. Eric's body trembled as Zach held a finger up in a "shush" gesture.

Eric bobbed his head frantically.

"Good, Zach." Scott kept his voice calm. "Now, let go of him slowly and make a zip-your-lips gesture."

Scott's fingers tightened on the binoculars. Eric had to keep quiet.

Zach did as instructed and picked up the pistol. He slipped the safety off and pointed the weapon at the water.

"No," Scott said quickly. "Not over the lake. At the ground. Point it at the ground." A bullet could travel a mile over water and hit someone on the other side.

Zach swung the gun down. He gave Eric a warning look, and Eric covered his mouth with his hands.

Scott planted his feet. "Okay. Good. Shoot the dirt, and then get off the phone fast so Eric doesn't fuck up and let Mole know he's alive."

Zach fired the weapon. He snagged the phone. "Done. Now what?"

Mole answered, "Leave the body. I'll have it taken care of. They're waiting for you at the warehouse."

"Okay." Zach tapped the screen off, dropped the phone in his pocket, and faced Eric.

"You haven't lost your edge since we worked together. Nice work." Lee said. "You got it from here? I'll man the station and put out an APB on Mole as soon as we hear back from your agents."

"All right. Can you send Tom to my apartment as backup? With Mole on the loose I don't want to take any chances."

"You bet." Lee handed the recorder dish to Scott and then left through the woods, phone to his ear.

Scott dialed Maddie's number. When she didn't answer, the muscles between his shoulders knotted. They'd taken every precaution, but Mole still could have gotten to her. Maybe Eric knew where Mole was.

Turning his attention back to the field, Scott frowned.

Zach stood in front of Eric. "Now I gotta figure out what the fuck to do with you."

Eric held his hands up. "Nothing. I'll disappear. We can pour some ketchup on the ground and make like I slid away. You know, like you didn't shoot me good enough."

"You insulting my skills?" Zach took a step toward Eric, who cowered back.

"No. No way. Hey, you don't want to hurt me. We're practically family. You know…your sister's in love with me. Wants to get married."

"Are you trying to *make* me shoot you?" Zach fisted a hand. "You spineless, lying fucker."

Zach launched himself at Eric, threw him to the ground, and slugged him in the face.

Scott shut off the recorder. Time to get down there before Zach killed the little prick with his bare hands. He ran through the woods and came up behind them.

Blood gushed from Eric's nose as he covered his face and whined like a stuck pig.

Scott tapped Zach's shoulder. "You need to get out of here."

He unclenched his poised fist, pushed off Eric's chest, and glared down at him. "Looks like you won't need ketchup." Zach glanced at Scott. "Sorry, but he had that coming for beating up Nikki."

Eric sat up holding a hand to his bleeding face. "What the fuck? You gonna arrest him for assault?"

"Looks to me like you tripped." Scott slapped handcuffs on Eric. "Where's Mole?"

Sweat streamed down Eric's face. "I don't know. I'll tell you whatever you need. Don't put me in jail. I got information on him. All kinds of stuff. I...won't even charge you for it."

Stupid fuck still thought Scott was on the take. He turned to Zach. "Go dark. You're in danger until we get Mole."

Zach glared at Eric, but then nodded and jogged toward his car.

After snapping cuffs on Eric, Scott pointed to him. "Don't make a move."

He dialed Kaitlyn's number.

No answer.

Nerves exploded in Scott's stomach. Neither of them were answering. He had to get to the apartment.

Eric squirmed and tried to stand. "Hey, I have rights. If you're going to arrest me—"

"Shut up." Scott picked up Zach's gun and yanked Eric to his feet. "Unless you can tell me where Mole is I have no use for you."

"I...I don't know. But he killed Gina. Blew up her car. That's worth something, right?"

Shit. No surprise there. Scott brought his face close to Eric's. "One last chance. Where is Mole? Nothing else matters right now."

Eric licked his lips. "I don't know, man, but I have more I can tell you—"

"Wrong answer. We're done." Scott read Eric his rights in triple-time on the way to the Impala. He threw him in the back, got into the driver's seat, and hit the accelerator.

Lee called.

"What do you know, Lee?"

"I sent Tom to your place. My GPS shows Kaitlyn's patrol car is there, but I can't get through to her by radio or phone."

Scott's thin grip on control slipped further. He floored it and took a turn that knocked Eric against the window. He yelped from the back. Screw him. No time for belting him in. If anything happened to Maddie...

Lee said, "Your overseas black-market buyer for that fake Clovis blade confirmed the money wired to Mole's offshore account. We got him, now. I put out an APB. We'll find him."

They had to, before he got to Maddie. Scott gripped the steering wheel tighter. "Okay. Keep me posted."

He hung up and got another call.

His lead DEA agent said, "I'm at the warehouse. The address was real. This place is full of meth. We arrested the dealer. Mole's done."

"All right. I want all available agents out there hunting down Mole. Coordinate with the chief so you're not tripping over each other."

"We're on it."

Scott's stomach bottomed out. They finally had their evidence, but where the hell was Maddie?

CHAPTER 41

SITTING in the back of Victor's car, Maddie twisted her wrists against the black leather seat. She tried to loosen the restraints biting into her skin as her mind raced to find a way out of the mess. Earlier, Mole had pulled over to the side of the road and talked crazy shit into his phone. Told Zach to shoot Eric. It sounded like Zach might have done it.

Impossible to imagine. Especially with Scott on the scene. But right now, she had her own problems.

Visions of Kaitlyn's and Lucky's motionless bodies on the ground haunted her. They had to be okay.

Sweat slicked her shirt, and saliva choked her. She needed to get free if she stood any chance against Victor. No doubt he had bad plans for her. She glanced out the window. They were on the road that led to the field survey site. Not far from it. Guess he wasn't taking her to the mansion. With all the woods around, he'd have plenty of places to dispose of a body. *Her* body.

If only she could get to her phone. Victor must not know she had it in her pants pocket or he would have taken it from her. Pressing the insides of her wrists together, she managed to wiggle a hand out. Her heart leaped.

She kept the gag in so he wouldn't know her hands were free. One step at a time. If she ever planned to see Scott again, she had to keep calm. Scott, who loved her and wanted a future together. Damn if she'd let Victor rob her of that dream.

Shifting on the seat, she slid a hand into her pocket and tugged out her new cell phone. She muted it and glanced at Victor who was intent on driving. She kept the phone low in her lap and typed a text to Scott. Her hands shook so hard she struggled to hit the letters.

Kaitlyn down. Victor has me. Field survey site. Gun.

She dialed the police number and stuffed the phone back in her pocket. Maybe they could trace her through the open call. The small town didn't have much technology.

Victor might notice her free arms, so she eased them behind again.

The car climbed the steep slope to the tip of the site. Her throat burned as she tried to swallow past the nasty gag. As if they were on a roller coaster, the closer they came to the top, the faster her pulse raced.

Her phone vibrated in her pocket. Probably Scott texting her back. Victor shot a glance at her. She couldn't risk pulling the cell out again. If the cops didn't find her soon, she'd be in big trouble. She was no match for the monster.

"Almost there. This is over, bitch. No one crosses me. You'll be the third today to pay." His cruel eyes stared back in the mirror.

Had he killed two other people, or was he including Kaitlyn and Lucky in the body count? Maddie's gut clenched as the image of them popped into her head again.

Victor stopped the car and got out. He rounded the front, and her lungs threatened to explode. She'd have to fight him. It was her only chance. She ripped the tape off of her mouth and spit out the gag.

He opened the door, grabbed her by the hair, and yanked her out. With the element of surprise as her only chance, she whipped her arms out, clawing at his eyes. She brought a knee up hard to his groin.

His massive thighs blocked most of the target, but she hit enough to make him grunt and bend over. He let go of her hair, but before she could run, he launched himself forward and knocked her onto her back, pinning her to the ground.

The weight of his body crushed her as she writhed to get out from under him.

No...oh no. He had her now. Terror exploded in her chest.

Rocks dug into her back and scraped her skin raw through her shirt as she thrashed beneath him. Unable to budge, she sunk her teeth into the massive cords of his neck. The coppery taste of blood mixed with salt filled her mouth. Her stomach roiled.

"Fucking whore." He shoved his meaty paws into the soft spot beneath her collarbone to push himself up. His open legs spread across her waist, trapping her.

She gasped for air and tried again to scratch at his eyes but couldn't reach his face. He'd kill her. Right there with his bare hands. She had no idea if the cops got her call or if Scott was anywhere close.

Victor's face, cheeks scraped and bleeding, contorted in rage as it darkened from red to near-purple.

"Once, I'd planned to fuck you. Now, I just want to watch your bones break." He hauled a hand back and slapped her across the face. Her head whipped sideways and smashed against the ground, causing her to bite her tongue. Searing pain burst into white lights.

She gagged and spit blood. Jesus, every bone in her body screamed in agony.

His weight lifted off her pelvis, and he jerked her up by the arm, twisting it in the socket.

"Time for you to fucking die." He pulled the gun from his pocket and held it to her head.

Spittle landed on her cheeks as he sneered in her face. Her sweat and blood-drenched clothes stuck to her skin. Unable to overpower him, maybe she could stall for time. "Wait. It's not too late." Her swollen tongue made it hard to talk. "I can change the survey. File a new one."

He grabbed her throat with his free hand and squeezed hard. "You lying, fucking bitch. Do you think I'm stupid enough to believe that?"

His fingers dug deep into the sides of her neck, taking her breath away.

"You can't unscrew what you did."

She pulled at his arm with her hands and he laughed. A sick, guttural sound.

"Enough games. Walk." He let go of her neck, and she dragged in a deep breath.

Lungs on fire, throat bruised, she weighed her options.

Nothing. She had nothing left.

He pushed her forward, shifting the gun to her back as they approached the cliff. "You love those fucking artifacts so much it's only right you die with them."

The cliff. He must plan to throw her body over. Sweat dripped into her eyes. God, no one could survive a fall from so high. Not with all the jagged rocks at the bottom.

He poked the gun into her back. "I can't wait to watch you splatter when you crash."

She pretended to stumble and fell to the ground. Anything to stall, but they were only feet from the edge now. Her heart threatened to explode.

"Get up, bitch." He yanked the back of her shirt, cutting into her neck. This was it. She could fight him, but he'd probably shoot her. The only card she had left to play was her phone.

"Look down." He shoved her closer to the drop.

When she refused, he gave her a push. Her feet skidded on the loose gravel, knocking pebbles off the cliff. They bounced on the rocks and fell to the bottom. Her mouth went dry.

She took a step away from the edge. "The...the cops are on their way."

Victor shook his head. "I'm done with your games."

"I mean it. I called from the car. I have my phone right here." She reached into her pocket, but Victor snagged her hand.

"I'll check it myself." He slid his hand inside and slipped the phone out, a sneer on his face.

He glanced at the phone and laughed.

The screen was shattered. Once again. The phone was dead.

Just like she was about to be.

CHAPTER 42

SCOTT DROVE the Impala through the twisted lanes away from the site like a stunt driver. Eric whined from the back. As if he had a right to complain.

Tom radioed. "I'm outside Maddie's apartment complex. Mole shot Kaitlyn and kidnapped Maddie, according to witnesses."

"What? Is Kaitlyn okay?"

"I don't know. She took a shot in the vest that didn't penetrate, but lost a lot of blood from a head wound. Wasn't conscious when I got here." Tom's voice faltered. "She's on the way to the hospital. A witness ID'd a photo of Mole as the man who dragged Maddie at gunpoint into the woods. No sign of either of them. We're still searching. He's not getting away after what he's done."

Scott gripped the steering wheel tightly. Nothing they could do but pray for Kaitlyn. Mole had Maddie. Where would he take her? Someplace private.

Scott pulled to the side of the road. He had to think. Some of his DEA agents were on the way to Mole's home. Others watched for him at the airport and train station. They didn't have much time. Unless he planned to use Maddie as a hostage, he could be torturing or killing her right now.

His phone beeped with a text. "Hold on, Tom."

The message was from Maddie.

Scott's heart hijacked a ride to his throat. She was still alive. He read the short text and broke out in a cold sweat. "Tom, I got a text from Maddie. Mole's taking her to the survey site. I'll reroute my agents from the mansion."

"I'm on my way," Tom said.

Scott made a U-turn, smashed the accelerator, and pushed the car to the limit as he radioed his agents for backup. If only he had stayed at the site. Sick fear for what Mole might do to her carved a hole in Scott's chest.

Lee radioed. "Scott?"

"I'm here. Mole has Maddie." Scott swerved the Impala around a bend and punched the gas again.

"We got a call from her number. She's at the site. At least it tracked her there before the line went dead."

Dead. The word bounced around in Scott's head like a pinball.

No. She couldn't die. He slammed a fist against the wheel. They were going to be together. He'd planned to buy a ring when this was over. Marry her, have babies, and live again. The bright vision of his future blurred into a black curtain of doubt.

"Did you hear me, Scott?" Lee asked.

"Roger." Scott gripped the steering wheel tight and rounded another sharp bend.

"I've got all units headed there and am on my way."

"Roger." Scott swallowed hard. Keep it professional. If he said any more, he might lose it. He'd heard the undercurrent of desperation in Lee's voice.

Mole had killed his brother. Damn if he'd take Maddie, too. Scott set his jaw and scanned the road ahead. Decision time. The right fork meant a straightaway and faster speeds. The left twisted up through the woods but cut the distance and time it would take to get there.

He veered to the left and channeled his focus on the driving. Trees whizzed past the windows as he raced up the snaking road, alternately hitting the brakes and flooring the accelerator. Eric's whimpers from the back faded as the rush of blood filled Scott's ears.

One mistake at this speed could smash the car into pieces on impact. He kept up the pace, fully in the zone. Nothing would stop him from getting to Maddie.

At last, the tree line from the opposite side of the cliffs loomed ahead. Out of roadway, he slammed on the brakes and bolted from the car.

He tore through the woods. Thorns and vines whipped his face and clawed at his clothes. Adrenaline coursed through his veins, fueling his speed. Visions of Mole's hands on Maddie propelled Scott through the forest.

If he didn't get to her in time, he'd lose everything. She'd breathed life back into him. Brought him back from the darkest place he'd ever been. He'd be lost without her light. Her joy. Her challenges and antics made him fucking crazy, but he loved her for them. No morning coffee together, no talks about the future. Lucky would sit by the door waiting for Maddie, who would never come back.

Sunlight filtered ahead through the thinning forest. He was almost to the clearing and pushed even harder.

He wouldn't be too late. Couldn't be.

Nerves stretched tighter than a guitar string, he charged out of the woods.

His heart soared at the sight of Maddie, alive, but then crashed. Mole held a gun to her back as she teetered on the edge of the cliff.

No!

If she fell, she'd die.

Scott snatched the pistol from his holster and raised it. He let out a half-breath and lined up the shot.

Sweat dripped into his eyes. Damn it. He swiped an arm across his face and repositioned. From this distance, even as an expert, it wouldn't be an easy shot. Never mind the fact that the woman he loved stood on a precipice and at any second could be pushed to her death.

Her clothes were covered in blood. Hot rage spiked the adrenaline already coursing through his body. This was all his fault. He never should have left her. What had Mole done to her?

No time to think about it. He had to make the shot. He wouldn't let Mole take another person from his life.

Time for action. He took a deep breath. "Freeze. Drop the gun."

Mole whirled around and pointed his gun in Scott's direction.

Like in the many raids Scott had led, the element of surprise threw the opponent off-guard. Mole's head whipped around as if searching for other threats.

Scott steadied the gun aimed at Mole and focused on controlling his breathing, still recovering from the sprint through the woods. "Put down the gun."

He assessed the wind speed that blew from behind. Steady and strong. It gave him a small advantage. From his distance, Mole would have to be an excellent pistol shot and need a heavy dose of luck to stand any chance of hitting Scott.

Time stood still as they faced off, and a million scenarios of how this might end played through Scott's mind. He'd never expected any to include the woman he loved in jeopardy. He didn't dare look at her again. He had to keep his emotions under control to handle the situation.

Had to save her.

And then, from behind Mole, Maddie lunged for his arm.

He fired an errant shot as she knocked the weapon out of his hand.

Mole grabbed her by the arm and pulled her against him as a human shield.

Shit. Scott forced his trigger finger to still. Maddie stood in the way of a clean shot.

"It's okay," she yelled in a hoarse voice. The desperation on her bloodied face cut him to the core. "Take the shot."

Sweat drenched his shirt. She didn't understand the logistics. A shot could hit either of them.

He couldn't risk it. He and Lee had been in worse situations. They'd come out on top. He would again. If he didn't let his emotions get to him.

Mole dragged her toward the ledge, keeping her in front of him. "Shoot and I take the bitch with me," he called out.

Fuck. Now they were close enough that a shot might push them both over. He didn't have a choice. He'd have to run toward them. Mole would try to get his gun. If he let go of Maddie, Scott would have a clean shot. If he didn't, at least they'd be away from the cliff and he could re-assess.

Before Scott could move, Maddie raised her leg and stomped her foot down, driving her heel into the top of Mole's foot. When he cursed and loosened his grip, she elbowed him and shoved off his chest. She twisted out of his grasp and dove for the gun.

Off-balance from her attack, Mole stumbled sideways, skittering along the edge of the cliff. His arms flailed as he tried to regain footing.

One fumbling step…two…and only inches now from the dangerous ledge.

Dust kicked up from his feet, and the loose stones made his efforts to stop his momentum futile.

Maddie secured the gun and pointed it at Mole with shaking hands.

One final flail of his arms and his massive body disappeared over the edge of the cliff. His agonized scream echoed through the bluffs.

Maddie lowered the weapon and slumped to the ground.

Scott's breath escaped with a *hiss*.

That had been too close. He sprinted across the field as sirens sounded in the distance. Reaching her at last, he gathered her into his arms. Jesus, it had come down to seconds. His heart continued to pound, still reacting to the thought of what he could have lost. "Are you okay?"

She gave a shaky nod and clung to him.

He wanted to hold her tightly and never let go, but bloody and bruised, she needed medical attention. He called for an ambulance, and then he ran his hands along her battered body, checking for injuries. Nothing broken from what he could tell, but he'd leave that to the experts.

Mole had nine lives and Scott wasn't taking any chances. "I have to check on what happened to Mole."

Maddie nodded.

He eased her back against a tree, kissed her forehead, and then headed to the cliff.

He ran parallel to the ledge and stopped several yards from where Mole had fallen. Pistol drawn, Scott cautiously peered over the edge.

The lucky bastard had caught himself in a tree growing out of the rocks. Mole's ass sat on the trunk. His hands clutched a jutting rock formation. Blood spread from where his pants had ripped at the knee and stained a flat rock surface above where he'd probably hit.

No cops on the scene yet. Nothing to stop Scott from finishing him off. He glanced at Maddie, bloodstained and slumped against the tree.

Red-hot fire burned in his chest.

He walked along the cliff edge to stand above Mole.

The bastard sneered and looked up at him. "This isn't over."

Scott stared into his eyes, finger on the trigger. One shot and it would be over.

"Scott, is he...gone?" Maddie had managed to stand, arms folded across her chest in a hug.

He couldn't do it. He wouldn't risk losing their future together by not playing by the book. And his training wouldn't let him do anything different. He had to trust that the law would dole out justice.

"Scott?" Maddie took a step toward him.

"It's okay." He waved her over.

She stepped nearer, and he drew her against him. Blood wet Scott's shirt where she rested her temple and gazed over the cliff.

He kept his gun trained on Mole. "I should kill him, but that's not good enough. He needs to rot in jail for the rest of his miserable life."

Mole sneered. "Fucking stupid, dirty cop. I'll take you down with me."

"You still don't get it. You've been outplayed." Scott scraped his boot along the edge, and dirt fell into Mole's face.

He snorted and spat. "You don't have anything on me."

"I witnessed attempted murder, and that's only the beginning," Scott said. "You're done."

"Anything a crooked cop says isn't going to mean shit."

"With my testimony, they'll have more than enough to put you away," Maddie said.

Scott stroked her arm, cradling her head to his shoulder, a protective hand covering her cheek. "She played you the whole time, you arrogant son of a bitch, and so did I. I'm not a dirty cop. I strung you along, always one step ahead."

Mole's nostrils flared, and his hands slipped on the rocks. He scrambled to regain his grip. His chest heaved from the effort, and blood dripped from the oozing scratches on his hideous face. His eyes narrowed as he glowered at her. "Should have finished you, bitch, when I had the chance."

The blood roaring in Scott's veins tainted his vision. It took every ounce of his control not to empty the magazine into Mole. "Biggest mistake you made was underestimating her. Look where it landed you. Dangling off a cliff with a tree up your ass."

Police cars roared up the dirt road. Scott radioed to Lee that Mole was disarmed. Tom, Lee, and Scott's agents got out of their cars and approached the cliff.

When his team reached the bluff, Scott pointed down at Mole. "Someone read him his rights and haul his sorry carcass to the station. Eric's locked in my car. He'll need processing, too."

Maddie slumped against Scott. He scooped her into his arms and carried her back to the spot under the tree away from the action.

Dropping to the ground, he held and rocked her gently. "I love you so much, babe."

So close. He'd almost lost her and his world.

Her body melted against his. She sighed and shut her eyes.

Alive.

He'd gotten to her in time. And he'd never let go of her again.

EPILOGUE

MADDIE TUCKED a beach towel inside her bag and shook her head. Hard to believe two months ago she'd almost died at Victor's hands, and today she was packing for a day at the lake like nothing had ever happened. A knock sounded on the door, and Lucky jumped to attention. Maddie's heart squeezed. Thank God, he and Kaitlyn had both fully recovered.

She opened the door. As usual, her body amped at the sight of Scott, shades perched atop his head, wearing a blue tank top that provided plenty of eye candy. A girl had to look.

Lucky whined, and Scott crouched down to hug him, dishing up a nice belly rub. "Hey, guy. You act like you never see me."

"I just need to grab my beach bag and we can go."

Scott glanced up and snorted as she turned away. "Hold on. What's that on your shirt?"

A giggle caught in her throat. She'd forgotten which one she had on. Of course, she'd worn it on purpose. A black T-shirt with white writing. *Archaeologists do it in the dirt.* She shrugged. "Eh, it's the only clean shirt I had."

"You know I own a lie detector. I might have to hook you up to it." He stood.

"As long as we hook up."

With a chuckle, he pulled her into his arms, and whispered against her ear, "That can be arranged." He nibbled her lobe, causing heat to pool between her legs. "But remember, I specialize in covert operations, so you'd better always shoot straight with me."

She wrapped her arms around his neck and smirked. "Oh, I've seen your under-the-covers action. And on the subject of shooting—"

"Smart-ass." He covered her mouth with his in a searing kiss. When he eased back, she rested her head on his chest. Safe and secure in his embrace, she let out a long breath.

"I'm so glad all the craziness is over."

"Me, too, babe. I still think about it. I almost lost you. God, if I'd been any later…"

"Shh." She held a finger up to his lips. "It all worked out. Eric and Victor are in jail, and the finds we dug up from his seized resort were enough to get the museum built."

"I hope you can get that curator job you're shooting for."

She sighed. "It's a dream. For now, I'm happy to dig the resort property and work on my doctorate. I never thought I'd give up travel, but everything I want is…here." She glanced up at him. "With you."

He took her hand, brought it to his mouth, and kissed her fingers. "I love you."

Her stomach fluttered. She'd never tire of hearing those words. "I love you, too. I worry, though. It's been a while now. Do you miss the action?"

Scott huffed and shook his head.

"What?" Maddie asked.

"Nothing. Just ironic. The question. I'll admit I wasn't sure what to expect with the DEA and police working together in the school system, but I'm anything but bored. Teaching teens about drug abuse prevention is a far cry from dodging bullets in Mexico. I'm okay with that. I can help in other ways that don't threaten my life…our life together." He tightened his grip on her hand and said in a soft tone, "I feel like Justin would want me to help keep others from getting hooked."

"I think so, too."

"Ready for some good news?" His eyes lit up.

"What?"

"They gave me the thumbs up today to start the program for the recovering addicts."

"That's awesome." She hugged him. He'd worked hard on setting that up. "You'll be helping people on both ends now."

"That's the plan." He gave her a quick squeeze. "Come on; let's go catch some rays."

She grabbed her bag and snapped a leash on Lucky.

After the short drive, Scott pulled into the Pebbles Beach lot along Oswego Lake. He handed her a bottle of water from the console. "It's pretty hot today. You should drink this before we head out."

She opened her door. "It's not that bad. I'll be fine. Let's just bring it."

"Nah, I don't have a cooler. The bottle will just get warm and leak chemicals into the water. Might as well drink it while it's cold."

She really wasn't thirsty, but he clearly didn't want to waste the water. Maybe some quirk he'd picked up from his time in Mexico. Rather than bring that up, she took the bottle. "Okay."

He popped the trunk and got out of the car. When he opened the door for Lucky, the dog bounded out, sniffed, and ran along the edge of the lot. Maddie drank the water as Scott pulled out a gym bag, her beach bag, and chairs. A gym bag? What a guy. "Do you want to put your stuff in with mine and just take one bag?"

"Eh, I'm good." He shut the trunk. "Let's go."

They made their way to the sandy beach area at the edge of the lake. The sun reflected off the water as children splashed and played. A huge seagull crept up to an unattended blanket, snatched a bag of chips from it, and squawked. Oh boy, someone was going to be pissed when they came back from the water and found their food missing. Rookie mistake.

The Captain's Inn restaurant behind the beach had a tiki bar with a guy singing Jimmy Buffett songs. Scott set up their chairs and towels. "I'm going to grab us a drink. Be right back."

"Okay."

Lucky raced to the water and barked, legs twitching in anticipation.

Maddie laughed. "I got it; I got it." She pulled his favorite stick from her beach bag, jogged to the shoreline, and tossed it in. Lucky swam out, fetched it, and came back. He shook, and then raced again to the water.

Several throws later, he dropped the stick in the sand and flopped onto one of the towels. Okay, well, that one would be his. He'd be out for a while. Maddie petted his wet fur, and her heart melted. This sweet dog had tried to protect her from that crazed Victor.

"How about a piña colada?" A frozen, creamy concoction appeared before her eyes.

Oh yeah. She turned around and planted a kiss on Scott's icy, coconut-laced lips.

Taking a seat in the beach chair she asked, "Heard anything from Zach lately?"

"Yeah. He's doing great at the police academy."

"He deserves a break. Good thing you and Lee were able to get that pardon and seal his records. Nikki's over the moon about sharing an apartment with him and going to cosmetology school. I think she was born to color people's hair."

"Don't let her near yours. I like it just the way it is." He reached across and tugged a curl. "Wild and unruly like you."

"I thought you didn't like that about me?"

He sighed. "You drive me crazy, but I love you. Things will settle down now."

Settle down. That sounded nice. She eased back in the seat.

After she finished her drink, she shut her eyes and soaked up the sun. So warm and comforting. She must have drifted off because Scott nudged her elbow. "I brought you a cold water."

"I'm fine. Thank you."

He shrugged. "Here, Lucky."

The dog jumped up and raced over to the collapsible bowl Scott trickled water into. Lucky slurped from the stream, licking the open bottle.

Maddie laughed. "He just laid claim to that bottle. It's his now." All this water. Now she had to pee. "Do you know where the restrooms are?"

"Yeah, over there." Scott gestured to a building next to the tiki bar.

"Okay. You got the dog, right?"

Scott waved at Lucky, who had settled back down to sleep. "I think I can handle the beast." He dug in the beach bag, "Do you want another drink? Lemme find my wallet."

"No. I'm good." Sheesh. The man must think she'd turn into a prune or something if she wasn't hydrated every second.

She glanced over her shoulder on the way to the restroom. Scott still dug around in his gym bag, muscles flexing. A spike of heat blazed south. She needed to get back to that hot guy as fast as possible. Maybe take a cool dip in the lake.

Or not.

Her flip-flops kicked up sand as she returned to the beach. She paused and shaded her eyes. On his hands and knees, Scott dug, a sand bucket beside him. What was he doing?

Lucky raised his head and wagged his tail when she approached, then flopped back down and shut his eyes. Tired pup; he'd sleep a long time.

"Scott?"

He looked up at her, "Yeah?"

"Umm…what are you doing?"

"Building a sand castle. Wanna help?"

She crossed her arms and stared down at him. "Where did you get the bucket and shovel?"

"I brought it." He went back to digging.

Okay, maybe she'd missed the memo, but they'd come out to chill and swim, and what the hell? "Knock yourself out. I spend my life digging. I think I'm good just relaxing here in the chair."

"Sure. You probably don't know how to build a castle anyway. You dig stuff up, not construct it."

"Hey, that's insulting."

He glanced up. "Sorry. I just meant that this is sort of the opposite of what you do. No offense."

"Seriously?" Irritation bit at her back, which was up now. "Fine. I'll prove you wrong."

He smirked as she stomped over and dropped to her knees.

"No, no, no." He waved her away. "That's too close. My castle is going to be big. You go over there."

She drew her mouth into a determined line and scooted over to the spot. "Fine. And just for the record, my castle is *so* going to make yours look like child's play."

"Game on." He handed her the shovel. "I'll use my hands. I don't need tools."

Oh, now he was really pushing it. The sun glistened off his sleek muscles, and she couldn't keep her eyes from tracing the outline of his oh-so-fine body.

"Better focus or you'll lose." The corners of his mouth twitched, and he dug with renewed vigor.

If he wanted a challenge, bring it on. She tossed the shovel to the side and buried her hands in the sand. Digging down a few inches, she stopped when she hit something hard. Probably a shell. The archaeologist in her leaped to all other kinds of conclusions. A bone, an artifact, a Clovis blade?

She used her fingers to clear the sand away and leaned closer to inspect. Not an artifact. A silver...something. She dug a path around and just below to push the object to the surface. A shiver of excitement passed through her. She extracted a small, sand-covered box.

After lifting it out, she dusted off the lid. What the heck? None of this made sense. "Scott, I found this..." She glanced up at him.

Bent on one knee, he reached out and took the box, holding her gaze.

Her pulse spiked, and the background blurred behind him. The sand, the sun, the noise of the kids playing on the beach. This couldn't be happening. She swallowed hard.

He opened the lid and a diamond ring, encased in velvet, glittered in the sun. His Adam's apple bobbed, and in a soft, deep voice, fraught with emotion, he said, "You told me once that you needed someone with a thick shell. Someone who could take a little fire. Someone who wasn't so sensitive that you had to tiptoe around them and not be yourself. Someone that you could...be wild with, if you wanted to. I want to be that someone."

She brought a hand to her mouth. He remembered. He'd heard her. And yes, he was the only man who fit the bill.

"I love you for all that you are, Maddie. I love your spunk and your fire, and God, you drive me crazy, but I can't imagine a life without you. Will you marry me?"

"Oh, Scott..." She dragged her gaze from his face to the box in his hand. "Is this why you plied me with drinks, so I would leave you alone long enough to bury this ring?"

"Guilty. But sweating on one knee here, waiting for an answer."

"Yes! God, yes!"

He slipped the ring on her finger, and she launched herself into his arms.

"I love you, Maddie." He kissed her soundly and then dragged his mouth to her ear. "Always have, always will."

She squeezed her eyes shut, overwhelmed by the love and his proposal. "Back at you."

He eased away and traced a finger across her shirt. "You're lucky there are women and children present, or I'd take you up on that slogan."

Maddie raised an eyebrow. "What about the guys? They get to watch?"

Laughter rumbled in his chest. "You're the worst."

The Scott she'd fallen in love with two years ago was back. He'd faced his demons and come out on top. Teasing, witty, sexy as hell, and all hers.

Forever.

At last, her world was grounded.

Thank you for reading! Did you enjoy? Please add your review because nothing helps an author more and encourages readers to take a chance on a book than a review.

And don't miss more from in the *Love Beyond Danger* series with LOVE ON THE LINE, available now. Turn the page for a sneak peek!

You can also sign up for the City Owl Press newsletter to receive notice of all book releases!

SNEAK PEEK OF LOVE ON THE LINE

Anne Cooper eyed the tray of tequila and kamikaze shots on the high table. Her friends grabbed one of each. Much as she'd like to join them, as the designated driver, she'd stick with water, and her stomach would thank her in the morning. Mixing shots was the kiss of death.

Mostly, she wanted to be there for Emily, who worked nonstop and deserved a night out to celebrate her birthday. With a spreadsheet and a calendar, Anne had compared everyone's schedules. Finally, she'd managed to find a date that worked for all of them. Thanks to her careful planning, she had all of her friends together. Her heart swelled with satisfaction.

Emily ran a hand through her curly red hair and pouted. "Have a drink. I want you to have fun. We can get a ride."

"Relax, I'm enjoying myself," Anne shouted over the band blasting alternative rock music from across the sports bar. Besides, she was more of a wine-sipping kind of girl. Hard liquor went straight to her head, and she didn't like to feel out of control.

She glanced at the guitar player jamming on the small stage. Maybe she could ask the band to play Emily's favorite song. Approaching a singer and drawing attention to herself made her pulse skitter, but what the hell. She'd do it for her best friend, who always had Anne's back. Besides, at thirty-two it's not like she was some shy teenager.

Trish, their server, was nowhere in sight. Anne pointed to her empty glass, using it as an excuse to slip away. "I'll be right back."

She weaved through the crowd, dodging servers carrying trays with pitchers of beer and fried wings. Baltimore Orioles pennants and Ravens pictures covered every inch of the walls. Even though she didn't follow sports, she at least knew the team colors, since her fifth-graders proudly wore their purple football jerseys to school.

The band announced they were taking a break, and the noise level returned to normal. Perfect. She'd grab a water and muster up the courage to make a request.

She spied an empty seat at the bar and hurried to the only open spot. As she slid the chair out, a man in the midst of an animated conversation waved a hand, bumping her shoulder. Cold soda spilled on her arm, and she jumped.

He whirled around, his mouth agape. "I'm sorry. I didn't see you behind me."

Her breath caught as eyes the color of emeralds stared down at her. Way down, because the guy stood an easy foot taller. Blond hair high-lighted his tanned face, which would be flawless if not for a few faint scars and a less-than-perfectly-straight nose that somehow added character.

Her heart thumped in her chest, and she blinked.

He snagged a handful of cocktail napkins as she held her arm away from her body so the drink wouldn't drip onto her jeans or shoes. At least some part of her brain hadn't seized. He placed a warm hand under her elbow for support and dabbed the napkins over her wet arm.

"Um...it's okay." She fumbled to take them from him, paying no attention to his bulging biceps. Not at all.

"Nice move, slick," came a voice from behind him.

Anne glanced at the beefy, dark-haired man with a shit-eating grin on his face.

"That's John. Ignore him. He has no manners," Mister Biceps said. He released her elbow, wiped his palm on his jeans and extended his hand. "I'm Wyatt."

She shook his hand, and an electric current tingled up her arm. Something in his eyes flashed. Maybe he'd felt it, too? Her gaze traveled from his massive chest to his broad shoulders. Either the place had shrunk, or this giant of a man had filled it. "I'm Anne."

"Hey, you gonna buy the lady a drink or what, superjock?" John asked.

Wyatt must have given a quick kick to John because he jerked on the bar stool and laughed. He leaned across the counter and said something to the bartender, who nodded, not breaking his rhythm pouring shots.

"My friend has a good point. Can I buy you a drink to make up for this?" Wyatt waved at her arm, which had bits of paper stuck to it from the napkin dabbing.

She brushed back a few strands of hair. Her stomach clenched. The guy was smoking hot, and the scent of his cologne was making her heady. Even so, she couldn't go there. The next guy she dated wouldn't be someone she met in a bar and knew nothing about. She'd closed that door and sealed the windows. But there he stood, jiggling the locks.

"Well …" She glanced across the room to her table. "I'm with friends."

The bartender placed a drink with a pink umbrella in front of Wyatt, and faced Anne.

"What can I get for you?" he asked.

"A water, please."

He filled a glass and slid it over to her.

Wyatt shook his head, plucked the umbrella from his drink, and twirled it in front of John's face. "Seriously? You ordered a Shirley Temple for me?"

John smirked and took a pull of his beer.

Anne bit her cheek to keep from laughing. This big, manly guy holding a pink paper umbrella was too much.

He dropped it on the counter and sighed. "I can't take him anywhere. My team lost tonight, so I'm the DD, but I *don't* drink Shirley Temples."

His eyes twinkled with humor, and her heart slammed against her ribcage. She needed to leave. Walk away right now before he made her laugh again. "Well, I gotta go."

Yet she didn't make a move.

Her gaze fell to the writing on his T-shirt. "No softballs here. We play hard."

This time she did laugh. Wyatt glanced down and winced. With a grin, he shrugged. "I'd regret the shirt choice, except it made you smile."

He made her smile.

"There he is. Hey, superstar." A tall blonde wearing stilettos, sprayed on jeans, and a clingy halter top strutted over, followed by an entourage of look-alikes. She gave Wyatt a peck on the cheek. "Sorry we're late. I see the party has already started."

Giggles came from the peanut gallery as they surrounded Wyatt, pushing Anne to the end of the bar. She shuffled in her Skechers. Sure, she liked to dress up and wear heels once in a while, but if she tried to pull off sky-high stilettos, she'd be limping for a week. Jeans and the T-shirt she'd bought off the clearance rack at Target were no match for these women's sexy, hip vibe. Heat crept up her neck like back in school when the popular girls called her a nerd.

Time to go to her table. She didn't fit in with this crowd. Picking up her water, she turned to leave, but Wyatt tapped her arm. He'd moved away from the women to stand next to her.

He rubbed his jaw. "Hey, I don't want to keep you, but…"

Her gaze flew to his, and he must have seen something in her eyes, because he didn't finish his sentence. He rocked back on his heels and shoved his hands in his pockets.

Great. She'd scared him away. Just as well. Didn't need a hot guy with groupies and an ego that probably needed constant stroking. She'd steer far away from that type.

When she dated again, it would be with a stable, responsible man. Someone who had a work ethic and wouldn't impulsively quit his job and expect to mooch off her. Someone she could count on, who wouldn't perpetually stand her up or not be able to commit to any plans for fear of missing something else more "fun."

Nope. She was so done with those guys. Looks didn't matter. Only, she couldn't deny that Wyatt's looks…well…the looks he gave her made her insides quiver oh-so-pleasantly.

"We usually come here after the games. Maybe see you around some-time?" He hitched an eyebrow.

John shook his head and coughed over what sounded like, "Coward."

The minions encroached on Wyatt, their laughter pealing. Still, he held Anne's gaze.

Something in her chest fluttered faster than the wings of a bird taking flight. Doubtful she'd run into him again, since she didn't get out much. "Maybe. Nice meeting you."

She hurried away before she changed her mind. Whatever expression he'd seen on her face had stopped him cold from asking her out. All for the best. Teaching, interviewing for vice principal jobs, and volunteer work kept her super busy. That's the way she liked it. Besides, she needed some space to get over the last breakup and time to do her homework on anyone new. He'd have to tick off the right boxes on her growing list of important attributes.

The band tuned their instruments, getting ready for the next set. She took a deep breath and pushed through the crowd to get closer.

The lanky lead singer, with sleeve tattoos and multiple piercings, paused to pick up his drink. She stood on her tiptoes and waved to him. "It's my friend Emily's birthday. Do you take requests?"

He leaned down. "Depends. What song?"

She told him, and he nodded in an I'm-so-cool way. "You got it."

His fingers fiddled with the guitar strings as his gaze wandered down her body. "Why don't you stop back when we take our next break?"

"Thanks, but I'm with the girls tonight."

"Bring them with you." He jerked his head in the direction of the drummer and bass player. "We love a party."

"Maybe next time." She smiled and walked away. Her face was on fire, but she'd done it.

His voice came over the mic. "Got a request from a pretty lady. Can't turn that down. This one's for Emily. Happy birthday."

Anne's friends let out a whoop from their table as she returned.

"Oh my God. My favorite song. Did you do that?" Emily high-fived Anne as the girls moved to the music. Worth the nerves to make Emily so happy.

Anne glanced across the bar at Wyatt. The group around him had grown. A guy clapped him on the back and another passing by gave him a fist bump. She ignored the tiny sinking of her spirits.

Wyatt was out of her league, and she'd promised herself she'd stick to her plan.

No room for players in her life.

***

Don't Stop! Keep reading now by grabbing your copy
of LOVE ON THE LINE today!

Don't miss book three of the Love Beyond Danger series with LOVE ON THE LINE and discover more from Diane Holiday at www.dianeholiday.com

* * *

Anne Cooper lives her life by the book and always has a plan. At thirty-two, if she wants to have her dream family, she needs to find a man who checks off the boxes on her ideal husband list. The hot football star who makes her heart stutter doesn't match a single one. She's not looking for a player. But spending time with Mr. Wrong feels so right.

Wyatt Pearson knows all about hard work—on the field. In the dating world, his celebrity football status has paved his way. He's blindsided when he meets Anne. She's smart, down-to-earth, and would rather grade papers than watch the Superbowl. For a chance with her, he has to up his game and take a risk. Stepping into all new territory, he approaches her from the heart.

As Anne and Wyatt fumble through their feelings, someone else is watching from the sidelines, plotting to win her affections. He's determined to have her, and if he can't...no one will.

* * *

ACKNOWLEDGMENTS

This is my chance to express my heartfelt thanks and gratitude to the people in my life who have supported me. And I guess, as usual, I'm going to do it Diane-style. With feeling, humor, and love.

My thanks and appreciation for everything these wonderful people have given to me in the process:

To my husband, Steve. He's right there all the time to remind me of what's important. Sharing my story. Enjoying my craft. Making people laugh and engage. He grounds me and keeps me from spinning off into the frenzied world of all the things I "should" be doing if I want to "make it." He tells me repeatedly that in his eyes, I have "made it." He makes me realize that everything in life is about balance. I trade off late work nights for sunny days boating with him because life is short and the most important thing is to live it with those you love.

To my daughter, Kelsey, who always asks about my writing. Plot points and the psychology of villains are her super powers (although I doubt she puts that on her resume). She's my biggest supporter, and it warms my heart to hear that her friends loved my book.

To the core group of girls Kelsey grew up with, my surrogate daughters, who did beta reads for me. They even hosted a lunch for me to sign books for them. Thanks Maureen, Kelsey, Anne, Tricia, Katie, Tess, and Meghan.

To my son, Brent. He makes me laugh all the time. Imagine my shock when he told me that he was reading my book aloud to his girlfriend so he could do "character voices." Too funny.

All kidding aside, a huge thanks to archaeologist and author, Rachel Grant. She answered my endless questions about archaeology, and I could not have written this book without her help and knowledge. I'm so thankful I attended her workshop and met her at an RWA conference in New York. Any misinterpretations or mistakes are my own.

To Mary Cain, my content editor. I never imagined I would get the chance to work with such a dedicated, thorough, professional editor. I'm honored by the time she devotes to my work and the way she pushes me to bring my writing to the next level.

To Tina Moss and Yelena Castle, co-founders of City Owl Press. These amazing ladies are the most supportive people I can ever imagine in the industry. Always on the cutting edge of marketing with complete transparency to us authors.

To my critique partners who are my constant support: Christina Hovland, CR Grissom, Renee Ann Miller, Dylann Crush, and Karen Alterisio. I couldn't have done it without you all.

To Caicos. RIP my unconditionally loving golden retriever who sat at my feet while I wrote both *Love in Hiding* and *Love Uncovered*. She inspired the scenes with the "favorite stick" and swimming to fetch. I miss her hugs and tail thumps. Anyone who has a pet in their life knows the feeling of complete love that comes from them. I'm grateful to this angel who came down to earth to spend time with me. I'd never be able to write about dogs and the pure love they give without having had her in my life.

To my readers. A million thanks to anyone who bought my book. I can't begin to explain how wonderful it feels to have my book published and being read. I used to sit under the moon at night, look up at the stars, and think, "Please, just let me find a way to share these characters, these emotions, and the joy and love that's so much a part of me."

This truly is my dream come true.

To everyone who served and continues to serve in the military. You and your family sacrifice so much to keep us safe. Every book sold adds to the personal donations I make to a non-profit organization that supports veterans.

ABOUT THE AUTHOR

DIANE HOLIDAY is an award-winning author who writes romantic suspense and contemporary romance with a healthy dose of humor. Her characters will make you laugh, cry, and root for them to the end. If you are sleep deprived because you couldn't put her book down, then she's achieved her goal. She and her husband, a retired Navy Captain, who  is her go-to for colorful slang and guy-talk, live in South Carolina on beautiful Lake Murray. Diane loves dogs and features one in each of her books. In her spare time, she volunteers at a rescue farm for large-breed dogs and another no-kill shelter national organization.

www.dianeholiday.com

facebook.com/DianeHolidayBooks
instagram.com/diholiday333

ABOUT THE PUBLISHER

City Owl Press is a cutting edge indie publishing company, bringing the world of romance and speculative fiction to discerning readers.

Escape Your World. Get Lost in Ours!

www.cityowlpress.com

facebook.com / CityOwlPress
x.com / cityowlpress
instagram.com / cityowlbooks
pinterest.com / cityowlpress
tiktok.com / @cityowlpress

www.ingramcontent.com/pod-product-compliance
Lightning Source LLC
Chambersburg PA
CBHW031204020726
47499CB00002B/475